THE

Shambles

Chloe Openshaw

To all the dedicated, unsung writers
who never gave up on their dream

1

THUNDEROUS HAILSTORM WAS ROLLING IN OFF THE YORKSHIRE Moors, the erupting weather front causing swirling balls of ice to fire like darts in all directions, a squally wind making it look like the vulnerable city was trapped inside a shaken snow globe. The usual bustling streets soon became deserted as people dived for shelter, leaving behind only those seeking temporary refuge in shop doorways and hidden crevices. On the busiest night of the year so far, the piercing sound of sirens echoed through the main arterial passageways as the emergency services attempted to keep alive the city's pumping heartbeat.

While brushing off the ice that had lodged in his hair on his way to work, Matron Matty Smith lingered outside the cumbersome double doors that led through to the intensive care unit at St Jude's Hospital, York. He took a moment to compose his emotions, bracing himself to face his last ever month of working the graveyard shifts before officially retiring. With his head lowered, he closed his eyes and prayed that all the drunks would stay away from the treacherous, wintery roads, and that the hospital would be able to avoid declaring a critical incident, a situation that would see the capacity of the ICU pushed to its limits. With a weakness to his posture, Matty drew in a deep breath before lunging out his arms and pushing open the doors, revealing the solemn, internal workings of the specialised care unit.

In the exact same way that he had always done upon first

entering, Matty looked up and scanned the room, digesting the initial state of the fragile unit. The very second that his eyes landed upon what had previously been an occupied bed, his heart sank. He noted how pieces of lifesaving equipment lay strewn and discarded on the floor around bed number two, and he could tell, without even having to touch them, that a slight warmth would still be clinging to the unoccupied, crumpled bedsheets. Matty didn't need to seek any formal confirmation about what had happened in his absence, his instincts and experience told him that the loveable, long-standing patient in bed number two, Ivy Hope, had sadly passed away.

Remaining in the doorway, Matty's lungs deflated and his frame collapsed like a puppet with severed strings. The familiar sound of medical alarms and bleeps failed to overshadow the fond memories of Ivy that swirled through his mind, a name he would never forget. His thoughts turned to Ivy's husband, Melvyn, who he had come to know well over the course of the past few months, and Matty wondered if someone had already made the telephone call to update the next of kin about the death of his loved one, a grim task that no member of staff ever wanted to make.

With his ID badge secured onto his scrubs, Matty finally made his way across the ward. For each bed that he walked past, he took a mental register of all the familiar faces who were still receiving care. Due to the open windows, he was unable to block out the sound of an approaching ambulance siren, a sound that over the years he had come to dread. He became swamped by a nauseating feeling of apprehension, knowing deep down that it was only a matter of time before the empty bed on his ward would become occupied, and he questioned how many more people's lives he could save before he needed to start fighting for his own. Pushing away his personal struggles, Matty hid his pained expression behind his face mask and dug deep to produce his professional façade.

'Hi, everyone,' he announced to his night-shift team, who had all congregated at the nursing station, awaiting the shift handover.

'Without reading the notes, we can all see that bed number two has just become vacant,' he began.

In unison, the team looked over to what was considered to be the jinxed bed, the bed that had earned itself a grim reputation.

Matty drew in another deep breath and forced out his mounting feelings of apprehension. 'Forget about the superstition, and once it has been prepared for a new patient, let's view that as a brand-new bed, a bed with no history, a bed with no tally,' he declared, pointing towards bay number two. He glanced out of the window and observed the blizzard, which showed no signs of easing as thick flakes of snow came cascading from the sky. 'With a bit of luck, we won't get any major incoming traumas this close to Christmas,' he added, taking another moment to watch the weather, knowing that the snow was settling on dangerous, frozen surfaces. 'But there's no better time to start believing in miracles.' Matty read the shift handover, the letters RIP scribbled next to the name Ivy Hope along with her time of death. 'I can see that Ivy's husband, Melvyn, hasn't been informed yet,' he announced. 'Can we make sure that her things are ready for collection, and I'll make the call to her husband now?'

Once the team dispersed to commence their duties, only Matty and his fellow Matron remained at the nursing station.

'Can I get you a brew before we start?' asked Marie. 'This might be our only chance tonight,' she added. 'The conditions out there tell me it's going to be a busy shift,' she concluded, indicating towards the window.

Without looking at her, Matty replied. 'I'm fine, thanks, Marie, but you go and get one. I need to call Melvyn Hope before I do anything,' he said, running his hands through his hair and arching himself back on his chair. 'I was hoping to reach retirement without having to make another of these awful calls.'

'Let me do it, I don't mind,' offered Marie.

Matty shook his head. 'No, I feel like I need to make the call, but thanks for the offer.'

Marie admired the dotting of festive lights scattered across the bank of computers. 'I can't believe this will be my last Christmas working with you. How many have we done together over the years?' she asked, placing a tender hand on his shoulder.

'Too many to count,' he replied, attempting to produce a smile.

'It's not going to be the same without you here,' concluded Marie, before walking away.

Looking up to check that he was alone, Matty removed his ID badge and pulled free the card, exposing a small, personal photo that was hidden behind it. Cradling the sentimental picture in his hands and with an aching heart, he lowered his head and prayed for his very own Christmas miracle.

2

WRAPPED UP IN A MATCHING HAT, COAT AND SCARF SET, CARRIE Hobbs weaved her way through the bustling York crowds while the sound of Christmas bells echoed from the festive cathedral in the distance. The moment she became engulfed in the epicentre of outdoor, artisan market stalls, the warming aromas of indulgent treats made her stomach rumble.

With her hand resting on the bar, Carrie made eye contact. 'Two large glasses of mulled wine, please,' she placed her order the moment the waiter looked her way. Whilst soaking in the jovial atmosphere resonating through the market square, Carrie spotted a familiar face heading towards her, a hand waving with excitement in the distance.

'You're still glowing, you do know that, don't you?' smirked Carrie as Lola made her way through the crowd, the friends sharing a prolonged embrace before taking their drinks and sitting down at a vacant table. With the festoon lighting shining on her friend's blushing face, Carrie came to a premature conclusion before the conversation had even gotten going.

'I don't even need to ask how the honeymoon went,' she giggled, her eyebrows raised enough to crinkle her forehead.

'My smile might give it away, but you can still go ahead and ask me,' Lola began, placing her bag on the floor.

'So, how was the honeymoon, my lovely Lola?'

Her eyes glistened. 'Oh, thanks for asking, Bali was amazing,' she grinned, brushing her copper-gold hair over her shoulder.

Carrie smirked. 'Tell me everything,' she requested, picking up her glass. 'But before you do, can I just make a teeny-weeny toast?'

The ladies raised their steaming glasses.

'To my beautiful best friend - here's to the next chapter in your life as the wonderful Mrs Cash,' she began, a depth of sincerity dripping from her words. 'May your life always be filled with this kind of joy,' she concluded, indicating towards Lola's radiant smile. The friends clinked glasses and Carrie took a sip of her drink, failing to notice that Lola never raised her glass to her lips. 'Although you're going to have to bear with me on the whole change-of-name thing, because I've known you forever as Lola Jukes, so Lola Cash is going to take some getting used to.'

Lola reached out and grabbed Carrie's hand. 'I missed you while I was away.'

Carrie sniggered. 'Behave. You were on your honeymoon, I really hope you didn't miss me!'

'I did, honestly! I must have talked about you every day, wondering if you were coping without me at work. I couldn't actually remember the last time we spent such a long period of time apart.'

'Probably primary school. Do you remember my dad insisted on taking me to the Isle of Man for a week, despite me saying I'd rather skip the holiday altogether and stay at yours instead?' Carrie recalled with fondness.

'I bought you this,' said Lola, reaching for her bag and taking out a little pink matchbox-size gift. 'For you.'

Carrie placed her hand over her mouth, trying to contain her emotions while taking hold of the present. 'Ah, thanks,' she replied, opening the package to reveal a keyring with the words *Work Wife* embossed in rose gold.

'I may have married Parker, but you've been like the family I never had, and I just want you to know that, no matter what happens in life, I'll always be here for you.'

Carrie stood up and leaned across the table, indicating for

Lola to stand too so that she could give her another hug. 'Thank you, my lovely Lola.'

The ladies sat back down.

'Anyway, we're not talking work tonight, that can wait until Monday morning. Tonight, it's all about the honeymoon of yesterday, and the hangover that shall come tomorrow.' Carrie took another extended sip of wine. 'So, tell me everything.'

Lola leaned back on her chair and smiled with a sense of contentment. 'It really was amazing. The place we stayed in was right on the beachfront, the resort itself hugged the coastline,' she explained, gesturing with her hand the curvature of the bay, 'but the views... Oh, the views!' Lola beamed. 'If I just close my eyes, I'm right back there. I can still feel the glow of the sun on my face and the way the ocean felt against my skin, warm and comforting.'

'Okay, enough,' mocked Carrie, holding up her hands. 'I mean, how perfect is your life right now?'

For a moment, whilst there was a pause in conversation, the sound of the cathedral bells became more prominent, ringing out the sounds of Christmas.

'My life hasn't always been perfect,' Lola sighed, recalling the time that Parker had cheated on her. 'It hasn't always been easy, you and your sofa know that more than anyone,' she laughed, remembering the many months that she had spent staying at Carrie's place across town. 'He hurt me so much, and if you'd asked me back then, I would never have dreamt that we could have moved past it and gone on to get married.'

'After everything that you and Parker have been through in the past ten-plus years, I think it's only made your relationship stronger. He knows how lucky he is to have you after coming so close to losing everything. It's just a shame that it took him acting like such an idiot to realise it,' Carrie replied. 'But look where you are now,' she concluded, admiring the wedding band on Lola's finger. 'You're now Mrs Cash, and happier than I've ever seen you before.'

Lola produced a grin that originated in the corner of her mouth but soon expanded, illuminating her entire face. 'I have a little secret.'

Carrie immediately put her glass down and leaned in. 'What is it? Tell me,' she requested the moment Lola fell silent.

'I'm pregnant,' she announced.

'Ah!' Carrie screamed so loudly that everyone around her peered over. Lola pressed her finger to her lips.

'Shush!' she requested, a sense of embarrassment making her body sink down in the chair.

'Does this mean I'm going to be an auntie?'

'Of course!' replied Lola. 'But it's still really early, so please wait before you go out and start buying goodness-knows-what.'

'And here's me ordering us glasses of mulled wine when I should have been looking at the mocktail menu. I thought it was unusual that you weren't keeping up with me.'

Lola laughed. 'I would be pregnant at this time of year,' she sighed, peering around at all the festive pop-up bars. 'It seems busier than ever this year, don't you think?' she added, taking stock of the evening market crowds, queues two or three deep at every stall despite the wintery weather conditions. 'I don't know why we've never capitalised on the evening trade.'

'Erm, there'll be no work talk until Monday, remember?' Carrie declared, waving her finger and tutting. 'So, what did Parker say when you told him the big news?'

Lola hid her face behind her hands. 'He doesn't actually know yet,' she revealed.

'What? Why?' Carrie looked puzzled.

'We've just had an amazing honeymoon,' Lola began to explain, casting her gaze to the floor. 'And although I know that Parker wants to be a dad, I'm not sure it was his immediate intention.' Lola's initial glow at revealing the news subsided. 'He's been talking a lot lately about this next year and what he'd like to do, and children weren't part of his plan. It's a surprise pregnancy, not a planned one. I think the amount of Sangria that I drank in Bali made any form of contraception null and void.'

'Listen,' Carrie began, taking hold of Lola's hand and pressing it with a firm touch. 'Although Parker might be shocked at first, you know that he wants a family at some point, he's told you that, and when he finds out the news, I'm sure he's going to be thrilled.' Carrie dipped her head to try and maintain eye contact with her best friend.

Lola wrapped her coat tightly around her body and an upturned expression appeared on her face, the chilly evening snap penetrating her warm, winter layers.

'I know, you're right. I'm just waiting for the right time to tell him. Maybe I'll wrap Christmas paper around my stomach and present myself on Christmas morning,' she mocked, running her hands through her wavy hair.

'So,' began Carrie, picking up her glass and indicating for Lola to do the same once again. 'I want to make another toast. Here's to special Christmas presents, and friendships that last a lifetime.'

Carrie downed her wine as Lola put her full glass back on the table.

'Let's go and celebrate with something we both love,' Carrie suggested. 'I've spotted a stall over there that has a chocolate fountain,' she added, before getting up and reaching for her bag.

'Thanks for always being there for me,' Lola said as the pair began to navigate the crowds, linking arms. 'Would you be a Godparent?'

Carrie paused, forcing the flow of the crowd to ebb around them. 'I would love to!' she replied, pulling Lola into a hug. 'We may not be actual sisters, but you've always felt like family to me,' she whispered into Lola's ear before pulling herself away. 'Now, let's go and eat our own body weight in chocolate. I've felt hungry ever since I arrived.'

3

*L*YING FLAT ON HIS FRONT, AIDAN DIVED BENEATH THE REAL Christmas tree ready to adjust its position at the base, wanting it to stand proudly in the lounge window.

'Right, let me know which ways it's tilting and I'll try and prop it up as best as I can.'

Standing a few paces back, near the door that led through to the kitchen, Holly inspected Aidan's work with an air of indifference, before her concentration returned to her phone.

'I'd say it's leaning to the left a bit,' she commented in a manner that suggested she wasn't really bothered if the tree was straight or not.

Still on the floor with his head buried beneath the dangling branches, Aidan did his best to alter the base.

'How's that? Any better?'

'It's okay, I guess,' she mumbled. 'I'm just not sure why we decided to get a tree so close to Christmas, and a real one at that,' she sighed, slumping herself into the single, cosy armchair and putting her feet up on the ottoman. 'The needles will fall and then I'll be spending all my time hoovering.'

Aidan wriggled himself out from under the tree and stood by the window, his hands secured inside his pockets.

'I've bought a tree because it's Christmas, and at Christmastime, it's nice to feel festive,' he sighed and released his hands, holding them up in frustration at having to defend his desire to have a tree, wishing he hadn't bothered. 'When we have children, they'll want a tree,' he added, 'so it's good practice.' He couldn't help but imagine how special it would feel to decorate the tree with the family he'd always craved.

'We can barely look after ourselves, let alone kids,' mocked Holly, inspecting her acrylic nails.

Aidan turned to face Holly. 'You're only saying that because you still like to have too much of a good time most weekends,' he replied, trying to think of the last weekend that they hadn't gone out in some capacity. 'I'm done with all the boozy late nights. I'm done with that phase of my life and I'm ready for something different. I thought you were, too.'

Holly pulled the cushion out from behind her back and held it to her chest. 'I'm only twenty-nine,' she began in a bold tone. 'I feel like if I still want to go out and enjoy a good social life, then that's okay,' she continued. 'And I thought that we'd both decided to just savour the feeling of being engaged, and then think about the serious stuff when we're ready,' she added, playing with the engagement ring twisted around her finger.

Aidan tried to gain eye contact.

'I would marry you tomorrow, you know that,' he began, walking towards the armchair and leaning down, 'and I'd start a family with you today, but I'm happy to wait,' he explained, looking Holly in the eyes and bending down to kiss her. 'I've never known what it's like to have a dad in my life and because of that, I want to give my children the childhood that I always craved,' he explained, recalling all the Christmases that he'd experienced as a child with separated parents, his mum passing away when he had just turned seventeen.

Holly met his gaze, witnessing for herself the sincerity in his eyes. 'It's not that I don't want to marry you, because I do, it's just...I don't want to rush in like my parents did, and then come to regret it later on.' Holly built up the courage and met Aidan's stare once again, taking hold of his hand. 'When I get married to you, I want to know in my heart that I'm ready to give you everything that you want in life, everything that you deserve. And until then, I want to savour the life that we have now, just me and you. Live selfishly, while we still can. Is that so bad?'

Aidan puffed out his chest and took a deep, gratifying sigh. 'Holly Benn, I'm not going anywhere, and when you're ready to become Mrs Holly Fogg, I'll be right here waiting to put another ring on that finger.' Aidan stood up and held out his arms, pulling Holly up when she placed her hands in his. He wrapped his arms around her waist and lifted her slight frame, her feet rising off the floor. 'Now, help me to hang some of these decorations on the tree, otherwise you know that I'm going to do a terrible job and you'll hate it all Christmas.'

Just at that moment, Aidan's phone buzzed.

'Are you okay?' asked Holly when she turned to look at him, witnessing that the sparkle in his eyes had dwindled. 'What is it?' she probed further, his look of sadness making her feel nervous.

'It's an email from a solicitor,' he replied, re-reading the words. Holly moved away from the tree and crouched herself on the floor by the single chair that Aidan had slumped himself in.

'Solicitors? About what?'

'My auntie has passed away.'

'Your auntie? The one you never knew?'

Aidan nodded. 'My mum's twin sister, Alice.'

Holly's eyebrows pulled together. 'Why has a solicitor contacted you about it? You never even knew her.'

With a sombre expression still cemented on his face, Aidan looked up. 'It's about her will,' he paused, and with an unfocused gaze, a look of disbelief spread across his face.

'And what does that have to do with you?' Holly added in a soft tone. She placed a hand on his thigh, noting his look of apprehension.

Aidan shook his head and his hand fell to his lap, releasing its grip on the phone. 'Apparently she's left something to me,' he replied, his small, shallow intakes of breath causing a light-headedness.

'What?' she asked, rubbing her forehead to try and smooth out the frown line that had appeared in her perfectly ironed out skin.

'It doesn't go into detail. The email is pretty short, and it just says that more information will follow.'

'I've never really heard you talk much about your auntie Alice.'

Aidan left his phone on the chair and stood up, pacing towards the window and taking in a deep breath. 'That's because there's nothing to say. She never had anything to do with me when I was growing up,' he began. 'Right up until the day that she passed away, my mum didn't have a good word to say about Alice, and from what I've told you in the past, you know that my mum was the type of person who loved absolutely everybody.'

'Why did they not get on?'

'All I know is that Alice didn't approve of my mum being a single parent,' Aidan paused, allowing himself to think back on his childhood. 'And because of that, Alice wanted nothing to do with us. She was embarrassed, I think. So, she and my mum never spoke, or had any kind of relationship once I was born.' With slumped shoulders and blank features, Aidan continued. 'Years passed, but when my mum became really poorly, she reached out, asking if Alice would come and be there for me.'

With a rigid posture and shaky voice, Aidan continued, despite the hurt he felt rising to the surface. 'I had just turned seventeen. I had nobody else in my life at that time; no mum, no dad. All I needed was someone to be able to call family, have a next of kin to write on forms, and a name to put down as an emergency contact,' he paused and fought back his emotions, pushing the hurt away. 'Taking care of my mum made me grow up fast, and it's a good job really, because there was nobody there to look after me once she was gone.'

'And then what happened?' asked Holly, taking the opportunity to talk about a stage in Aidan's life that he had always been reluctant to share.

'Alice refused, I guess, because I never saw her. Not once.'

Holly walked over to where Aidan was standing and nuzzled herself underneath his arm. 'Why, in all the years that we've been together, haven't you spoken about all this to me?'

'Because Alice wasn't a part of my life. I didn't know her. I never met her, so why would I talk about her?' he replied, looking down to meet Holly's gaze.

'And what about your dad? I know you don't like talking about him either, but when your mum died, did he not try to get in touch?'

'Nope. He left my mum after I was born, and that's it. There isn't anything else to tell.'

'And you've never tried to find out who he was?'

Aidan's facial expression remained nonchalant. 'Nope. In my mind, I don't have a dad, and I don't have an auntie, as tough as that sounds,' Aidan defended, his words clear and decisive. 'My mum was dying and her own twin didn't have the compassion to come and see her, or even attend the funeral to pay her last respects. My mum stopped considering Alice as family way before she passed away, and I did the same. As far as I was concerned, I had no family left after my mum died.'

Holly released herself from his embrace and walked to get Aidan's drink, passing it to him.

'Here, I think you need this,' she suggested, watching as Aidan finished the glass. 'So, I'm confused…' Holly began, walking to take a seat on the chair, 'if this relative of yours, Alice, was never part of your life, or never even met you, then why on earth would she leave something to you in her will? It just makes no sense.'

Although the lights on the tree were shining and flickering in Aidan's eyes, his feeling of festive cheer disappeared. 'I don't know,' he sighed. He walked over to a table at the far side of the room and took hold of his wallet, which housed a picture of him and his mum. He rummaged through the various compartments and removed the treasured image, revealing a crumpled photo hiding within.

'This is the only photo I have of Alice, I found it in my mum's purse after she passed away. This is Mum, and that's Alice,' he explained, pointing to each of the young women in the photo, the twins looking similar, even in their late teens. 'My mum must have been pregnant with me in this photo.'

Holly studied the photo, examining the surroundings.

'God, they do look similar, don't they? Where was this taken, do you know?'

With a heavy sigh, Aidan shrugged. 'I'm not sure. Mum never showed the photo to me, but deep down it must have meant a lot to her if she carried it around in her purse,' he said, taking hold of the picture and scrutinising its details.

Holly sat herself on the sofa and crossed her legs. 'Maybe the will is Alice's way of making things up to you, her way of saying sorry for everything that she did wrong to you and your mum.'

Aidan shook his head and peered out of the window.

'This was a woman that refused to go to her own twin's funeral, and who left her only blood relative orphaned, for want of a better word,' he explained. 'She's probably left behind a trail of debts that need sorting, and I've been tracked down as her only blood relative.' A sinking feeling developed in the pit of Aidan's stomach. With flushed features and a well of emotions threatening to break through to the surface, he left the room.

Holly heard a phone buzz, so got up and walked to the chair, spotting Aidan's phone still abandoned on the cushion. Upon seeing the new email notification pop up on the screen, she unlocked the phone and opened up his inbox. 'Aidan!' she shouted, continuing to read the new email from the solicitor.

Aidan appeared in the doorway a few seconds later. 'Are you shouting me?' he asked, his eyes glossy and red. Holly kept her focus on the phone, reading the email again to ensure she was correct in what she was saying.

'The solicitors have sent a further email,' she explained through a shaky, disbelieving voice. 'They want you to attend a meeting about the details of the will,' she added, turning her head to look up and meet his gaze. 'You won't believe this, but Alice has left you a house in her will,' she revealed. 'It looks like you need to take a trip to France.'

4

STEPPING INSIDE THE CONVERTED HORSEBOX THAT WAS TUCKED into a secluded nook at the top end of The Shambles, Lola opened up the customer hatch of her brownie business with a weary sigh. Resting her elbows on the countertop, she allowed her mitten-covered hands to cup her chilled cheeks. The open hatch framed the early-morning, star-speckled sky, the glittering scene stretching out towards the horizon. Before the chaos of the day began, she allowed herself a few quiet moments to admire York Minster as it rose from the cobbles, the mighty cathedral standing guard over the festive city. If she closed her eyes, Lola could almost hear the city's history echoing down the maze of side streets, just like she had experienced as a child during enchanting school field trips.

At Christmastime, the city that Lola had always called home felt particularly special. Through her admiring eyes, the rows of quaint shops illuminated the narrow pavements with a magical torch, the window displays enticing passers-by to step over their cobbled thresholds. She closed her eyes and savoured the momentary nugget of stillness, the cool breeze working to brush away any lingering feelings of pre-dawn sleepiness.

'I need coffee,' she muttered to herself after a few seconds, rubbing her eyes and yawning, stretching out her torso. Her lungs expanded with the sudden influx of oxygen, encouraging a surge of energy to seep into her weary limbs. She bent down and flicked the switch, the revving sound of the coffee machine breaking the peaceful morning ambience. For Lola, the day had begun.

'Morning!' she announced the moment Carrie arrived, her business partner pushing her way in through the door before closing it with force.

'Can you believe it?' Carrie replied, pushing her back against the door so that it took her weight. 'I've left my gloves at home and I've forgotten to switch on the slow cooker, which means not only am I going to have freezing hands all day, but when I get home tonight, an uncooked chicken casserole will be all that's waiting for me,' she huffed, before taking her bag off her shoulder and allowing it to fall to the floor. 'I'm sure that these dark mornings have never felt so brutal.' Carrie rested her head against the door and allowed her shoulders to sink, her fatigued limbs feeling the brunt of the relentless, early-morning rises. 'The day can only improve,' she added, making sure the fastener on her body warmer was zipped to the top and secured beneath her chin.

She reached down and picked up two chalkboards, stepping back onto the cobbles and hanging them at either side of the central hatch. Above the wheel trim, she filled canisters with folded napkins, sachets of sugar, and wooden stirrers. Stretched up on tiptoes, she hung two hanging baskets of flowers and ensured the fabric bunting sat central, before scurrying back inside and locking the door.

'That's it, I'm done!' she exclaimed, allowing herself to slide down the door, her body only stopping when her bottom touched the ground.

'Not feeling it today?' Lola asked while cradling a hot water bottle against her chest, white beads of mist emerging from her mouth whenever she spoke. 'I have to agree, the winters feel like they're getting colder, and the dark mornings are tough.'

Over the past six years, Lola and Carrie had devoted themselves to running their business, establishing an idea that had flourished as they holidayed beneath a cool Caribbean breeze.

Inside the snug interior of the horsebox, Carrie switched on the electric heater, working up the courage to say what was on her mind. 'Maybe we should seriously start to think about renting some space. We'd have our own toilet, central heating, and we could finally expand our product range like we've always talked about. We know that our brownies are a big hit, but there are so many other treats we want to try, and we just don't have the room here.' Carrie adjusted her bobble hat and zipped up her fleece until it, too, was secured beneath her chin. 'It'd be nice not to feel cold to the core in winter, and like we're sat in an oven during the sticky summer months.'

Uncharacteristically so, Lola remained quiet.

'We could even hire some extra help, a Saturday assistant, and then give ourselves some additional time off. Now wouldn't that be nice?'

Lola perched herself on her usual bar stool. 'Come and sit down,' she requested, moving out the other stool to encourage Carrie to also take the weight off her feet. 'There's something we need to talk about.'

With a concerned look on her face, Carrie stopped what she was doing and sat beside her friend, placing her hand on Lola's thigh and pressing it with a gentle touch. 'What is it? Is the baby alright? Is Parker alright? You're not poorly, are you?' she rambled.

Lola blew her nose for what felt like the hundredth time that morning. 'I think I have a cold coming on, but other than that, I'm fine, and so is the baby. I just want to talk to you,' she began, encouraging her foot to stop tapping and her heart to sink back into her chest. 'And if I delay this chat any longer, I'm going to go out of my mind.' Lola ran her hands through her hair and drew in a deep breath before looking up at Carrie. 'I've finally made a decision. I've made up my mind and nothing will change it,' she added, the defiance in her words making Carrie's heart drop.

With a shake of the head, Carrie dropped her gaze, her look of concern changing in an instant to an expression of sadness. 'You're leaving York, aren't you?'

Lola pressed her lips together and nodded. 'I am,' she confirmed.

'You've finally decided to go travelling?' asked Carrie in a hesitant voice.

Lola's shoulders loosened and she lifted her head, making eye contact. 'Yeah, it just feels like the right thing to do,' she began, looking up at Carrie, fearful of the expression that she would be met with. 'If we don't do it now, it'll be too late and the opportunity will have passed us by,' she concluded, admitting to herself that her wishes for the future could stretch beyond the castle walls.

Carrie couldn't help but feel disheartened. 'You haven't mentioned it for a while so I just assumed that you'd both decided against it, or that you'd managed to talk Parker out of the idea altogether.'

Both ladies fell silent for a few seconds.

'What about the business?' Carrie asked. 'You're not going to want to come back and work in our rusty tin once you've seen the world and had a glimpse of what else life has to offer,' she added, pointing out towards the horizon.

Lola released a trickle of low-level giggles and shook her head in disapproval. 'We promised each other that we'd never call our thriving business a rusty tin.'

'I know, but it is a rusting horsebox, at the end of the day,' Carrie admitted with a jovial tone. 'Is this all because of Parker? He shouldn't be encouraging you to do something that you really don't want to do. It's a massive decision and I can tell that you're upset,' she said, noticing the glossiness in Lola's eyes and handing her a tissue.

Lola looked up and met Carrie's gaze. 'Parker isn't making me do anything. I'm just upset because my decision means that I'll be leaving you, and all of this,' she explained, looking around the interior of the converted horsebox. 'But I'm also sure that it's the right decision. I've been thinking about nothing else for the past two or three months, and the more I think about it, the more it just feels right.'

'It feels right for who? You or Parker?' Carrie felt quick to ask in the most supportive voice she could muster. 'You hate travelling. If you venture across the border into Lancashire, you think you've been on holiday. And when we went to The Bahamas way back when, you felt homesick the entire time.'

Lola gazed out onto the cobbles and admired the view that she loved so much, a view that, over the years, had become etched into her memory. 'It feels right for both of us,' she began, turning back to look at Carrie. 'Parker has *always* wanted to take a career break and explore life beyond the city walls, and it'd be nice to share those experiences with him before we settle down and have our baby,' she explained, caressing her stomach. 'If we go now, or at least straight after Christmas, we'll have been away for a good few months before this little one even starts to fully show, and who knows, maybe at that point Parker will have had his fill and he'll be ready to come home.'

'And what about what you want? Don't you want to start looking after yourself and putting yourself first for once? You're growing a human being and I'm sure the process will be easier on your body if you're settled in one place, eating the right kind of food and getting plenty of sleep. What about morning sickness? How will you cope with that on the road?'

'We won't be roughing it, and I'm sure I'll be fine for at least the first couple of months,' she reassured her friend, recalling the guidance provided by her doctor. 'And I want to show Parker that I'm willing to do this for him, even though travelling might not be high up on my list of priorities.' Lola played with her wedding rings, still getting used to wearing a diamond on her finger. 'I've invested so much into this place, and I love it, you know I do. This business has been the centre of my life for the past six years. But now I'm married, I need to think about what Parker wants, too.' Lola produced a genuine smile that couldn't be faked. 'I love him, Carrie, and I just want to make him happy.'

'I know, but–' Carrie began.

'And before you say it, I'm not just doing this to make him happy. This is my choice, this is what I want. And anyway, what could be so bad about setting off on a road trip with the man that I love?'

Carrie drew back her shoulders before speaking. 'It just feels like you're agreeing to do something which I know, deep down, you really don't want to do.'

'I want to make him happy, Carrie. But more than that, I want him to feel ready to settle down and have our baby, and I know that if he's given the opportunity to get this travel bug out of his system first, he'll be more prepared for what comes next.'

Carrie sat upright and cleared her throat, a serious tone to her voice. 'So, as your business partner, I will agree to this arrangement only if we hire a temporary assistant to replace you, and then once you return from your amazing adventures, and realise that you can't live without me, or our rusty old tin, we are able to pick up where we left off. You'll just be a silent partner for a while. And if you don't want to come back to the business, then that's okay too, and I'll buy you out, if that's what you want,' she confirmed, laying her hands in her lap.

Lola stepped down from her stool and wrapped her arms around Carrie. 'Thank you for being such an amazing friend, I couldn't do any of this without your support.'

'I bet Parker's so excited.'

Lola paused before answering, anticipating her friend's reaction. 'I haven't told him yet,' she mumbled.

'What?'

'I wanted to speak with you first, make sure that you're happy to hold the fort while I'm away.'

Carrie smiled and said the only thought swirling through her mind. 'What will I do without you? 'Who will I chat to all day long? I'll end up talking to myself, and then people will think I'm a bit odd and won't want to buy our brownies anymore.' Carrie's body visibly sunk into the stool. 'I'm going to miss you. I love you like you're my sister, and I can't imagine doing this without you.' She wiped away her few stray tears and buried her face into Lola's shoulder the moment her best friend stood up and wrapped her arms around her.

'I'll miss you too, so much,' Lola replied. 'You're the only person in this entire world that I could spend so much time with in a two-metre-square space, and not want to kill them after just one day.' Lola sat back down on her stool with her head lowered.

'Hey, where's all your excitement suddenly gone?' Carrie asked, spotting Lola's sombreness. 'You're planning on being whisked away by that gorgeous man of yours. I know I'm amazing company, but even I can't compete with an offer like that.'

Lola's face became alight with colour and life. 'Well, even though I've just got back from my honeymoon, we both know I'm no expert when it comes to travelling, you said it yourself, but I've been doing my research and I've become a bit obsessed,' Lola began, a change occurring in her facial expression the moment she started speaking. 'There are so many wonderful places that I didn't even know about, Carrie, and so many things I now want to experience for myself.' Lola became lost in her own world of imagination, falling in love with the romantic idea of travelling. 'I want to go swimming in Mykonos and wake up to some gorgeous French sunrises,' she said. 'I want to experience new skies and sink my feet into some soft, tropical sand until the sun sets. But, most of all, I just want to laugh and feel happy.' Lola turned to Carrie and shrugged her shoulders. 'Why should I just settle for the view from our lovely hatch, when the man I love is offering me a front-row seat to some of the best views that life has to offer?'

Carrie's eyes brightened and she spoke with a light tone of voice. 'I'm convinced,' she smiled, holding her hands up in a show of surrender. 'You should definitely go,' she said. 'I'm very jealous, and I'll be sitting right here when you get back, ready to hear all about your sunsets and sandcastles.'

A smile broke out onto Lola's face. 'Oh, you won't have to wait that long to hear about what I'm getting up to, I'll be ringing you on a daily basis with travel updates, and to make sure that you're not scaring away all of our customers,' she laughed.

'So, are you still planning on telling Parker about the baby on Christmas morning? Maybe you could hold a map in your hands at the same time. Do you think he'll get it all from that?' Carrie asked, getting off her stool and busying herself with preparing for the day ahead, trying to mask her sadness and put on a brave face.

'Well,' Lola began with a chirpier sounding voice, 'I have a plan of how I want to tell him. I've seen a campervan that I've put a deposit down on, and then come Christmas Eve, I'll take him to pick it up and reveal everything,' she explained, her hand resting over her stomach. 'And then we'll set off straight after the Christmas holidays, before the start of the new academic term.'

'Blimey, you'll barely have any time to pack.'

'Yeah, I know. Parker submitted his career break request back in the summer, hoping that after six months, I'd agree, so from that point of view, there'll be no hold-ups.' Lola looked out from the hatch and scoured her section of The Shambles, wondering how many times she'd walked across the charming collection of historic cobbles.

'I'm happy for you, honestly I am,' Carrie gushed. 'All I want is for you to be happy,' she added, placing her arm around Lola's shoulder. Carrie smiled as wide as she could, hiding her real emotions that were tumbling through her mind like a pile of autumnal leaves on a blustery day. 'It's crazy to be talking about babies and travelling when Parker doesn't even know. He's going to be blown away.'

5

THIS YEAR WOULD BE DIFFERENT, THAT'S WHAT MATTY TOLD himself as he took hold of the single Christmas present that he had purchased a few days earlier in town. The wooden photo frame had the words '*Love Dad xx*' carved into the surface. From a brown envelope, he pulled out a photo, the image on the front of a man holding a baby in one arm, with his other hand gently but firmly wrapped around the hand of a toddler. The quality and clarity of the photo depicted its age. Taking hold of a black pen, on the back he scribbled, '*My Family*'. After removing the glass front from the frame, Matty placed the photo inside and secured the back, before turning it over to see the final product.

Through glossy eyes, he admired the photo that, although he'd looked at it a thousand times before, now took on a new sense of life in its personalised frame. It was the same family photo that had always been hidden beneath his hospital ID badge, the same photo that was taped to the inside of his locker, the same photo that was displayed in his wallet, the same photo that had retained pride of place next to his bedside table, and the same photo that stood in a small photo frame on the lounge windowsill. He wiped his eyes and gazed down at the street, spotting that the shops were now open. After wrapping the frame and placing it into a brown bag, the gift tag reading '*To Aidan, Love Matty*', he grabbed his keys and wallet, put on his coat, and headed out onto The Shambles.

'Hi, Matty,' Aidan announced the moment the shop bell

jingled, and he looked up ready to greet his next customer. 'I have your order all ready, let me just run and grab it.' With that, Aidan disappeared into the back workshop.

Matty lingered in the shop, his work bag draped over his shoulder and across his chest and the brown gift bag clutched between the fingers of his left hand. A flurry of nerves made its way through his body, and he just wanted to hand over the gift bag and leave.

'Here we are,' announced Aidan when he appeared from out of the back. 'It's a bigger order this month, treating the family for Christmas?' he asked.

Matty took hold of the bag with his free hand and shook his head. 'It's actually for my work colleagues. I'm retiring at the end of January, so I thought I'd make this Christmas extra special for them.'

'Oh, wow, hanging up your stethoscope. So, big changes are on the cards for you. Have you got any exciting plans for your retirement? Take up golf, or travel the world maybe?'

Matty paused. 'I'm actually hoping to spend more time with family.'

'Oh, that's great, I've never seen them in here with you, you'll have to introduce me one day,' he commented, realising for the first time that his regular customer had always visited the shop alone. 'After all these years of talking to you, I sometimes think I know you better than I know some of my own friends.'

'I do come in here a lot,' said Matty, lifting his head and making eye contact.

'Well, because you've been such a loyal customer to me over the years, have this order on me, a Christmas gift from me to you, and to all your team on the ward.'

Before Matty could reply, the shop door swung open and two delivery men entered.

'Anyway, I best get on,' Aidan added, before taking hold of the order form from the delivery man. 'See you soon, and Merry Christmas.'

Matty walked out of the shop, disappointed that he'd failed to find the courage to hand over the gift bag. 'You too, and thanks for the order,' he concluded.

Zipping his coat up and pulling his hat over his head, Matty looked up at the sky, flecks of snow landing on his face, the freezing flakes melting on his warm cheeks and merging with a trickle of tears that he could no longer control. A feeling of loneliness stole his remaining glimmer of hope, and in that moment, it felt like his heart would always be deprived of love.

6

'PLEASE, YOU GO. I'LL BE ABSOLUTELY FINE,' LOLA INSISTED AS she lay huddled up on the sofa, the glow from the fire warming her face. 'I've got a stash of paracetamol, a hot water bottle under my feet, a tacky rom-com at the ready, which you'll hate, and I'll be in bed by nine, asleep by five-past.' Lola took hold of the television remote and hovered her finger over the play button. 'You go out as planned,' she continued, followed by a stream of phlegmy sneezes. 'I've got a dose of flu that you need to stay away from. Enjoy your Christmas night out with the team and I'll see you in the morning.'

Parker bent down to Lola's eye level. 'Are you sure? I'd much rather stay and make sure that you're okay. I can make you a constant supply of warm drinks and restock your tissues,' he explained, looking at the scattering of crumpled Kleenex on the floor. 'I haven't seen you look this rough in years.'

Lola squinted hard and crimpled up her nose. 'Thanks for that, I always look awful without makeup on,' she joked, running her fingers through her unwashed hair and trying to recall when she last ran a toothbrush over her teeth. 'Just don't go mad on the alcohol. I'm hopefully taking you somewhere special in the morning, remember?' she said, determined to stick to her plan of taking him to see the camper van that she'd bought.

'And you're still not going to give me any clues as to what we're doing?' Parker asked, getting up and checking himself in the mirror. His shoulder-length, wavy hair had been scooped into an effortless, messy bun, his defined features and stylish clothes always working to make him stand out in a crowd.

'Nope,' Lola replied, waving her arm out to try and get him to move away from the television.

'Are you sure you're going to be okay tonight? It feels like you're still running a temperature,' he asked, feeling her forehead.

'I'm fine, honestly. Now, get going before you miss out on all that exciting algebra talk,' Lola mocked, pulling the blanket up to her eyes and hiding her face, anticipating Parker's reply. 'And before you say it, I know you don't just teach algebra,' she laughed as Parker shook his head in dismay.

He leaned in and ruffled Lola's hair, before pulling the blanket up to cover her entire head. 'You should come to one of my lectures. Maybe you'd learn something, and then you could give Carrie a hand with the books,' he mocked, kissing Lola on the cheek. He walked over to the side table and grabbed his keys and wallet. 'Text me later so that I know you're alright,' he shouted before leaving the room, 'I love you.'

The cool, late-December evening snapped at Parker's skin, making him immediately regret not grabbing his coat, too. He stuffed his hands into his trouser pockets and speed-skipped down the street, encouraging his blood to pump and his body to warm up.

The full length of Candle Crescent had been decorated with miniature Christmas trees, all lit up with delicate, warming lights that twinkled in people's eyes as they passed. Clusters of naked garden trees stood heavy with frost, each outstretched branch pearly-white and glistening under the reflections provided by the dotted lampposts. A flurry of snow remained mounted in secluded crevices where the wind had encouraged it to bed down for the night, adding a quintessentially festive feel to the street.

Upon approaching the busy city centre, the hustle and bustle drew Parker into its embrace. His pupils dilated when his eyes absorbed the collection of bright lights that were radiating from the busy bars and restaurants.

'Ah, here he is!' announced Ed the moment Parker stepped foot into the bar. 'The man himself. After not showing up for the meal, we were just having a wager on whether you would turn up at all.' Ed and Parker had been best friends since the age of eleven, the pair sharing their love for maths during after-school clubs.

Parker made his way through the crowd and towards the bar, greeting his other lecturer pal, Max. 'Lola isn't well, she's full of flu, or something equally as grim, so I actually wasn't planning on coming out at all,' he explained. 'And I'm only going to stay for a few. I want to get back and make sure she's alright.'

Parker ordered a drink, forgetting that he hadn't actually eaten anything since lunchtime.

Ed planted his hands on Parker's shoulders in a playful way. 'Any excuse not to let your hair down,' he joked, ruffling Parker's bun. 'In all the years I've known you, I've never pictured you actually settling down and keeping your eyes on just one lady, but you've definitely proven me wrong. You've got a ring on your finger and you're willing to sacrifice a good night out so that you can go home and be a good husband. You're a changed man.'

Parker took a mouthful of his drink. 'I'm not making excuses, she's really rough,' he defended. 'And you make me out to be some kind of womaniser, which we all know I'm not. I've just never found the right woman who I wanted to settle down with.' Parker took another mouthful of his beer, the liquid highlighting the emptiness in his stomach.

'But you've certainly played the field. Is there any woman in York that hasn't shared your bed?' Ed asked in a playful manner.

Parker rolled his eyes and already regretted his decision to join in with the Christmas celebrations. 'Anyway, what have I missed?'

Ed produced a wry smile. 'I was just trying to find Max a suitable lady,' he explained, peering around the room and placing his arm over his friend's shoulder. 'And I think I've just spotted a perfect match,' he announced as his eyes landed on two ladies sitting together by the window, perched on bar stools and sipping on what looked like two colourful tequila sunrises.

'I don't need setting up, thanks,' Max replied, shaking his head with embarrassment and diverting his attention to the bartender before ordering another round.

'You're the only one in the department who's still single, so let us help you out,' Ed continued, walking off in the direction of the two women.

'Has he had a few already?' Parker asked.

'Yep, because he's freaking out. He said that Sophie has been talking to him about starting a family, and he doesn't think he's ready. I'm not sure if he'll ever be ready. And if I'm going to survive a night out with him, I need a few shots to help dilute his eagerness to milk this night for all it's worth. He's much more manageable at work with a lanyard around his neck, don't you agree?' Max joked, ordering a round of tequila. 'Get this down your neck,' he added with a toast. 'Cheers to Christmas, and a few weeks without maths, students, or emails.'

'Sounds like a plan to me,' Parker replied, raising his empty glass towards the bar and ordering another round. 'Same again, please,' he asked, and no sooner had the drinks appeared, than they, too, were downed. Parker looked across the room to check on Ed, who was deep in conversation with the two women he'd spotted. Just as Parker looked across the room, one of the girls caught his eye and smiled with purpose. Parker turned back around and ignored the flirtatious gesture, pretending he hadn't noticed. 'Well, it certainly looks like he's making the most of things,' he said to Max, shaking his head. 'I hope Sophie isn't waiting up.'

Max cast a disapproving glare across the room. 'I don't know why Sophie hasn't left him. She must really love him to put up with all his crap.' Turning back around, Max watched Parker empty his fourth drink within half an hour. 'Steady on! Looks like you're making the most of things too,' he mocked. 'Lola is back home sick and here's you necking drinks like it's last orders.'

'Just catching up.'

'So, how's married life?'

'Great.'

'Is there a but?' Max questioned when he sensed hesitation.

Parker emptied his bottle. 'I know Lola wants to start a family, but I wanted to travel first, experience a bit of life outside of York. How amazing would it be to travel through Europe together, as a married couple, and live a little before we start a family? Once a baby comes along, all that freedom goes away.'

'And what does she think about this?' asked Max, already anticipating his friend's response.

'We've chatted on and off about the idea of travelling for the past twelve months, maybe longer. But The Brownie Box is finally booming, so it's not great timing for her,' Parker continued to explain. 'And she loves it here. York is home and Lola is a homegirl at heart.' Parker didn't want to thrash the battle aloud, but his annoyance seeped out regardless. 'And I know she's conscious about her age, her best fertility years passing her by,' he sighed and shook his head. 'We're only twenty-nine, so you'd think that time was on our side, but apparently not.' Parker glanced over towards the window, searching for Ed, but instead locked eyes with one of the ladies, who, for a second time, held her smile until her affection was reciprocated. Flustered, Parker turned back around so that he could keep his back towards the window.

'So, there's good news, and bad news,' Ed announced upon his return, standing amongst his friends. 'Max, unfortunately, neither one is interested in getting your number, which is only their loss, my friend,' he explained, tapping Max's arm.

'And what's the good news?' asked Max.

'The good news is they're both single, and extremely attractive,' laughed Ed, doing his best not to stumble over his drunken slurry of words.

'Why is that good news when you and Parker are taken?' Max

asked, shaking his head in befuddlement at his friend's twisted logic.

Ed produced a wicked kind of smile. 'Because it's always good to know that we have options in life, if we want them.'

Parker jumped on the reply. 'You have options at the canteen. You have options on Netflix and where to go on holiday. But when you're engaged and thinking about starting a family, other, more exciting options are limited.' Parker placed another empty bottle on the bar and ordered another drink.

'Don't order another,' protested Ed, 'we're moving on now.'

The bartender placed Parker's order on the bar. 'You two go, I'll have this, then I'll follow,' he replied, tapping his card on the machine. 'I want to give Lola a quick call and check on her anyway.'

Ed and Max headed out the door and down the street, making their way towards the next bar. Parker downed his last beer and also made his exit, loitering outside and taking out his phone. Time had passed him by, and he'd failed to hear his phone as a message from Lola had come through at 21:45. It read, *Off to bed. Exhausted. Love you xx*

Just as he began to compose a reply, someone approached from behind.

'You're not leaving already, are you? Was your friend's company that bad?' The woman from the window seat had followed him outside. The fresh air, combined with the large amounts of alcohol that Parker had consumed, left him feeling light-headed and woozy.

'I'm not leaving, we're just heading to another pub,' Parker replied, trying to concentrate on his message, the words appearing blurred on his screen. 'In any case, we were doing a pretty good job of drinking that place dry,' he joked, the world through his eyes momentarily spinning when he looked up.

'I thought you might have come over for a chat, or at least that's what I was hoping for,' the woman replied, maintaining eye contact and taking the opportunity to flirt up-close. She zipped up her jacket and took out a bobble hat from her clutch bag, pulling it over her head.

Parker grinned internally at the flirtatious comment. 'I think my mate did enough talking for everyone tonight. I'm sorry if he was pestering you and your friend, he doesn't get out much, and when he does, well...' he paused as thoughts of Lola flashed through his mind, and he attempted to wriggle himself out of the conversation. 'I actually best get going, make sure he's not making an idiot of himself somewhere else.'

Parker slipped his phone into his pocket before completing his message to Lola, an awkwardness evident in his demeanour.

'I'm actually calling it a night. It's way too busy out tonight and I can't be bothered fighting the queues at the bar,' the woman explained, adjusting her hat so that it fit snug around her ears. 'Would you mind walking with me, I mean, just until I get home? My friend has decided to stay out, and even though I live just around the corner, I'm not a big fan of walking alone when it's so late.'

Parker pressed his lips together and looked up the street, hoping to see his friends so that he could elect Ed as chaperone and, in the process, get himself off the hook.

'You know what, I'll just walk super quick, don't worry,' she added when Parker didn't offer. 'Night,' she said, turning and walking away.

Guilt shuddered through Parker's drunken bones, encouraging him to pace after her.

'You know what, I think I'll call it a night too,' he began, walking alongside her. 'I'll walk you home and then I'll walk myself home. I've had enough Christmas spirit for one night.'

The woman slowed her pace and smiled at Parker, the look of attraction in her eyes melting away the frosty mist lingering in the air.

'That's super kind of you, thanks so much. I'm not that far away, just the other side of the square on Poets Nook, the opposite end to Jigsaw Lane. Do you know it?'

'I do,' replied Parker. 'I've lived in York all my life so there aren't many parts that I'm not familiar with.' He diverted his gaze, blinked hard a few times and drank in a few sobering breaths. 'York is amazing at this time of year, with all the hustle that the markets attract, but I much prefer it when it's not quite so packed.'

She waited until his gaze returned. 'I'm Holly, by the way. It's nice to meet you,' she said the moment he faced forwards. She allowed her arm to brush against his as they walked side by side out of town, an inner glow radiating when he didn't retract from her touch.

'Parker,' he replied, placing a hand on his chest and nodding. 'And that was my friend Ed you were talking to, if he didn't introduce himself, which I'm guessing he probably didn't.'

Holly laughed. 'He was just going on about this weird tale of falling off a gondola in Florence.'

Parker laughed. 'It's a story that always comes out, and each time he tells it, something more spectacular has happened since the last retelling.'

'He seemed very proud of his gondola moment.'

Parker couldn't help but admire Holly's beaming smile as they walked beneath a lamppost, the reflections accentuating her natural features. He found the way that she paired her tatty old bobble hat with a pair of high heels and a dress endearing, her blonde, curly hair bouncing on her shoulders. Even though he didn't want to admit it, her giggles and smile were infectious.

'This is me,' she announced as they passed Jigsaw Lane and turned onto Poets Nook, pausing outside a front door which had been painted a vibrant shade of pink, accentuated by what looked like a handmade wreath.

'Nice door,' Parker commented. 'Stands out from the crowd,' he added, peering around, noting that every other door blended into the background.

'Thanks so much for walking me home, I really appreciate it,' she said, rummaging in her bag for her keys. 'I hope it wasn't too far out of your way.' Before Parker could reply, Holly continued with her sentence, blurting out a question in one quick breath. 'Do you want to come in?' She looked down at her feet, not quite believing she had been so forward, embarrassment stealing her smile. 'I make a good brew, and I have some fancy biscuits in the cupboard which are great to dunk, that's if you're a dunker,' she said, hoping to fill the awkward pause that had developed in the conversation.

In a moment of drunken madness, Parker reverted to his old ways. He plunged his left hand into his pocket and wriggled his wedding band, wondering if it would release. 'I best not,' his voice of reason finally replied, though his feet didn't back away.

Noting Parker's unwavering stance, Holly placed the key in the lock and eased the door open, taking a step inside, sheltering herself from the bitter breeze that was swooshing the length of the lane. Maintaining eye contact, she removed her bobble hat and coat, hooking them behind the door. With her hands, she ruffled her hair, bringing her flattened curls back to life. Seeing her for the first time in full view, Parker could admire her outfit, a pale gold, mid-length sequined dress that wrapped around her frame, accentuating her chest with a plunging neckline, and her slender, long legs.

'I really best get going,' he finally replied, trying hard to drag his eye away from the lure of hers. He peered down at the floor and plunged both hands back into his pockets.

Holly leaned against the door, half concealing herself but still leaving a narrow gap of opportunity, and then looked up. 'You can't go now,' she said, admiring the blanket of snow that had begun falling from the sky. 'At least wait until it's stopped,' she added, opening the door a little wider for Parker to follow her inside. The mixture of flattery, his own weak will, and the copious amounts of alcohol that he'd consumed, all worked to pull Parker's feet forwards, and he followed Holly inside before closing the door behind him.

7

AN INCESSANT POUNDING PENETRATED DEEP WITHIN PARKER'S skull, dragging him out of a heavy sleep, and although his brain had begun the process of awakening, his eyes remained shut. He felt parched, and the taste of alcohol clung to the inside of his mouth, discouraging him from swallowing. His ears detected a few unfamiliar noises; the annoying sound of a clock ticking loudly in the background, the banging of internal doors coming from next-door, and the high-pitched tone of a barking dog.

With his body submerged beneath the covers, the glow of the clock shone on his face, encouraging his eyelids to finally open, albeit by the narrowest of margins. The clock at the side of the bed came into focus, signalling that it was 05:23 a.m. Parker massaged his temples in an attempt to ease his pounding headache. On the back of his neck, he felt a warmth, followed by a gentle kiss against his skin that encouraged an outbreak of sensual shivers. Expecting to see Lola, he rolled over and squinted through bloodshot eyes.

'Good morning,' whispered Holly as a flushness crept across her cheeks. Parker squinted and an immediate wave of regret washed over him like a tsunami. He struggled for breath and his heart pounded beneath his chest.

'Are you feeling okay?' she asked after a few seconds, when Parker failed to speak.

'Hi,' he finally replied, rubbing his eyes and pressing his hand against the side of his head. 'Morning,' he added, peering around the room, everything looking sickeningly unfamiliar beneath the sombre glow that was emanating from the bedside lamp.

'How are you feeling?' Holly asked again, reaching out her arm and laying it across his bare chest.

The touch of her skin now made him feel uneasy. 'Delicate,' he began, 'I don't think I've ever drunk quite so much in such a short space of time.' Becoming aware that he had no clothes on, Parker scanned the bedroom, searching for his belongings.

Moving her body closer to his, Holly grinned. 'I had a great time last night,' she confessed, pulling the duvet up to her nose and shying away the moment she released the comment. 'I don't think we slept for more than a couple of hours.'

On his side of the bed, guilt soared through every bone in Parker's body, causing his limbs to feel listless 'I'm married,' he revealed out of nowhere.

The room fell silent. In the light of the new day, all the passion, all the romance and all the excitement of the previous evening disappeared in an instant.

'I'm engaged,' she replied.

Parker turned to face Holly. 'I'm so sorry, I should never have—' he began, but was quickly interrupted.

'You don't need to apologise. We're both adults,' she began. 'I saw your ring last night in the bar, before you took it off. I knew it was too good to be true that a guy like you would be single.' She moved her arm back over to her side of the bed. The photo of her and Aidan on the bedside table came into view, and for the first time since being in the bar the previous evening, she thought about her fiancé.

The pair lay still in bed, neither one knowing what to say.

Parker ran his hands through his hair, the reality of the situation stealing his breath. He recalled removing his wedding band the previous evening, his promise to Lola already destroyed despite having only just declared his vows. 'My wife and I are newlyweds, just back off our honeymoon.' He shook his head, wishing that he could go back in time and do things over. 'I'm so sorry,' he began, turning to look at Holly. 'I really shouldn't have done this. I love my wife and she deserves so much better.' Parker thought back to Lola, remembering how unwell she had felt the previous evening. 'I best get going.' Parker leaned over to kiss Holly on the cheek, and he hated admitting to himself that the previous evening had felt so good, that she had felt so good against his skin. Before he could pull away, Holly turned her head and kissed him on the lips, wrapping her arm around his back and drawing him back to her naked embrace.

Parker leant over her body, allowing his chest to press against the warmth of hers. He kept his eyes closed and ran his hands through her hair, inhaling her perfume and savouring how easily she made his body come alive.

'I thought you were going,' she smirked as Parker reciprocated the kiss, her legs wrapping around his back, securing his body in place. 'Or do you want to stay right here?' she teased, kissing him again.

Parker looked Holly in the eyes, and yet blurred visions of Lola distorted how she now appeared. 'I'm leaving. I'm sorry, I shouldn't have done this,' he replied, peeling back the bedcovers. He scooped up the trail of clothes that were scattered across the floor, each item of clothing acting as a ghastly reminder of the previous evening's sordid antics, and walked out of the room.

Holly slipped an oversized jumper over her head and eased her legs into a pair of night-time shorts. She followed Parker downstairs; her trail of clothes also scattered across the floor.

'I loved last night,' she announced gently from the kitchen doorway, watching Parker grab his wallet and keys. Her hands clung to the frame for support. 'I hate myself for saying this, but last night was amazing, and I didn't think about my fiancé once, and I know you felt the same.' She waited for Parker to say something, to agree with her, or at least to smile with flattery.

Parker remained silent, unwilling to accept that everything

Holly had said was right. 'I'm married,' he replied, shaking his head and avoiding eye contact, knowing that the more he admired Holly, the more tempted he might be to take her back upstairs, his attraction to her undeniable. Instead, he fumbled with his wallet and phone, preparing to leave.

Holly lowered her gaze too. 'You knew what you were doing last night, even though you'd had a drink.' Holly watched Parker pick up his phone, recalling the moment they had taken some photos together earlier on in the evening, their wild behaviour captured on his camera.

Parker stopped what he was doing, momentarily hating himself for knowing that she was right. 'I did know what I was doing, but that doesn't make it alright. I'm not that person anymore.'

She walked over to where he was standing and infringed on his personal space, allowing her hair to tickle his arm, her breath to fall on his neck.

'Don't go. Stay here, stay with me, at least for a few more hours.'

She slid her hand beneath his shirt, sensing his excitement, and relished the way that she could feel his skin reacting to her touch. Taking hold of his hand, she guided him across the room, wrapping his arm around her back so that he was once again caressing her body. At the bottom of the stairs, Parker paused.

'I can't do this, I need to go,' he muttered, looking up at her, remembering exactly why he'd been unable to resist her allure the previous night, her full lips and blue eyes temptation alone. 'You're amazing and you deserve way better than me.' Parker made his way to the front door, easing his feet into his shoes and turning the key. Holly followed and placed her hand on the wood, pressing the door shut.

'Have a shower before you go, you don't want your wife smelling my perfume,' she suggested, once again taking hold of his hand, knowing that deep down he really wanted to stay.

Parker turned to look at Holly, loathing himself for still finding her attractive, even in pyjama shorts and a scruffy t-shirt. He took hold of her waist and pulled her close, pressing her body against his before kissing her and releasing all of his passion onto her lips. 'Bye, Holly,' he whispered into her ear, before opening the door and slipping away into the darkness of the early morning.

Outside, a sheet of puffy, white snow had fallen since he had last stepped over the threshold. Parker's footsteps left impressions on the ground the moment his feet sank into the blanket of soft snow, his prints trailing from Holly's front door all the way down the street. A barrage of thoughts tumbled through his blurred mind; in one minute, he practised how he was going to confess everything to Lola in the hope that she could forgive him, and in the next moment, he felt confident that he could keep his secret and convinced himself that she never needed to know. Deep in thought, Parker didn't notice the person walking towards him on an otherwise deserted street.

Upon approach from the other end of the street, Aidan looked up to offer a polite acknowledgement to the passing stranger. 'Morning,' he announced when their eyes briefly met. Witnessing Parker's dishevelled appearance, Aidan smirked to himself as he realised that the person he had just passed was obviously only just on his way home after a good night out, recalling how in the past, he had also done the walk of shame. Aidan continued walking down Poets Nook towards his home, the street completely deserted now that Parker had turned the corner and vanished.

In the quietness of the early morning, Aidan ran through what he wanted to say to Holly. The weight of his boots left a trail in the snow, each step sinking next to those indentations made by Parker only minutes earlier. Aidan rummaged in his pocket for his keys, and it was this distraction that prevented him from noticing the fresh set of footprints in the snow that lined the steps to his own front door.

'Holly?' he called out in a soft tone once inside. He placed his travel bag down and removed his coat, noticing the disarray in the kitchen; empty wine bottles and glasses left abandoned on the island. 'Holly?' he said again, peering through to the lounge, spotting her clutch bag and pair of tights on the sofa. He made his way upstairs, stepping over a pair of high heels, Holly's gold, fringe dress draped over the bannister. He peered into the bedroom just as he heard the sound of the shower being turned on, the noise diverting his attention away from the heavily crumpled duvet.

'Holly?' he called out again, knocking on the bathroom door as it stood ajar. He peered his head around, steam from the shower filling the bathroom. 'Hi,' he announced.

Her head swung around upon hearing a voice. 'Bloody hell, Aidan, you scared me to death!' she exclaimed, turning the shower off and grabbing a towel. 'Why did you creep up on me like that?'

'I shouted from downstairs, you just didn't hear me,' he smiled, walking over and planting a wet kiss on her moist lips.

'What the hell are you doing here? I thought you'd be on a plane to France by now,' she questioned, a look of confusion appearing on her face as their lips parted.

'Marry me,' he blurted. 'Come with me and elope. Let's go and get married and do away with all the fuss.' He placed his hands on either side of her face and drew it closer to his 'I know you're scared because of what happened in your past, but I'm your future, and I want to spend the rest of my life with you,' he declared, looking Holly right in the eye.

Having had her shower cut short and not yet brushed her teeth, Holly could still taste the previous evening in her mouth; the wine, the nacho crisps she and Parker had eaten in the early hours, and she could still feel the way that Parker's skin had felt against hers.

She diverted her stare and pulled her head away. 'I'm really confused right now,' she began, avoiding the question. 'You're meant to be on your way to France to sort out all that solicitor stuff.'

She grabbed hold of her robe and wrapped it around her body, brushing past Aidan so that she could leave the room. She walked into the bedroom, panicked by what she might find, her eyes immediately spotting Parker's scarf on the floor. 'You could have called me to let me know about the change of plans,' she shouted, scooping up the scarf and stuffing it in her clothes drawer.

'Why are you mad? I wanted to surprise you and be hopelessly romantic, isn't that what all women want?' Aidan muttered, still lingering in the bathroom, allowing his head to lean against the wall, his heart and hopes deflated. 'I thought at least you'd be pleased to see me.' Aidan could feel his confidence draining with every second that Holly avoided responding to his marriage proposal. He skulked through to the bedroom, not really knowing what to say to fill the awkward silence, and lingered in the doorway.

'So, was it a good night last night?' he asked, noting the state of the bedroom despite Holly's quick attempt to tidy.

'I guess so. Jess and I had way too many drinks, but it was okay,' she replied, putting on a pair of jogging bottoms and a clean t-shirt, trying to shed her feeling of guilt, her body feeling heavy beneath the weight of betrayal. 'Town was so busy, so we pretty much ended up staying in one place the whole night. It was nothing special.'

Aidan watched as Holly fidgeted with her clothes. 'That's a shame. Your Christmas night out with Jess is one of the best party nights of the year, isn't it?' he began. 'I mean, I know my proposed trip to France to sort out the solicitor stuff wasn't the most exciting of offers, but you still chose your night out with Jess over spending a few days in France with me at Christmas.'

Holly looked up at Aidan. 'It's always been something we've done on the last Saturday before Christmas, sort of our tradition, and I didn't want to let her down, but maybe it's time for new traditions,' she said, looking into his eyes and approaching him in the doorway.

Aidan took hold of her hand and guided her towards the bed and sat, signalling for her to join him.

'You don't want to marry me, do you?' he asked, despite not really wanting to hear the truth. 'I love you so much, but I'm ready to start the next chapter in my life, and I want to be with someone who wants the same things as I do.'

Holly sat down alongside him, resting her hands in her lap.

'Ask me again,' she requested, holding his hand tightly. Aidan looked confused, so she continued to speak. 'I didn't know until last night, but I'm ready for the next chapter, too.' Images of her and Parker flashed through her mind, and she now hated herself for how much she had betrayed her fiancé. 'I'm done with the endless nights out in town, I've had my fill of the social scene in York, and I'm so done with being scared of marriage just because my parents went through a messy divorce,' she explained, her emotions brimming in her eyes. 'I didn't think I was ready to let go of the carefree life that I've been enjoying for so long, but I am, I really am,' she continued, running her hand across Aidan's cheek in a bid to not only convince him, but to convince herself. 'I have a wonderful man wanting to spend the rest of his life with me and build a future together, and that's exactly what I want, too. So go on, ask me the question again.'

Aidan bent down and got on one knee, taking hold of her hand. 'Holly Benn, will you run away with me and get married? I can't promise a perfect wedding with seating plans, confetti, and fancy trays of fiddly-looking food, but I can promise you I'll always try my best to make you happy.'

Holly got down off the bed and crouched on the floor beside him, gently placing her arms around his shoulders.

'I can't think of anything better than running away and marrying you, Aidan Fogg,' she replied, planting a kiss on his lips.

Aidan hugged her back, squeezing her tightly. 'I love you so much, Holly.'

The pair sat on the floor together, their backs pressed against the bed.

'So, when do we go? Where do we go?' she asked, smiling at the thought of escaping the house and the suffocating memories of the previous evening.

'Well, it's Christmas Eve, so our options might be limited.'

Holly looked at Aidan in a way that she hadn't done for years, seeing him for the incredible man that he was, unsure of how she had nearly thrown it all away. 'Is it too late for us to go to France for Christmas?' she began, thinking back on Aidan's original plans. 'Did you cancel the flights? What about the meeting with the solicitors, I thought you had to sign all the paperwork? We could combine both at the same time - get married in Paris, one of the most romantic cities in the world, and then go and sort your family stuff out.'

'I cancelled my flights and the meeting with the solicitor,' Aidan began. 'But I'm sure we could get some cancellation seats if we try, and the sooner I get the solicitor stuff sorted, the better,' he explained.

'Then let's do it. I'll look for flights to Paris, and you contact the solicitors and see when you can go and sign the paperwork,' she confirmed, kissing him repeatedly like it was their first time. Aidan stood up and helped Holly off the floor.

'I'll go and make us some coffee while you finish getting ready,' he suggested, walking out of the bedroom and heading downstairs.

In the kitchen, Aidan switched on the kettle and, while waiting for it to boil, spotted Holly's phone on the side unit, the light flashing to indicate that she had a new notification. He pressed the side button and saw that she had a new message from Jess that began with the words, *Tell me everything*. He unlocked her phone with her password and opened the notification to reveal the contents of the full message.

Tell me everything that happened between you and the hot guy from the bar. Still love you even though you left me early xx

The longer he stood reading the words, the more Aidan's heart raced. He could feel his face flush and his hands tremble as he read the message over, making sure he understood the words. Without thinking, he opened up Holly's gallery, knowing that in nearly all situations in life, Holly rarely missed an opportunity to take a photo. Just as the kettle boiled, a photo appeared on the screen of Holly in bed with another man, both parties smiling for the seductive selfie. His heart shattered and an internal pain stole away his ability to breathe. He shook his head and dropped his shoulders, the weight of disappointment too heavy to carry. He scrolled to the next photo, and upon looking closer, Aidan realised that the picture had been taken upstairs, in his bed.

Without thought, he threw the phone down and walked through to the hall. He peered upstairs, listening to Holly as she brushed her teeth. He grabbed his keys, put on his coat, and threw his travel bag over his shoulder before walking out, slamming the front door behind him. With his emotions laid bare on his face, he wiped his eyes with the back of his hand and walked away.

Now that the sun had begun to rise and light shone over the street, Aidan spotted the only other set of footprints that were visible in the snow. In that moment, he realised that the stranger he'd passed on the street had been the man that had slept with his fiancée, the man in the photos. With a trail of tears lining his footsteps, he continued to walk away, the pink door on Poets Nook soon falling out of sight.

Back at home, Holly heard the front door slam from upstairs as she continued to brush her teeth. 'Aidan?' she called out from the landing. When there was no reply, she made her way downstairs and peered around, spotting the steaming kettle that was waiting to be poured. Then, her eyes landed on her phone. She walked over and unlocked the device, the photo of her and Parker appearing on the screen.

8

WITHOUT ANY FAMILY TO SPEND TIME WITH ON HIS DAYS OFF, and with no real friends to call upon, Matty stepped outside his flat ready to go for an early-morning, solitary walk down by the canal. Securing his earphones in place, he headed across the city on foot, the sheets of snow and ice crunching beneath his shoes as he walked. He always felt particularly lonely during the build-up to Christmas, a time traditionally spent in the company of loved ones, and yet he had nobody of significance to love and embrace around the warming coals of his fire at home. The moment he reached the centre of the festive city, Matty looked on with envying eyes each time a family unit of any guise walked past him, their broad smiles and trails of laughter only heightening his inner sense of social isolation.

He turned up the volume on his phone, hearing that the local radio station was reporting on a major accident that had just happened on the outskirts of town. The moment he heard the initial report, his stomach churned and he felt a surge of nerves flood through his body. He took out his phone again and saw that he'd had several missed calls from work.

'What's going on?' he asked Marie when she picked up the phone. 'I've just heard that there's been some sort of accident.'

'There's been a massive pile-up on Lendal Bridge, multiple fatalities already confirmed and an unknown number of casualties heading our way. I know you're on annual leave, but they need as many people on shift as possible, that's why they've called you. If you don't want to come in, which you shouldn't have to, just turn your phone off. They can't say anything about it because you're not on call today.'

'I've just stepped out to go for a walk,' he replied. 'I can hear the ambulances,' he added, removing one of his earphones. 'I'll head straight in and just borrow some uniform.'

'The bridge is blocked so they're struggling to gain access,' she replied. 'It's going to be a long day followed by a long night, so be sure that you're rested enough before you offer to come and work. I know what you're like, you've given your whole life to this bloody place.'

'You know me, I just can't stay away, not when there's a major incident,' Matty admitted. 'I didn't really fancy a walk anyway, it's all a bit too cheery in town for me.'

'By cheery you mean that people are actually smiling and having a good time?' she questioned, knowing that Christmas wasn't his favourite time of year. 'Maybe you should join in with some of the festivities that are on offer,' she encouraged. 'You might actually enjoy a festive tipple while listening to some carolers.' Down the line, she heard the sound of Matty's disapproving groans, and before she could offer any further words of persuasion, her attention became diverted when a fellow colleague pushed a piece of paper in front of her. 'Actually, forget about all that stuff and come in, if you can. I don't think our vacant bed number two is going to stay that way for much longer, and I'd appreciate your support.'

'I'm on my way.'

9

*L*OLA OPENED HER EYES AND COULD TELL THAT SHE WAS FEELING better. The fog that had been befuddling her head for the previous few days had now eased, and her body no longer ached with an unyielding intensity. She looked over at Parker's side of the bed and became immediately confused, his pillow empty and the covers untouched. Reaching out her hand, she grabbed her phone and pressed the side button, expecting to see a string of messages and missed calls while her phone had been on silent, and yet no new notifications appeared. She pulled back the covers, sunk her feet into a pair of well-worn slippers and walked through to the lounge. She was a little unsteady on her feet, so allowed her hand to follow the line of the wall, offering her body support.

'Parker?' she announced, expecting to see him passed out on the sofa, knowing that his thoughtfulness could have made him reluctant to disturb her sleep.

The room was in darkness, and with a stretch of the neck, she could see past the door frame, noting that Parker's shoes weren't scattered near the front door in their typical, abandoned style. Walking back through to the bedroom, she dived back beneath the covers to keep warm. A nauseating feeling of worry brewed in the pit of her stomach as to why her husband hadn't come home last night, and images of him lying in a hospital bed made her hands shake.

She scanned her last message to him, noticing that it had been read, but that Parker hadn't been online since the previous evening. Just as she opened up her contacts page ready to give him a call, she heard the sound of the front door opening.

'Parker?' she shouted, peering towards the front of the house. A few seconds later, the bedroom door eased open. Still dressed in the previous night's clothes, and looking blurry eyed, Parker appeared.

'Hi,' he announced, rubbing his hands, his body shivering. 'It's so cold out there. Have you seen that it's snowed?' he asked, walking over to the bedroom window.

Relief flooded through Lola's body, images of her husband lying drunk in a ditch were quickly replaced by thoughts of where he'd been all night. She glanced over towards the window, rage brewing that he hadn't immediately offered up an apology of any kind. 'I can see that it's snowed,' she commented in a very matter-of-fact tone. 'Are you just getting in now?' she questioned, a look of disappointment spreading across her face. 'You look like hell, like you've been up all night.'

Parker ran his hands through his thick, wavy hair and tied it back into his usual messy bun. 'I had a few too many and by the time I looked at my phone last night, I knew I'd wake you up if I came home, so I spent the night on Ed's sofa,' he explained. 'I didn't want to risk disturbing you, knowing that you were under the weather and probably already fast asleep.' Parker walked over and perched himself on the side of the bed next to Lola, reaching his hand out and pressing it against her forehead. 'You're looking much better,' he added, smiling. 'Are you feeling better?'

She turned her face to the side, brushing off his hand. 'Yeah, a bit,' she replied, sitting up and straightening out her pyjama t-shirt. 'I thought you were just having a few and then coming home? Isn't that what you said right before you left?' she asked, detecting the pungent smell of alcohol still lingering on his breath.

Parker allowed his body to fall back on the bed, his arms resting over his eyes. 'That was the plan,' he began, leaning his head to one side to look at Lola, 'but I was late to the party, so the boys made it their business to help me catch up.'

He closed his eyes, unwelcome flashbacks from the previous night running through his mind like unwanted ghosts. He could still smell the lingering scent of Holly's perfume, he could hear her voice whispering into his ear, and he could feel her delicate touch all over his skin. Wishing he'd had a shower before leaving her house, a haunting sense of paranoia clung to his skin.

Lola blew her nose. 'It's a good job my nose is still blocked because it looks like you haven't showered in a while,' she commented. 'Did Ed kick you out before you had chance to shower?'

Parker could feel his heart beating beneath his chest, his face flushing and the smell of Holly's perfume continued to tease his senses. 'I wanted to get home to you, so I didn't bother. I'd imposed on him enough by spending the night on their sofa.'

Parker felt his phone vibrate in his pocket.

'You're popular,' she added upon hearing the phone buzz again in close succession.

'It'll just be the lads,' he brushed off, keeping his mobile wedged into his pocket. 'They'll be comparing hangovers, no doubt.'

'So, how was it, apart from the alcohol and stinking hangover?' Lola asked, resting her back against the headboard.

The answers Parker had rehearsed on his way home disappeared from his memory, leaving him tongue-tied. 'Erm, we had a few drinks and a laugh, that's about it really,' he replied. 'Ed was being his usual self and entertained everyone.'

'Was it busy in town?' she continued to question in a blasé manner, her disappointment in his behaviour lingering just beneath the surface.

'Yeah, packed. We couldn't sit down, which you'd expect at this time of year.'

'Anything exciting happen?' she asked in another nonchalant tone.

Parker's phone buzzed, again.

Lola raised her eyebrows and smiled. 'Something must have happened for you to be getting so many messages. The lads never text you unless there's something interesting to talk about, and I'm assuming it isn't work-related.'

Eager to end the conversation, Parker pulled himself up and stretched. 'Ed was trying to set Max up, so he's probably digging for the gossip.' He stood up and took off his jumper, walking towards the bedroom door. 'I'll go and have a shower, then get us something to eat. I'm starving.'

Lola's frustration bubbled over. 'You could have at least messaged me,' she began in one quick breath. 'I woke up wondering if you were in hospital somewhere, or lying somewhere waiting to be found,' she explained, 'and you don't even bother apologising.' She bowed her head, the hurt that had been hiding beneath the surface now evident all over her face. 'This isn't how married couples behave, this isn't even how you behave when you're dating,' she scoffed, throwing her phone on the bed.

Parker stood in the doorway and allowed Lola to have her say, her anger making him sink to new depths of guilt. He opened his mouth, ready to turn and apologise, but Lola beat him to it.

'We haven't spent a night apart for so long, and it was awful waking up alone, not knowing your whereabouts or even if you were alright,' she concluded, her heart craving an apology, or better still, a tender kiss followed by him owning up to the fact that he'd been a complete idiot. 'I got that sinking feeling in the pit of my stomach that something terrible had happened to you,' she added when Parker continued to stand in silence. 'Don't you have anything to say?'

Parker paused in the doorway. Part of him just wanted to be able to get a shower and wash away all traces of Holly in a bid to convince himself that last night had never happened. With his head lowered, he couldn't even bear to look at Lola, let alone say anything that was going to make things better.

His silence infuriated her. 'Since when do we stay out all night and sleep on other people's sofas? Didn't we used to do that in our early twenties?' she questioned, aggravated. 'If you think that this is the best way to start a marriage, then you're mistaken, and I'm mistaken in assuming that you've changed. It seems like you haven't grown up at all.'

He finally swung his body around, guilt spreading quicker than a roaring bushfire. 'Everything you're saying is right,' he began. 'I should have messaged you, and to be honest, I thought I had,' he explained, recalling the moment that he had begun composing a message, right before Holly approached him outside the pub. 'I knew I'd had too much to drink, and I didn't want to risk waking you up, that's all. So, I'm sorry,' he apologised, shaking his head. 'I passed out on Ed's sofa and now I'm here, feeling awful that I didn't come home, and worse still, that I didn't send a message so that you wouldn't have worried about me.'

Parker leant against the doorframe, loathing that he could still smell Holly and taste her skin.

'Honestly, I'm an idiot and I'm sorry for worrying you. I don't want to be the person that lets you down, the person that I once was. Really, I don't.'

Lola took a deep breath, digesting his sincerity. 'You're not an idiot, Parker, I just hate some of the choices you make, choices that make me feel bad.' She flattened out her hair and rubbed her eyes, trying to prevent herself from getting upset. 'All I've ever wanted is to feel that you put me first, that you think of me first, and you've managed to do that for so long, and then something like this happens, and I feel like I mean nothing to you all over again.'

Parker walked over to the bed, resting on his side and taking hold of her hand. 'You mean everything to me, and I don't deserve you, Lola.'

Lola looked up, her eyes glossy with fresh tears. 'I chose to spend the rest of my life with you and all I'm asking in return is that you love me, and treat me how I deserve to be treated,' she began, sniffling back her sadness at the situation. 'I don't care if you get drunk and sleep on Ed's sofa. I mean, it's not ideal, but all you had to do is let me know, send me a message so that I didn't worry, and everything would have been fine.'

Looking into Lola's eyes made Parker realise just how stupid he'd been, and how close he'd come to throwing everything away, again, all just for a moment of passion with a stranger.

'I'm sorry,' he began. 'I do love you, so much, and I don't know why I act so stupid sometimes, and I don't blame you for being so upset.'

Lola drew in a composing breath. She couldn't help but love Parker, even though he'd hurt her again.

'Have you forgotten about our plans this morning?' she asked, eager to change the mood.

'To be honest, I had forgotten,' he began, his body language deflated. 'But let me shower, have breakfast, and then I'm all yours, I promise,' he added, leaning over and kissing her gently on the cheek. 'Do you forgive me?' he asked, peering deep into her eyes.

'I'll think about it,' she agreed, unable to resist his charm. 'I'll forgive you quicker if you brush your teeth,' she said, wrapping her arms around his waist and pressing her head into his torso before delivering a gentle kiss. 'I'm sure I can taste alcohol on you.'

'I'll give myself a onceover and then I'll come out looking and smelling like a new man,' he reassured her, getting up and heading into the bathroom. The sound of the shower came resonating into the bedroom.

In a moment of haste, Lola grabbed her phone and began texting Sophie, Ed's fiancée.

Hi Sophie, hope you're okay, haven't seen you at The Brownie Box in a while, stop by soon and we can catch up over coffee and sugar! Odd question, but did Parker spend last night on your sofa?

She shook her head in frustration at herself the moment she pressed send on the message, disappointed that after so long, she once again found herself questioning Parker's loyalty.

Changing into a fresh set of clothes, Lola walked through to the bathroom and grabbed Parker's clothes off the floor. 'I'm going to put a wash on before we head out,' she called to him, closing the door behind her. Flustered, she rummaged through his trouser pockets and grabbed his phone. Continuing to walk through to the kitchen, she placed his mobile on the worktop without turning it on. Biting her bottom lip and pulling at a stray hair at the base of her neck, she walked away from the phone and threw Parker's clothes on the floor next to the washing machine, loathing her out-of-character behaviour.

Feeling slightly hopeless, she slumped her body on the floor next to the washing machine and rested her weary head back. With her sinuses still congested, she took hold of Parker's shirt, pressed it against her face and inhaled, her instincts screaming that something wasn't right, something didn't *feel* right. Frustrated at her blocked nose, she closed her eyes and inhaled again while the material was pressed against her skin, the faint scent of unfamiliar perfume or body spray making its way up her nostrils.

'So, where are we going this morning?' Parker asked upon entering the kitchen, making Lola jump and quickly get off the floor before stuffing the clothes into the machine. He placed some bread in the toaster and flicked on the kettle before reaching up for the medicine tin and grabbing the tub of paracetamol, shaking the bottle to make sure they hadn't run out. 'You haven't told me anything.'

Startled by his entrance, Lola slammed the washing machine door and pressed the button. 'Wait and see,' she replied.

At the far end of the room, Parker's phone buzzed again. Lola continued putting the washing powder away, watching him from the corner of her eye.

'I might put this on silent. I get the impression that the lads are going to annoy me today,' Parker commented, grabbing his phone off the counter. He pressed the side button, shocked to see that there were three messages, all from Holly, failing to even recall the moment that they had exchanged numbers, much of the previous twelve hours still a boozy blur in his mind. The first part of the message read, *Can we talk? It's Holly xx*

'Is it the lads?'

Parker tried to delete the first message, an alert popping up before he could do so, asking if he was sure about the requested action. 'Yep, it's just Ed. He'll be like this all day so I'm just going to ignore it,' he replied, turning it off and putting his phone in his pocket. 'So, come on, tell me where we're going this morning. Do I need to bring anything or wear anything special?' he asked, buttering two slices of toast and liberally spreading one slice with lemon curd for Lola.

Lola checked her own phone, waiting for a reply from Sophie. 'I'm taking you to see something,' she began, noticing that Sophie was in the middle of typing a message. 'You don't need to wear anything special,' she added, taking a bite of the toast, the tangy spread awakening her dulled senses. 'You hate the smell of lemon curd. Is this your way of making it up to me?' she asked.

'Just let me spoil you today,' he began. 'So, that's all you're going to tell me, that we're going to look at something?'

'Yep, it's a surprise.'

Parker wrapped his arms around Lola's waist and kissed her on the neck, making her hairs stand on edge. 'I love how thoughtful you are,' he whispered, before tending to the boiled kettle.

'Make them to-go. If we don't get going, they'll think we're not coming,' she said, walking out of the room and through to the lounge. Her phone vibrated in her pocket, and with a slight nervousness, she swiped across the screen to unlock it.

Hi Lola! Lovely to hear from you. I'm trying to cut down on treats so staying away from your delicious brownies. There are too many temptations at this time of year as it is!

Sophie had responded. Her second message followed seconds later.

Ed has just made me promise not to say anything, so please don't let on that this came from me, but Parker didn't stay here last night. Ed last saw him at The Mill. Sorry. Always here if you need to chat xx

Lola could feel her cheeks blushing, and her hands trembled like she'd gone too long without food. A sickening feeling made her want to throw up, and everything that she'd pictured in her mind about her future disappeared. All she could think about was where Parker had stayed, and with whom. She deleted both of Sophie's messages when she heard Parker shouting.

'Would you like some more toast?'

She walked back into the kitchen, her fears masked with a poker face. 'No, thanks,' she said. 'So, did you get to chat to Sophie last night, or this morning before you left?' she asked, taking another bite of toast.

'I saw her briefly before I left and just said thanks for letting me stay over,' he replied, mulling over in his mind how to go about telling Lola everything, knowing that it was the right thing to do, knowing that he loved her and wanted to make their marriage work.

'Shall we get ready to go?' he asked, his nerves getting the better of him.

Lola turned off her phone and looked up. 'Yeah, I just need to borrow your phone to check the directions to our destination. My Google Maps isn't working for some reason,' she requested in a steady tone, pushing down her emotions and walking through to the lounge, trying to hide the emotion that was bound to be showing on her face.

'Give me the postcode and I'll check for us, you know I'm way better with directions,' he replied, unwilling to give her his phone, his fingers working to delete and block Holly's number the moment Lola disappeared from sight.

Lola walked back towards Parker and smiled. 'No, this is my surprise, remember? Let me do all the work. You just need to go upstairs and find my pink hat and scarf from the airing cupboard,' she insisted, taking the phone from his hand and indicating in a playful manner for him to go upstairs.

'Sure, no worries,' he replied with reluctance before running upstairs. The moment he left the room and she could hear his footsteps, she walked into the lounge and closed the door, pressing the side button on his phone to unlock the screen, tapping on the WhatsApp icon without hesitation. The message at the top of the list was from Ed the previous night, asking what time he would be at the pub. She then quickly opened up Facebook, Instagram and Messenger, searching for clues. With nothing on any of his social media accounts, she looked up and breathed easy, relief momentarily flooding through her heart. As an afterthought, she thought to open up his gallery, at which point, her stomach dropped, and she burst into tears. The last photo in Parker's gallery was of him asleep in someone else's bed, naked, with a woman lying next to him, the smirk on her face and ruffled hair telling the whole story. Upon seeing the photo, Lola pressed her back against the wall and buried her face in her hands, unable to halt her tears. With her vision blurred, she looked at the photo again before casting the phone to the floor.

She heard Parker's voice bellow from upstairs. 'I can't find your pink hat, will the grey one do?' he shouted.

Lola opened the lounge door, grabbed her coat and keys and ran out of the house, her woolly slippers sinking into the snow until the soft material became soggy. She fumbled to get the keys into the ignition, urging the car to start and take her away, her eyes turning back to the house every other second to see if Parker had followed her. Just as he appeared in the doorway, she pressed her foot down on the accelerator and headed down the lane. The street was still quiet and the city began to disperse a dusting of pearly snowflakes; perfect conditions for those fortunate enough to be tucked up inside a chocolate box cottage ready to savour a magical Christmas Eve.

10

*H*AVING TO DIVERT ACROSS TOWN TO AVOID THE LENDAL BRIDGE accident, Matty continued to battle his way to the hospital on foot. Heavy snow continued to fall and accumulate in whichever crevices the wind had drifted, every rooftop dressed with a white-peaked hat. On untreated surfaces beneath the picturesque billows of snow, sheets of ice remained hidden, making conditions dangerous, and every time his trainers slid on the ice, his heart skipped. He hated the fact that work remained his priority, even on his days off, and he yearned to have something, or someone, more important in his life than the hospital.

'I'm going to make changes in the New Year,' he announced the moment Marie picked up the phone.

Taken aback by his out-of-character statement, Marie encouraged her friend to open up. 'What changes?' she asked, having always been curious about his personal life, an aspect that Matty always kept guarded. 'Please tell me that you're still retiring.'

'I am, I'm talking more about changes to my personal life,' he admitted, his honesty causing Marie to get upset. 'I don't want to feel so alone anymore.'

Marie dabbed her face. 'You'll always have me in your life, even after you've retired,' she replied. Having always respected Matty's request for privacy, Marie yearned to know more about the person she had spent so much time with over the years, and yet whom, beneath the surface, she knew little about. 'I know you don't like talking about personal stuff, but I'd like to know more about your family, your life outside of work.'

'I don't have a life outside of work,' he was quick to reply in a sombre tone. Having finally admitted his darkest secret aloud, Matty heard how terrible it sounded. 'I go to work, I eat and then I sleep. There isn't much else to say.'

Marie could sense his sadness. 'What about family?' she asked with a sense of hesitance, knowing that she had stepped over a line that, in the past, she had always respected.

Matty changed the subject. 'I'm nearly there, can you find me some scrubs?'

'I've been and got you some already,' she replied, knowing that she had pushed him too far.

'It's a bloody nightmare out here,' he said, the wind sweeping across his face, the freezing temperatures stinging his eyeballs. 'Access to the hospital is going to cause havoc and delay people getting to us.'

'When there's a delay, we know that the odds are already stacked against us.'

Matty's heart plummeted. 'I know, I'll be there as soon as I can.'

Slipping his phone back into his pocket, he momentarily felt like he was in some kind of horror film, with the sound of emergency sirens blasting through his ears. It felt as though a sense of panic was being swept through the city. With a quickening pace, his diversion took him through an area of the city that he didn't usually visit, and he meandered down a deserted stretch of road called Swan Lane; a little side street running parallel to the river. Crossing the road in haste, Matty slipped, regaining his balance and narrowly avoiding a tumble. Taking a moment to calm his nerves, he spotted the sheet of black ice lining the entire stretch of road, and he made a mental note not to walk the same way home, knowing that the surface was lethal.

11

With the image of his fiancée in bed with another man still spinning through his mind, Aidan continued to make his way down Poets Nook, his feet picking up pace at the thought of Holly chasing after him. At the first crossroad he came to, he took a left, not really knowing in which direction to head, but desperately wanting to disappear into the architectural shadows of the street and make himself invisible. Beneath the dim light of each lamppost that he passed, all he could think about was the photo of Holly, naked with another man. He stopped walking and hunched himself over at the side of a wall, his stomach churning with the intention to vomit. He crouched and cradled his head, driving his face into the crevice of his arm, the material of his coat soaking up his tears. He took out his phone and called Annie, his closest friend and work colleague, but she didn't answer, and he couldn't bring himself to leave a voicemail, not knowing what to say. With his phone running out of battery, he turned it off and put it back in his pocket.

After a few deep breaths and shakes of the head, he stood up and continued to make his way through the quiet, suburban side streets of the awakening city, weaving his way through unfamiliar parts that he had rarely explored. After a brisque ten-minute walk, confident that even if Holly attempted to uncover his whereabouts, she would be unsuccessful, he joined a section of road that didn't have any streetlights; a deserted side road called

Swan Lane. He paused for breath and rested his arms on some railings, watching the turbulent nature of the canal as snow fell and the breeze picked up in strength. He pulled up the collar on his coat and dropped his bag, wondering if he could face a busy day at work, or if it was a better idea to hide himself away and live for a few hours steeped in waves of denial, contemplating if it was possible to salvage his relationship.

Just as he dropped his head into his hands, the sound of a car skidding made him look up. Within the space of about ten seconds, Aidan watched as the vehicle's driver completely lost control on the icy road. The wheels of the car crashed against the curb and caused it to spin, the car momentarily travelling along the road on its roof until it crashed against another curb at speed and landed back on all four wheels. Ricocheting, the driver's side of the car ploughed into a lamppost, bringing the car abruptly to a halt.

Aidan scrambled for his phone while running towards the scene of the accident, his freezing fingers fumbling in the icy conditions to dial 999.

'Which service do you require?'

'Ambulance,' he said breathlessly as he continued to run down the street, frantically looking around for any other witnesses. His phone beeped, indicating that the battery was running out.

'Connecting you now,' replied the emergency services call handler.

'Hello, can I take your name?' asked the paramedic once the call connected.

'Aidan Fogg,' he shouted, the incident now only a few yards away.

'Where are you Aidan?'

As he ran, he looked around and searched for a street sign. 'Er, I don't know, I'm in York, near the canal, on the eastern side.'

'And what's your phone number, just in case we get cut off?'

'07700 116311. My battery is low,' he explained in a splutter at the sound of his phone beeping again.

'What's happened, Aidan?'

'A car has crashed. It skidded on the ice and the driver lost control,' he explained through a series of frantic breaths. 'The car crashed into a lamppost and I'm running towards it now. I don't know how many people are inside.'

'Okay, Aidan, I'm going to get someone there as soon as I can, but there's been a major incident declared due to a collapsed bridge, so access to your side of the canal is an issue right now. I need you to—' Just as the paramedic was about to continue with her sentence, Aidan's phone ran out of battery and turned itself off. He reached the car the moment his phone lost power, the bonnet of the vehicle completely crushed, the driver's side the worst following impact with the lamppost. He peered in through the driver's window.

'Are you alright?' he shouted upon spotting the female driver, panicking at the sight of the blood running down her face.

The woman inside the car didn't respond.

'Help!' he shouted, peering around in the hope that he'd spot another passing pedestrian. A wave of panic surged through his body when nobody appeared, the secluded side street completely deserted, causing his hands and body to shake. He peered back in through the driver's window again, searching for more passengers before realising that the driver was alone. He wrapped his fingers around the dented door handle and attempted to pull it open, the crushed metal making entry to the vehicle impossible. After he tried to open all of the locked doors, he scrambled back to the driver's side, wiping the snow away with his coat sleeve, the glass fractured.

'Can you hear me?' he asked, hoping that the sound of his voice would cause the driver to respond. 'An ambulance is on its way,' he added when the woman didn't reply.

Inside the car, Lola's eyes remained closed, her breathing shallow. After passing out upon impact, she finally began to come round, her eyes working hard to open. She felt an immediate pounding in her head the second she regained consciousness, her traumatised brain trying to make sense of the situation and yet failing to decode the scrambled scraps of information available. She moved her lips, ready to speak, and yet without realising it, her lips didn't actually move. Her battered body remained pinned in place by her seatbelt, the right side of her head bleeding where her skull had smashed against the window the moment her car performed a summersault. She attempted to speak again, and yet her lips remained sealed, failing to receive the message from her brain.

As the minutes passed, Lola moaned subconsciously as her central nervous system acknowledged her injuries, and stabbing pangs of pain resonated throughout her body. With her hair strewn across her face, her vision remained blurred even when her eyes stayed open for long enough for her to focus, the pounding deep within her skull making her feel like she was about to vomit.

Help,' she finally mumbled, the word only audible to herself.

Outside in the snowy street, Aidan spotted Lola's attempt to talk and moved his face closer to the glass to peer through the fractured window.

'Oh, thank goodness,' he mumbled, as relief that the driver was alive flooded through his body.

'Did you say something?' he asked, willing her to speak again. He watched as the driver attempted to move her head in fractured movements, her posture gravitating back towards its original position each time. 'Are you alright? Can you hear me?' he shouted while knocking on the window, desperately trying to get Lola to turn her head fully and look at him. 'Help is on its way, I've called for an ambulance,' he said in a reassuring tone, partly to calm the driver, but also to steady himself, 'and then they'll get you out of there,' he added, his fingers still trying in vain to prize open the door. 'The doors are jammed so I can't get you out,' he said in frustration. 'Are you okay? Can you hear me?' he repeated, his panic transcending his words. He peered up and down the street in desperation, taking himself towards the back of the car and covering his face with his hands, never in his life feeling so alone, so frightened and so helpless. 'I'm still here,' he reassured upon walking back to the driver's side door. He crouched on the floor and peered in. 'I'm still here.'

With a slow-motion movement, Lola turned her head to face the driver's window, her attention gravitating towards the male voice that she could just about detect. Her breath produced mist over the cracked glass, the distorted sight of Aidan's face coming into focus the more she paid attention. In her mind, she was screaming as loud as she could, replying to each of his questions and begging for help, and yet in reality, no sound emerged from her mouth. A warm trickle of blood continued to ooze down her face, the fracture to her skull the source of the bleed. The moment Lola's head turned to face the window, Aidan produced a beaming smile and wiped the window again with his coat to avoid cutting his hands.

'Hi, my name is Aidan. Are you okay? Can you tell me your name?'

Summoning every ounce of strength, she mumbled through bloody lips, 'Lola.'

'Lola, I need you to keep looking at me. Can you do that for me?' he requested, losing hope as Lola's eyes began to close. 'It's really important that you stay awake for me until the ambulance gets here. Can you do that for me?' he added, tapping his finger on the glass.

Lola's eyes reopened, albeit with a struggle, as though she had been deprived of sleep for weeks.

'Where do you live, Lola? Can you tell me that?' Aidan asked, desperate to keep her alert. 'What's your surname?'

Grappling with a muddled mind, all Lola wanted to do was sleep. She could feel pain and she could sense an internal stream of panic sweeping through her body. Amid her confusion, she knew that she'd suffered some kind of trauma to her body, though she couldn't exactly pinpoint the origin of her pain. Her head pounded like a drum, throbbing like she'd never experienced before, as if her brain was banging against her skull, trying to escape. Her skin felt alive, the cold temperature penetrating her core, and it felt as though her internal organs may freeze. The soft tones of Aidan's voice provided her with a sense of hope that, despite everything she knew was occurring, she would be okay, she would be rescued, and she would survive this horrific accident. Melancholy thoughts of all the things she hadn't yet achieved in her life played through her mind like an old film, the pictures distorted and cracked, and her confusion meant that she couldn't decipher between her dreams and reality. It felt like someone was shining a torch directly onto her face, a light so bright that even though her eyes were closed, she couldn't help but feel the need to squint.

'Lola, can you tell me your last name?' Aidan repeated when he could see that Lola's eyes were rolling behind their lids.

'Help me,' she finally replied, the words being sent from the depths of her brain.

The desperate sound of Lola's plea struck straight through Aidan's heart. 'I'm here, Lola. Can you tell me where you're hurting?'

Lola paid attention to the screams of pain coming from every inch of her body.

'Everywhere,' she muttered, as tears began to roll down her blood-smeared face.

Upon sight of her tears and the blood still weeping from her head, once again, Aidan looked around in desperation, hoping to see the blue flashing lights of an ambulance. With the road still deserted, he took out his phone and tried to turn it on, the lack of battery preventing the screen from even illuminating. He peered in through each window, trying to see if Lola had a mobile with her.

'Lola, do you have a phone?' he asked when he failed to see one.

'I don't know,' she mumbled, her words slurred.

'Lola, I'm going to go and get some help, but I'll be back, I promise,' he explained, getting ready to stand and assessing which direction would be the best to try and find help.

Summoning all her strength, Lola moved her head and peered out of the window. 'Don't leave me,' she gasped, her words barely able to be heard.

Without thought, Aidan crouched back down, his knees resting in the icy snow.

'Okay, Lola, I'm right here,' he reassured her, peering back in through the window. 'Does anyone know where you are?' he asked in the vain hope that a loved one might be out searching for her.

Aidan spotted tears rolling down her cheeks, a look of such terrible sadness brimming in her eyes that couldn't be ignored.

'Are you in more pain?' he asked. 'Where does it hurt now?'

In the midst of her turmoil, her memories threw her another obstacle to overcome and, remembering what she'd seen on her phone before leaving the house, she began to cry.

'My husband...' she managed to whisper, before allowing her head to fall away from the window, revealing to Aidan the extent of the blood loss. 'He cheated on me,' she concluded, allowing her head to rest.

Aidan tapped on the glass. 'Lola, I need you to do something for me. Can you look at me?' he asked, waiting for her to respond.

She moved her head so that she was looking towards him. With her vision further blurred, she was only able to make out vague shapes.

'Okay, I need you to grab that scarf on the seat and press it against your head where it's hurting. Can you do that for me?'

He watched as Lola squirmed, the grimace on her face conveying how much of a struggle it was just to move her arm.

'Perfect,' he encouraged when she grabbed hold of the scarf, scrunching it in her hand and pressing it against her delicate head. 'Now if you can, apply a bit of pressure...'

After Lola had done as requested, her eyes began to close.

'Lola, I'm just going to see if I can smash the back window, I'll be back in a minute. I'm not leaving you, I promise.'

Aidan moved to the rear of the car, searching the surrounding area for a brick or something hefty that he could lunge towards the glass in order to smash it. With the window frozen and nothing more than a handful of rocks and his own brute force to use as leverage, his attempts at smashing the glass failed, leaving Lola trapped inside. Looking down in desperation, he realised his feet were sitting in pools of water, which, upon closer inspection, he soon realised was actually petrol, the tank having ruptured upon impact and now spilling out onto the road. Another desperate glance up and down the street confirmed that nobody in the nearby area had heard the crash, and that nobody was coming to their rescue.

Stepping away from the leaking petrol, Aidan walked back to Lola's side of the car. 'Lola, what should we talk about while we wait?' he said, doing his best to keep both of their spirits raised. The winter snap swirling around the exposed stretch of canal attacked his skin and penetrated his clothes, his body temperature taking a tumble. His teeth began to chatter and he lost all feeling in the tips of his fingers. 'Maybe you can give me some advice?' he began in an attempt to fill the eerie stillness.

He leant his head against the window, trying to get as close to Lola as he could. 'Like you, I've just found out that my fiancée has cheated on me,' he began, thoughts of Holly not far from his mind. He diverted his gaze, making sure that Lola was still awake, checking that her eyes were open and that she remained conscious. 'And I don't know what to do,' he explained. 'I love her so much, we were about to get married,' he continued. 'She slept with someone in our bed,' he added in dismay, the disgust spilling through his words.

Freezing and feeling like he was losing the ability to think, Aidan turned to look at Lola, panicking when he saw that her eyes were now closed.

'Lola, wake up!' he shouted, tapping on the window. 'Open your eyes, the ambulance is nearly here,' he lied. 'I can hear it in the distance, just stay awake for a little bit longer,' he pleaded. 'What kind of music do you like, Lola?' he asked, staring into her eyes. He began to sing the first song that came to mind. *'So don't go away, say what you say, say that you'll stay, forever and a day, in the time of my life, 'cause I need more time, yes I need more time just to make things right.'* His voice was shaky, his trembling emotions getting the better of him as he watched Lola's head continue to bleed, the dark-red blood saturating her forehead.

'Am I dying?' he heard her mumble.

He took a sharp intake of breath and pushed away his own fears. 'No, you're not dying, we're going to get you out and then everything will be alright,' he shouted, his tears falling off his cheeks as he watched Lola's head fall to one side, her chest still. Without thought, he stood up and, with one mighty force, smashed his foot against the back window behind the driver's side. The glass shattered beneath the force. With his arm covered by his sleeve, Aidan cleared away the glass and reached inside, pressing the handle, and after a few attempts, he managed to force the battered door ajar, squeezing himself through the narrow gap.

'Lola, I'm here,' he whispered, forcing his upper body between the two front seats and scooping her head into his palm so that she was once again in a more upright position. 'Lola, can you open your eyes for me?' he encouraged, wiping away her hair so that her face wasn't obscured. For the first time, Aidan saw Lola's features and admired the way her copper hair fell onto her shoulders, and the dotting of her freckles scattered across her nose and cheeks. He couldn't help but be drawn in by her eyes. 'That's better,' he smiled the moment she forced her eyelids to part.

'Will you do me a favour?' he asked, pressing his hand against her skull, stemming the flow of blood. 'Will you keep this safe for me?' he asked, removing a brown leather band from his left wrist. 'It means a lot to me because my mum gave it to me,' he began. 'She told me that it would always remind me to be strong, even when times are tough,' he explained, his emotions once again getting the better of him. 'And now I need you to wear it,' he added, placing the band around Lola's wrist and tightening it. 'I need you to be strong and I need you to fight,' he said, holding her limp wrist in his hand. 'And then once all this is over and you're alright, once you're safe, you can give it back to me. Is that a deal?'

Lola produced a meek smile and cast her gaze down towards her wrist. Through a sudden surge of energy, she began to speak. 'I'll make you some of my brownies,' she mumbled, the words only just loud enough to be heard. 'That's what I'm good at.'

Aidan beamed at her sudden responsiveness, encouraging her to keep talking. 'I'll hold you to that promise,' he said.

Just as the conversation drew to a natural pause, the cathedral in the distance began to ring its bells.

'Lola, can you hear that?' he asked, arching his head. The majestic sound of the mighty bells ignited Aidan's hopes.

Lola looked into his eyes. 'It's the cathedral,' she whispered, and a slight smile appeared across her tired features.

Aidan drew in a deep breath and looked out of the window. 'The sound of the bells reminds me of my mum,' he muttered, more to himself than to anyone else. He drew in strength, allowing the moment of spiritual optimism to fill his lungs. 'Do you like the sound of the bells?' he asked, turning back to look at Lola, only her head had fallen to the side again and her eyes were closed.

'Lola, open your eyes!' Aidan urged. 'Lola, please, open your eyes,' he pleaded again, but her head remained fallen to one side, the life that was once evident in her eyes now hidden from the outside world.

In the distance, a siren echoed through the quiet streets and all those families who were safely tucked up inside gravitated towards their windows, the strange lure of morbid curiosity tearing them away from their festive preparations. Those who had little hands abandoned the task of hanging up their empty stockings, while others momentarily turned their backs on a freshly cooked breakfast, all just to witness what was occurring beyond their windows.

Within a few seconds, the flashing lights of an ambulance illuminated the chilling scene unfolding on Swan Lane. Before the vehicle came to a complete halt, the lights settled on Aidan and Lola, who were lying at the heart of what the emergency crew initially imagined would result in a Christmas Eve tragedy.

12

THE MOMENT THAT MATTY WALKED ONTO ICU, HIS EYES WERE drawn towards bed number two; it was still empty, and an immediate surge of relief flooded through his body.

'I'm so glad that you're here,' said Marie when she spotted him.

Matty walked to the nursing station and reviewed a shift handover, noticing that the names of his five inpatients still remained the same. 'Have we had an update on the accident?'

'Downstairs are feeling the brunt, but so far, there's been nobody earmarked for us,' she replied. 'They were talking about extending our capacity at one point, converting the adjoining theatre to allow for three more beds,' she continued, a look of dismay lodged on her face.

The internal red phone rang, alerting the team of a potential new patient requiring the specialised treatment provided in the ICU.

'Here we go,' he muttered. With the phone pressed against his ear, Matty answered the call. 'ICU, Matty speaking.'

'We've just been told of another RTA, a separate crash to the one on the bridge. Happened down by the river, some place called Swan Lane, wherever that is,' the person downstairs in A&E relayed. Matty could feel an additional surge of adrenaline coarse through his body, his heart pumping beneath his scrubs. He thought back on his early morning walk to work, realising that he'd passed the exact site of the accident that the person on the other end of the phone was now describing.

'Do we know any more?' he questioned.

'It's a head injury and there's been a delay in rescuing the driver. I'll keep you posted, but it's more than likely that you'll be needed.'

Matty put the phone down and turned to address his team, who had all congregated around the station, awaiting an update following the call.

'We have a possible incoming but no ETA as yet. It's a head injury so let's prepare bay two and I'll update you all when I know more.'

When the team dispersed, Matty walked over to a window and looked out across the city. He surveyed the landscape, wondering who it was in need of their help and the life-saving support that bed number two could offer.

'Are you okay?' asked Marie, placing her arm around him. 'I'm worried about you.'

'I'm fine,' he reassured, turning and offering her a faint glimmer of a smile.

'What you said on the phone, about being lonely…' she began.

Matty interrupted. 'I was just having a moment. I'm fine, honestly. It's just this time of year, when you walk past houses and spot everyone inside having a good time, you can't help but crave a little of that happiness for yourself.' Knowing that he'd uncharacteristically let his real emotions slip through the net again, he lightened his tone and brushed over it. 'It's just the thought of leaving this place, really. After so many years of having a purpose, the thought of life without it is just a little daunting.'

Marie looked out of the window too. 'Can I ask you a question? Why have you never really talked to me about your personal life? We've known each other for so long, and yet you're always so vague, you never let me in or tell me anything.'

'Like I said, there's nothing to tell,' he replied. 'I go home, I eat, and I sleep, and then I come back here. You know everything there is to know.'

'But I've seen you looking at that photo in your locker, and the one beneath your badge, so I know there are other people who mean something to you in your life.' Marie remained by his side and gave him a gentle nudge with her hip. 'I might be able to help if you give me a chance.'

Matty wanted to open up more than ever before, but he knew that once he started to unpick the poignant details of his life, there'd be no going back.

'You can't help me, nobody can,' he said, before turning and walking away.

13

THE SOUND OF THE APPROACHING SIRENS MADE AIDAN CLENCH his eyelids together and even though he wasn't religious, he released a grateful prayer. His hand continued to prop up Lola's head, her body listless. His own limbs felt frozen and detached from his body, his teeth chattering incessantly.

'They're here, Lola,' he whispered when the lights shone with a brighter intensity as the emergency crew approached. His eyes landed back on Lola to see if her chest was continuing to rise and fall, but all he witnessed was a deluge of dark red blood. Down her face, signs of injury continued to trickle from open wounds, her clothes were smeared with blood, and now the palms of his own hands were disguised.

Outside, the ambulance crew jumped down from their van. 'Let's go,' one of them announced just as a police car also arrived on scene.

'Hi, we've just arrived,' the other paramedic announced to the officer, grabbing his bag and approaching the mangled vehicle.

Inside the car, Aidan heard the voices, the paramedic's tone deep. He attempted to shout whilst moving his head to look out of the window, his voice nothing more than a weak, croaky whisper. 'They're going to get you out,' he muttered to Lola the moment a torchlight shone into the car, pausing when it hovered over their bodies. Aidan manoeuvred his free arm and took hold of Lola's hand, squeezing it tightly.

'Are you okay?' the paramedic asked, unable to gain access past Aidan's body.

Aidan attempted to move his head so that he could make eye contact. 'I'm okay, but Lola isn't moving. She's not spoken for ages and she's bleeding from her head,' he cried, all the panic that he'd been containing now spilling out. 'I'm not sure if she's even breathing,' he added, turning back to look at Lola, her body still.

'What's your name?'

'Aidan.'

'Is Lola your girlfriend? Your wife?' the paramedic added upon spotting the wedding rings on Lola's fingers as he attempted to get a better view of her injuries.

Aidan shook his head. 'No, I don't know who she is, I just saw the accident happen and stopped to try and help.'

'Aidan, can you tell me if you're hurt too?' the paramedic asked whilst checking Aidan's body for any sign of bleeding.

He shook his head. 'I wasn't in the car when it crashed.'

'Aidan, can you tell me where you think Lola's hurt?'

'On her head, it's been bleeding the whole time,' he said, his words interspersed with erratic breaths.

The paramedic pressed his hand against Aidan's leg. 'Aidan, listen to me. You've done a brilliant job. My name is Sam and we're going to get you both out, but what I need you to do for me is to just remain still, it's really important that we get you both out as safely as possible. Can you do that for me?'

Aidan nodded and rested his head back down.

'Great, now just let me see in here,' the paramedic said, scanning the scene inside the car. 'Aidan, can you do me a favour?' he asked. 'I can't reach Lola, so I need you to press your fingers against her neck, like this,' he explained while pressing his fingers against his own neck. 'Tell me if you feel a pulse.'

Aidan did as instructed and pressed his three middle fingers against Lola's neck, her soft skin feeling cold even against his freezing fingertips. 'I can't feel anything,' he said in a panic, his eyes welling.

'Try again, and just give it a few seconds,' suggested Sam in a calming voice.

Aidan pressed his fingers against her neck again and felt for a pulse, the slightest murmur beating against his fingers.

'I can feel it!' he cried, looking over at Sam and smiling.

'Perfect, you're doing brilliantly.' Sam turned to look back down the road. The fire engine came rolling down the street. 'Aidan, we're going to get you both out, and I'm going to talk you through it, but for now, I need you to just remain calm. I'll be back with you in just a minute, is that okay?' he asked, looking back to check on Aidan.

Aidan nodded and rested his head back down, his fingers remaining pressed against Lola's neck, her faint pulse rate providing him with a flicker of hope. Aidan heard a commotion occurring outside the car as bright, white lights came beaming in through the smashed windows, along with multiple voices that he didn't recognise. The blue flashing lights of a second ambulance added to the commotion, the pandemonium causing a new sense of panic to set in.

'Sam!' Aidan shouted.

Sam leant back into the car. 'I'm here,' he reassured, once again pressing his hand against Aidan's leg to offer a physical form of reassurance. 'We're just assessing the best way to get you out due to the way the car has been crushed.'

'Is Lola going to be okay?'

Sam momentarily diverted his gaze, which Aidan spotted. 'I'm not going to lie to you Aidan, because that's unfair, but what I will say is that we're going to do everything we can, okay?'

Aidan rested his head back down, his legs feeling numb with cold. 'Okay.'

This time, Sam reached out his hand and took hold of Aidan's when given the command.

'Right, they're ready to get you both out, so, what I need you to do is stay still. It's going to be noisy, but everything will be okay, I promise,' he reassured with a smile before wriggling his way back out of the car.

Inside the vehicle, Aidan took hold of Lola's hand the moment the emergency services turned on the hydraulics, the machinery revving into life. The booming sound of the generator vibrated through every one of Aidan's bones, his ears paining at the deafening sound.

'It's going to be alright, Lola,' he reassured his new friend as the cutters began to sever the mangled car roof, tearing the sheet of metal apart before moving onto the driver's door. Aidan watched people appear through the open crevices once the car had been pulled apart, and never had he felt so relieved to see the faces of others.

'Aidan, we're going to get Lola out first, and then we'll be back for you,' shouted Sam when he appeared in the gap in the roof.

Aidan nodded and remained still, his hand still gripping Lola's. Within seconds, someone leaned into the car to unbuckle Lola's seatbelt.

'We're ready!' the man shouted as Lola's body became free.

Another paramedic appeared, placing an oxygen mask over Lola's mouth and nose before doing a check on her entire body, the seatbelt having pinned her in place and prevented her from moving.

'Let's get her out,' the paramedic ordered once she had done the necessary checks, spotting that Aidan was still holding her hand. 'Aidan, you can let go now, we're going to get her out,' the paramedic smiled, pressing her hand against his. 'We'll look after her, I promise,' she added, noticing Aidan's hesitation to release his grip. 'Then we'll come and get you, and you'll both be in the ambulance together, okay?' she added with a gentle nod.

Aidan slowly released his grip and let go of Lola's hand, watching as she was lifted from the vehicle, placed on a waiting stretcher, and taken to the ambulance.

'You okay?' asked Sam once Lola had been moved, taking her place in the car and taking hold of Aidan's hand.

'I'm good,' Aidan smiled, 'just cold.'

'We're going to get that sorted, it's your turn now,' he replied, moving aside so that another paramedic could assist. With help, Aidan walked into the ambulance and got checked over and a hyperthermic sheet and blanket was wrapped around his body.

'I'm okay, honestly, I'm just cold,' he reassured as Sam assessed him for any injuries.

'We just need to make sure that you don't go into shock,' he advised as the doors to the ambulance closed.

Aidan looked to his left, seeing Lola lying on the stretcher, her whole body covered by blankets and the female paramedic inserting something into her arm.

'Did you say that she's your wife?' Sam asked, spotting him gazing at Lola.

He shook his head. 'No, I've never met her before,' he replied. 'And yet I feel like I've formed this strange kind of bond with her. Is that normal?' he asked, his emotions pouring through his words. 'She's a total stranger.'

Sam nodded and smiled. 'Completely normal in situations like this, we often see complete strangers forming friendships that last for lifetimes.'

'Is she going to be alright?' he finally asked as the ambulance pulled away, the sirens once again blaring through the streets. Aidan waited for the reply and felt his heart sink at the look of uncertainty that flashed in Sam's eyes.

'She's stable for now, but when we get to the hospital, her head injury will be assessed,' he finally replied.

'Can I hold her hand?' he asked.

'Sure,' agreed Sam, manoeuvring a chair so that Aidan could sit alongside the stretcher.

He held out his hand and scooped up Lola's, resting it on the bed alongside her body.

'It feels warmer than it was,' he announced, refusing to divert his attention. He played with the band that he'd placed around her wrist. 'Don't forget our agreement,' he began, looking at Lola as her eyes remained closed. 'You're going to keep this safe for me, and it will remind you to be strong, and once you're better, you're going to make me those brownies you talked about. Is that a deal?' he asked, hoping and praying that, somehow, Lola would suddenly open her eyes and respond. She remained silent.

'Aidan, we need you to let go now, we're about to arrive at the hospital,' the paramedic explained, at which point the ambulance pulled up and came to a complete standstill.

'Is this the RTA head trauma?' asked a man who was wearing blue scrubs the moment the doors swung open. He stepped inside and conferred with the paramedics before Lola's stretcher was unstrapped. 'Right, let's get her inside,' the A&E doctor ordered, at which point, Lola disappeared.

14

INTERRUPTING THE SOMBRE STILLNESS THAT HAD ENGULFED ICU for the past hour, the red phone on the nursing station rang again, and all the staff turned to look in the same direction. Closest, Marie picked up the phone before placing it down a few moments later.

'Our expected patient has arrived downstairs, and she'll be stabilised before undergoing scans,' she began. 'It's a bad head trauma and we'll know more details soon, but in the meantime, let's get prepared,' she announced.

Each member of the team made themselves busy, maintaining their readiness to receive the next patient. Matty paced to the double doors, securing his face mask in place, wrapping a gown over his uniform, and pulling his gloves over his hands. He peered through the glass panes in the doors, keeping an eye out for an approaching gurney, still wondering who his next patient would be. He turned back when the corridor remained empty, and took a final glance at bay number two, the empty space surrounded by waiting machinery and equipment.

In his moment of quietness, he wondered if he'd miss the adrenaline rush that accompanied the moments before receiving an incoming patient. Slipping his ID badge out of its holder, he looked at the hidden photo beneath, acknowledging that there was more to life than just the hospital, more to life than always trying to save the lives of strangers.

Marie spotted him out of the corner of her eye, witnessing an expression that she'd secretly spotted on his face so many times before.

'Are they your children?' she asked in a moment of bravery, standing behind him and admiring what looked like an old family photo.

Matty replaced the photo behind his badge and ignored the question.

'I'm sorry about earlier, for prying, but I'm concerned about you, that's all.'

'There's no need to apologise,' he replied, looking back through the doors. 'But I'd prefer it if we didn't talk about it,' he added, at which point, Marie skulked away and sighed, her head lowering with disappointment.

In that moment, when the only person that cared for him had turned her back on him, Matty knew that the time had come to stop cowering, and instead turn to face the people that he cared for so deeply, even if he felt unsure of how their affections would be reciprocated. Knowing that there was someone heading his way that was potentially fighting for their life, Matty didn't want to waste another moment of his own life feeling like a coward. He longed for his own house to become a home, a space filled with love and laughter. He longed to mean something to someone, and he longed to love, and be loved, and only he could make those things happen. But more than anything, he didn't want to end up being one of those people who had no next of kin to call upon during the times in life when nobody wanted to find themselves alone.

15

CHRISTMAS AT ST JUDE'S ALWAYS FELT PARTICULARLY SPECIAL. During the lead-up to the big day, the nursing staff on all of the wards wore elf hats as part of their festive uniform. Groups of local carol singers performed a mini concert to all inpatients twice daily, and there was always a heartfelt visit from Father Christmas on the children's ward, *Sunshine*. But this year during Christmas Eve, all of the typical festive cheer had been postponed the moment a drunk driver had ploughed his work van into Lendal Bridge, the accident causing multiple fatalities and blocking all access to the eastern side of the city, causing the area to spiral into chaos.

'You can wait over there,' a nurse practitioner advised, witnessing the befuddled expression plastered across Aidan's face the moment he arrived in the bustling reception area of A&E. He heard the lady speaking to him, and yet he couldn't divert his attention away from Lola, watching the speed at which she was ushered through the double doors at the end of the corridor. The lady placed a hand on his arm.

'We'll update you when we know more,' she continued to explain. 'Why don't you take a seat and get a warm drink from the machine? You look frozen.'

'He needs to be assessed too,' Sam advised before he was about to leave, the empty stretcher by his side.

Aidan saw the bloodstains on the bed, knowing that they were from Lola. He shook his head. 'No, I'm fine, honestly,' he reassured.

'Sit and wait a while then,' Sam insisted. 'At least until you know she's in good hands,' he added with a reassuring smile before leaving.

'That's a good idea. Your wife won't be happy if she finds out you didn't follow medical advice,' added the nurse, who was still standing by Aidan's side, watching as his eyes remained glued to the double doors where Lola had been whisked away.

'She isn't my wife, I don't know who she is,' Aidan replied.

'Then why don't you sit here? I'm sure she will appreciate the fact that there is somebody here for her, even though you're a stranger,' she said. 'At least wait until you know how she's doing, otherwise you'll always wonder. I'll come and let you know as soon as I have an update,' advised the nurse, squeezing his hand before she walked away.

The moment Aidan sat, he felt the weight of his worry dragging down his shoulders and the burden placed upon him during the past few hours could be seen in his pale complexion. Before he had time to collect his thoughts and stitch his composure back together, the lady sitting next to him invited herself to partake in polite conversation.

'I bet they're here for the free minced pies,' the elderly lady to Aidan's right announced, poking him in the ribs. 'My next-door neighbour told me that the pies are from Aldi this year and according to Jeremy Vine on BBC Radio 2, they're the best on the market,' the lady grinned, her full set of false teeth falling lopsided as she laughed. Aidan produced a weak smile in acknowledgement and then looked in the opposite direction, the waiting area brimming with a mismatch of people from all corners of the city.

'I'd get comfy if I were you,' she continued, pulling out some knitting needles from her bag. 'You could be in for a long wait, Christmas Eve is one of the busiest nights of the year in here, too much alcohol and not enough sense,' she explained. 'Would you like a drink of my water?' she asked upon taking out a clear bottle from her bag. 'I've added a touch of gin, as it's Christmas,' she admitted with a smile. 'It'll go nicely with the minced pies when they finally decide to bring them out.'

Aidan shook his head. 'No thanks,' he replied, running his hands through his hair.

With his clothes still damp from sitting in the snow, it dawned on him that in all the commotion of the ambulance and fire brigade appearing, he'd left his bag at the scene of the accident, and having just walked out on his fiancée, not only did he not have a change of clothes, but he had nowhere to stay either. While trying to think about what he was going to do once he left the hospital, all his mind could focus on was Lola, and the look of hope that had momentarily flickered in her eyes. In his mind, he could still hear the sound of the machinery that had been used to tear the car apart, his bones still feeling the aftereffects of the vibrations.

Each time the doors of the emergency department flung open, Aidan's head swung around and he was brought back to reality. He didn't know who he was expecting to appear, or what he was expecting to see, and yet each time when a stranger appeared, it filled him with a strange sense of disappointment. In his moment of vulnerability, he hoped that somehow Holly had heard about the accident and that she would dash to the hospital to collect him, begging for his forgiveness and willing him to come home. With each stranger that entered, his hopes for a reunion dwindled.

With his phone not working, he gazed up at the clock, watching the minutes turn into an hour, the bustling emergency department drowning as more people arrived. Beginning to assume that the nurse had forgotten that he was even waiting, Aidan got up and began to head for the exit.

'I was just coming to find you,' announced the nurse who had spoken to Aidan earlier. 'I have an update for you, do you want to come through?' she asked, guiding him towards the lift and going up a level, pausing at some double doors at the far end of the corridor. 'We've managed to find out where Lola lives and who her next of kin is, and we're trying to get through to him now, but I thought you might want to see her after what you both went through together.'

The nurse pressed the bell located at the entrance to ICU, and moments later, Marie appeared at the doors.

'Marie, this is Aidan. He arrived with Lola and was the one who called for the ambulance. He waited with her until it arrived,' the nurse announced when the doors opened. 'He isn't related, but he'd like to see her after everything that's happened, if that's okay with you?'

'Yes, of course, come in. My name is Marie, I'm one of the senior nurses on duty today,' she replied, smiling in acknowledgement at her colleague before allowing the doors to close. 'Just follow me, I'll take you over to her,' she added, making her way across the ward. 'Don't be too alarmed by our face masks, gowns and shields, it's all just standard uniform in here now.'

'Is she okay?' Aidan mustered the courage to ask, unable to gauge anything from Marie's demeanour. Once submerged in the room, Aidan looked around at the handful of patients on the ward, unable to recognise Lola.

Marie stopped near the nursing station, wanting to give Aidan an update before reuniting him with Lola. 'She's as well as we could have hoped for,' she began. 'Lola's been through quite a trauma, and although her CT scan came back clear, which is a miracle given the nature of the accident, there are still many uncertainties until she wakes up.' Marie spotted Aidan's facial expression alter, her own heart pumping. 'It's so hard to predict outcomes when it comes to head traumas, but there's much to feel positive about,' she tried to offer some degree of reassurance.

Aidan's emotions poured out the moment he heard the news, and without thought, he wrapped his arms around Marie, almost crying with relief.

'Thanks for letting me know,' he replied with a shaky voice.

Marie pressed her hands against Aidan's back, tapping gently. 'You're welcome,' she whispered.

Embarrassed, Aidan pulled away. 'Sorry,' he apologised, looking away and straightening out his clothes. He searched the room for Lola, desperate to see her again. 'I can't explain it, but I feel like I have this bond with her, and yet I have no idea who she is,' he explained, his eyes once again becoming wet as he caught sight of her.

Upon overhearing the conversation, Matty looked up from where he was seated behind the nursing station, his heart falling to the floor at the sound of Aidan's familiar voice. His hand released its grip of the chart he had been reviewing, and the papers scattered over the desk. Having been praying for a miracle for what felt like a lifetime, he could barely believe his eyes when he saw Aidan stood before him, his hopes for a family reunion coming earlier than expected, and not at all in the context that he'd hoped. In the seconds that followed, while the conversation between Marie and Aidan continued, Matty forgot where he was, his breathing slowing as the world around him blurred from existence. Behind his facemask, his expression evolved from shock, to disbelief, to one of unmistakable love. He wanted to stand and join in with the conversation, and yet his feet remained planted to the floor, shock sapping all his strength from him, along with his ability to function.

'Could you pass me the tissues?' Marie asked Matty, and when he didn't reply, she leaned over the nursing station and grabbed the box herself, noting that Matty remained still, his gaze focused forwards and unwavering. She pressed her hand against his arm. 'You okay?' she whispered, her words dragging Matty out of his solitary moment. He nodded before looking down, busying himself and pretending to type on the computer.

Marie walked back towards Aidan and offered him a tissue. 'It can feel very overwhelming in here, so just take your time before we go over to her,' she reassured with a slight tilt of the head. 'It sounds like you were quite the hero and helped to save her life.'

Aidan shook his head in protest. 'I didn't save her life,' he was quick to correct. 'I just stayed and talked to her.'

Marie jumped on his words. 'You called an ambulance and you stayed with her, that all means that you helped to save her life.'

The pair walked over to bay number two, the curtains on one side shielding the area from the rest of the ward.

'Please, don't be too alarmed by all the machines, I know it can be intimidating at first,' she explained.

Aidan shuffled on the spot and with a look of hesitation glanced at all the equipment attached to Lola. 'As long as she's okay,' he replied.

'She's sedated at the moment, just to let her body rest, but you can stay with her for a few minutes if you'd like,' Marie offered, pulling up a chair for Aidan. 'We're just monitoring her, and although I can't give you any specific details about her condition, she's doing much better than we first thought.' Aidan took a seat at the side of the bed when Marie indicated for him to sit. 'Take a few minutes,' she concluded before walking away.

With the various machines beeping in the background, Aidan looked up at Lola, her head wrapped in a secure bandage, additional cuts and grazes scattering her forehead and left cheek. A row of stitches ran the length of her right eyebrow, and both eyes appeared swollen and puffy in appearance. Without thought, he reached out and took hold of her hand while she slept, her skin feeling warm against his. He noticed the wedding rings on her finger and wondered who her husband was. After only a few minutes, the calmness of the ward was interrupted, the bank of monitors in the middle of the room sounding an alarm, and within seconds, a team of staff wearing various uniforms all rushed to one of the patients, and a curtain was quickly whipped around.

'I'm glad you're okay,' he whispered to Lola, not really knowing what else to do or say. He stroked her skin in an attempt to provide comfort in a room that felt so intimidating, with the alien machines, the surgical appliances, and the peculiar noises all serving to unsettle even the hardiest of souls.

He spotted his wristband on her bedside table and took hold of it, securing it back around her wrist.

'You remember our deal, don't you?' he whispered, with fears that she would never wake up still running through his mind. 'Once you're ready to go home, you can give this back to me,' he explained, in the back of his mind knowing that he'd probably never see her again. 'It's always reminded me to be strong, and I want it to help you to be strong now,' he added. 'And you can make me those brownies that you told me about, one of those would go down nicely now with a cup of tea,' he smiled, Lola's facial expression remaining unchanged. He spotted the gents' over in the corner of the room. 'I'll be back in a minute,' he said to Lola, bending over and whispering near her ear so that he wouldn't disturb anybody.

Aidan dashed to the toilet, taking a moment to splash water over his face and take in the enormity of the day so far. His face looked drawn, bags were hanging beneath his eyes, and he almost didn't recognise his own reflection, his appearance dishevelled. After a few moments, he opened the door and peered back into the room. At the side of Lola's bed, he caught sight of the same female nurse talking to a man who he assumed to be Lola's husband. The man was kissing Lola on the forehead.

Parker had his back towards the room, so Aidan was prevented from getting to see his face. He lingered outside the toilet door, waiting for his opportunity to leave the ward without being noticed.

'She's going to be staying in for observation, at least for a few days, because of the fracture to her skull,' Aidan overheard Marie explain, 'and because of the type of head injury sustained, she's likely to suffer from the effects of severe concussion for at least a few weeks, if not longer.' Aidan watched as the man who was stood by Lola's bed took hold of her hand, the nurse continuing to talk through her condition.

'The concussion could affect her concentration, she could have episodes of dizziness and suffer from headaches, and her memory could be damaged,' the nurse continued. 'But we'll monitor her closely over the next few days just to make sure that she's stable and that there's no change to her condition,' Marie continued. 'The gentleman who stayed with Lola really did save her life. He was here just now, I thought you might want to talk to him,' Marie explained looking around to introduce Aidan.

At that moment, Aidan pushed open the doors and left the ICU.

16

MARIE LOOKED AROUND AGAIN FOR AIDAN. 'HE MUST HAVE left,' she explained. 'I'll be back to check on Lola soon,' she advised Parker, who remained seated by his wife's side. On the floor, she spotted a single black glove. Leaning down, she picked it up and held it in her hand. 'Is this yours?' she asked Parker, who in turn shook his head.

'Are you okay?' asked Marie when she returned to the nursing station and spotted that Matty was still seated behind the desk.

'Think I've got a bit of a cold coming on, that's all,' he replied, wiping his face.

Marie didn't believe his explanation. 'You don't know the patient in bed two, do you?' she asked, recalling the look of shock she had spotted in Matty's eyes only moments earlier.

He shook his head. 'No, I don't. Why do you ask?'

'I thought you looked a little emotional when I saw you look up.'

'I'm a little tired and the day has only just begun, maybe that's the look you spotted.'

Marie glanced over her shoulder. 'Do you know where Aidan went? He was the guy who was just sitting with Lola before her husband arrived.'

'I think he left. Why?'

'Can you believe that he's a total stranger to her? He happened to see the accident, called for an ambulance, and stayed with her the whole time. If only there were more people like him in the world.'

Matty had watched Aidan walking across the ward, and no matter how much he had wanted to, he hadn't prevented him from leaving and instead, allowed him to walk away.

'There are kind people out there doing good,' he smiled.

'I think he's dropped his glove, that's all,' she replied, looking at the grey woolly mitten in her hand. 'And I was a bit concerned about him. It looked like he was still in shock and apparently they were trapped in this weather for some time. I think I'll just go and check that he's okay,' she explained in a concerned tone.

'Here, let me,' Matty offered with an eagerness about his posture, standing up and taking hold of the glove and grabbing the opportunity that had presented itself. 'You must be ready for a sit-down,' he suggested, indicating for her to take his seat.

Matty headed towards the exit and pushed the doors open. With his mask still secured over his face, he walked through the artery of corridors, scanning all the visitor seats that he passed. His heart remained lodged in his throat, his mind swirling in rhythm with his tumbling emotions. He scanned the faces in the waiting area of A&E, concerned about Aidan's welfare and desperate to lock eyes with him.

'Can you check if a patient called Aidan Fogg was admitted?' he asked the girl downstairs on A&E reception.

'No, there's nobody under that name. Why?' she asked, turning to see that Matty had already left.

With the glove clenched in his hand, Matty continued to search the hospital, and yet there was no sign of Aidan, it was like he had just vanished. Disheartened at the missed opportunity, Matty took a moment to gather his emotions, wiping his face on his scrubs. The moment he raised his head and peered out through one of the many windows located at the front of the site, in the distance, he spotted the familiar figure of Aidan walking away. Desperate to prevent him from leaving and without thought, he banged on the window and shouted, and yet Aidan remained unawares, and continued to walk away. Just as Matty turned to run towards the exit, his bleeper sounded, signalling an emergency back on the ward. He stuffed the glove into his pocket and took another look outside just as Aidan was about to vanish from sight. With a slow shake of the head, Matty silenced his bleeper before turning his back on his answered prayer, and ran back towards the ward. All he could think about was Lola, and prayed she wasn't the unfolding emergency.

Out of breath, he reached the doors to ICU and peered through the glass panes, noting that a number of staff members were congregated around bed number five. With a sense of relief rushing through his body and whilst ignoring his own emotional needs, he took a deep breath and rushed to join his colleagues in their attempt to save another patient's life.

17

PARKER HAD REMAINED BY LOLA'S BEDSIDE FOR OVER TWO hours. As each minute passed, he waited with patience for her body to move. He willed to see her fingers twitch, or even better, for her to open her eyes, and smile back at him. He cupped her cold, delicate hand between his, and although the medical staff had reassured him that she was just sleeping off the medication, he couldn't breathe easy until she woke up. The stubborn hands on the wall clock seemed to have come to a standstill, the agonising wait feeling like a life sentence, and in his mind, punishment for his adulterous actions only a few hours previous.

'Can I get you a drink?' asked one of the healthcare assistants when she spotted Parker clock-watching. 'A cup of tea can pass a good fifteen minutes in here.'

Parker did his best to engage, so took his eyes off Lola and looked up at the lady. 'No, thanks,' he replied. 'I'm sure she'll be awake soon,' he concluded, looking back at Lola.

The lady offered a sympathetic smile and then walked away, her experience telling her that Lola could be one of those ICU patients that, despite everything that the doctors might try, may never wake up.

Parker swallowed his fear and took a deep breath, admiring Lola.

'Wake up, Lola,' he whispered, cradling her hand. 'You're missing one of your favourite days of the year,' he commented, sensing the spirit of Christmas Eve as it echoed around the corridors. 'Please, wake up. I love you so much, and I can't do any of this without you.'

He lowered his head, allowing his tears to speckle the floor. Outside, daylight turned into Christmas Eve darkness, the light beyond the window sinking into the misty horizon. As the hours passed, a building anxiety led Parker to encourage Lola to wake. He took out his phone and placed it on her pillow to play some music on a low volume, knowing that her daily routine had always been filled with an eclectic array of songs. He gently brushed the hair away from her eyes and stroked her hand. 'I love you, Lola,' he whispered.

'Is she still doing okay?' he asked when Matty came over to record Lola's observations.

Matty checked the monitors and scribbled something on the chart. 'As expected,' he replied, continuing to check Lola's other vitals. 'She'll wake up when her body is ready. We see this a lot with patients who've been through such a traumatic accident, and the body is a very clever machine, knowing what it needs, and when,' he concluded before putting down the chart. 'You look shattered, why don't I get you a cup of tea?'

Parker shook his head. 'I'm fine, but thanks.'

The moment that Matty walked away, Parker looked back at Lola, searching for any signs of her awakening, and feeling disappointed as she remained dormant. The incessant beeping of machines in his periphery pierced his woozy head and added to his already banging headache, his features dark, drawn and heavy. Guilt weighed down on his burdened shoulders. He knew deep down that everything that had happened that morning was because of him, and all he wanted was for Lola to wake up so that he could tell her how much he loved her, and how sorry he felt for betraying her trust, and for breaking his wedding vows.

A firm hand pressed on Parker's shoulder. 'Would you like me to come and sit with you, keep you company?' asked a member of the hospital chaplain. Unaware of the approaching footsteps, Parker jumped and turned around, inadvertently dropping Lola's hand.

'No, I'm okay, but thank you for asking,' Parker declined, offering up a reassuring smile so that the vicar would leave. 'She'll be awake soon,' he concluded, before turning back to Lola. As he did, he saw that her eyes were beginning to open, and within seconds, two members of the nursing staff appeared at the bedside.

'Looks like she's starting to come round,' Matty commented as he pressed on Lola's wrist. Parker's relief spilled out in one uncontrollable wave of emotion, his eyes welling with tears.

'Oh, thank God!' he exclaimed, standing up and getting out of the way so that the nurses could get closer.

Matty and Marie adjusted the pillows.

'Lola, can you open your eyes for me?' Matty asked.

Parker remained stood a few paces back, praying that her eyes would open again, only this time, stay open for longer.

'This is quite normal. She will be very groggy initially, and it may take her some time to fully come round,' he explained. 'It's always good to have a familiar face here for when she does fully wake up,' he added, 'but it's important that you don't ask her too many questions or bombard her with too much new information initially. It can be overwhelming until we know the extent of her concussion. Remember, she's experienced quite a significant trauma and she'll be dazed.'

'Can I carry on talking to her though?' he asked, scared to do the wrong thing and make the situation worse than what it already felt.

Matty offered a warm, reassuring smile that resonated through his eyes. 'Of course, hearing your voice will certainly help her to feel at ease,' he replied, adjusting the drip attached to Lola's arm. 'I'll come and check on her in a little while, but if you're concerned at all, just press the buzzer.'

Matty and Marie stepped aside before walking away, allowing Parker to regain his position. He sat down slowly and took hold of Lola's hand.

'Lola, can you hear me?' he asked with a gentle tone.

Submerged within her own private world, snuggled beneath the covers, Lola squinted and then blinked hard, trying to keep her eyes open. Feeling dazed, she tried to focus on her unfamiliar surroundings and realised after a few seconds that she was in a hospital bed, the railings pressing against her free hand. Her head pounded and she could feel a tightness where the bandages were wrapped around her skull, protecting her wound. Her mouth felt dry, and her stomach was hurting to such a degree that she'd never experienced before. She tilted her head to the side, spotting Parker, who was sat beside the bed. Her mind felt blank and peaceful, the usual stream of chaotic thoughts momentarily silenced. She blinked a few more times, allowing her eyes to adjust to the brightness of the room, the noises surrounding her feeling unfamiliar, and daunting in their consistency.

Parker leaned over and kissed her on the cheek, nuzzling his head against her neck. 'I'm so glad that you're okay, I've been so worried,' he whispered. 'I love you so much, and I want you to know how sorry I am,' he explained, his guilt spilling out through his words, despite the nurse's warning not to overwhelm Lola with too much information.

Lola heard Parker's words, though they didn't fully register, her mind still stuck in some sort of fog. She pulled her arm out from under the covers and pressed her hand against her head. 'What happened to me?' she asked.

Taken aback, Parker turned to see if any of the nurses were available. When nobody appeared, he answered her question with a sense of hesitance.

'You were in an accident. Don't you remember?' he replied tentatively.

Lola's eyebrows pulled together. 'An accident?' she questioned, her fear rolling down her cheeks and tumbling onto the pillow. 'What accident?'

Parker looked around again, hoping that a nurse would come

over and reassure them both that this type of memory loss was normal, and to be expected. All the nurses were busy, so he got up and sat on the edge of the bed, positioning himself closer to his wife. He wiped away the tears from her cheek.

'You were in a car accident this morning. You're in St Jude's now, but you're going to be absolutely fine. You hit your head and you've got a concussion.'

Lola began to cry as she peered around her surroundings again, the sight of the hospital ward, the machinery, and all the medical staff inducing pangs of fear to course through her veins. She gazed down at her body hidden beneath the covers, making her own assessment based on how she felt.

'Am I okay?' she asked, fearful of the answer.

Parker nodded, his beaming smile offering the reassurance that she needed. 'You're awake and talking to me, you're going to be fine.'

'Have I got any broken bones?' she asked, trying to sense if she could feel all of her limbs.

Parker shook his head. 'But you have had some scans and been stitched up in a few places,' he replied.

Lola tried to raise her head off the pillow. 'And what about the bandage?'

'Don't worry, your mind is fretting when all I need you to do is rest,' he replied, easing her head back down onto the pillow.

'I love you,' she cried, continuing to look at Parker for reassurance. 'How long have you been here?' she asked, gripping his hand, fearful for him to leave her alone.

'The accident was this morning, I got here shortly after you arrived,' he explained. 'I've spoken to the nurses, and they've all said that you've been so lucky,' he began, his emotions rumbling in his throat. 'It could have been so much worse, Lola, I could have lost you,' he cried, lowering and shaking his head. 'I love you so much and I can't imagine what my life would be like without you by my side.'

A comfortable look of warmth appeared on Lola's face. She extended her arm and, with a gentle touch, raised Parker's chin. 'You can't get rid of me that easily,' she mumbled, leaning up slightly. 'We're married now, remember.'

Parker smiled. 'You haven't forgotten the important stuff then,' he joked. 'Are you in pain?' he asked when he saw a grimace appear on her face.

Lola squinted and eased her head back onto the pillow. 'It feels like I've been hit over the head with a sledgehammer.'

'I guess you kind of have been,' he began. 'They've already spoken to me about the headaches you're likely to suffer with for a while, which means when you come home, you have to rest and let me take care of you, for a change.'

Lola's eyes opened wide and she turned to look at Parker. 'Was the accident my fault?' she suddenly thought to ask. 'Was there another car involved?'

Parker shook his head. 'The police said it looks like you lost control of the car and skidded on some black ice. The car rolled over before you crashed into a lamppost.'

Lola relaxed. 'Oh, thank God.'

An empty feeling stirred in the pit of Parker's stomach and he momentarily broke eye contact, wondering if she would be able to recall seeing the photo of him and Holly right before she had left the house and sped away in her car. 'Can you remember anything about the accident? Anything about this morning?' he asked, holding his breath, his right knee bouncing.

Lola thought for a moment. 'I don't remember anything,' she suddenly realised. The realisation caused her to break out in tears, the feeling unsettling.

Parker couldn't help but release a slight sigh of relief that his sordid secret had remained just that. 'The nurses have said that memory loss is normal, and not to worry, it will come back, it'll just take some time,' he reassured.

Lola heard the Christmas carols being sung in the distance.

'What day is it?' she asked when her brain also failed to recall that information.

'It's Christmas Eve, Lola,' he replied with a beaming smile. 'Your favourite day of the year.'

Matty appeared by the bedside. 'Well, hello. My name is Matty, I'm part of the team who has been looking after you since you arrived at St Jude's. How are you feeling?'

'My head hurts,' replied Lola, touching her bandages once again.

'It will do, but we're giving you plenty of pain relief to help, that's why you've been asleep for some time,' he explained. 'You've had quite a nasty bump to the head, Lola, causing a fracture, which is why you may feel a little confused, but you've been really lucky.' Matty scanned Lola's chart before scribbling something down. 'As we've explained to your husband, you've had a CT and an MRI scan of your head to rule out any internal bleeding or swelling that could have caused permanent damage to the brain, and the pain you'll be experiencing now will slowly start to improve over the next week or so.' Matty checked the bandage, inspecting the wound beneath. 'The stitches in your head will naturally dissolve as the wound heals.' He went quiet for a moment while checking Lola's temperature and blood pressure. 'We've already performed some tests to determine the extent of any damage to your memory,' he began to explain, looking up at her. 'But I still need to ask you a few questions. Can you remember what happened before the accident?'

Lola produced a look of upset and shook her head, already knowing the answer.

Matty got a little closer and perched on the bed. 'And that's normal. Due to the nature of your injury and based on your results, we anticipated that there might be some temporary memory loss in the form of retrograde amnesia, which means that memories from right before the accident can become lost. It may take you a few days, or maybe a few weeks to regain your full memory function, but it will hopefully come back in time, just try not to worry too much. The main thing is that your short-term and long-term memory haven't been impaired. You've been so lucky, Lola, it was a terrible accident and yet here you are, awake on Christmas Eve, with your husband by your side,' he said, trying to offer reassurance. 'We'll need you to spend a little bit of time with us, just so that we can monitor your progress, and then you can go home and recover fully in the comfort of your own bed.'

Matty got up and turned to Parker. 'Now, why don't you two have a little chat before saying goodnight? Lola will tire really quickly, so it's important that she gets sufficient time to rest,' he explained. 'You can come and visit her anytime tomorrow, at Christmas we try to remain flexible on visiting times. We understand that family is super important at this time of year,' he concluded before walking away.

Parker took hold of Lola's hand. 'I love you so much. When I got the phone call, I couldn't even breathe. The thought of losing you was just too much,' he sobbed, closing his eyes and allowing his tears to fall.

'I'm okay,' she reassured, pressing his hand between hers. A charming grin settled on her face as she met his gaze. 'I might look a little frightening with this on my head, but maybe a bit of sense will have been knocked into me,' she added, the pain preventing her from laughing with too much expression.

'Please rest,' Parker insisted when he saw her grimaces of pain, pressing his finger against her lips. 'I need you back home with me as soon as possible. Can you hear the carol singers outside?' he asked as the melodic echoes of the choir penetrated the walls.

Lola closed her eyes as instructed, the comforting sounds of Christmas playing in her ears. Whilst she tried to rest, she couldn't stop her brain from making its attempts to piece together the parts of the day that remained elusive.

'Should I get going?' asked Parker when he sensed Lola was beginning to fall asleep.

She shook her head on the pillow. 'Don't leave me yet,' she cried, holding his hand tightly. 'I'm scared.'

Parker leaned over and delivered a warm, gentle kiss to her lips. 'Don't be scared,' he began, looking into her eyes and smiling. 'You're safe, and all you need to do is rest,' he continued, pushing away his own fears. 'I'll come and visit you tomorrow and hopefully take you home, if you're allowed.'

'But what if they don't let me? And what if I still can't remember anything?' she cried, her bottom lip trembling. 'I'm scared that my memory might be permanently damaged.'

'You're panicking and overthinking things. This is exactly what they said not to do,' Parker tutted. 'You've had a nasty bump to your head and now you're suffering with a concussion and some temporary damage that will rectify itself, which the doctors aren't overly concerned about, so neither should you be,' he confirmed. 'It's Christmas Eve, please rest,' he begged. 'The more you sleep, the sooner you'll be able to come home with me.'

Lola closed her eyes and offered a slight smile. 'You're right. I'm sure that everything will come back to me, and then all this will start to make sense.'

Upon hearing her defiance, Parker felt clammy beneath his jumper, his posture stiffened, and he felt a shiver sweep through his body as a quiver rumbled in the pit of his stomach. 'There's something important I need to tell you,' began the start of his confession.

'What is it?' she asked, her eyes opening.

The look of fear in Lola's eyes, her vulnerability, scared away what was meant to be Parker's moment of honesty. 'I've changed my mind about travelling,' he began to explain. 'All I want is to be with you. I know that you're ready to start a family, and I am too,' he revealed. 'I thought I wanted to travel and I know we've spoken about it a lot, but everything I want is here, in York, with you.'

'Really?' she replied. 'Why the sudden change of heart?'

Parker pointed to her bandaged head. 'This has made me realise what's important in life, and that's you.'

'How are we doing?' asked Matty, interrupting the conversation.

Lola smiled. 'Can I go home?' she asked. 'I don't like hospitals and I think I'd rest much better in my own bed, like you said.'

Matty shook his head. 'I'm afraid not,' he was prompt to reply. 'We need to keep you here, just for observation. Let's see how you are tomorrow once the doctors have done their rounds. It'll be them that you need to convince, not me.' He paused and reviewed the charts. 'I actually need a moment alone with Lola, if that's okay?' he asked, turning to look at Parker.

'Oh, yeah, sure,' he replied, standing. 'There's nothing wrong, is there?'

Matty shook his head. 'No. We do need some details from you, so if you could go over to the nurse's station, they'll assist,' he advised, pointing across the room.

'I won't be a second,' Parker said to Lola with a smile.

Matty took Parker's place and rested on the bed.

'There's something I need to tell you,' he began in a much softer tone, 'and I wanted to do it without your husband present, just in case he isn't aware of the situation.'

'What is it?' Lola asked, a topsy-turvy feeling bubbling in her stomach.

Matty took hold of her hand. 'It appears as though, during the trauma of the accident, your body suffered a great amount of stress, and as a result, you have sadly lost your baby. I'm so sorry, Lola,' he explained. 'Did you realise that you were in the early stages of a pregnancy?'

Lola nodded and began to cry. 'I'd only just found out and I hadn't told my husband,' she explained, looking across the room to where Parker was standing.

'The trauma of the accident resulted in a miscarriage; you were just gone eleven weeks.'

Lola closed her eyes, attempting to block out the huge amount of sadness engulfing her body. 'I feel a pain in my stomach,' she muttered, placing her hand over her abdomen. 'Is that normal?'

'There will be some discomfort. You've been through a major trauma, Lola, your body will hurt all over for a few days, if not weeks,' he explained, taking hold of a tissue and handing it to her. 'I'm a firm believer that everything happens for a reason, even if we don't fully understand it at the time,' he explained, offering up a glimmer of hope in Lola's darkest hour. 'When I heard the paramedics talking about the state of your car over the radio before you were brought in, I expected the worst when you arrived, and yet here you are, and we're already talking about you going home. It's a miracle that you've only suffered from relatively minor injuries. Hold onto that, even if things seem sad and upsetting right now. You have a lot to be grateful for.'

Parker approached the bed after speaking with the other nurses. 'That's all done, are you okay?' he asked when he saw Lola crying.

'Here, you take my place,' Matty said, getting up off the bed. 'I'll leave you two to it.' He turned and walked away.

'Are you okay?' asked Parker, dabbing away a few stray tears. 'What did he want to talk to you about?'

Lola couldn't bring herself to tell the truth, not yet. 'He was just going through what I should expect when I get home, stuff that I can and can't do for a while,' she replied. 'It's all just a bit overwhelming. I was fine this morning and now I'm here, and I can't even remember what happened to me. It's like a whole part of my memory has been erased,' she explained just as an image of the accident flashed through her mind, the sound of the car skidding across the road ringing through her ears.

Parker's phone buzzed in his pocket. 'You're going to be okay,' he reassured her, before taking out his mobile and reading the message. The moment Lola saw his phone, a feeling of great unease rocked her bones and she felt upset, and yet she had no idea why.

'I best get going, leave you to rest. I'll be back in the morning,' Parker said, kissing her on the cheek. 'I'll bring some fresh clothes in the hope that I can take you home with me.'

'Bye, see you tomorrow,' Lola replied, holding back tears as she watched Parker walk away.

Outside in the distance, the cathedral bells rang, a special Christmas Eve service getting underway, and the sound brought out her sobs. She rolled over and scooped herself into the foetal position, bringing her arms into her chest, resting just below her pillow. She allowed all the emotions of the day to seep onto the sheets, her upset intensifying the longer the bells rang, a sound that had never before stirred up such emotion. For the first time in her adult life, Lola felt alone, and scared. The bandages wrapped around her head felt suffocating, and the pounding in her skull acted as a constant reminder of the accident that she had been at the epicentre of, an accident she couldn't remember anything about.

As she wiped her eyes, for the first time since waking, Lola spotted the brown wristband that had been secured with purpose around her left wrist. Sitting upright, she inspected the bangle, concluding that the chunky, ill-fitted accessory looked out of place on her slender wrist, and wondered where it had come from, knowing that it wasn't hers. Resting her head back down, with weariness taking control of her body, she played with the leather in her fingers and for reasons she didn't understand, found comfort in the soft leather during what felt like her darkest hour.

18

'WHY DON'T YOU GO HOME? MOST OF THE OTHER STAFF WHO offered to come in on overtime have already left and you're no longer the matron on duty,' offered Marie. 'We're over the wave now,' she confirmed, 'and you're meant to be on annual leave, remember?'

'I don't expect you to understand, but I don't want to go home, not right now.'

'Then help me to understand. You've looked upset all day,' she said, pressing her hand against his. 'I might be able to help.'

Matty shook his head.

'The photo you look at...' she began. 'Is someone you care for poorly? Because even if you don't want to talk to me about it, there are services out there, you just have to be willing to ask.'

'Nobody is sick,' he said. 'So, can we just leave it, please? You really aren't helping.'

Marie released his hand. 'No problem.'

'I'm going to go and take a break,' he said, walking away.

Unwilling to go home until he felt sure that his new patient was stable, Matty approached Lola's bedside. Even though a fresh team of staff were now on duty, while she slept, Matty checked Lola's vitals again, monitoring her progress personally, unwilling to let go of the reins. Reassured that there were no changes to her condition, and with his own eyes struggling to remain open, he retreated to the staff room, lying down in the darkness with his arm covering his face. His thoughts scrambled from one thing to another, his tiredness causing his emotions to surface. Beneath the darkness, he allowed himself a private moment of weakness, an outpour of tears after such an emotionally draining shift. He recalled the events of the past day, wanting to place them in his memory bank for future reference, and with the hope for future opportunities of storytelling. In his mind, he pictured the way that Aidan had cared for Lola, despite knowing that she was a complete stranger to him, and he beamed with a sense of pride like never before. Matty recalled the way that Aidan's voice had sounded, but most of all, he remembered the way that his heart ached when he saw Marie offering Aidan comfort, wishing more than anything that he had been the one placing his arms around his shoulders.

The staff room door creaked open.

'Matty, Lola's unsettled and her vitals have dipped a bit. She's asking for you,' Marie announced through a crack in the staff room door.

Matty's heart fell through to his feet and he looked over to Marie before getting up. 'I'm coming,' he replied. 'Is she okay though?' he asked, panicked.

'I think she's just had a bad dream and her meds need topping up,' she replied, walking away.

In the darkness, all Matty could think about was the upsetting telephone call that he'd recently been asked to make, the one where he'd informed a next of kin that their loved one had sadly passed away in his care. Beneath the stillness engulfing the staffroom, the sound of the widow's sobs continued to stalk his memory, hearing with clarity the very moment that someone's heart had been broken by the devastating news. Refusing to find himself in a similar situation, he secured his face mask and adjusted his scrubs before pushing the door open and heading straight towards Lola's bedside.

'Are you okay?' he asked, checking her observations before

perching on the side of her bed. He took hold of her hand and held it tight.

'I was having a nightmare,' Lola replied, crying, her face saturated with sweat and tears. 'I could hear the sound of my car crashing, and I couldn't stop it, I couldn't do anything to stop it happening,' she explained, pressing her eyes closed to try and block out the unwanted images which were swirling through her mind.

'Keep your eyes closed,' soothed Matty, his tone soft, and calming. 'It was just a nightmare,' he added. He took hold of a tissue with his free hand and dabbed Lola's face. 'You're safe now, and there's nothing to be afraid of,' he continued, watching as Lola's mind sank back into a state of rest, her exhausted body soon sending her back to sleep. Matty watched the monitors, making sure that things remained stable. Once he felt reassured that she was asleep, Matty released Lola's hand and took a seat by the side of her bed, resting his head back when the enormity of the day once again caught up with him.

Although she didn't understand the motivations that were driving his behaviour, the moment that Marie spotted Matty asleep in the chair by Lola's side, instead of waking him, she placed a blanket over his legs and turned down the lights in the bay, allowing him to rest. She removed his ID badge so that it didn't press uncomfortably against his skin, and in the next moment, found herself sliding out his identity card. With a careful touch, she took hold of the hidden picture, scrutinising the old photo, wishing that she knew more about the people who clearly meant so much to her colleague. When Matty's body twitched, Marie returned the photo and placed the ID badge on the side table, determined not to give up on her mission to help a friend that deep down she knew was really struggling.

19

*D*URING THE DEPTHS OF THE NIGHT, THE WARDS LOCATED AT the extremities of St Jude's adopted new personalities, transforming from bustling epicentres to eerie hollows. Beneath the dim lighting of bed number two on ICU, Lola's head thrashed from side to side as she tried to sleep, ambiguous sounds rattling through her nightmares. With clammy skin and night sweats continuing to attack her body, she imagined a car skidding out of control, the sound of her own screams hollering until the vehicle crashed. She opened her eyes wide and this time, sat upright, breathless.

Having awoken an hour or so after he'd fallen asleep by her side, Matty appeared back at her side within moments. 'Are you okay?' he asked, checking all her vitals before administering some additional pain relief.

'Another bad dream,' Lola mumbled, her mind disorientated and jaded. Matty nodded with understanding.

'We see it a lot with patients who have been in bad accidents,' he began, encouraging Lola to lie back down. 'Things will ease, and time is a great healer. I'll go and make you a brew,' he said with a smile, pulling the covers up to her chin. 'Oh, and Merry Christmas, Lola,' he added, before turning and heading across the room.

Lola looked over at the clock to see it had just turned five-thirty on Christmas day morning. Teary, she relaxed her head on the pillow and thought about all the families who would be creeping downstairs to see if there had been a delivery under the tree, realising that she had never felt so alone.

'Don't cry,' Matty said when he returned with the tea. 'It's Christmas, and you're not allowed to cry on Christmas Day.' He pulled a tissue out of his pocket and handed it to her.

'Thanks for being so nice. I didn't think you'd still be here,' she said, having expected to see another fresh set of faces.

'I offered to stay,' he began to explain. 'It allows those members of staff who have young families to have a precious day off,' he replied. 'But I'll be going home soon, otherwise I might just fall asleep in one of the beds myself.'

'Do you have a family at home waiting for you?' she asked, a pensive look appearing on her face.

A lump appeared in Matty's throat that, no matter how hard he tried, refused to budge.

'Maybe a cold turkey sandwich will be waiting for me later,' he replied, his voice croaky.

'This isn't the Christmas I expected,' Lola sighed, adjusting the bandage on her head.

'You'll be able to go home and join your loved ones soon. But for now, enjoy that brew, I don't make them for everyone,' Matty said with a wink, walking away and allowing Lola to sip on her steaming mug of sugary tea.

Even on Christmas Day, the aromas of warm minced pies and sticky, spicy fruit cake weren't enough to drown out the sterile smell that greeted Carrie the moment she stepped through the hospital doors of St Jude's a few hours later.

'Hi,' she mouthed from across the room the moment she spotted Lola, who was sitting up in bed, dressed. Carrie approached the bed and flung her arms around her best friend, lingering in the embrace for longer than normal. 'God, I've been so worried about you,' she whispered in Lola's ear, still unwilling to release her grip. 'How are you?' she asked as their bodies parted.

'It looks worse than it is,' Lola commented, noticing Carrie's reaction to the bandages around her skull.

'Merry Christmas,' Carrie whispered in Lola's ear when she went back in for a second embrace, the sight of Lola's injured head causing her to well up.

'Merry Christmas,' Lola replied, relishing how good it felt to hug her best friend. 'I've missed you.'

Carrie sat on the chair next to the bed, pulling it as close as she could. 'It's only been a day since I saw you, and yet it feels like a lifetime,' she confessed. 'I was going out of my mind yesterday. You always reply to my messages, and as the day went on, I knew there must have been something wrong,' she explained. 'I could just sense it in my stomach and then when Parker called me, I just knew. Are you sure you're alright?'

'I'm fine, honestly,' Lola reassured, taking hold of Carrie's hand. 'Apparently it's some sort of miracle given how bad the accident actually was,' Lola continued. 'I guess I was just lucky. My car, not so much.'

'So, what happened? Tell me everything.'

Lola looked blank. 'This is the *really* frustrating part. I can't remember,' she said, shrugging. 'I've been told I was driving my car yesterday morning and lost control, skidded on the ice and hit a lamppost head-on,' she explained, still feeling dissociated from the events. 'Nobody else was involved, thank goodness, so I've only myself to blame.'

Carrie felt Lola's legs beneath the covers. 'And you don't have any broken bones?'

'Nope. I have a pretty nasty cut to my head,' she explained, placing her hands over the wound, 'and I have a bad concussion that is temporarily affecting my memories of the accident, but apart from that I came out pretty much intact,' she explained, pulling a funny face.

'Well, someone must have been watching over you,' Carrie smiled.

'It's just my memory that's causing me a problem. It's like yesterday has been completely erased from my mind – like it didn't even happen.'

'You've got a memory like a sieve anyway,' Carrie laughed, 'so there's nothing new there,' she added, trying to dispel the look of worry that she could see brewing in Lola's eyes. 'You're not really concerned, are you?'

Lola shrugged. 'It's just an awful feeling not being able to remember something, a whole day of your life where something so significant occurred,' she said. Suddenly, Lola's facial expression changed, and with a shaky voice, she asked Carrie a question. 'Did I tell you what I was doing yesterday morning?'

Carrie nodded straight away. 'Yeah, of course. You were going to take Parker to see the campervan that you've bought.'

Lola nodded. 'Oh, yeah, so I was,' she began, smiling with recognition. 'But if that was the plan, then why was I out driving alone, and on Christmas Eve morning too? Had my plans changed? I just can't remember,' she said in frustration, flaring her hands again and allowing them to fall on the bed.

'Well, you'd been poorly. Maybe you'd woken up still feeling groggy so weren't up for it. But then why would you be out alone?' Carrie questioned as she too tried to piece together the puzzle. 'Have you asked Parker where you were going?'

'He said I was going out, something about a surprise, which sounds about right because that's all I would have told him,' she explained. 'I wonder if the van company had changed the plans at the last minute or something.'

Carrie took her phone out of her pocket. 'Here we go,' she began, scrolling through her messages. 'You texted me late in the evening saying that you were starting to feel a bit better and that you were excited to show Parker the van, smiling face and thumbs-up emojis. Can you not check your phone?'

'I don't even know where my phone is. I'm guessing crushed in my knackered car somewhere.'

With a sense of hesitation in her voice, Carrie asked a question. 'Have they said when your memories of the accident will return?'

'Could be days, weeks, maybe never. Who bloody knows?' Lola

said in an exasperated tone. 'Every head injury is different, or so I've been told, and whilst they can guess, it's all a bit unknown, I think.'

'But your short-term and long-term memory are fine? It's literally just the day of the accident?'

Lola nodded in agreement.

'Then there's so much to be thankful for, isn't there?' she began. 'And is it so bad that you can't remember the accident? Wouldn't something like that cause you to have nightmares? Just imagine if you could remember the exact moment that you crashed, the pain you felt and the worry of waiting for the ambulance to arrive. I think I'd rather have that stuff erased,' Carrie tried to convince her friend. 'Or maybe this is just your body's way of avoiding having you suffer from any type of post-traumatic stress. I think you've been through enough.'

'Maybe,' agreed Lola in a half-hearted way, her tone unconvincing.

'What about the baby?' Carrie whispered.

Lola looked away to try and hide her tears, her reaction answering Carrie's question.

'Oh, Lola. I'm so sorry,' she replied, leaning down and scooping up Lola's body, holding her tightly. 'Are you okay, or is that a stupid question?'

Lola rested herself back onto her pillow. She blew her nose before taking a deep breath and replying. 'I know it doesn't look like it, but I'm actually alright,' she began. 'I have to believe that the timing just wasn't right. It wasn't meant to be.'

Carrie offered Lola another tissue. 'That's a good way to look at it. You're going to make a great mum when the timing is right.'

'Yeah, I know, that's what I keep telling myself.'

'So, if the accident was yesterday morning, does this mean that Parker doesn't even know about the van yet, and your decision to go travelling?'

'He has no idea. And I guess it doesn't matter now, because

he told me yesterday that he doesn't even want to go travelling anymore. Maybe it's all been a blessing in disguise.'

'What?' Carrie asked, surprised. 'For as long as I've known Parker, he's wanted to go travelling,' she said, a befuddled expression on her face. Carrie stretched her arm out and touched the leather band, noticing it around her friend's wrist for the first time. 'I haven't seen this before,' she commented. 'It doesn't feel like something you'd buy for yourself. Is it a gift from Parker? He didn't ask me for any help this year on what to buy you for Christmas.'

Lola smiled and looked down at the band, pressing it against her skin and feeling the leather between her fingers. 'I don't know where it's come from, I'm guessing that Parker bought it for me, but I really don't remember, and he hasn't mentioned it,' she explained. 'And I know it looks a bit odd on my wrist, but I kind of like the way it feels.'

At that moment, Matty approached the bed.

'You starting to feel more like yourself?' he asked.

Lola nodded and smiled. 'I am, but my headache is just the same,' she replied, pulling herself up a little. 'And I still can't remember the accident, or arriving here. It's all gone.'

He nodded in understanding. 'And I'm sure that the doctor has reassured you that this is all very normal when someone suffers from a head trauma and concussion. The headaches will ease over the coming weeks, and the blank spots in your memory will hopefully start to return in time.'

'So, can I go home today?'

'Well, your observations were a little unstable overnight so we'll have to wait and see what the doctor says. Maybe you'll make it home in time for some leftover turkey sandwiches tonight, or tomorrow at worst. We just need to be certain that you're okay before discharging you.'

'Ah, that sounds like good news,' Carrie said softly, reaching over and pressing Lola's hand. Matty leaned in and had a look under the bandages.

'If it wasn't for the man who called an ambulance and stayed with you all that time, things might have been very different,' he announced.

Lola raised her eyebrows and momentarily froze. Through a shaky, disbelieving voice she replied, 'What man?'

Matty stopped what he was doing and looked equally puzzled. 'Did your husband not explain?'

Lola shook her head.

'Oh, right,' he replied. 'Well, a passing stranger saw the accident and called for help,' he began. 'But there was a delay in the ambulance arriving because of another accident in town that had caused problems accessing the bridge,' he continued. 'And so, this kind-hearted man stayed with you the whole time, talking to you and making sure you remained awake,' he explained. 'He even came with you in the ambulance, holding your hand the entire time, or so the paramedics told the staff in A&E upon arrival. And he even waited here, at your bedside, until your husband arrived. That we are certain of because we met him ourselves. From the way he was acting, with so much care and looking so worried, I assumed that he must have been a family member of yours. It wasn't until afterwards that we discovered he was just a passing stranger.'

Carrie and Lola looked at one another in disbelief.

'Apparently, that stretch of road down Swan Lane is pretty deserted at the best of times, so had this stranger not seen the accident, it could have been even longer before you were found, and then who knows what the outcome would have been,' Matty concluded.

Lola looked perplexed. 'I had no idea,' she replied, shaking her head as tears began to trickle down her face. 'Do you know his name? Who was he?'

Although tempted to reveal Aidan's identity to the woman whose life he had saved, Matty decided to simply relay the facts that any other member of the team would have known. 'I don't know. He disappeared once your husband arrived,' he explained. 'And he didn't speak with anyone before leaving, so we have to assume that he wanted to remain unknown, an unsung hero if you like. But he really did save your life.' Matty walked away, leaving Carrie and Lola alone to digest the news.

'Oh, my goodness, how crazy is that?' Carrie announced. 'A total stranger saved your life and you didn't even know it.'

Lola rested her head onto the pillow. 'Why didn't Parker tell me?' she questioned, failing to understand how he could have forgotten to tell her something so crucial.'

Uncharacteristically, Carrie jumped to his defence. 'Parker sounded absolutely distraught when he called me,' she began. 'I bet he just forgot because he was too busy making sure that you were okay. The whole thing will have just been a blur in his mind.'

'Him and me both,' replied Lola, wishing more than ever that she could recall the face, or the name, of the man who had saved her life.

20

THE STREETS OF YORK WERE QUIET AS MATTY MADE HIS WAY TO the hospital on Boxing Day evening, the roads still covered in snow, with miniature icicles hanging from tree branches like outdoor, festive ornaments. Each house he passed remained illuminated, twinkling lights shining on the people tucked away inside. He tried to avoid feeling too envious as he peered in at the extended families who were savouring time together, a joy he had never had the opportunity to experience, and he couldn't help but imagine how his own house would look all lit up whilst family gathered around the open fire, sharing in stories and making memories.

He diverted his attention and instead looked down as he continued to walk. In his mind, he knew exactly what he was going to say to Lola when he reached the hospital, and he'd rehearsed the words over and over, thinking of little else for the past twenty-four hours. Feeling that it was the right thing to do, he wanted to reveal Aidan's identity to Lola, or at least offer up the information that the stranger who saved her life worked in town, his business located on The Shambles. Knowing that the reunion would help with Lola's ability to recall aspects of the accident, Matty knew that it would be a missed opportunity if the pair were never able to reunite.

With the main access bridge still closed for repairs, he made his way past Swan Lane, pausing when he spotted the skid marks ingrained into the tarmac, the crumpled lamppost, and the small bits of debris still littering the road. He pictured how Lola might have been trapped, from which direction Aidan might have spotted the accident and then called for help, the scars on the road telling their own tale of events like a picture book.

To the side of the road, near the embankment, Matty spotted an abandoned bag lying beneath a bench. He walked over and, with caution, picked it up, unzipping it to reveal the contents. Inside, amongst some clothes and toiletries, he spotted a passport. Fumbling in the cold, Matty opened the pages, shocked to see Aidan's passport photo staring back at him. He crouched on the floor and admired the picture, taking a private minute to acknowledge the feelings that were swirling through his heart, feelings he no longer wanted to ignore. He took hold of a t-shirt, pressing it between his fingers before burying his face in the material to conceal his moment of sadness, his tears transferring to the cotton. Never had Matty's heart ached with such a great intensity, and he placed a hand over his chest, feeling like it might stop pumping altogether. With his emotions running high, Matty returned the contents and grabbed the bag before continuing his walk to work, thinking about when he might be able to return the belongings, and what truths may be spoken in the process.

Changing with haste into his scrubs, the moment he arrived in the staff room, Matty placed Aidan's bag into his locker and then secured his face mask around his ears. Pushing his way through the double doors to ICU, he felt ready to talk to Lola and looked up, but she was nowhere to be seen.

Bay number two was now vacant.

His heart began to pump at an irregular rate again. His palms felt sweaty and a light-headedness rocked his composure. He searched for clues that would tell him what had happened in his absence, a nauseating sense of dread weakening his posture when he spotted that the whiteboard behind the nursing station had been updated, Lola's name erased. There weren't any obvious signs that an emergency situation had arisen, all the equipment was where it belonged as far as he could tell, and the bed had been made, ready for a new patient.

'Where's Lola?' he asked Marie the moment she appeared, the pair walking to the nursing station.

'Well, hello to you too,' she replied.

'Sorry, I'm just a little shocked that she's not here. I thought they'd have kept her in for another day of observations after her numbers dipped.'

'No, she was discharged not long ago, according to the handover sheet. Isn't that great news?'

Matty lost his words, along with his ability to speak. Everything that had been running through his mind for the past twenty-four hours no longer existed. 'Brilliant news,' he finally replied.

'But guess what?' she exclaimed, a glow about her face, continuing with her sentence before Matty could reply. 'The stranger who arrived with her in the ambulance, apparently he called the ward and spoke to a member of staff, wanting to know if Lola was doing okay. Isn't that such a nice thing to do? There really are some genuine souls out there.'

'Really nice,' Matty replied. 'I couldn't place him at first, but it came to me earlier where I'd seen him before,' he revealed.

'Really? Where?' she asked, intrigued.

'I think he owns a shop in town, somewhere down The Shambles. I just knew he was familiar.'

'Well, maybe he and Lola are destined to reunite after all, because I know she lives in town, I saw it on her record. Wouldn't that be a perfect ending to a story that could have turned out so different?'

Matty struggled to conceal the emotions that were tumbling through his body.

'Are you okay?' Marie asked, placing a hand on his arm when she spotted his glossy eyes.

'When I saw the bed empty, I thought we'd lost her, I thought that that dreaded bed had taken another life from us,' he revealed, pressing his face mask against his eyes, dabbing away his sadness.

Marie indicated for Matty to sit and she pulled a chair alongside his, unable to resist the opportunity to say what was on her mind. 'I don't know what's going on, Matty,' she began, her voice tender. 'I don't know why Lola meant so much to you. I don't know why you won't tell me anything about your home life. All I know is that I'm your friend, a dear friend, and I'm here to help, if you'll let me.' She looked down at her lap, frustrated by the sense of helplessness that no matter how hard she tried, she couldn't rid herself of.

Matty took in a deep breath. 'After a lifetime spent by myself, trapped inside my own world and with my own thoughts, it's hard to comprehend that anyone would actually care for me so much,' he began, taking hold of her hand. 'And even though I can't find the words to explain all of this right now, I know that in time, the words will come, and hopefully you'll still be there by my side, ready to listen. And for that, I can't thank you enough.' The pair exchanged a mutual smile of understanding, and Marie took in a deep breath before speaking.

'I will always be here for you, Matty,' she began, her voice cracking beneath the weight of emotion. 'And I'll be ready to listen whether it's a day from now, or a year from now.' Satisfied that she had done all she could to make an impression, Marie straightened out her torso and drank in another deep breath. 'But for now, let's crack on and clear all of this paperwork off our desk before that blasted red phone rings again and we lose the opportunity,' she smiled, winking at Matty before getting up and walking away.

21

AFTER WALLOWING THE FESTIVE PERIOD AWAY STAYING WITH Annie, his friend and work colleague, Aidan left the house for the first time in days and ventured back to Poets Nook. Safe in the knowledge that it was the first working day back in-between Christmas and New Year, he knew that Holly would be leaving for work. With his car parked at the far end of the road and hidden out of sight, he sat spying on his own front door. He saw that the lights were on in the bedroom, and deducted she must be home. Taking out his phone, he scrolled through Holly's raft of messages, deleting her words of apology the moment an image flashed through his mind of her in bed with another man. Opening up his internet browser, he searched the online local papers for any news reports of the accident he'd witnessed on Swan Lane, his mind able to focus on little else since Christmas Eve. Having spoken to hospital staff, who had refused to give him any details about Lola, Aidan searched social media platforms for a 'Lola' from 'York', yet failed in his bid to uncover her identity.

Outside, and on cue, Holly stepped out onto the street before locking the front door, getting into her car and driving away. The moment her car turned the corner, Aidan got out and scurried across the road, rummaging for his keys and letting himself in. Although it'd only been a week since he'd left, the house he had once called home felt hostile. The smell of Holly's freshly sprayed perfume drifted through the air, the crumbs from her breakfast toast were still scattered on the chopping board, and her slippers lay abandoned near the front door, a breath of warmth still lingering on the material. Aidan urged himself to walk past all of the personal items that served as reminders of the good times he'd experienced with Holly, and the love they'd once shared. He swung open the wardrobe and grabbed a bag, stuffing in his personal belongings.

His phone rang in the silence.

'Hello?' he answered.

'Have you arrived?' asked Annie on the other end of the line.

'I've just come in now,' Aidan began, continuing to pack. 'I'm just taking my clothes; she can keep everything else.'

'Are you sure you don't need any help? I can pop over, it's no bother. The shop is ready for opening so I can leave the others to manage for a little while.'

'I'm sure, thanks. You've done enough already by letting me stay on your sofa. Speaking of which, I've just been told that the flat I've found to rent is ready, and I can pick up the keys this afternoon, so that's some positive news, I guess.'

'I'll bring pizza over tonight and maybe a few drinks.'

'Beer will help, especially as I've lost my passport and wallet. I went back to where I remember leaving it on Swan Lane, but my bag wasn't there. It's definitely been taken.'

'How annoying,' replied Annie.

'I know. Anyway, I best get cracking, I'll text you in a bit,' Aidan replied before hanging up and putting his phone back in his pocket. He walked through to the bathroom and grabbed his toiletries, unable to avoid looking at the silly photo of him and Holly wearing sombreros; a photo taken on their first holiday abroad together.

Downstairs, the front door banged, making him jump. His heart started racing. He walked out onto the landing and glanced down. Lingering at the front door, Holly stood on the doormat, peering at a pair of Aidan's abandoned shoes that hadn't been there when she'd left for work.

'I thought you'd be back at work today,' Aidan announced as Holly looked up and met his gaze.

'I am, I just forgot my purse,' she replied. 'Why haven't you answered any of my messages?' she asked.

'There's nothing to say.'

He walked away and disappeared back into the bathroom, leaving Holly standing alone. He heard her footsteps climbing the stairs. With each additional step she neared, he fought to rein in his emotions, so that at least on the outside, his demeanour appeared unperturbed.

Stood outside the bathroom door with her heart in her hands, Holly fidgeted as she waited for Aidan to appear.

'So, that's it?' she asked. 'You've got nothing to say to me, after all the years we've been together, after everything that's happened? You're done with us?'

She took a tissue out of her pocket and captured the welling tears in her eyes just as the door opened and Aidan appeared, walking straight past her without making eye contact.

'You can't just keep ignoring me, Aidan.'

'What else would you like me to do?'

'Talk to me, work things out, fight for us. Anything apart from just pretending like I don't exist.' She followed him through to the bedroom, standing back and watching as he cleared out his drawers.

Aidan stopped what he was doing and momentarily turned to look Holly straight in the eye.

'Did you give me a second thought when you brought another man into our home, into our bed?' he spat in anger, all his frustrations spilling through his words. 'The thought makes me sick,' he added, turning away from Holly and grabbing his bag. '*You* make me sick.'

'Stop, please,' she said, grabbing his arm and preventing him from leaving the room. 'Just let me explain. We've been together too long not to at least talk about it.'

Aidan took a look at his watch. 'You've got two minutes,' he declared, his ambivalent expression unwavering.

'Can we not at least sit down?' she requested when he began making his way downstairs, continuing to gather his personal possessions.

'Nope, I really don't want to be here for any longer than I need to be.'

He walked through to the lounge and peered around the room, scanning for anything important that he might have missed, picking up the one family photo of him and his mum that he had displayed in a frame.

'It was a mistake, Aidan, just a stupid mistake after too many drinks.' Holly placed herself in the doorway, hoping to prevent him from leaving. 'And I'm so sorry for how much I've hurt you.'

Aidan continued to busy himself by looking through drawers, sorting through anything important that he needed to take.

'Is that it?' he asked with indifference when Holly fell silent.

'Less than a week ago, you were begging me to elope. You wanted to marry me and spend the rest of your life with me, and now you can't even look me in the eyes,' she replied, shaking her head and watching in dismay as he continued to collect his belongings.

'I thought I knew you, but clearly I was mistaken,' he began. 'I trusted you and I shouldn't have.'

'I made a mistake, fuelled by alcohol—'

'Don't blame the alcohol,' he interrupted. 'From the photo that I saw, it looked like you were fully in control of the situation.'

'Please, Aidan, just talk to me,' she begged as he tried to get past her and leave the room.

'So, who was he?'

Holly shook her head and dropped her gaze. 'Why does it matter who he was?'

'Because I want to know, I think I deserve that much given the fact that this man spent the night in my bed,' he began, dropping his bag and pressing his back against the wall. 'You want to talk, so talk to me. Who was this guy that meant so much that it was worth losing everything?'

Holly moved away from the door and stood in front of Aidan. 'Just some guy,' she muttered in a meek voice, trying to make the words insignificant.

'How long has it been going on for?'

'It was just the one night. I met him in town.'

'You've thrown everything away for a one-night stand. Wow, I really meant that much to you?' he commented with sarcasm. 'Well, I hope it was worth it. I hope he was worth it.'

'It meant nothing, it was just a stupid mistake. Can't we work through it, together?' she asked, trying to take hold of his hands.

'I'd never be able to trust you again,' he replied, pulling his hands away. 'If I'd got on that plane to France, would you ever have told me?' The look on Holly's face confirmed his suspicions. 'You wouldn't have, would you?' he said, speaking in an unsteady voice and curling his lip. 'You really do make me sick.'

Aidan grabbed his bag and walked through to the hallway, sinking his feet into his shoes. 'I've already paid the rent for this month and next,' he said. 'You can keep the deposit, I don't want it. I don't want anything from you.'

'Please, Aidan, I love you.'

A pained expression appeared on his face, his eyebrows furrowing. 'You love me?'

Holly's tears rolled down her cheeks, her face turning blotchy. 'I know I've messed up, but I do still love you, and I want us to be able to get past this.'

'You know what? I should be the one apologising,' he said with another hint of sarcasm.

'What? Why?'

'I knew you weren't ready. I knew you didn't want to marry me, not really, not deep down, but I pushed you into it anyway, so I guess in a way, this is all my fault.'

'I did want to marry you, Aidan, I was just struggling with the thought of starting that next stage of my life.'

He drew in a deep sigh of resignation. 'If you loved me, I don't think it should have been such a struggle, so really, you've done me a favour.'

'I still love you,' she cried, her face blotchy and red.

Without looking up, Aidan asked the question that he couldn't get out of his mind. 'What was his name?'

'What?'

'What was this guy's name, who was such a mistake?'

'Why does it matter?'

When Aidan placed his hand on the door handle and pressed down, ready to pull it open, Holly gave in and answered his question.

'Parker Cash.'

Aidan paused in the doorway and turned back to look at Holly.

'And have you deleted his number off your phone? Have you told him to never contact you again? Have you deleted the photo of you and him in our bed?'

Holly fumbled and her face couldn't disguise the truth.

'I thought not. Well, I hope he was worth it,' Aidan concluded before walking out and slamming the door behind him.

22

MATTY STOOD ON THE SHAMBLES AND COLLECTED HIS NERVES, remaining just out of sight from Aidan's shop window. With the travel bag clenched in his hand, he went over what he wanted to say so that his specific string of words would become second nature and when the time came, he wouldn't need to think on the spot. His mouth felt dry, and his stomach churned with anxiety. The moment a customer entered the shop, the sound of Aidan's voice travelled out onto the street, interjected by rumbles of laughter.

'Morning,' announced Aidan as Matty walked into the shop. 'How are you?' he asked, continuing to restock the display counter with a selection of sale items.

'I'm good, thanks,' Matty replied, holding the bag in his hand. 'I think this is yours,' he blurted, holding it up. 'I was walking down by the canal the other day when I spotted it near a bench. I saw your passport and wallet inside and I haven't had time to return it since. I've been putting in some overtime and working nights, with the hospital being so busy.'

Aidan's face lit up and he walked round to the other side of the counter. 'Wow, really?' he asked in surprise, taking hold of the travel bag and looking through its contents. 'I thought I'd never see this again.' Rummaging inside, Aidan took hold of his passport and wallet. 'These are what I've been worried about,' he explained, waving them aloft. 'Thank you so much for returning it, I really appreciate it. I'd had a manic day when I left it down by the canal. It was some time before I even realised that I'd left it behind if I'm honest. I think I need to start looking after my things a little better.'

'No problem,' Matty smiled. 'Like I said, I'm just sorry it's taken so long, it's a busy time of year.'

'I read online about the accident that happened on Lendal Bridge over Christmas. I bet that was a busy few days at the hospital.'

Matty nodded. 'It's always busy at this time of year. Too many people drink driving, and way too many fights and accidents fuelled by alcohol. We've had some awful weather to contend with this year too.'

Desperate for an update on Lola, Aidan grabbed the moment of opportunity that had presented itself. 'Which department do you work in? I'm not sure you've ever spoken about the specifics of what you do.'

'I'm a ward nurse. Well, a matron, actually.'

Aidan took a moment before replying. 'The only reason I ask is that I know there was another bad crash on Christmas Eve, a woman lost control of her car. She was travelling by herself. I've heard some of my customers talking about it and I was wondering if the driver was okay.' Aidan tried to appear aloof and yet inside, felt desperate to hear any additional news relating to Lola.

'I don't really get to hear much about who is being admitted down in A&E or what's going on in the bigger picture. The hospital is so huge, with so many wards, that there's only really time for me to focus on those patients that I'm personally treating,' he explained. Despite practising what he wanted to say, Matty couldn't bring himself to speak truthfully, knowing that if he had revealed the truth about his involvement on ICU that day, it would only have led to more questions that, as yet, he just couldn't bring himself to answer, especially to Aidan, the fear of rejection keeping his words held hostage.

'Did you get to enjoy some time off?' Aidan asked, aiming

to conceal his disappointment, stepping aside and allowing his colleague to serve the waiting customer.

'Not much, but can't complain.'

'Any exciting plans for tonight? There're the usual big celebrations here, I suspect. The Minster's bells will be chiming in the New Year, along with the firework display. That's usually pretty spectacular.'

'Just a quiet one at home for me,' Matty replied, punishing himself inside for not finding the courage to open up to Aidan and letting another opportunity pass him by.

'Same here, actually. Let's hope that next year is a good one. I could do with a better year than the one that we're just about done with.'

'Has it been a tough?' Matty asked.

'Not the best. I've had some family stuff to deal with just recently, and I was also engaged, up until about a week ago,' he revealed.

Matty could see the hurt concealed within Aidan's eyes, and had never before felt so much love. 'I'm sorry to hear that.'

'Don't be. I'm sorry for offloading all this onto you. I guess you've just caught me at a bad time,' he explained. 'Anyway, I best get on. I can feel that it's going to be a busy one today, people tend to go crazy in the sales. Happy New Year to you.'

'Happy New Year to you, too,' replied Matty as he opened the shop door and walked away. From across the road, where he positioned himself just out of sight again, Matty watched through the shop window of Fudgy Nook, unable to bring himself to walk away. He observed how Aidan naturally fidgeted with his wrist despite not wearing the wristband that over the years, Matty had observed was always secured around his wrist, Aidan once having shared the story that the item had been gifted by his late mum.

In a moment of clarity, Matty recalled a conversation he'd had with Lola about a band that had appeared on her arm. When asked by Lola on the ward, Matty hadn't been lying when he said he hadn't known who had placed it there, but now, in a moment of quiet observation, he realised that, actually, he did have a good idea who had gifted it to her, and given what he had witnessed relating to the kindness offered from one stranger to another, the answer had been obvious all along.

23

Through Lola's eyes, the house had never appeared so dismal, so bleak – so January. The Christmas decorations had been removed and stuffed back into the loft, leaving a gaping void in the lounge, and it felt like life had returned to normal for everyone, except her. Lola remained sat watching daytime television, squandering another day away, when her phone buzzed.

'Hi,' announced Carrie when Lola answered. 'I thought I'd give you a quick ring before what I hope will be a lunchtime rush. How are you doing?' she asked.

Lola didn't answer immediately, giving herself time to think of a suitable reply. 'I'm doing okay.' Lola heard Carrie shrug.

'I've known you for long enough to know when you're lying to me,' Carrie responded like a school teacher gruelling a pupil for hiding the truth.

'Life just feels difficult at the moment, you know, since the accident.'

'Things will get better, it'll just take time for your body, and your mind, to heal,' she reassured in a soothing tone.

'I know, I don't think it's just the accident though,' she added, her lungs releasing a sigh that deflated her entire chest.

'What else is going on?'

'Things with Parker just feel…'

'Just feel what?' she asked when Lola failed to complete her sentence.

'Things just feel weird between us, and I don't really know why,' she revealed. 'He's actually let it slip that before I went out on Christmas Eve by myself, we'd been arguing, over nothing really. Apparently it was down to the fact that he was a bit hungover from the previous night, and that's why I was out in the car on my own. I stormed out of the house apparently, and now he's feeling guilty and sort of responsible for what happened.' Lola held out her hand in an exasperated manner. 'And I want to talk to him about the fact that I've bought us this campervan, but I honestly don't know how to broach the subject now because he just doesn't seem interested anymore.'

'Well, people are allowed to change their mind, I guess. And anyway, isn't it a good thing? I'm sure you were only entertaining the idea of leaving York because of him, despite what you told me.'

Lola exhaled. 'Maybe. I just feel like my life has been turned upside down and I can't make sense of anything.'

'Why don't you come into town so we can have a coffee and a proper chat, in person? It sounds like we're overdue a good natter,' Carrie suggested. 'Getting out of the house would do you some good.'

Lola hadn't ventured away from home for weeks, using her sporadic episodes of dizziness as an excuse when, in reality, she just felt a bit lost, for reasons she couldn't explain to herself, let alone others.

'I'm not sure, I haven't been out since—'

'Come on, please, just for me,' persuaded Carrie when she anticipated an excuse coming her way. 'Just a coffee, then you can go home and rest all afternoon,' she added.

'Alright, but just a quick visit.'

Once she'd hung up, Lola sank her feet into a pair of boots and wrapped a coat around her body. She took a quick glance in the mirror, covered her hair with a hat, and applied a thin layer of lipstick before heading out of the door.

Nervous, she made her way on foot towards the town centre, the atmosphere outside doing little to improve her mood, the decorations hanging off the higgledy-piggledy buildings looking particularly sad when not illuminated. The cold air swept across Lola's face, stinging her skin and drying out her lips. Her boots skidded on ungritted patches of pavement, adding to her unsettled nerves. Although she told herself that walking past the site of the accident wasn't a great idea, not yet, within minutes she found herself approaching the particular stretch of deserted road down near the river.

In the distance, she spotted the lamppost that she had crashed head-first into, and despite the repair work that had been carried out, evidence of the crash could still be witnessed in the steel. One pace at a time, she made her way down Swan Lane, when all of a sudden, she remembered the screeching sound that her car had made the morning of the accident, the noise sending shivers through her body. Beneath her coat, her body quaked, her posture collapsing. Her eyes opened wide, unable to blink, and a haunted look appeared on her face.

'I've just remembered something,' she announced the moment Parker answered his phone.

'I'm just about to head into a lecture,' he whispered. 'Are you okay?' he asked, failing to hear her statement.

'Sorry,' Lola replied, taking a look at her watch. 'I didn't think.'

'It's okay. Are you alright?'

Lola couldn't tear her eyes away from the lamppost. 'I've just had a mini breakthrough and I wanted to share it with you.'

'We'll talk tonight, I need to get going,' Parker insisted.

Disheartened, Lola replied, 'Sure, see you tonight,' before hanging up.

Taking a seat on a nearby bench, Lola took the weight off her shaking legs while her eyes remained focused on the site of the accident. She spotted the markings on the road where her tyres had skidded, and the sound her brakes had made continued to course through her mind like the accident was happening right this second. Tears tumbled down her face in recognition of her breakthrough, her first memory of the accident rising to the surface and breaking through the fog that continued to hinder her memory. Closing her eyes and placing her hands over her face, she tried to place herself in the heart of the accident, hoping that other memories would surface, and yet no matter how hard she tried, the sound of her car screeching was the only thing she could recall. In her pocket, she felt her phone buzz, and a message from Carrie popped up on the screen, encouraging Lola to leave the riverbank and continue into town.

With her mind focused on Swan Lane, Lola arrived in the centre of town without recalling anything about the walk, her body working on autopilot. She peered over to The Brownie Box where she could see that Carrie had a queue, the lunchtime rush beginning, so she pulled her phone out and replied. *Sorry, got distracted so won't make it in today, we'll reschedule, promise xx.* Once the message had been sent, she headed to the opposite end of The Shambles and took refuge from the wind in a café she seldom visited, *Time for Tea.*

'Hi, what can I get you?' the lady behind the counter asked when Lola approached.

Lola scanned the menu before placing her order. 'Er, I'll have a pot of tea and a jam scone, please.'

The lady took payment before handing Lola her receipt. 'Find a table and I'll bring it over.'

Lola gravitated towards the window, sitting on one of the three vacant window stools and removing her coat. She watched the people as they passed by out on the cobbles, and yet her mind remained at the riverbank as she willed herself to recall more.

'Here you go,' said the waitress as she placed down a tray. 'Let me know if you need anything else.'

Out on the street, The Shambles was busy with lunchtime activity, a raft of local workers heading out to purchase lunch. She found her attention returning to the interior of the café when the door opened.

'What can I get for you today?' the waitress asked Aidan as he walked into the café. 'Are you going for your usual soup and sandwich, or will you surprise me today?'

Aidan walked over to the counter and produced his most convincing laugh. 'No surprises today, just the usual, thanks.' He lingered near the counter and waited for his order, failing to notice those patrons around him, including Lola, who remained seated in the window with her back to the room.

'Here we go,' announced the waitress as she handed Aidan the takeaway bag.

'Thanks, have a great day,' he replied before walking towards the door. Just before he reached out his arm to grab the handle, the smell of Lola's perfume drifted into his nose, causing him to look up immediately. His heart raced the moment the smell entered his system, the scent of the perfume transporting him right back to Christmas Eve and the ambulance ride when he'd travelled alongside Lola, holding her hand. He turned to the right, at which point he spotted a lady sat in the window, alone. Panicked, he felt his face flush and his heart race.

'Have I forgotten something?' shouted the waitress upon noticing Aidan lingering near the door.

He shook his head. 'I'll surprise you today after all and I'll sit in, if that's okay,' he responded, taking a seat in one of the vacant window stools near Lola and placing his lunch on the bench. With a glance to his side, his heart cantered the moment his eyes settled on Lola's soft, familiar features. He took out his phone, sending Annie a quick message.

Can't believe it. I'm sat next-door and Lola is here. What should I do?

Within seconds, a reply came back. *Talk to her!!! You've been trying to find her and now you have x*

'Hi,' he announced, turning and addressing Lola with a warm smile. With so much expectation surging through his mind about how their first meeting following the accident would go, he felt so embarrassed when she produced a meek smile, the look on her face conveying the fact that she had no clue as to who he was.

'I didn't mean to interrupt,' he quickly added, trying to salvage the embarrassing situation. 'I own the fudge shop next-door and we're having this special event next Saturday. I'm meant to be handing these out, but I've been doing a terrible job,' he said, pulling out a promotional card. 'This will get you a discount on the day, if you're interested.'

With reluctance, Lola held out her hand and took hold of the card. 'Thanks,' she replied before returning her gaze to the street outside.

Deflated, Aidan reached out for a second time. 'Are you planning a trip?' he asked, peering down and spotting that she was looking at a map on her phone.

Lola took a moment to reply, hoping that the stranger would take the hint and leave her alone. 'Sort of,' she finally answered, somewhat rudely.

Her standoffish response caused a sense of heaviness to rush over Aidan, reality falling short of the emotional reunion he had romanticised in his mind.

'I'm sort of planning a trip too, anything to escape this grim, British weather,' he replied, turning back and peering out the window, his hopes, and heart, deflated.

Lola continued to bury her head in the map, internally tutting at her out-of-character rudeness. Just as Aidan stood to leave, she extended an olive branch. 'Where are you planning on travelling to?' she asked after an extended pause, turning her body to face the stranger in polite acknowledgement.

Aidan allowed his body to collapse back onto the stool, an overwhelming sense of relief working to lift his spirits. 'Southern France. I have some family stuff to sort, but I'm thinking that it's the perfect reason to have a road trip while I'm out there.'

He glanced up to meet Lola's gaze, confident that she would recognise him, and yet she looked at him like he was a total stranger, as though they'd never before crossed paths.

'It's actually my husband's idea to go travelling,' she admitted, finally warming to the conversation. 'And even though I'm not keen on the idea, I'm now trying my best to get excited about all the places I could visit,' she added, pointing down to her map of Europe. 'To be honest, if it was just up to me, I wouldn't need to travel very far to find happiness. There's this quaint campsite that my family used to visit during the summer holidays, when I was in primary school,' Lola began to explain, a little spark flickering in her eye at the memory. 'It's not that far away from here, and it had this amazing lake that I'd spend all my time swimming in,' she continued. 'So, if it was up to me, I'd start my travels there.'

Although Lola didn't spot it, Aidan's eyes glistened the moment they began to chat, his broad smile lighting up their corner of the quirky café.

'Sounds idyllic,' Aidan smiled. 'My main problem with the thought of travelling is trusting people to run my business while I'm away. I struggle to relax if I have a weekend off, let alone weeks, or even months.' Aidan fiddled with his shirt sleeve and cringed at his own admission. 'I think I've just described myself as a total control freak, which I hope I'm not. I've just invested a lot into the business to throw in the keys and leave it in the hands of someone else.'

Lola nodded. 'I get it. I have my own business too, and it can be hard to let go.'

'Oh really? What's your business?'

'You might know it, it's The Brownie Box just up the street. I've already spent so many years in a tin can, so travelling in an actual campervan wouldn't really be too dissimilar.' Lola found herself offering up a genuine smile for the first time in weeks, and she loved the way it felt. A lightness appeared in her limbs while a warmth radiated through her chest, encouraging her more relaxed nature to shine through. 'I thought I knew most people's faces who work around here. I guess I'm not that observant after all,' she concluded, trying to recall if she and Aidan had rubbed shoulders before.

'I'm mostly tucked away in the workshop at the back,' he grinned. 'Well, I best get back. I was only meant to be nipping out to buy lunch,' Aidan smiled. While putting on his coat, he spotted the scar on Lola's head, the same wound that he had watched bleed profusely, the same wound that he'd pressed his hand against in an attempt to stem the flow. The image of blood trickling down Lola's face was one that still stalked his nightmares. 'If you can, come to the event next Saturday. Like I said, we're just next-door,' he explained, pointing to his right. 'I'll make sure you get a good discount, you'll need lots of sugary snacks if you're going on a road trip,' he laughed. 'Anyway, nice to meet you. Sorry, I didn't ask your name.'

'Lola.'

'Mine is Aidan. Hopefully see you at the event on Saturday,' he concluded, before opening the door and stepping out onto the cobbles. He walked past the café window and dived into his own shop next-door, his smile leading the way. He put his things behind the counter, and without saying anything, quickly gave Annie a thumbs up before stepping back out onto the bustling street. Just out of sight, he peered back to the café window, spotting that Lola remained seated. Maintaining his inconspicuous demeanour, he stood and observed, his heart dancing the moment his admiring eyes landed on his wristband, the leather strap still fastened with purpose around Lola's delicate wrist. His hopes of a reunion were reignited.

24

WITHOUT BOTHERING TO ROLL OVER IN BED AND GLANCE AT the clock, Lola could feel that it was an ungodly hour just by the weight of her body. With her eyes wide open and gazing up towards the ceiling, the thoughts in her mind fluttered like a feather caught in a gusty wind. Outside on Candle Crescent, she could hear that the road was unusually quiet, indicating that it must be the few precious hours of silence that occurred once the late-night bus service stopped, and before the early morning service commenced.

Having made the decision to give up on getting any sleep, Lola peeled back the covers and eased herself out of bed at 02:35am. She grabbed hold of her phone and jumper before treading carefully across the bedroom floor and out onto the landing, easing the door closed behind her. Beneath the deep darkness of the night, she crept downstairs and turned on the table lamp in the lounge. Crouching to her knees, she bent down and plunged her arm underneath the sofa, pulling a piece of paper free, the glow of the lamp illuminating her words. Through her tired eyes, she studied what she'd already scribbled down; a messy timescale of all the events leading up to her accident. On the left-hand side of the landscape piece of paper, she'd written *Thursday 23rd* and underlined it, and then on the right-hand side she'd written the words *Waking up in St Jude's,* in bold capitals.

Despite a pounding headache, she closed her eyes and dragged herself back in time. She allowed her mind to wander, hoping that forgotten memories would be unearthed, and yet no matter how hard she tried, not a single recollection came to mind. In frustration, she rubbed her temples, trying to coerce her brain to release the withheld information. Exasperated, she skulked through to the kitchen seeking something to numb her pain, easing the cupboard open and reaching for the medical tin. The moment she took hold of the old biscuit tin and reached for the pills, her whole body trembled as goosebumps covered her skin. An image flashed through her mind of Parker standing in the exact same spot on the morning of the accident, painkillers in hand. Inquisitively, she peered around the room, trying to flesh out the entire scene that had developed just before she had left the house that nearly fatal morning. When her mind remained blank, she sensed her frustration mounting. Hungry, she opened the fridge and reached for a yoghurt, her arm knocking a jar of lemon curd, the glass smashing the moment it made impact with the floor. The instant the tangy aroma reached her senses, her mind once again regressed, taking her back to Christmas Eve. This time, her recollections told her that she'd been standing in the lounge, upset, and holding her phone.

Walking back through to the lounge, she closed the door, went and sat in the far corner, and dialled Carrie's number.

'I know you're probably asleep, and I'm sorry for waking you, but I need someone to talk to,' Lola apologised when Carrie finally answered her phone.

'What time is it?' Carrie mumbled, her eyes trying to focus on the alarm clock positioned next to her bed. 'Are you okay?'

'I've had a breakthrough,' Lola announced, trying to keep her voice down so that, upstairs, Parker wouldn't stir. 'I've remembered some things from Christmas Eve, stuff that happened before the accident,' she said in a ramble, her words rolling into one another.

'Right. Why are you whispering?'

Lola looked up, listening for movement. 'Parker's asleep and I don't want to wake him. I'm sat in the lounge on my own.'

Carrie rubbed her eyes, encouraging them to remain open. 'So, what do you mean you've had a breakthrough?' she asked when her brain began to emerge from its state of slumber.

'I've remembered something about Christmas Eve,' she announced with excitement. 'And I know that Parker has already explained his version of events, and I agreed to move on and try and forget about it, but I haven't been able to move on, Carrie, because I just feel that something isn't right. I *know* something else happened that day that he isn't telling me about.'

'And now you've remembered what that is?'

'Sort of,' Lola replied.

Carrie pulled herself up in bed and rested against the headboard, wrapping the duvet around her body, accepting the fact that she was now fully awake. 'What do you mean?'

'Well, I've remembered bits, like the fact that Parker took some painkillers that morning, and he never takes them, and I know that he made me some lemon curd on toast, and he loathes the stuff, Carrie, he always has done, and he's always refused to make it for me, saying that the smell makes him feel physically sick,' Lola explained with mounting enthusiasm.

'Right, so, what does that mean?' Carrie questioned, struggling to follow Lola's train of thought. 'He'd been out in town, hadn't he? Drinking. And he was late back, so that would explain the painkillers to ease his hangover.'

'Yeah, but I think I was upset too. I was in the lounge with my phone, and he was upstairs, at least I think he was,' she explained with a crumpled brow. 'And I don't know why I was upset.'

'Have you looked through the messages on your phone now that you're back up and running?'

'Yep. There's nothing.'

'And what about your gallery and social media accounts.'

'I've checked everything, there's nothing.'

'And you're sure you weren't just annoyed that he'd stayed out and drunk too much? He was hungover, you were annoyed and stormed out, and so he did spoil the surprise that you'd taken time to arrange. I'd have been annoyed had it been me.'

'No,' she replied, shaking her head. 'He's done stuff like that before, I kind of expect him to drink too much and come home late when he goes out.'

'So, why were you upset then?' quizzed Carrie. 'And you're sure that the weird wristband doesn't have anything to do with all this? Maybe Parker gave it to you as an early Christmas present and you didn't like it, making you feel upset, or disappointed by the fact that after all these years, he still doesn't know your taste?'

Lola looked down at her wrist, still puzzled by the band. 'He said it wasn't from him, so I must have got it at some point after the accident. But that bit is still all blurred out in my mind,' she replied, her voice conveying that she felt exasperated by the whole thing.

Putting the phone on speaker, Lola took a look at the screen to see what time it was.

'Oh my God!' she declared.

'What?' exclaimed Carrie on the other end.

'It wasn't *my* phone in my hand that morning, it was Parker's phone I was holding. I remember feeling something on the back, a sticker from one of the pubs that he'd been to that night.'

Standing in the dimly lit room, Lola's face turned ghostly, the whites of her eyes shining through the darkness.

'He's hiding something from me, Carrie. I know he is, and I'm going to find out the truth.'

25

'Y OU'RE JUST GOING TO HAVE TO SUCK THIS UP,' SAID MARIE, AS Matty walked onto the ward for the very last time. 'I know that you didn't want a fuss, but people here care about you, I care about you, and we couldn't just have you leave without doing anything,' she said in an apologetic tone. 'So, let's get it over with now, and then it's done,' she said, indicating for him to leave the ward and head back out.

'Where are we going?' he asked, confusion spreading across his face.

'To the staff room.'

'What about the ward?'

'We have cover,' smiled Marie. 'So, don't worry.'

More than anything else, Matty hated attention from others and dreaded situations where he knew that all eyes would be on him.

'You know I didn't want this.'

'I know you didn't, but like it or not, we're your friends, your work family, so you have no choice,' she replied, opening the door to the staff room and allowing Matty to walk in first.

The moment he stepped through the door, he was greeted with a sea of familiar faces, colleagues from every department in the hospital had turned up to say their goodbyes. With a raft of cards and presents piled up on a table, Marie silenced the room so that she could say a few words.

'We know that you don't like a fuss, so I'll keep this short and very sweet,' she began. 'I just want to say a huge thank you for all your hard work and commitment over the years. You've spent more time here than you have at home, and on behalf of all the patients you've cared for, thank you from them, and thank you from us.' Marie began to cry, at which point, Matty placed his arm around her.

'I'll be popping in for chippy lunch Fridays, so you're not getting rid of me completely,' he smiled, reigning in his own emotions, his era of working at St Jude's coming to an end.

'So, what are you going to do tomorrow?' Marie asked.

'Tomorrow, I'm going to try and do all the things that I've delayed for the past twenty something years,' he said, his jovial tone underlined with sincerity. Everyone in the room smiled and clapped. 'Thanks for all this,' he said, noticing the pile of gifts. 'I've ordered pizzas for everyone, so at lunchtime, make sure you come and help yourselves to a slice on me.'

As people wished him well and the room began to naturally disperse, Matty gave Marie another hug.

'Are you okay?' she asked, sensing that he still wasn't quite himself.

'Why are you always so nice to me?' he replied, wrapping his arm around her waist.

'Because you're my friend, and I just want you to be happy,' she replied.

'Once I'm done with this place at the end of my shift, I'm going to work on making myself happy, I promise,' he said. 'And it's not going to be easy, but I am going to do it, and when I do, I'll be telling you all about it,' he reassured, a smile lighting up the defined features of his face.

'You do know that you kept your promise?' she announced, her eyebrows raised.

'What promise was that?'

'The promise that all of our patients were going to see

Christmas. And they did, even the patient admitted to bed number two on Christmas Eve.'

A sparkle shone in Matty's eyes.

'I love that Lola Cash was the last patient that I admitted onto the ward. She was always going to make it home safe and well.'

Marie's face lit up. 'I knew it!' she exclaimed. 'I knew there was something special about her that you weren't telling me.'

'I'll tell you everything, in time, but for now, I just want to get through this last shift.'

'Well, I've been told that you can leave early. You don't even have to finish your shift, so you can make a dash for it before they change their minds. They rarely let people finish early, you know that, so you're an exception.'

'Thanks, Marie, for everything,' he said, removing his lanyard. 'I'll take them up on their offer and get myself out of here. I'll let you know how I'm getting on,' he said, at which point, he left the room, the significance of the day feeling so overwhelming that all he wanted to do was hide his crumbling emotions.

With all of his goodbyes said, Matty opened his locker and, for the first time in years, removed the photo that had been attached to the door, placing it in his bag with care. He took one last look at his empty locker before walking away from ICU, finally ready to confront the demons that he felt were forever haunting his heart.

26

With the main lights in the kitchen dimmed and scented candles dotted around the dining table, which had been set for two, a romantic ambience had been staged. The background selection of love songs humming away through the speaker added to the atmosphere Parker had worked hard to create.

'Hi, where are you?' he asked Lola when she answered her phone.

'I'm choosing a bottle of wine, like you asked me to do,' she replied, scanning the wine selection and trying to pick one that she thought would pair well with dinner. 'What did you say you were cooking for tea?'

'I told you, it's a surprise. Anyway, be quick, it's nearly ready.'

Parker hung up the phone and checked himself in the mirror, adjusting his choice of shirt, the one which he knew Lola was particularly fond of. After checking on tea and fixing dessert, the doorbell rang just as he placed a bunch of fresh flowers next to her plate.

'That was quick. Did you forget your key?' he began to mock before he'd fully opened the door, expecting to see his wife.

'Hi, Parker,' replied Holly. 'How are you?'

Parker looked up and down the street, watching out for Lola. 'What are you doing here?' How do you even know where I live?' he spat as his throat tightened. He took shallow, rapid breaths, an intense feeling of shame taking hold of his emotions.

'You wouldn't answer my messages.'

Frustrated, Parker spoke through his teeth with a forced restrain. 'There's nothing to say.'

'Can I come in?' Holly asked before pushing her way inside. 'Is your wife here?' she asked, looking around the lounge and hesitating when her eyes landed upon the table.

'What are you doing?' he asked, quickly shutting the door. 'She'll be back any minute.'

'I have feelings, you know, and when you blocked my number, it really hurt me,' she began, her tone softening. 'What happened between us felt like more than just a one-night stand, at least for me,' she confessed, taking the courage to look up into his eyes. 'I've been trying to pretend like it didn't mean anything, but it did, and I felt like it meant something to you, too.'

Parker shook his head. 'Look, I'm really sorry,' he began, leaning his back against the front door. 'I'm married, and what I did was wrong. I didn't know what else to do but block your number so that Lola wouldn't see any of your messages.'

Holly's facial features were downturned, her eyes appearing wet and dull. She allowed her body to press against the wall, and she peered down at her empty hands. 'I've lost everything because of you. My fiancé knows what happened, and has moved out.'

Parker shook his head. 'I'm sorry to hear that, and I'm sorry that I hurt you, that was never my intention, but that night was a mistake.'

'It didn't feel like a mistake when we were together. It felt right.'

Parker ran his hands through his hair and a pain developed in his jaw from clenching his teeth. 'I want to try and make my marriage work,' he confessed.

'If your marriage was that strong, why did you spend the night with me? Why did you kiss me the following morning? And why did you look at me the way that you did?'

Parker searched the floor for answers, his heart galloping beneath his chest as he listened out for Lola's return. 'I don't know,' he replied. 'All I can say is I'm sorry, for everything.'

Holly looked over at Parker. 'I don't want you to apologise. I made the decision to spend the night with you, I just didn't like the way you treated me afterwards. It made me feel like I meant nothing to you, like I was worthless.'

'We did have a great time together, and it did mean something to me too,' he revealed through a reluctant sigh, thus far having refused to acknowledge, even to himself, what his true feelings were about what had happened that night. 'But I do want to make my marriage work.'

Outside, he heard footsteps approaching the front door, so he pressed his face against the spyglass.

'It's Lola, my wife,' he muttered in a panicked voice, taking hold of Holly's arm and guiding her through to the back of the house. 'Please, Holly, please leave,' he spluttered as he opened the door, a desperate look appearing on his face.

'Unblock me on your phone and I'll leave,' she requested, taking hold of his hand. 'I understand that you're married, but we can at least be civil, be friends. I think we owe each other at least that much respect after what happened between us that night,' she concluded, releasing a satisfied sigh.

Parker nodded, taking quick breaths. His limbs felt quivery, and his muscles were twitching beneath his shirt. 'I will, I promise.'

'Now. Unblock me now so I know that you're a man of your word,' Holly encouraged, remaining stood near the door.

Parker grabbed his phone and fumbled for a few seconds. 'There, done. Now, please leave before she comes in,' he spluttered, looking back towards the front door and hearing the creak as it opened.

Holly stepped out and walked away, disappearing through the back garden and out of sight just as Lola appeared in the kitchen.

'What's going on?' Lola questioned.

'What do you mean?' Parker snapped, a flustered expression spread across his face.

Lola removed her coat and hat while peering around the kitchen. 'All the candles? Is this all for me? I thought you were just making us dinner.'

Parker breathed a shallow sigh of relief and his tone changed when he realised that she hadn't seen Holly leaving. 'I wanted to make a special effort for you,' he explained, walking around the table to pull her chair out, his eyes spying on the garden every few seconds to ensure there was no sight of Holly. 'Things have felt like such a struggle since Christmas, and I just wanted to make sure that you know how much I love you.' He leaned down and delivered Lola a kiss, unable to recall the last time that they'd shared a passionate moment.

A shine radiated from her eyes. 'I don't think you've kissed me like that since our honeymoon,' she confessed, relishing the way that Parker's lips felt against hers, his touch still having the ability to make her skin tingle with excitement, encouraging her to push away the doubts that were running through her mind. 'I don't know why things have felt so difficult. Between us, I mean.'

'Here you go, I hope it's edible,' he joked, placing a bowl of homemade lasagne down in front of her. 'You know my cooking isn't all that great.'

'Why do you feel things have been so difficult?' Lola continued once Parker had taken a seat.

'It's just been pretty stressful, what with coming back from the honeymoon, and then the accident. I don't feel we've had the best start to our married life.' Parker's eyes darted between the garden and Lola, his soaring levels of adrenaline causing a jumpiness that he struggled to control.

'Are you okay? You seem a little on edge,' Lola remarked, spotting his fidgeting hands and somewhat rumpled appearance.

Parker was just about to reply when his phone buzzed.

'Why don't I put that on silent?' he suggested, jumping up and grabbing his phone off the side unit near the back door. 'The last thing I want is for anything to spoil our romantic evening.' He took a quick glance at his phone, relieved that it was just an email from work.

From the kitchen table, Lola's brow wrinkled when she watched how Parker reacted with his phone, his behaviour confirming what she already suspected. 'Anyone important?' she asked when he sat back down.

'Nope, just work stuff. It can wait. So, how is it?' he asked, looking down at Lola's plate.

'It's delicious, and all the more reason for you to start cooking for us more regularly.'

Parker put down his fork and leaned back in his chair. 'So, how are you feeling about getting back to work? Do you feel ready for it?'

'Physically I feel ready,' Lola began. 'I mean, the headaches have gone and the dizziness isn't an issue, thank goodness.'

'I sense some hesitation,' he pressed.

Through vacant eyes, Lola looked up at Parker with hesitance. 'I don't really feel like I've dealt with the accident, emotionally I mean.' A lump appeared in her throat whenever she spoke or even thought about the accident. 'How can I understand what happened and move past it when I can't remember for myself what I went through?' she asked with a long, slow sigh, her arms hanging by her side in defeat. 'And I know that you've told me as much as you know, and that you're eager for me to forget about it, but I can't just forget that something traumatic happened to me.'

Lola sensed the tension in Parker's voice as he began to speak.

'You've been able to remember the sound of the car skidding, everything else might come back too. But if it doesn't, then like I've said before, so what?' he questioned. 'I just don't see why you can't be grateful that you're okay. It was a terrible accident, and even though it's a miracle that you managed to walk away pretty much unharmed, you're sabotaging things in the here and now, because of what? Because you can't recall every single thing that happened. I just don't get it.'

Lola pushed away her bowl and crossed her arms in front of her chest.

'And I don't get why you're not being more supportive or understanding. First you told me I went out that morning to sort out a surprise for you, then you let it slip that we'd actually had a fight because you'd come home drunk, and I get this feeling that there's more to the story than you're letting on.'

Parker pushed his seat back and stood up, storming out of the room and walking upstairs, closing the bathroom door behind him. Without thought, Lola took hold of his phone and unlocked the screen. Her hands began to shake, and although she didn't know what she was looking for, her instincts told her to search.

She flicked through his Facebook messenger and Instagram private messages, and found nothing untoward. Just as she heard the toilet flush, a new message appeared on screen, the number not linked to any of Parker's contacts. Lola opened up the message and read the words.

I'm sorry for just turning up. I really do hope you can make a go of your marriage.

Her face turned white in an instant, her lungs forcibly expelling all breath as her mind tried to process the meaning behind the message, wondering who he'd been talking to about the state of his marriage. She felt her stomach tighten and her face flushed as her shock turned to anger. The sound of the bathroom door opening made her quickly mark the message as unread before placing the phone back down on the table.

'I'm sorry,' Parker said upon reappearing in the kitchen. 'You're right. I do need to be more supportive and help you through this, no matter how I feel,' he continued. 'I'm just scared in case you're forever waiting for something that might not come,' he added, crouching down and taking hold of her hand. 'But, whatever you want to do, I'm here for you, alright? As long as it takes and whatever you need from me, I'm here.'

Parker delivered a tender kiss and allowed his lips to linger on hers, his hands placed at either side of her face.

Lola forced out a smile and pushed all of her emotions away, offering Parker an embrace.

'My memories will return, I'm sure of it. It's just going to take time, and I need you to have some patience with me in the meantime,' she whispered into his ear. His arms were wrapped firmly around her back in reciprocation of her affections.

Parker's phone buzzed again, and from her vantage point over his shoulder, Lola caught sight of another message from the same unknown contact. She squinted to read the words before the notification disappeared.

I will never regret what we did xx

Internally seething, she pushed herself away from his body and looked him in the eye.

'Are you sure there isn't something that you're not telling me about the accident? About Christmas Eve? About us?' she asked, fighting the urge to grab his phone and read the full message thread for herself. 'I just need to know the truth, from you,' she added, her chin falling into her chest. 'Whatever that is.'

Struggling to mask his emotions, he smiled and scooped her face between his hands.

'The truth is, I don't deserve you, and I love you more than I can explain,' he replied.

Over on the table, his phone vibrated again, encouraging him to stand up and reach for it. He quickly turned it off before placing it into his pocket.

'Now, let's have some dessert.'

Lola spotted a grimace appear on Parker's face that she had seen on him before, an expression that confirmed her husband was lying, her stomach churning as she anticipated the level of betrayal that he had committed this time, the words from the text message jammed in her mind.

'I'll pass,' she replied, standing up and walking out of the room. 'I've lost my appetite.'

27

*L*OLA SNUCK OUT OF BED, LEAVING PARKER IN A DEEP SLEEP. Walking over to his side of the bed, she checked his phone. The messages from the previous evening had been deleted. She crept through to the bathroom and had a wash, pulled her hair into a messy bun, and applied a subtle layer of makeup. Checking that Parker hadn't stirred, she tiptoed downstairs, scribbling the words, *Couldn't sleep, going to do some shopping and then meeting Carrie afterwards. Be back in time for tea,* on the back of an envelope, and leaving it next to the kettle. She unlocked her phone and turned off the app function that allowed Parker to see her location. Then she grabbed her coat and bag before slipping out through the front door and locking it behind her.

With hesitation, she paced towards The Shambles, towards hers and Carrie's pitch.

'Oh, my goodness,' announced Carrie as she saw Lola approaching The Brownie Box. She lunged her body through the open hatch and jumped down, running eagerly towards her friend.

'Blimey, we should spend more time apart if this is the reception I get afterwards,' Lola smiled, the two ladies embracing in the middle of the street like they were long lost friends.

Lola looked over Carrie's shoulder upon hearing footsteps.

'Erm, there's a customer waiting,' she commented, spotting the man standing at the hatch.

Carrie took hold of Lola's hand and guided her towards the

side door of the van.

'You're coming with me,' she insisted, pulling Lola inside The Brownie Box. 'Now sit here.'

While watching Carrie serve the early morning customer, Lola revelled in the comforting feeling of being back at work.

'It feels so nice to be back, but odd at the same time,' she commented once the customer had left, and Carrie had taken a seat. 'I'm not sure why I feel so nervous.'

'Don't be nervous, it's just me,' Carrie reassured her. 'What's wrong?' she added, reaching out and taking hold of Lola's hand when she spotted her eyes glossing over.

'Parker–'

Carrie slumped her body back onto her stool and her shoulders dragged low. 'What's he done this time?' she sighed before Lola had even finished her sentence.

A pained expression appeared on Lola's face that she couldn't disguise. 'I think he's done something stupid,' she replied through a scratchy voice, her eyes wet and heavy with sadness.

'How do you know?'

'Last night he got a text message, and I'm guessing it was from another woman.'

Lola hung her head and covered her face with her hands, scooping together her torrent of emotions, her body shaking as she sobbed. Now that she'd voiced her concerns aloud, she could no longer live in denial that everything was okay in her new marriage. Carrie stepped down off her stool and wrapped her arms around Lola's slumped shoulders.

'I'm so sorry,' she whispered.

'I knew I couldn't trust him, not really,' Lola continued to sob. 'I made myself believe that he'd changed,' she said. 'Actually no, he made me believe that he'd changed, and that he'd never hurt me again.'

Carrie dragged her stool over so that she was sitting close to Lola, their knees touching. 'Have you asked him about it? Asked him what's going on?'

Lola shook her head. 'He doesn't even know that I saw the message. He has no idea.'

'Could you have got the wrong end of the stick? Could the message have been from a friend that you don't know about?'

Lola recalled the words in the message. 'Unlikely.'

Carrie's expression was one of anger. 'Surely he wouldn't do that to you, not again?'

Lola drew her body up until her posture appeared sturdy. 'I don't know, but I'm going to find out,' she began, taking a deep inhale, her nostrils flaring. 'I won't let him baffle me with any of his bullshit like last time.'

Another customer appeared at the hatch.

'Hi. You're back again. What can I get you today?' Carrie asked when she spotted the waiting customer.

'A regular cappuccino, please.'

From where she was sitting, Lola looked up when she heard the customer, the sound of his voice oddly familiar.

'Hi,' she announced when she stepped down off the stool and saw Aidan.

'Oh, hi,' he beamed upon spotting Lola. 'So, this is your place?' he added, peering around inside The Brownie Box.

'Your place is much warmer, and less leaky in winter, I suspect,' Lola joked, looking to the roof where the rain tended to flood in on those days when the wind blew in an unfavourable direction.

'Are you coming over to the shop? It's my big event today.'

Aidan handed Carrie the money for the coffee and lingered near the hatch, warming his hands on his steaming cup of coffee.

Lola smiled. 'Sure,' she grinned. 'Give me ten minutes and I'll be over to check it out,' she concluded, before watching Aidan walk away.

Carrie raised her eyebrows. 'And who, might I ask, is that?' she smirked. 'He's become a bit of a familiar face these past few days, I'm starting to think I might know why judging by the smile on your face.'

'He owns Fudgy Nook, the shop just at the other end of the street,' Lola replied in a casual way, her eyes becoming bright and engaged. 'I was sitting in the café the other day and he happened to be sitting next to me,' she began to explain. 'And I guess we just sort of got talking.'

'Oh, I see.'

'No, it's obviously nothing like that, I'm married,' Lola defended. 'He was just so easy to talk to, and it's really weird, because he seems familiar, and I don't know why. Maybe I've served him before,' she pondered, allowing a genuine smile to break across her face. 'Though he hasn't mentioned being a customer.'

Carrie shook her head. 'He's definitely not been here before this past week, I'd have remembered a hunk like him.'

'Who says the word hunk?' Lola laughed, getting ready to leave. 'Anyway, I'm going to go and get myself some free fudge,' she added, opening the door. 'Thanks for the chat. I'll ring you tonight.'

Carrie gave Lola a hug before closing the door and peering through the hatch. 'Let me know how things get on at home. I'm here anytime you need me.'

'Thanks, and I'm sorry I'm leaving you in the lurch a bit, I mean with the business,' Lola replied, resting her chin on the counter momentarily. 'Hopefully my life will sort itself out soon,' she added, before walking away and waving.

The Shambles had begun to get busy as people made their way to work and Lola navigated the cobbles, Fudgy Nook coming into view in the distance. A huddle of people congregated outside, all waiting to enter the quaint, sugary cavern. When she crossed the street and approached the window, Lola took out her phone and saw that Parker had sent her a message.

Just seen your note, have a great day, see you later.

She looked at Parker's whereabouts on her app, noticing that he'd already left the house himself and was heading away from Candle Crescent. She found herself already questioning where he was going, and why he hadn't added that information to his message.

'I'm so glad you came. Let me give you a little guided tour,' Aidan offered as he appeared on the street, beaming at Lola.

Lola's adrenaline rushed and she felt flustered. 'It's pretty busy, maybe I'll come back another day,' she suggested, noticing the name badge attached to his apron, *Aidan Fogg, Manager.*

Aidan rushed his words. 'You're here now. At least come and get a goodie bag,' he suggested, leaning his body towards the shop. He felt a fluttery sensation in his stomach as Lola returned his smile and agreed.

'Okay, just a quick look,' she said, following him through the shop entrance. 'I have to admit, I don't think I've been in here for some time. With leftover brownies to eat every day, I don't have much need for any more sugar in my life.'

'There's always room for more sugar,' Aidan felt quick to reply. 'Here, let me show you where it all happens, while it's busy in here,' he suggested, guiding Lola through to the workshop towards the back of the building.

'Wow, this is amazing,' Lola gasped upon sight of all the fudge lined up on the central island, ready to be boxed up. 'People in York really do like their sugar, don't they?'

Aidan took hold of a tray full of fudge nuggets. 'All over the country, actually. We ship everywhere. Here you are, as promised,' he offered out the tray. 'These are a few new recipes that I'm trying out. See what you think, I need your honest feedback.'

'Aidan, got a second?' asked one of his colleagues, appearing in the doorway. 'I've got a bit of a fussy customer asking about allergies and I'm not sure of the answer.'

'Take a seat,' Aidan offered, pulling out a stool for Lola to perch on. 'I'll be back in a minute.'

Once Aidan had disappeared, Lola wandered around the workshop, a few photos pinned to the wall capturing her attention. As she leaned in to get a closer look, she saw the photos were of

Aidan, and someone who looked to be his girlfriend, or wife maybe, with her arms wrapped around his waist. In one photo, they were kissing while taking a selfie. She lowered her head and dragged her gaze away from the photos, her chest growing tight when she momentarily forgot to breathe, and although she didn't want to admit it to herself, she felt a strange sense of disappointment at the sight of the romantic photo.

'So, what do you think?' Aidan asked when he re-entered the room.

Lola's voice dropped and she went quiet. 'Delicious,' she replied, swallowing.

'Here, it's definitely best when accompanied with a nice cup of tea,' he suggested, placing two mugs down on the bench and indicating for Lola to sit.

'You'll never get rid of your customers if this is the service you always offer,' she replied with a smile.

'You're the first customer that I've ever made tea for.'

The moment the little flirtatious comment escaped from his lips, Aidan felt his skin flush.

'So, how are the travel plans coming along?' he asked in a chipper tone.

'They're not, really,' Lola shrugged.

'You're still not convinced it's a good idea, but your husband is. Is that right?'

'Kind of,' she began, taking a moment to pause the conversation and take a sip of the tea. 'He came up with the idea of travelling originally, but after the–' Lola paused before mentioning the accident, negotiating her words to avoid bringing it up. 'But now he's just not sure that's what he wants anymore.'

She cringed and fidgeted, pulling her knees together beneath the bench.

'I'm really sorry, we've only ever met each other twice, and on both occasions, I've done nothing but talk about my problems,' she apologised. 'It's just so strange,' she began, looking up and meeting Aidan's eyes. 'It just feels so easy to talk to you, and I don't really know why.'

Aidan maintained her stare, willing Lola to remember who he was so that they could talk about the accident and share in the experience that had impacted only the two of them.

'It's like I know you, or I've spoken to you in the past, but I just can't remember where, or when.'

A look of frustration became evident on her face.

'We work in the same city, on the same street, we have probably walked past each other hundreds of times in the past,' Aidan explained.

Unconvinced, Lola resigned to nodding in agreement.

'Yeah, you're probably right.'

She took a glance at the photos pinned to the wall again before looking at Aidan.

'So, I'm sure you said the other day that you're planning to travel too. Didn't you have some family stuff to do?' she questioned. 'I hope your wife is more on board with the idea of travelling than my husband is.'

Aidan took a moment before replying, a hard edge unable to be masked in his voice when he replied. 'I'm not married,' he began. 'I nearly was, but we're not engaged anymore, or even together.'

'Oh, I'm sorry.'

'Don't be,' Aidan smiled. 'She cheated on me, so I left the relationship,' he revealed in one quick breath so that his emotions wouldn't have time to spill out for her to hear. 'So, I'm now thinking about travelling alone. I do have some family stuff to sort out in France, so that'd be a great place to start.'

'Are your family French?'

'No, at least I don't think so. I just had this auntie who sadly passed away, and she's left me something in her will, and that just happens to be in France. My mum passed away when I was seventeen, and I've never met my dad. I don't even know who he is.'

'Wow, that's amazing, I mean about France,' Lola fumbled.

Aidan shook his head. 'Not really. My Auntie Alice wasn't a

part of my life, so I don't have any positive expectations concerning her will,' he explained, releasing a dejected sigh. 'I'm thinking that it's all going to end up costing me, I'm already having to pay for flights,' he joked with a half-hearted shrug, resignation etched in his voice. 'You're right, you know.'

'Right about what?' Lola asked before finishing her tea.

'I find it so easy to talk to you. I haven't told many people about my relationship ending, and only my ex-fiancée knows about the will stuff, and here's me spilling my life story to you.'

Aidan couldn't disguise his upbeat expression and genuine smile when looking at Lola, her eyes drawing him into her world. He admired her splash of freckles and the fact that she didn't wear much makeup to try and conceal them.

Lola tilted her head and allowed her stare to fall away, her voice softening. 'Well, at least by talking to each other about our problems, we're saving money on therapy. Isn't that what everyone does these days, get in touch with the state of their mental health?' She took out her phone and flicked through the screens, pausing when she saw that Parker was now at the other end of town. 'Anyway, I best get going, I think I need to walk off all this fudge that I've eaten.'

'Let me go and get you a goodie bag,' Aidan offered before dashing through to the shop. While he was gone, Lola sent Parker a message.

I'm still in town, just going to do some shopping. What you up to?
She hid her phone in her bag when Aidan reappeared.

'Here you go,' he announced, holding a brown bag filled with treats. 'Don't eat it all at once, you'll make yourself sick,' he joked.

'Thanks, how much do I owe you?'

'On the house, in exchange for my therapy session,' he offered. Aidan took hold of one of his business cards and scribbled his mobile number on the back. 'I'll pop this in too, just in case you need another one of our counselling sessions, or if you have any emergency fudge situations that I can help out with.'

In the background, she heard an Oasis song playing on the radio and she felt her body temperature immediately elevate when a flashback of the accident followed.

'Are you okay?' he asked, noticing the haunted expression appear on Lola's face.

The moment she looked into his eyes she knew that she and Aidan had already crossed paths, and in a more poignant manner than just strangers passing on the street, and yet despite scouring her memories, she just couldn't place how she knew him.

'Just a sugar rush I think,' she lied.

'I was going to ask you if you fancied being a tourist with me tomorrow because I have the day off. We could get in some practice for if – or when – either one of us does decide to go travelling.'

Concealing the torrent of emotions that were rumbling beneath the surface, Lola smiled, walking through the shop.

'Sure, that would be great,' she began. 'But I don't want to mislead you,' she added. 'I am married, and although we're going through a bit of a rocky patch, I do love my husband and I just want that to be clear.' Lola felt awkward, unsure where to look.

Aidan smiled, putting Lola at ease. 'We're new pals, that's all, and you can never have too many friends in my opinion,' he began. 'I like your company and we're business neighbours now so there's nothing wrong with us just hanging out if you're comfortable with that.'

'Absolutely,' she smiled.

'Brilliant, then meet me near the bridge at Waterfront Way at around ten, and I'll have something exciting lined up for us.'

'Okay, see you tomorrow,' Lola smiled before stepping out onto the street and walking down The Shambles.

She took out her phone and opened up the app. Her heart sank as she realised that the dot to indicate Parker's whereabouts had now disappeared. She opened up her messages and read his reply to her earlier text.

Just watching a film and waiting for you to come home.

Knowing that he was lying, she dialled their landline number. After seven rings she hung up, knowing that he was never going to answer the phone, because he wasn't home.

28

SINCE TURNING HIS BACK ON THE HOSPITAL FOR THE VERY LAST time, Matty had fallen into a world of isolation, observing life like a spectator instead of being an active participant. It was like he was cupping a snow globe and peering inside, watching others live their lives whilst he remained still, silent, and alone. His daily routine stagnated, and he found he couldn't break the monotonous cycle that he'd succumbed to. He fluttered the mornings away by meandering the side streets, taking time to select some lunch. Once he'd found a vacant bench, he would then rest and watch the world go by while his meal digested, only heading home when the chill penetrated to his bones, and fatigue set in.

'Hi, I thought it was you! How are you, Matty?' asked Aidan when he spotted a familiar face sitting on one of the benches in town. 'Mind if I sit with you? I'm on my lunch break and if I don't leave the shop, I end up having a working lunch,' he added before sitting at the opposite end of the bench. 'Not at work today?'

Matty's heart raced and he could feel that his words were going to jam in his throat. 'No work today,' he announced. He cleared his throat and offered up more of an explanation, 'I've officially retired.'

'Oh yeah, I remember you telling me. Wow, congratulations!' Aidan replied in between bites of his sandwich. 'I hope this doesn't mean that you won't be coming into the shop anymore,' he added. 'I don't mean because you won't be buying anything, it's just I think the team would miss chatting to you. I know I would. You're one of our favourite customers,' Aidan smiled. 'You always have something nice to say, and unfortunately, the same can't be said for all of our customers.'

'Thanks,' Matty replied. 'I'll still be popping in for sure. I think I'd start to have withdrawal symptoms otherwise,' he joked.

'Did you have a good New Year?' Aidan asked, making polite chit-chat.

'Quiet,' shrugged Matty. 'And yourself?'

'Quiet too.'

When Aidan didn't elaborate, Matty asked a leading question. 'So, no big party with friends, or family?'

Aidan shook his head. 'Most of my friends already had plans, and I actually don't have any family.' The moment that the words left his mouth, Aidan heard how awful it sounded, and a heaviness weighed on his heart like it had always done in the past whenever he confessed to having no family. 'I recently found out that my auntie passed away. She was my only remaining blood relative, not that I actually knew her. And since then, since my fiancée and I broke up, life has been a little tough.'

Matty's heart raced at the window of opportunity that had presented itself. 'I'm sorry to hear that,' he began.

'Don't be. It's absolutely fine,' Aidan interrupted. 'It's been just me for so long that it feels like the norm now,' he continued, turning to face Matty. 'You must have seen your fair share of broken families over the years at the hospital. I'm sure I'm not the only one who's alone. I have friends that I consider family. I guess it proves that there doesn't always need to be a blood connection.'

'It's always nice to have someone to call family, isn't it?' Matty replied, looking out across the bustling market square. 'Otherwise, life can feel so lonely.'

Aidan offered Matty a crisp when he spotted that his smile had faded. 'Would you like one?' he asked. 'I feel bad that you were enjoying a nice peaceful moment, and then I came along and have managed to make us both feel miserable,' he laughed.

'No, thanks,' he replied. 'It's just nice to chat. Since leaving work, life has been a little hard for me too.'

'I'm sorry to hear that. Anything that I can help with? I'm not great at dispensing advice, but I'm good at listening, or so I'm told.'

Matty fought hard to open up the shutters that had been closed on his emotions for so long. 'I'd like to form a relationship with my family, people that I haven't spoken to in so long. I just don't know where, or how, to start.'

Aidan offered a clenched half-smile upon hearing Matty's quandary.

'Start simple, I guess,' he began. 'Maybe drop them a message, or give them a call. You could say that although time has passed by, you'd like to try and build some bridges. Then see what they say.' He turned to Matty to gauge his reaction.

Matty scratched his face, wishing that the answer to his problem was as easy as picking the phone up and saying hello. 'I'm just not sure how it'd be received.'

'You'll never know until you try. And if they're not interested, then at least you tried. What more can you do?'

Matty glanced at the gift bag that was placed next to him on the bench, the same bag that he took out with him every day in the hope that he'd find the courage to offer it to its intended recipient. He urged himself to take Aidan's advice; take a simple step into the unknown. Matty knew that this was the perfect moment that he had been waiting for, and yet the fear of rejection silenced the confession that was lingering on his lips. Just at that moment, Aidan's phone rang.

'Oh, this will be work,' he said, reluctantly pulling his phone out of his pocket. 'I best get going, but thanks for keeping me company,' he said, standing and grabbing his bag. 'Stop by the shop soon, and keep me posted how you get on,' he concluded before walking away.

In defeat, Matty's shoulders fell, and all he wanted to do was retreat back to his flat and hide himself away from the world; a world that he found so difficult to find his place within.

29

'YOU CAME!' AIDAN SAID WITH A SMILE WHEN HE SAW LOLA approaching, his grin beaming from his face as a nervousness fluttered in his stomach.

'You're joking, right?' she asked when she spotted the tandem bicycle that was resting against his body.

Aidan laughed. 'Well, my original idea was for us to have a bike of our own, but it appears that on a day like this,' he began to explain, pointing to the glorious blue sky, 'everyone in York has the same idea, and this was the only option left.'

Lola pressed her hands against both knees and felt the stiffness she suspected was wedged deep within her muscles. 'I haven't ridden a bike for a good decade, maybe longer,' she said in an apologetic tone. 'I'm not even sure I'll remember how to ride a bike, let alone trying it tandem.'

'You never forget how to ride,' Aidan reassured her. 'And there's nothing more quintessentially touristy than to ride a bike through the streets of York. It's the best way to experience everything. Wouldn't you agree?'

Lola shook her head and released a trickle of infectious giggles. Her tone lightened, and she spoke in a bubbly voice.

'I do agree that we would definitely look like tourists.'

Aidan shrugged his shoulders. 'Well, I'm game if you're game,' he said, casting his leg over the bike and securing his helmet in place. 'What do you say?' he asked, holding out the other helmet for Lola. 'You never know, you might actually enjoy the experience.'

With a sense of hesitation detectable in her body language, she took hold of the helmet and swung her leg over, taking a seat behind him. 'If we fall, I will accept absolutely no responsibility,' she laughed, looking around to see if anyone was watching them. 'When you asked if I wanted to spend a day being a tourist, I thought that maybe we'd go for a nice walk, or go and admire The Minster, or better still, have a nice relaxing pot of tea and slice of something at Bessie's. But oh no, we're riding tandem. If this was the type of friend I knew you were going to turn out to be, I might have reconsidered.'

'So, we're friends now, are we?' Aidan asked, his eyebrows raised.

'We'll see if we're still friends by the end of this bike ride,' Lola teased, easing her helmet over her head.

Aidan took a deep breath and conjured up a spritely tone of voice. 'So, are we ready?' he asked with all the enthusiasm of a tour guide, before pushing off and beginning to pedal. 'Let's go.'

'Oh, my goodness!' Lola shouted as the wheels began to spin in motion, suddenly realising that even if she wanted to stop or get off, she wasn't solely in control of the situation and therefore had no choice but to pedal too. 'Now might be a good time to tell you that I was involved in a serious car accident just before Christmas, and that I'm still recovering from a concussion,' she laughed. 'And I'm not sure that riding tandem was part of my suggested recovery plan.'

Aidan applied pressure to the breaks and pulled over. 'Wait a minute,' he smirked, trying to maintain a serious expression. 'You've only just told me that you've been in an accident, and now I'm riding a bike with you. Maybe this isn't a good idea after all,' he jested.

'There was ice on the road,' she laughed, the first time she had been able to talk in a light-hearted way about the accident. 'Black ice, I might add.'

'Then it's a good job that it's sunny today, otherwise we'd be in trouble,' Aidan joked before pulling away again. 'Let's try extra hard not to fall off or crash,' he added, looking back to see her reaction.

'Don't look at me, look ahead!' Lola shouted, a slight sense of panic edging into her voice as the bike veered towards the middle of the road.

'We're doing alright,' Aidan encouraged, steering them onto the cycle path that navigated the circumference of the city. 'At least if we do fall off now, we're not going to get run over by a car, or a bus,' he joked.

Lola replied in a bubbly voice. 'Well, that's reassuring,' she said, secretly loving the thrill of seeing the city in a way she never had before. With the sun beating down and the breeze igniting her skin, acting as a reminder that her senses still worked, she couldn't help but beam with joy. 'I really do feel like a tourist,' she said, admiring the scenery through a fresh pair of eyes. 'I've always called York home, but I can't remember the last time I took any time out to savour all the magic that it has to offer.'

'Perfect, then my idea is working,' Aidan commented. 'On our right, we have the National Railway Museum, which just so happens to be the largest train museum in the world,' he declared in his best tour guide voice.

With the gentle breeze continuing to move over her face, Lola's eyes began to water, a feeling of liveliness flooding through her body.

'You'd make a good tour guide,' she said. 'Maybe the fudge business isn't your calling after all.'

Aidan smiled but shook his head. 'I'd soon get bored reciting the same script over and over again,' he explained. 'And I think I'd be a fair-weather guide. Can you imagine how miserable it'd be to do this when it's raining, or snowing? And York gets its fair share of dark, dank days.'

'Then I'm honoured that I get to be your one and only

customer,' Lola smiled, relishing the feeling of the wind blowing through her hair, her legs already tiring. She couldn't help but admire Aidan, his broad shoulders rocking in time with his legs as they peddled. An immediate wave of guilt washed over her, and she thought about what she had told Parker about her plans for the day.

'I'm not sure that my husband would approve of me riding tandem with a strange man,' she revealed. 'Maybe you'll have to offer him the same service.'

'I'm not a stranger,' Aidan defended. 'You just said it, I'm a friend, and if he would like to experience any of my tandem services, then I can sort him out, no problem.'

'He probably hasn't even noticed that I'm not there,' Lola mumbled, recalling how Parker had been glued to his phone before she'd left the house.

Remembering what Lola had revealed to him the morning of the accident, that her husband had cheated on her, Aidan asked a poignant question.

'You and your husband are going through a tough spell?' he asked in an attempt to eke out some snippets of truth, trying to establish what Lola could, and couldn't, recall about the events of that day.

Lola took a moment before replying. 'I guess so. We've been struggling for a while now, and I just know that he's not being completely truthful with me, about where he's going and what he's doing, so I'm going to find out what's going on.'

Knowing the truth about the state of their marriage for himself, Aidan remained quiet. The pair continued to cycle along the designated route that led round to The Minster, the building rising in the distance. 'Well, I'd like to offer you some advice but my relationship history isn't exactly perfect.'

'I'm not sure a perfect relationship exists anymore,' Lola replied. 'Or maybe I just make the wrong choices,' she sighed, the cathedral coming into view. 'Oh, wow,' she exclaimed the moment the sun shone through the stained glass.

'Do you visit the cathedral much?' Aidan asked, turning to witness Lola's reaction.

The pair continued to cycle towards the cathedral, emerging themselves in the atmospheric bustle.

'I don't really, and I know I should try to more often because people travel from all over the country to admire it, there just never seems to be enough hours in the day,' Lola admitted, looking at The Minster in a way she had seldom done before.

Aidan stopped pedalling and the bike came to a natural stop, the pair staying seated and holding onto the railings that were located next to the cathedral with their free hand.

'Before she died, my mum used to bring me here a lot, mainly to admire the windows and to listen to the choir, not to be involved in any kind of formal service. She wasn't religious in that sense.'

The tone of Aidan's voice changed as he spoke, a tender sense of nostalgia mixed with sadness engulfing his words.

'I'm sorry to hear about your mum.'

Aidan turned to Lola and smiled. 'It was a long time ago now, being here just brings back happy family memories. With my auntie recently passing away, I've found myself thinking about family a lot, and how I don't really have any.'

'Have you ever thought about trying to track down information about your dad?' she asked, recalling an earlier conversation.

'I have, but I always conclude that if he'd wanted to reunite, then he would have done it by now. He chose not to be involved with my life, a decision that I have respected.'

'Carrie is my family,' Lola began to share. 'My parents separated when I was in primary school, and life after that just became really hard,' she opened up, a pained expression appearing on her face. 'I became trapped in the middle of their divorce and they both seemed more focused on using me to get a one-up on one another. So when I was seventeen, I moved in with Carrie and her family. I've never looked back.'

'Could I ask you a favour? And it's absolutely fine to say no, given that we haven't really known each other for that long.'

'We've known each other long enough to feel comfortable riding tandem,' Lola laughed.

'True, but this is a bit more serious.'

'What is it?'

'You know I told you that my auntie passed away?'

Lola nodded.

'Well, apparently it was her wish for her ashes to be scattered here, in York, and I wondered if you'd be there, you know, just—'

'Of course,' Lola interrupted when Aidan began to stumble over his words.

Her eagerness to console him warmed his heart, his happiness flushing onto his face.

'I'm not sure when it is, or what even happens. It's all a bit of a mystery, if I'm being honest with you. I've just been asked to honour the last wishes of someone I didn't know, and someone who disliked me immensely, and if you're there, it'd make it easier, and I'd have someone else to blame if it all goes wrong.'

Lola raised her eyebrows. 'I'll do anything but hold the ashes,' she joked. 'I admire the way that you're able to put your own feelings aside for the sake of someone else's. It means you'll never have any regrets.'

'Exactly,' Aidan agreed. 'Now, back to our tour. Did you know that The Minster is the largest gothic cathedral in Northern Europe?' he asked, pointing and trying to change the topic to hide his embarrassment. 'Another useless fact that you didn't need to know.'

Lola admired the grandeur of The Minster while listening to the sound of Aidan's voice, his tone somehow becoming more familiar as he spoke, a sense of calm taking hold. Without warning, the bells of The Minster rang out, bellowing its hourly chime across the city. The chimes startled Lola, her heart skipping a beat as the vibrations echoed through her entire body. In that moment, her mind took her back to the day of the accident, and she felt like she was once again trapped in her car, recalling how she had heard the sound of the bells in the distance, the noise reminding her that she was still awake, still alive.

'Are you okay?' Aidan asked, turning and witnessing the haunted look on her face. 'Did the bells make you jump?'

Turning slowly, Lola looked up at Aidan.

'When I crashed my car, I was trapped for some time, and I've just remembered that I heard the bells. At the time, the sound felt calming, but now–'

'But now?' he asked, encouraging her to finish her sentence.

'But now, everything associated with the accident still makes me feel anxious, and I try not to speak about it. I sometimes remember all these little random snippets of information, things that happened to me, but nothing helps to piece it all together.'

As a tear escaped from the corner of her eye, Aidan reached out with his thumb and wiped it away, his stroke slow and soft.

The moment he touched her face, his hand pressing against her skin, Lola met his gaze. 'We've met before, haven't we?' she asked. 'The sound of your voice, I know I've heard it before, I just don't know where, and the way you just touched my skin, it feels so familiar, and I don't know why. I don't know where we've met, but you just make me feel so–'

'I make you feel what?' Aidan asked, a longing tone to his voice.

Lola shook her head. 'I don't know. I just get this strange feeling and I can't explain it.'

She looked away, becoming lost in her muddled stream of thoughts.

'In your shop yesterday, a song came on the radio, and it made me think of you. I know that sounds odd, and I'm not some crazy person or a stalker, I promise.'

Aidan saw the look of helplessness in her eyes as she struggled to piece together her memory of events.

'You're right, we have met before,' he began, ready to tell her everything. Just as he'd got the words out, Lola ducked behind his back, failing to hear anything that he'd said. She stared into the distance, a deep frown appearing on her face.

'Oh, my God!' she erupted. 'That's Parker, my husband.' Lola pointed towards a bench located at the other end of The Minster. 'He said he was meeting a friend today at the library to talk through a new work project, or something like that,' she said, continuing to stare with intent. 'It doesn't look like he's meeting a friend in the library, does it?'

With Lola's attention diverted, Aidan knew his moment to speak truthfully had gone, and he felt deflated.

'You can leave if you want, I can ride the bike back to the shop,' he said, watching how intently Lola was looking at Parker, all her thoughts and attention now with him.

'Would you mind?' she replied, dismounting. 'I feel like I need to see where he goes. I know that sounds awful, and I'm really not that kind of person, it's just–'

Aidan interrupted. 'I understand, you go.'

Lola began walking away, holding her hand up to wave him off whilst trying to shield her broadened smile. 'Thanks for the ride. I loved it,' she shouted, before scurrying off into the distance.

Aidan looked up at the cathedral and, although disheartened at Lola's early departure, he could sense that the person who he had originally met on Christmas Eve was once again on the cusp of stepping back into his life. The manner in which his heart ached felt more revealing, his body's way of letting him know that it wasn't just a person who was about to re-enter his world, it was the prospect of finding love.

30

As the days turned into weeks following his retirement, Matty was beginning to display the behavioural characteristics of a recluse. Despite a promising routine initially which saw him venture beyond his front door, he now rarely found the motivation to step outside and he'd become loath to even open the blinds on his windows. The sofa in his lounge had become his new bench, and most mornings, he found himself sitting alone while trying to ascertain what day of the week it was, the days no longer holding any significance, or purpose. He couldn't recall when he had last spoken to another human being, and although he'd thought about calling Marie, he kept his mobile phone switched off.

Despite his attempts to sever all contact, the noise from the street below drifted in, serving as a reminder that, although he didn't want to be part of it, life beyond his window continued to pass by.

Below Matty's window out on The Shambles, Aidan arrived at his shop across the road.

'I thought you'd be out all day,' Annie commented as Aidan approached the counter.

'Lola had to dash off, so here I am,' he replied. 'But I did manage to get her on a tandem,' he smiled, his mind still absorbed by thoughts of their biking expedition. 'And we managed not to crash.'

'Sounds cool,' Annie replied.

Aidan grabbed his apron and peered out onto The Shambles.

'That's a bit odd,' he commented, looking up at Matty's flat.

'What's odd?' Annie questioned.

'Come here,' he said, placing himself in the window and looking out across the street.

Annie stood by his side. 'What am I meant to be looking at?'

'Have you ever seen Matty's blinds closed for so many consecutive days?' he asked, pointing up at the darkened windows.

'So what?' she shrugged before walking away. 'He could be on holiday, he could be having a lie-in, he could be feeling unwell, and besides, what's it got to do with us?' she asked.

'I just get this feeling that something isn't right, and he's a friend of ours, isn't he?' he asked, seeking confirmation.

'He's been a great customer for us over the years, and we obviously all like chatting to him when he comes in, but I wouldn't really call him a friend.'

'Well, you know what I mean. We know him, and I think we have a duty to make sure he's alright.'

'I'm sure he has family and friends to do that,' Annie replied, turning and walking away.

'When have you ever seen anybody going in or coming out of his front door?' Aidan questioned.

Annie's forehead creased. 'Now that you mention it, I'm not sure I've seen anybody going in or out. But that doesn't mean that they don't, it just means that you work me too hard, so I don't have time to stop and notice,' she joked.

'The last time I saw him, he was telling me about how he was finding things difficult since retiring, and that he was hoping to build relationships with some of his estranged family,' Aidan explained, recalling their previous conversation on the bench. Annie had left the room, uninterested. 'I'll be back in five minutes,' he shouted, before leaving the shop and walking across the street.

He knocked on Matty's front door, then waited. He looked up, watching for signs of life, and yet the blinds remained closed. Unperturbed, Aidan rattled his knuckles against the door again.

Inside his flat, Matty assumed that the person knocking was another nuisance caller and listened for the flapping of the letterbox that typically followed, knowing that he'd find a flyer on his doormat asking if he was interested in selling his flat. Once sure that the person had given up, he got up and went to look at the front door only to find that the mat was empty. He peered through his peephole, seeing only the usual stream of pedestrian traffic, and so turned and walked away, sinking himself back into the safety of his sofa.

Within the darkness of his lounge, Matty covered his face with his hands, unable to prevent himself from sobbing. Through hazy eyes, he saw the brown gift bag that was still sitting on the counter top, and it acted as a reminder of what felt like his own personal failings, his inability to face his fears or confront the consequences of the bad decisions that he had allowed to happen in the past. Unable to stop the self-sabotaging thoughts running through his mind, he lay down and closed his eyes, hoping that it would all stop, and that maybe soon, it would be his turn to rest in peace.

31

*L*OLA REMAINED NEAR THE CATHEDRAL, TOOK OUT HER PHONE and saw that she had a message from Parker that read, *I'm just having a catch up with Ed now. See you later xx.* Her heart cantered and when she looked up again, Parker had disappeared. She instantly opened up the app on her phone to check his location, tracing his route through the city centre, a route taking her away from the library and towards a suburban part of town. Breathless and with an avalanche of emotions running through her mind about what she was about to uncover, Lola paused when she noticed that his dot on the map hadn't moved for a while.

Upon arrival at Parker's last known whereabouts, Lola remained hidden behind a parked van, shielding herself from the row of houses where she suspected he was visiting, and waited. She didn't know anybody that lived on the street, a thought that made her even more jittery. Peering around, she couldn't see him anywhere, the street dotted with obstructions; trees, lampposts and vehicles all making it harder to spot him. When the door of a nearby house opened, making her jump, she immediately looked up.

She saw Parker standing at a front door, an attractive woman by his side. Unable to hold herself together, Lola began sobbing. She turned away, shaking her head as waves of disappointment flooded her heart. Her muscles stiffened and her stomach fought off the desire to be sick. Wiping her eyes, she looked back across the street, watching an embrace unfold, spotting how the woman put her hand through Parker's hair, stroking him. From behind the van, Lola watched the woman kiss Parker's neck and how she took hold of his hand, pulling him back as he attempted to walk away. Unable to watch, Lola's skin bunched around her eyes and she allowed herself to crouch. Resting out of sight on the curb, she gripped her stomach and tried desperately not to vomit. She glanced down at her wedding rings, anger causing her to pull and grapple until they came off. Within her chest, she felt her heart ache with an intensity she'd only experienced once before, and in a split moment of mental weakness and vulnerability, she lowered her head and wished that she hadn't survived the accident.

'He's a bastard!' she announced the moment Carrie answered the phone.

'Lola? What's going on?'

'You were right. I should have listened to you. You knew him better than I did all along.'

Carrie lowered the hatch on The Brownie Box and placed a sign on the shutter which stated, *Back in five minutes.*

'Lola, where are you? Do you need me to come?'

'I've seen him with another woman, Carrie. I'm outside her house right now.'

On the other end of the line, Carrie shook her head and placed her hand over her face.

'Lola, don't do anything silly. Tell me where you are and I'll come and get you.'

'How could he do this to me again?' she sobbed, her tears streaming down her face. 'He promised me that he'd never cheat on me again. He made me believe that he'd changed. He let me marry him, for God's sake,' Lola ranted, her anger and hurt pouring inexplicably through her words.

'Tell me where you are. I'll come and meet you and then we can talk,' said Carrie, hurrying to grab her coat.

Lola stood up and wiped her face with her coat sleeve, checking that Parker had gone.

'I'm going to go and knock on this woman's door,' she declared. 'I need to know, Carrie. I need to know from her mouth what's gone on. I need closure, and to know for myself that my marriage is over.'

'Lola, please don't. Wait until you've calmed down. You don't want to see this woman when you're upset, it'll only make it so much worse.'

'I can't possibly feel any worse than I feel right now. I'll call you later,' Lola concluded before hanging up the phone.

She blew her nose and took a deep intake of breath before standing. Looking both ways before crossing the road, she slowly approached the door that Parker had emerged from, and with a gentle knock, she tapped on it.

'Hi,' Holly said when she opened the door and saw Lola standing there, not speaking. 'Can I help you?' she asked.

Upon setting eyes on Holly, Lola knew she'd seen the woman before, and then it came to her; she was the girl in the photo that was pinned to the wall in Fudgy Nook, the woman with her arms wrapped around Aidan.

'I'm Parker's wife,' she announced.

The colour drained from Holly's face and she felt a sudden weakness creep into her limbs. She peered up the street with a sense of desperation.

'I'm sorry, I don't know who you are,' she added, before trying to close the door in Lola's face.

Lola held her arm out to prevent the door from closing.

'I'm not angry with you and I'm not here to fight. I just want to know the truth,' she explained with a level of maturity that she didn't know she had. 'Please, can I come in?'

Holly dropped her chin to her chest and allowed the door to swing open.

'Sure, come inside.'

Shielding her body behind the door, Holly watched as Lola entered her home.

'Just go through to the lounge, that way,' she indicated, pointing towards the right.

Holly followed her unexpected guest into the lounge, taking a seat at the opposite end of the room and struggling to find the courage to meet Lola's gaze.

'What do you want to know?' she finally asked, breaking the tension-filled silence.

'I need to know what happened between you and my husband,' Lola replied with a shaky voice. With a concerted effort, she forced her limbs to relax while she shifted her body in the chair, trying to find a comfortable position. 'Tell me everything, from the beginning.'

'Well,' Holly began, 'erm…'

Her halted dialogue frustrated Lola.

'It's okay, you can tell me. I won't be angry. I don't blame any of this on you. He's done it before, and if I was honest with myself, I knew that he'd do it again.'

Holly crossed and re-crossed her legs, also unable to sit still.

'Well, we met in a bar in town the night before Christmas Eve,' Holly began, trying to look anywhere but in Lola's direction. 'Then what?'

Holly's hands wouldn't settle and she fidgeted with her nails.

'We got chatting and he walked me home,' she admitted in one quick breath.

'Then what?' Lola asked, fighting to keep her tears under control.

'Then,' Holly began, shaking her head, 'he came inside.'

Holly could feel her cheeks burning and she willed one of her friends to knock on the door, or for her phone to ring so that she could escape from the room.

Lola nodded with a sense of resignation. 'And you slept together?' she asked when Holly went quiet.

Avoiding eye contact, Holly nodded. The confirmation sent a sharp pain coursing through Lola's heart, and she pressed her hand to her chest, seeking strength and comfort in the moment that she knew her marriage was over. She couldn't help but close her eyes tightly and wait for the pain to pass.

'How many times has it happened?' she asked, taking a moment to look at Holly and wonder what it was she had that she herself didn't.

'Just once,' Holly was quick to defend.

'Then why was he here just now, if all this happened before Christmas?'

Holly once again stammered over her words.

'I wanted to talk to him.'

'About what?'

'I wanted to know for sure that it was over between us. I needed the closure.'

Lola took in a deep breath before asking her next question.

'And what did he say?'

Holly looked up, tears in her eyes.

'He said he wants to make his marriage work. He said that I was a mistake, and that he didn't want to see me again.'

The revelation didn't do anything to take away the hurt that was still tearing through Lola's devastated heart.

'But you have met up with him before today, haven't you?'

Holly nodded. 'But we didn't sleep together.'

'And that's supposed to make it okay?' Lola laughed.

Holly remained silent.

'And you've messaged him, haven't you?' Lola asked, recalling the messages she'd seen on his phone the night they were meant to be having a romantic dinner.

When Holly simply nodded, Lola continued. 'Well, as far as I'm concerned, you're welcome to him,' she announced with a sense of defiance. She sat up in her chair and straightened out her posture. 'My marriage is over. He's all yours now.'

The two women sat in silence for a few seconds. Lola took another glance at Holly, hating how pretty she was, and how perfectly her hair fell.

'Well, there's nothing more to say, is there?' Lola announced. 'Could I use your bathroom before I leave?'

'Sure. It's up the stairs and to the right.'

Lola left the room and headed upstairs, wanting to leave the house looking better than when she'd arrived, her attempt to scrape together as many parts of her dignity as she could. As she made her way upstairs, she peered at the décor, still comparing herself to the woman who had managed to destroy her marriage. Once hidden behind the bathroom door, she took a long look at herself in the mirror, trying to straighten out her flyaway hair and touching up her concealer, hiding where her tears had left unsightly trails in her makeup. Once she'd washed her hands and felt like she had some control over her composure, she lingered on the landing and spotted the open bedroom door. Without entering, she paused in the doorway, realising that she'd seen the distinctive wallpaper and the framed picture before. A memory of Christmas Eve rattled her composure once again, and when she spotted the duvet, she knew exactly where she'd seen it.

'I'll be going,' she announced once she'd made her way downstairs.

'I'm sorry, Lola,' Holly offered.

Lola shook her head and produced a smirk. 'No, you're not.'

'I am sorry for hurting you,' Holly offered with sincerity.

'Don't be sorry, you've done me a massive favour,' Lola replied, reaching out for the door handle. 'You're welcome to him,' she concluded, before stepping out onto the street and walking away, shielding her fresh batch of tumbling tears.

32

READY TO BREAK ALL CONFIDENTIALITY RULES, MARIE SNUCK into the manager's office at the end of her shift and unlocked the filing cabinet, the one which had all the personnel files for all staff members concealed inside. Quickly, and knowing that her boss had just gone for her tea break, Marie flicked through the files, trying to find Matty's in the hope that it hadn't been removed now that he'd left the trust.

With her heart in her mouth, Marie found the file and flicked through the internal pages, taking a picture on her phone of his address. She then looked for the name of his next of kin and emergency contact, seeing her own name next to each. With a distant, dull empty stare, she replaced the file and locked the cabinet.

'Hi, Marie. I thought you'd already left,' announced her boss, appearing suddenly at the door.

Flustered and digging in her pocket for a tissue, Marie replied.

'Oh, I couldn't find my keys, and I remembered talking to you in here this morning,' she explained, looking around the room. 'They must be in my desk drawer. I'll go and have another look,' she concluded, opening the door. 'See you tomorrow.'

With a heavy-footed walk, Marie made her way out of the hospital and across town, checking her phone to make sure that she knew where Matty's flat was located. Her downturned facial features couldn't be hidden, so many troubling thoughts tumbling through her mind. She scrolled through her contacts and tried calling Matty's number again, her call log letting her know that she'd tried calling the same number 23 times over the past week, the call failing to connect each time.

'Hi Matty, it's Marie,' she began when it went to voicemail again. 'I'm worried about you, and even though I know you'll be mad, I'm on my way to your flat. See you soon,' she said, ending the call.

Upon arrival at The Shambles, a street she'd walked along so many times over the years, never realising that her friend lived in one of the flats above the shops, she peered at the door numbers and paused, checking her phone again to ensure she had the right door. She reached out and knocked. Despite a stream of people walking past her, Marie became oblivious to the world, her sole focus now on Matty's wellbeing.

When no answer came, she knocked harder, her knuckles hurting beneath the pressure. She searched for a doorbell or a side entrance and found nothing, so tapped on the door again.

There was still no reply from inside.

Bending to her knees, she pushed open the letter box and peered through, seeing the bottom of the stairs and a few letters scattered across the floor.

'Matty, it's Marie. Please come to the door,' she shouted. 'I'm worried about you, and I need to know that you're okay.'

No reply was forthcoming.

She took a step back and peered up, noticing that the curtains were drawn and that there were no signs of movement behind. She rummaged through her bag and took out a piece of paper, scribbling a note requesting for him to call her, and pushed it through his letterbox.

'Matty. Please come to the door if you're home,' she begged, sensing a warmth on her face from the central heating system, an indication that someone was home.

After nearly ten minutes of trying, Marie could sense that

people were starting to stare at her from the café opposite, making her feel uncomfortable. And so, after knocking for a final time, with reluctance, she turned and walked away, vowing to return the following day.

33

'TELL ME WHAT I SHOULD DO,' LOLA PROMPTED WHEN CARRIE picked up the phone. 'I can see him in the distance. He's alone on the bridge.'

'I told you last night, I don't think you should meet up with him today,' Carrie began. 'He's got all this weird ash scattering business to take care of, and he doesn't need to know right now that the man his wife slept with was actually your husband.'

'I could just avoid telling him, at least for today.'

'Really? You think you could do that? You're friends with him now, aren't you? So, you wouldn't want to keep a secret from him, and it'd be hard to keep this secret, not that I think it'll make any difference to him.'

'What do you mean?'

'His fiancée slept with someone behind his back. Why does it matter who that person was? It won't change what happened. He's already left her, and he's moving on with his life.'

'It's different though because that man just so happened to be my husband. It'd be weird if I knew that and didn't tell him.'

'I think you should forget about Aidan's feelings and focus on your own,' Carrie began. 'You've just found out that Parker has cheated on you, and instead of taking care of yourself, you're too concerned about how everyone else is feeling, which is a testament to your character, and why you're such a lovely person, but sometimes, it does you no favours.'

Lola remained silent, unable to even think about what Parker had done without wanting to cry, or scream. Irrationally, she clung to the hope that it had all just been a bad dream, or at the very least, a silly mistake that she and her husband could work through and overcome as a couple.

'You can stay at mine for as long as you want, you know that, but sooner or later, Parker will come knocking, wondering why you're avoiding going home.'

Lola peered out from behind the tree, noting the nervousness in Aidan's body language.

'He's by himself, Carrie, waiting for me to go and stand by his side while he throws his auntie's ashes off a bridge.'

Before Carrie could speak, Lola spoke again.

'I think he's just seen me. Gotta go.'

She walked out from behind the tree and headed towards Aidan, holding her hand up in acknowledgement.

'Oh blimey, is that it?' she asked, spotting a small box cradled in his hands. 'I've never been to an ash scattering before, so I'm a little unsure about what to expect.'

'I'm scared to death that I'll drop it. I mean, how awful would that be? I know I didn't have any kind of relationship with my auntie, but I wouldn't want to accidentally drop her ashes next to a public rubbish bin where people throw empty takeaway trays and God knows what else.' Aidan gripped the box tighter. 'Thanks for coming. I know this is all a bit weird.'

'It is a bit odd,' Lola replied, looking around at the surroundings. 'So, why here, do you know?'

Aidan shook his head. 'All the information I have been given has been through the solicitors in France,' he began. 'This was part of my Auntie Alice's last wish, to have her ashes scattered here, and this was the date and time that the solicitor advised would be best. So here I am.'

The view from the middle of the Skeldergate Bridge took Lola's breath away, the River Ouse glimmering in her eyes as the early-morning sun beamed down, casting shadows across the surface of the water like a scene extracted from a watercolour painting. The three ornate arches also served to provide picturesque reflections, and for a moment, Lola could understand why the location had been chosen for such a poignant moment.

'It's pretty,' she commented, admiring the view, her and Aidan the only people around at that time of the morning. She leaned her arms on the railings and lowered her head, her eyes mesmerised as the water rippled below, the melodic sound enchanting. 'So, what happens now?'

Aidan looked at the box of ashes in his hands, the shadow of someone approaching in his peripheral vision distracting his attention. Turning to his left, he spotted a young woman standing by herself at the far side of the bridge, stopping and leaning over to admire the morning view. He turned back to Lola.

'Should we wait until that person walks away?' he asked, indicating with his head towards the woman who was still lingering.

'Probably best. She might wonder what we're doing otherwise.' Lola continued to gaze out over the horizon, her demeanour distant and standoffish.

'Are you okay?'

She took a breath before answering, ensuring that what she was about to reveal was the right thing to do.

'We're friends now, aren't we?' she began.

'Yeah, for sure,' Aidan felt quick to confirm.

'And as my friend, I'd like to think that you'd always tell me the truth, because to me, that's what friendships are based on.'

A pang of guilt like nothing he'd experienced before knocked Aidan off balance, knowing that he was purposefully keeping such a big secret from her.

'What's wrong?' he asked, able to detect the serious look in her eyes.

'I know who it was that Holly, your fiancée, slept with behind your back,' she revealed, maintaining her focus out on the horizon.

'And I think you deserve to know. I don't think it's right that it's kept from you, especially when we're friends.'

Aidan followed Lola's gaze and looked out towards the horizon, the sun beaming in his eyes.

'How do you know?' he asked, puzzled, knowing that Lola didn't know Holly, or share any of the same friends.

'Because the man she slept with was my husband,' she replied in a low voice. Lola felt Aidan turn to look at her, but she maintained her glance. 'And I'm sorry.'

Aidan digested the information, processing all the details in his mind.

'That means that Parker, that's your husband's name, isn't it? That means that Parker was the man that I walked past when I was on my way home from the airport, having changed my mind about going to France on Christmas Eve.'

He turned to look at Lola, who had now turned to meet his dejected gaze.

'I remember kind of laughing to myself, you know, because when I walked past him, he looked like he was on his way home after a night out. The walk of shame, if you like.'

'I've only just found out,' Lola confirmed. 'After our bike ride, when I saw him and had to dash off, I followed Parker to Poets Nook, and I saw him and Holly stood at her front door, hugging.'

'So, what did you do?'

'I went and knocked on her door,' she explained, pulling in a deep breath. 'I already had suspicions that Parker had cheated on me, I just didn't know when, or who with, and with my memory still bad after the accident, nothing was making any sense.'

'And Holly told you everything?'

'Yep. She told me that they met in town and then he went back to her place,' Lola said, before retracting her words. 'Sorry, your place,' she corrected. 'I haven't confronted Parker about it yet and I stayed with Carrie last night after I found out. I'm just too mad to be able to have a civilised conversation with him,' she explained. 'Not mad because he cheated on me, though admittedly that's not great news to hear as a newlywed, but the fact that he continued to lie about it, even when I asked him, even when I suspected something was wrong, he still lied, he still tried to cover it all up and pretend like nothing happened.'

Lola looked away, trying to gather her thoughts.

'I'm sorry that my fiancée slept with your husband,' Aidan added after a few seconds of silence.

Lola turned and looked at him. 'And I'm sorry that my husband slept with your fiancée.'

The pair looked out across the water, the coming and going of nature in the river providing a welcome distraction.

'Are you going to be able to forgive him?'

Lola didn't need to contemplate her reply.

'Absolutely not. My marriage is over. It never really got going, if I'm honest. I knew deep down that I couldn't trust him, and he proved me right for a second time.'

Looking over towards where the woman had been standing, Lola saw that she was still there, alone, and now standing a little closer to their spot on the bridge.

'It doesn't look like she's going to leave any time soon. Do you think we should just start?'

Aidan took another glance at the stranger, the young woman, in his opinion, looking a little out of place, standing alone at that time of the day, no bag or personal belongings with her.

'You don't think she's a jumper, do you?'

Lola laughed. 'No, she'd have picked a more dangerous bridge to jump off if that was her intention.'

'True,' he agreed, smiling and peering down at the water.

'So, what do we do now?'

'I guess I should say a few words and then just open the box and let the breeze do its job.'

Aidan paused and seemed a bit lost for words, nothing appropriate coming to mind.

'Why don't you just say how you feel?' Lola suggested when she sensed Aidan struggling.

Aidan lowered his head, as if to pray, and began to speak in a soft and sincere tone.

'I'm sorry, Alice, for whatever happened in the past that made you feel like you didn't want to be a part of our lives. I forgive you for how much hurt you caused me and Mum, and I hope that you will forgive us for anything that we did to make you feel unwelcome, or unloved. It was never my intention to hurt you, and I would have liked it had we been a part of each other's lives.'

'Perfect,' Lola added when she sensed his words had concluded.

Aidan lowered the box over the edge of the bridge and opened the lid, allowing the contents to fly away amid the breeze, a small plume of grey ash being carried away into the distance.

'I think your words were perfect.'

Aidan looked over to his left, catching sight of the woman who he thought had been crying.

'She looks upset now. Do you think I should go over?'

Lola looked unsure. 'Too late,' she replied, watching as the woman walked away. 'I hope she's okay.'

Once the stranger had gone, Aidan turned back to Lola. 'Well, if there is a positive to be drawn from any of this family stuff, I think this experience has made me want to find out who my dad is,' he began, looking down at the empty box of ashes. 'And that's something that I never thought I'd want to do.' Aidan felt a warm sensation filling his lungs when he admitted to his curiosity. 'I was never sure that my mum would have approved of me wanting to find my dad, but if it makes me happy, I know she'd have been okay with it.'

'That's a big decision,' Lola said with raised eyebrows. 'Imagine if it's somebody that you see in town, or somebody that comes into your shop, or even someone that you already know, but who you don't like. How tough would that be?'

'Not as tough as learning that he doesn't want anything to do with me,' he confessed, his greatest secret out in the open.

'I'm sure that wouldn't happen. Who wouldn't love you?' she admitted, her bold statement escaping from her lips before she had the chance to stop it. 'Anyway, I best go and see Parker,' she said. 'I can't put it off for any longer.'

'Thanks for coming, I'm not sure I would have said anything had you not been here to give me a nudge.'

In a moment of quiet reflection looking out over the water, Lola felt the wristband beneath her clothes.

'Are you okay?' he asked, noting her sudden quietness.

'I still have some things to sort out in my mind, you know, stuff to do with the accident that I was in,' she began. 'My life is a bit of a shambles at the minute, and until all the pieces of the puzzle come together, I don't think I can move on. It's like I'm stuck in the mud.'

'Is there anything I can do to help?'

'No, but thanks for asking.'

Aidan grinned as the sun shone in his eyes. The moment he reached out his arm to waft away a fly, she noticed a bangle on his left wrist, identical to the one still wrapped around hers. She felt her face flush, and in that moment, a clear image appeared in her mind of her and Aidan trapped inside her car. For the first time since the accident, she remembered with certainty that Aidan had been there with her, holding her hand, and she could hear his voice telling her that everything was going to be okay. She could smell the scent of his deodorant and she could feel the warmth of his breath as they lay together, waiting for help to arrive.

'You look lost in thought.'

'Sorry, I didn't mean to go quiet.'

In the reflection of the water, Lola caught sight of her silhouette, and Aidan's by her side, the image making her glow on the inside, and smile on the outside.

'I can finally feel that my memory is coming back, which is such a massive relief,' she confessed. 'Because for the first time in months, I'm starting to feel like myself again. I know what happened and I don't feel that there are any more nasty surprises waiting to knock me down. I can start to move on with my life.' She turned to look at Aidan, her face shining.

In that moment, Aidan's pulse raced and he felt sure that, after all this time, Lola had finally remembered what had happened between them on Christmas Eve, and the burden that he had felt on his shoulders to reveal the truth, could be removed. A tightness appeared in his chest in anticipation of what she was about to say, a moment of awkwardness lingering in the air.

'I best get going,' she announced, knowing that before she could open a new chapter of her life, she needed to close the one with Parker.

'Well, thanks for coming today, I really appreciate it,' said Aidan, his shoulders dropping and a heaviness appearing in his body.

Despite picking up on his broken demeanour, Lola turned to walk away.

'No problem, I'm glad that I could help you,' she said, taking a few slow, easy breaths. 'See you soon, Aidan,' she called back over her shoulder, drawing upon all of her willpower to go against what her heart was telling her to do - to run back and wrap her arms around the man who she knew with certainty had saved her life.

34

'I WAS BEGINNING TO THINK YOU'D CHANGED YOUR MIND,' SAID the salesman when he saw Lola approach the forecourt. 'I've never had a customer leave their purchase here for so long after they've paid in full.'

Lola took a moment to admire the vintage campervan that she'd originally bought as a surprise for Parker. She ran her hand across the pastel green-coloured paintwork, which paired perfectly with the stripy pop-top roof. The spare wheel on the front was covered by a baby blue roundel that gave it its distinctive vintage identity, and Lola fell in love with the idea of the van for the very first time.

'I'm sorry that I've messed you about,' Lola apologised.

'No problem at all.' The salesman held out his hand and passed her the keys. 'It's all yours, enjoy.'

Lola walked to the front of the van and sat behind the wheel, putting the key in the ignition and turning it. The sound of the revving engine made her heart perform somersaults and her excitement could be seen on her face. She buckled in her seatbelt and wound the window down.

'Thanks again,' she shouted, before pulling onto the main road.

For the first time since the accident, Lola found herself behind the wheel, her nerves bouncing. Once she got the feel of how the van drove, she relaxed and made her way home, pulling up to her front door for the first time since witnessing the embrace between Parker and Holly.

Feeling safe in the knowledge that on a Wednesday afternoon, Parker had lectures, she opened the front door and stepped inside. The house that had once felt warm and homely, now felt cold and devoid of any love. She walked upstairs and took out her suitcase from the spare bedroom, opening it up and laying it flat on their bed, her bikini from their trip to Bali still inside, along with a scattering of sand. Without too much care or thought, she filled the case with her clothes.

'I just needed to hear your voice,' she said when Carrie answered the phone.

'Why didn't you let me come with you? I knew how hard it was going to be for you today.'

Lola looked around the room, her wedding dress still hanging on the back of the wardrobe door, waiting to be dry cleaned and put into storage.

'I needed to face this alone, and anyway, he's in lectures all afternoon, so I know he won't be home until tonight.'

'Perfect, so grab everything you want because you really don't want to have to be going back there anytime soon.'

Flustered, Lola scurried about the room.

'I'm just grabbing my clothes and some personal stuff, I really don't want anything else. He can have it, all of it.'

Carrie paced around in The Brownie Box before stepping outside and leaning her back against the wall.

'Don't make any rash decisions. Once the dust has settled, you might regret not taking everything that's yours,' she suggested. 'It could be a costly mistake.'

Lola meandered from one room to another, admiring the home that she had helped create, her personality ingrained into the design.

'I honestly don't want it, Carrie. Everything reminds me of him, and I want a fresh start. I need a fresh start if I'm going to be able to forget about all this and move on with my life.'

Carrie heard a customer at the hatch. 'As long as you're sure,' she said. 'Look, I've got to go, there's a customer. Call me back if you need me.'

Lola slipped her phone into her back pocket and continued to pack up her belongings, stuffing some clothes, her laptop, a bunch of family photos, and a few keepsakes into her suitcase before wheeling it towards the front door, just as it opened.

'What's going on?' Parker questioned when he opened the door, pushing the case out of the way.

Lola moved away from the door. 'I thought you were lecturing this afternoon.'

'They all got cancelled,' Parker replied, looking down at the suitcase. 'What's going on?'

'I'm leaving,' Lola replied.

'Leaving? Why?' he questioned. 'Is this why you've been at Carrie's?'

'You still can't be man enough to tell the truth, can you? It's pathetic, you're pathetic.'

Lola looked at the floor, shaking her head in disapproval.

'At least tell me what I've done,' Parker insisted, closing the door and throwing down his keys.

'I know about Holly, she told me everything,' Lola began. 'I know that you slept with her. I know that you've met up with her since. I've seen the two of you together with my own eyes, so don't try and deny any of it.'

Lola felt a sluggishness infiltrate the pace of her heartbeat, her body feeling weak as she remained lingering in the hallway. 'What more is there to say?' She could see Parker taking a few shaky breaths, rendering him speechless.

He took a step back and leaned his shoulder against the door for support.

'Nothing to say?' Lola added when he failed to speak. 'Thought not. I'll get going then.'

'Wait, you can't just leave without us talking about it. We're married for goodness' sake,' he finally replied, taking hold of her arm when she leaned down to pick up the suitcase.

She looked down at his hand in disgust, at which point he released his grip.

'There really is nothing to talk about,' she asserted in a tone of voice Parker had seldom heard. 'The first time that you cheated was your mistake, this time it was mine. I should have known better than to trust that you'd changed. I should never have married you.'

'Lola, please, just let me explain,' he begged, running his hands through his hair and pacing the hallway.

She released her grip of the case.

'Did you sleep with her?' she asked, turning to face him, wanting to hear the worst of the details from his own mouth.

He paused before answering, his eyes darting before he covered his face with his hands.

'I did but–'

'Then there's nothing to talk about,' she interrupted. 'I believed that you'd changed. I trusted what you were telling me and that you'd never cheat on me again, and look what happened, you went and broke my heart for a second time.'

Lola sobbed, frustrated with herself for showing Parker how much she was hurt, how much she still loved about him.

'I was ready to put my life on hold for you and to go travelling the world, like you've always wanted. How naïve of me,' she shouted, her hurt now turning to anger. 'You let me marry you and make a fool out of myself. How could you? Do you not care for me at all?'

Parker thrashed his arms into the air. 'It was just a bloody mistake,' he defended. 'One stupid night which has made me realise how much I love you, how much I'm ready to start a family with you.'

Her eyebrows pinched together with anger. 'You should have known that before you married me, it shouldn't have been something that you still needed to figure out!' she exclaimed before allowing her body to go limp with defeat. 'You've hurt me too many times, Parker, and now I've had enough. I can't do this anymore. I want a divorce.' She cradled her head in her hands, shielding herself from the pain. 'You can either buy me out of the house, or we can sell. I really don't care.'

The house that had once felt like a home fell unusually silent. Parker allowed his back to slip down the door until he sat on the floor, his knees pulled to his chest.

'How did you find out?'

'I remembered something that happened on Christmas Eve morning and after that, things just began to piece together in my mind,' Lola added, smiling apathetically through her trail of tears. 'I remembered holding your phone that morning and feeling upset, but I just couldn't remember why,' she began, a strange sense of satisfaction brewing in her stomach. 'And then last week, I saw a message on your phone, a message that I now know was from Holly.'

She took a moment to compose herself, the pain that was stirring in her heart hard to ignore.

'So, I followed you to her house. The rest is history.'

Parker looked defeated, hanging his head low. He found himself unable to formulate a suitable reply. His body began to sway, and he covered his face again with both hands. At a loss for words, he felt his eyes fill with tears at the thought that his marriage was really over.

'I now know that I got into my car that morning feeling devastated and heartbroken because I'd seen a photo of the two of you in bed together,' Lola added, courage that she didn't know she had now gaining momentum. 'I was upset. I was distraught, and I got into my car not knowing what else to do. The roads were lethal with ice and because I was crying, hysterical actually, I skidded and nearly killed myself, all because of you.'

Parker continued to remain silent, only able to release a grief-choked exhale. He didn't know where to look or what to do with himself, his body continually shaking.

'And the worst part of it all, if that wasn't bad enough, is that you continued to lie to me, even after the accident.'

Lola forced her tears to stop, anger making way for bitterness.

'You never wanted me to remember anything about the morning of the accident, did you? Because that would have meant that I'd also remember that you cheated on me.'

Parker's continued silence began to infuriate her.

'Why didn't you just tell me? You knew that my memory was going to come back sooner or later, and then what? Were you just going to hope that you could talk your way out of it? Do you know how sick that is?'

'I was about to tell you when I came to see you for the first time in the hospital. The guilt was eating me up and I just wanted you to know everything, but the nurse interrupted–'

'And you couldn't have told me once the nurse had left? You should have tried to tell me every day. You should have been man enough and had the guts to own up to your mistakes. But no, instead you lied to me. When I first asked you about what had happened that morning, you said that I'd just nipped out, and then because you couldn't keep track of your own lies, you then let it slip that we'd actually had an argument. But I remember it all now,' she explained with a satisfying smile. 'When you got home on Christmas Eve morning, you actually told me that you'd stayed at Ed's place, didn't you? Because you'd had too much to drink. And I had messaged Sophie to see if you were telling me the truth, and she confirmed that you were never there. And then once you spoke to me after the accident and you realised that I hadn't remembered anything, your story changed and you didn't mention about apparently staying at Ed's, or the fact you only got home that morning, right before the accident.' The hurt and disgust could be heard in every one of Lola's words as she laid out the truth.

Parker shook his head in defeat, a look of embarrassment falling from his expression, and in that moment, he had nothing to say.

'There were so many opportunities for you to just be honest with me, and yet you just kept on telling me more and more lies. You don't even know what it is to be honest, do you?'

Parker suddenly stood up and his body became animated, his speech rushed in an attempt to save the marriage he could feel slipping from his grip.

'I was scared of losing you. I knew I'd made such a stupid mistake, and after the accident, after everything that you'd already been through, I just didn't want to hurt you even more. I felt so much guilt. You were in that car because of me, I know that. I knew that the accident was my fault, and you could have lost your life because of it.'

'Thankfully, there was someone there who helped to save my life, another detail of that morning that you failed to tell me about. Did you not think that I'd want to know something like that?'

'When I arrived at the hospital, all I cared about was that you were okay. Yes, in hindsight, I should have told you what I knew,' Parker explained, shaking his head. 'I should have thanked the guy before he left, but all I was concerned about was you.'

A sense of resignation could be heard through Lola's voice. 'From the moment that you stepped foot through that woman's door, our marriage was over. All the mistakes and lies that you told me afterwards didn't really matter anyway, the damage had already been done.'

'In my mind, I just hoped that, given time, we'd be able to work through the problems that I knew were there.'

Lola laughed. 'Well, you thought wrong.' Without even thinking, she took out her wedding and engagement rings from her pocket and left them on the side table. 'I'm leaving. This marriage is over, and I don't ever want to see you again.'

'Where are you going to stay?' Parker asked with an air of concern in his voice. 'Carrie's?'

'That's really no business of yours.'

Parker shook his head and his eyes filled with tears.

'I do care about you, Lola,' his voice was weak and cracking as he reached the end of his statement.

She stood up.

'Clearly you didn't care about me quite enough,' she responded, pulling on the handle to open the door. She stepped outside, walking a few paces down the path. From the doorway, Parker caught sight of the van.

'Is that yours?' he questioned.

Lola laughed and nodded her head. 'I actually bought it as a surprise for you, for us to go travelling in together,' she began, a sense of formality in her voice. 'How stupid of me. This was the surprise that I had planned on showing you on Christmas Eve,' she added, her tears falling to the floor. She turned back to look at Parker, all the love she still felt for him making her momentarily question her decision. 'I was planning this for you, and all along you were in bed with another woman.'

He followed her down the path.

'Please, Lola,' he began, his tears joining hers on the ground. 'Please don't leave. I love you so much and I promise that, if you'll let me, I'll remain by your side for the rest of our lives,' he added, taking hold of her hand. 'I know that I've made a mistake, loads of mistakes, but I can honestly say that you're the only woman that I have ever loved, and you're the only woman I would choose to be the mother of my children.'

He took hold of her other hand and pulled her close, working her into his chest before wrapping his arms around her body, pressing her tight.

Lola closed her eyes and savoured his warmth, inhaling the smell of his aftershave for what she knew would be one last time. She felt his heart beating against her cheek, and she never wanted the moment to end.

'I deserve better,' she began, pulling herself away from his embrace and shaking her head with defiance. 'I want to be with someone who knows how lucky he is to have me,' she cried, her words being released in between torrents of tears. 'I want to be with someone who isn't constantly looking or waiting for something better to come along; someone prettier, someone thinner, someone funnier.'

With a heavy heart, she opened the gate and unlocked the van, placing her case inside before turning to take one final look at Parker.

'Oh, and I was pregnant,' she declared, 'but I lost the baby in the accident,' she added, smiling when she saw a look of shock spread across Parker's face. 'Isn't it strange how life always seems to work out for the best in the end?' Lola slammed the door behind her, before starting the engine and setting off down Candle Crescent. Watching Parker in the rear-view mirror, she forced herself to keep driving and made a promise to never go back.

35

Carrie was sitting eating her tea, the kitchen window slightly ajar to get rid of the smell of curry that lingered throughout the house. Outside, she heard the sound of her driveway stones crunching beneath the weight of a vehicle. Curious, she put down her fork and walked towards the window, pulling apart the curtains to reveal the garden. The moment she peered outside, the origin of the noise became apparent.

'Fancy a road trip?' shouted Lola when she pulled up onto Carrie's driveway. With her head stuck out of the campervan window, she waved with the excitement of a schoolchild. 'Isn't she fabulous?' she asked when Carrie appeared at the front door.

Carrie gazed at the vintage van, a puzzled expression becoming lodged on her face. 'She?'

'Oh, she's definitely a she; loyal, trustworthy and reliable,' Lola laughed before stepping out. 'Grab your coat and I'll give you the grand tour.'

Carrie wrapped a coat around her body before stepping outside. Beneath the warm, subtle light emanating from the house, she couldn't help but admire the van as the pristine paintwork sparkled. 'When you told me that you'd bought a van, *this* isn't what I expected,' she said, walking the perimeter. 'This is stylish, this is chic,' she commented, peering in through the windows.

'You didn't think I was going to go travelling in anything other than something fabulous, did you? Who needs a savings account anyway?' Lola pulled the side door open, exposing the camper's interior. The first thing Carrie saw was a suitcase and brimming shoulder bag.

'You've really left him then?'

'Let's not talk about that right now. Let's just feel happy that I have this amazing van in my life,' Lola joked, pushing the case aside and indicating for Carrie to join her.

Carrie stepped inside and took a seat, her eyes focused on Lola. 'It's okay to be upset. It's normal to feel sad when your marriage ends, you don't have to hide anything from me. There's no shame in it,' she explained, reaching out and taking hold of her friend's hand.

Lola forced out a smile as she slid the camper door closed. 'I know, and I might be unable to stop crying later, but for now, let's just feel excited that this lovely girl is all mine.'

Carrie relaxed into the seat and looked around the interior, admiring the quaintness of the soft furnishings. 'It really does feel homely and has everything you'd want,' she smiled, spotting the appliances and home comforts.

Lola lay down on the bed and put her hands behind her head. 'It does feel so cosy, and it'll make any journey feel a bit special.'

Carrie wanted to share in Lola's excitement, but she couldn't help but clasp her hands together. 'You're not actually going travelling though, are you? By yourself, I mean,' she asked, taking a deep breath. 'Because going travelling was all Parker's dream, not yours.'

Lola sat up and allowed her legs to dangle.

'My dream was to live happily ever after with my husband and our baby, but that plan didn't work out the way I was hoping, and with everything that's happened, I feel like I just need to get away,' Lola began, her passion for what she was saying seeping through her words. 'This city feels so suffocating now, and *everything* reminds me of Parker.' Lola took a moment to collect her emotions so that she could articulate what she wanted to say with composure. 'We built our life together here, and everything has a memory attached to it,' she explained. 'And could you imagine if I saw Holly in town every day? She'd be a constant reminder that my husband cheated on me, again, and I just don't want that. I want better for myself. I deserve better.'

'But you can't just run away. This city is *your* home too.'

Lola stared down at the floor with her neck bent forward. 'I know, and I'm not running, but I am choosing to temporarily leave.'

She released an audible breath in the hope that some of her internal pain would be encouraged to leave her body too.

'Some time away will help me to lick my wounds without the world watching, and then I can move on, figure out what I want in life.' Lola raised her head and began to speak in a brighter tone. 'The idea of travelling might never have been my dream, but maybe it was my destiny all along,' she added. 'In any case, I have this van, whether I want it or not, and I don't actually have a place to call home anymore, so there's no better time than now to see what else is out there, beyond the city wall.'

Carrie couldn't disguise the disappointment in her expression as she shrugged her shoulders weakly.

'You can stay with me, you know that, for as long as you want. My home is your home.'

Lola looked at Carrie and smiled, reaching out and squeezing her hand.

'I know, and I really appreciate it. But I just feel the desire to go somewhere, anywhere, and be a bit of a free spirit for the first time in my life. See which direction life guides me towards.'

'But your business is here, I'm here.'

'I'm not suggesting that this will make for a permanent change, far from it. But I think I'm the one who now needs to get this travel bug out of their system,' Lola revealed. 'And then hopefully I'll return, and we can pick up where we left off, and you can hire someone to step into my shoes while I'm away.' Lola stood up and adjusted the curtains. 'It will be so hard for me to leave the business, leave you, but it's what I need to do. You can understand that, can't you?'

Carrie took an extended breath in before nodding.

'I'll just miss you. You're not just my business partner, you're my best friend. You're my family.' Lola sat back on the bed and patted the mattress, encouraging Carrie to sit next to her, both their legs dangling.

Beneath the glow of the lamp, Lola smiled. 'I have a little secret,' she revealed, a raft of giggles following the announcement.

Carrie sat up and turned to face Lola. 'Tell me everything,' she insisted with a sense of urgency.

Lola smiled broadly, wearing nothing but a silly grin on her face. 'Well, I know who the mystery man is, the man who saved my life.'

'And you've known this for how long without telling me?' Carrie was straight to ask.

Lola's eyes sparkled, a blush appearing in her cheeks. 'I've only really just found out for myself because my memories are finally coming back.'

'Oh, that's amazing! I know how worried you've been,' Carrie gushed. 'What a relief and you can finally put it all behind you now. So, who is the mystery man?'

Lola turned to give Carrie her full attention. 'It was Aidan.'

Carrie's facial expression conveyed her sense of surprise. 'Really? Aidan? Your new friend, Aidan?'

Lola nodded. 'Yep.'

'Oh, my goodness, how romantic. If only he had given you the kiss of life,' she joked. 'And now you two are friends, which is amazing. Almost a perfect ending to the story.'

'He doesn't know that I know, at least I don't think he does. I haven't told him yet.'

'But it makes no sense. Why hasn't he told you himself after all this time?'

Lola blew out her cheeks and then released the air with a huff. 'I don't know why he hasn't told me.'

'You need to ask him.'

'I only remembered when we were releasing his auntie's ashes, and the time obviously wasn't right. It wasn't appropriate.'

Carrie raised her eyebrows. 'Blimey.'

'But that's not all.'

'There's more?'

'He was the one who put this on my wrist,' she explained, fiddling with the band in her fingers.

'Do you know why?'

'Nope, that bit is still unclear in my mind.' Lola turned away to gather her thoughts, her gaze becoming distant. 'But I'm going to find out.'

A frown appeared on Carrie's forehead as she tried to work everything out in her mind.

'Is it me, or is it all a bit twisted? Aidan saved your life, and by coincidence, his fiancée and Parker were having an affair. What are the chances of that?' Carrie spotted a rosiness in Lola's cheeks. 'Are you blushing?'

'No,' Lola was quick to defend, cringing and touching her cheeks to try and conceal the blush.

'Really? Tell me the truth.'

'Well, I think there's something between us, or at least the potential to be something. We've spent so much time together lately.'

Carrie's voice became strained. 'You know I only want you to be happy, don't you?' she began. 'But you've just had your heart broken, and I don't want you getting hurt again. There are so many emotions that you're dealing with, and I don't want you jumping with both feet into something new without being sure.'

Lola shook her head. 'I know you're only looking out for me and it's still my intention to leave. But I just get this lovely feeling when I'm around him that's hard to ignore,' Lola explained. 'I need to meet up with him and talk about the accident before I set off travelling. I need closure on this whole thing and he's the only one who witnessed what happened. I want to say thank you to him for saving my life, I owe him that much.'

36

MATTY TIDIED HIS FLAT, MAKING SURE THAT EVERYTHING WAS in its place and that nothing was left outstanding. He placed the brown gift bag on the dining table in the middle of the room so that it was noticeable, and then he grabbed his keys and headed down the stairs. Out on The Shambles, the street remained quiet, not a soul to be seen on the cobbles, which was unsurprising given that it hadn't even reached 4:30am. Pulling his collar up around his neck, he checked that his door was locked before walking away and disappearing into the dusky backdrop of the awakening city.

With his head lowered, he walked towards the canal, his pace quickening, his legs marching in time to his frantic heartbeat. In his mind, the world failed to exist, and as such, he didn't notice the delivery drivers that were making their morning drop-offs. With his head still downcast, Matty failed to notice the handful of swans that were gliding across the water, and he failed to hear the birdsong, his mind only listening to the constant stream of toxic thoughts that had been ram-raiding his brain for the past few weeks, thoughts that he wanted to put an end to.

Having broken free from the city limits, Matty headed towards the outskirts of town and in the direction of the Morris Bridge, the mighty steel arch that ran across one of the busiest arteries leading into York. With his mind consumed, his legs carried him forward, moving on autopilot. With the bridge soon in sight, his senses suddenly awakened, and he could hear the deafening roar of the road as commuter traffic began to flow. He could feel the coldness of the wind as it callously swiped across his face, and he could see the spot on the bridge where he was going to stand. With heavy feet, he walked a bit further, the bridge now only steps away. Daring to look up, he spotted the cathedral in the distance, the sight of the central tower rocking his composure.

A woman passed the spot where Matty had now positioned himself on the bridge. Out on a run with her dog, she looked up and smiled, offering a welcoming acknowledgement to the man who she mistakenly assumed was out on an early morning walk. Matty didn't respond to the lady's polite exchange, instead looking down at the traffic, the stream of articulated lorries roaring beneath, the sound of their engines bold and intimidating. His eyes unfocused and he became lost in a trance, and once again, the wider world failed to exist. He placed his hands on the bridge's safety railings, feeling the steel against his skin, and braced himself for the climb, and for the fall. At that moment, touching recollections from his childhood ran through his mind in an act of sabotage. He could hear his mum's voice echoing through his ears, recalling how her soft tones once filled his heart with love. The scent of a newborn baby infiltrated his nose, and he could feel the way the wispy strands of hair had tickled his face the moment he leaned in to deliver a first, tender kiss. Lost in his thoughts, Matty failed to hear someone calling his name.

'Hi, Matty. I thought it was you,' Lola called out again, approaching him from behind. 'Do you remember me?' she asked, unaware of what she had interrupted.

Matty released his hands and turned to look. 'I do, of course. Hi, Lola,' he began, his facial expression blank, his nerves tattered and his heart feeling like it was about to explode from his chest.

'Not working today?' she asked, joining him, leaning her hands on the railings and looking down over the stream of constant traffic.

Matty shook his head, his silence an indicator that he felt a reluctance to engage in conversation.

Matty's quiet, standoffish demeanour made Lola regret stopping, and she wondered if perhaps Matty found it annoying when patients stopped and talked to him in public.

'Looks like we're in for a nice day,' she commented, remarking the light now being cast by the slow-rising sun. When Matty didn't reply, she filled the silence and made one last attempt to continue with the conversation. 'Did I ever thank you?' she asked, her sight now focused on the cathedral that was peaking above the rest of the city horizon.

'Thank me for what?' he questioned.

'For encouraging me to be patient,' she replied, turning to face him. 'I felt so scared that my memory might never come back, and all along, the only thing that kept me sane was hearing your voice in my mind, reassuring me that I just needed to give things time, and that everything would be okay. And you were right, my memories have returned.'

Matty didn't divert his gaze as he replied. 'I'm glad that I was able to help you,' he said, the sadness behind his eyes drowning out his ability to see the world clearly.

'Are you okay?' she asked, his personality a far cry from the one that she warmed to while she had been a patient in St Jude's. 'Why are you out so early? I thought I was the only crazy one that liked to be the first person up, enjoying the city while it's fresh, and quiet.'

Matty drew in a deep breath. 'I retired from the hospital and ever since leaving, I just feel so lost,' he revealed, unable to hold back his feelings any longer, his innate need to self-preserve kicking in in the eleventh hour.

Lola witnessed the sadness lurking in his eyes. 'It must be a big adjustment, leaving the hospital after so many years,' she began. 'So, why don't you listen to your own advice and give yourself some time to adjust?' she smiled, nudging his shoulder with hers. 'Be patient with yourself until you find a new norm, a new way of life, without work being at the centre of everything,' she continued. 'There's so much that life has to offer, and if I know anything, it's that when life feels hard, and unfair, there are better things to come just around the corner. Am I right?'

'Maybe,' he shrugged.

'Well, I have some news that will prove that you were right, prove that I'm right,' she began to explain in a lighter tone. 'You know that I was asking for details of the man who arrived with me in the ambulance that day?' she began, her smile growing. 'Well, I managed to find out for myself who he is, or at least I've remembered who he was. Isn't that great?'

Matty turned to face her, the thought of Aidan making his heart ache and causing his thoughts to slide back to the dark side. 'That's great news.'

'So, you were right all along. You told me to be patient, and that everything would turn out okay,' she said in a soft, gentle voice. 'So, now you can do the same, and know that everything will turn out okay.'

Matty didn't adjust his gaze despite Lola's upbeat tone of voice and attempt to make him smile.

'I had no clue that something so amazing would come out of something so terrible,' she continued.

'Something amazing?' he questioned.

'Yeah, the man who saved my life is now a part of my life, and he's such an amazing person. I'm lucky to be able to call him a friend.'

Lola thought about all the things she wanted to say to Aidan when they next saw each other.

'And if I could, I'd have liked to have met his family and have the opportunity to learn more about him, thank his parents for raising such an amazing person.'

Lola looked out over the bridge, the constant stream of cars making her vision go blurry.

'Why can't you thank his parents?' Matty asked when Lola's words registered in his mind, curious of the reply.

'Well, his mum passed away when he was seventeen, and he's never known his dad,' she began. 'But all that's going to change I think,' she revealed, failing to realise the significance of her words, and how she herself had just saved a life.

'In what way?' Matty asked, his demeanour changing amid the awakening breeze.

'Well, Aidan–' she began, turning to place her hand on Matty's arm, '– that's his name, by the way. He's decided to find out who his father is. Isn't that great? I'm not sure why I'm telling you all this when you're probably not really interested, but my point is, although you feel unsure about life right now, better things are coming, you just need to be patient,' she encouraged, before taking a look at her watch. 'Well, I best get going, I'm actually meeting up with Aidan in a little while and I don't want to be late,' she said. 'Take care, Matty, and look after yourself,' she said, easing herself away from the railings. 'Why don't you stand on one of the other bridges, one with better views. Standing here isn't peaceful at all,' she said, turning and walking away.

With his constant cycle of disturbing thoughts having been broken, Matty released his hands from the railings and, with caution, took a slow step back from the barrier separating him and the road below. With Lola's words fresh in his mind, he took another step back from the edge and told himself that today was not the day to give up on life.

37

*L*OLA FELT CONSUMED BY NERVES THE MOMENT SHE TURNED
down onto Swan Lane, spotting Aidan sitting on a bench in the
distance. The sound of the river echoing in her ear worked to calm
her mounting levels of tension, the fresh morning air filling her
lungs with courage. She paced towards the scene of the accident
with her head high, glad to have chosen the poignant location as
a meeting place.

Aidan stood up. 'Hi,' he said, smiling at the sight of Lola. 'Are
you okay?' he asked when she neared.

Lola nodded, wrapping her coat tighter around her body the
moment the wind scowled around her face. 'It's freezing,' she said,
trying to curtail her hair as it also whipped around her cheeks.

'Shall we go and chat somewhere a bit warmer?'

Lola shook her head. 'I'd prefer to stay here, at least for a
minute, if that's alright?'

Taking a seat, Lola peered towards the scene of her accident.

'I need to make my peace with this road, and I think you'll be
able to help me achieve that.'

Aidan took a seat next to her, the nerves that were rattling
through his body causing his legs to shake beneath his jeans.

'I assumed from your choice of location that you've remembered
that I was there with you on the day of the accident.'

'I have,' began Lola, still staring out before her. 'I'm just not
sure why you've kept it a secret from me,' she continued, turning

to face him. 'Why didn't you tell me who you were when we met in the café that very first day?'

Aidan smoothed down his jeans and, with strain in his voice, responded to her question.

'I didn't know what to say. I could tell that you had no idea who I was, so it was hard for me to know what to do for the best.'

'And I understand that, but since that day we've obviously become good friends, and yet you still didn't tell me who you are. You could have helped me to remember what happened, you knew I was struggling with it.'

'But I would have had to lie to you as well,' he revealed.

'Why?'

'Because while you were trapped inside the car, you told me that your husband was cheating on you, I obviously didn't know at that point that it was my fiancée he was in bed with.'

The pair fell silent for a moment.

'And once we'd met in the café and started to become friends, I realised that you and your husband were still together, and that you hadn't remembered that he'd been unfaithful.' Aidan clutched his hands. 'I just didn't want to tell you something that you hadn't yet remembered. I didn't want to be the reason that your marriage ended,' he replied, turning to meet Lola's eyes. 'I felt like you needed to remember everything in your own time.'

'Did you give me this?' she asked, revealing the wristband.

He nodded. 'I did. My mum gave it to me before she died, saying that it would always remind me to be strong and to never give up, and in that moment, when I felt so scared because I wasn't sure if you were going to be okay, if you were going to make it, that's what I felt like I needed you to do, be strong.' Aidan took a moment before continuing. 'And we made an agreement. Do you remember what it was?'

Lola looked a bit confused. 'No, I'm not sure.'

'I told you that you could look after it and only give it back to me when you had recovered.'

Lola wriggled the band off her wrist. 'Thank you for lending it to me. I've worn it every day since, and in a strange way, it did sort of help me to get through this past couple of months. It gave me comfort and I wasn't sure why, until now.'

She handed the bracelet to Aidan.

Aidan smiled. 'I knew you'd take care of it for me,' he said, slipping the band over his wrist. 'It's felt strange without it, so I had to go out and buy something similar. How stupid is that?'

'It's not stupid at all, I understand.'

Lola looked up and gazed across the street. 'So, you saw the accident?' she asked next, remaining faced forwards.

Aidan's gaze darted and he became very aware of his environment, images of the crash flashing through his mind like unwanted bolts of lightning. 'I did,' he confirmed. 'I was on foot and saw your car skidding, like you'd lost control on the ice, and then the car collided with the lamppost.'

Lola could tell from the sound of his strained voice that recalling details of the accident was just as challenging for him as it was for her, so she turned to look at him. 'I understand if you don't want to talk about it.'

'I don't mind, really, and I actually think it'd help because I've been bottling it all up, having nobody to talk to about it, at least nobody who really understands.'

'In that case, I'd like to know everything so that I can move on,' she said. 'Because although things are starting to come back, there are still parts that are sketchy in my memory.' She closed her eyes and replayed Christmas Eve in her mind. 'I left my house upset that morning and set off in haste, not really realising how dangerous the roads were.' Taking a breath before continuing, Lola opened her eyes and imagined that her car was travelling down the road right before her. 'And I lost control, the sound of my brakes came screaming through my ears, and before I knew it, I crashed head-on. Is that how you saw it?'

Turning to Aidan for reassurance, she was met with a nod.

'Yep, and then I called for an ambulance as I ran towards you, but there'd been trouble with the bridge due to that big accident, so they said that help was going to be delayed, and at that point my phone ran out of battery.'

'Oh really? I didn't know that. I assumed the paramedics would have been talking to you the whole time, until the ambulance arrived.'

'It was over an hour before they came.'

'So, then what happened? I remember my head was hurting, but memories of being trapped in the car are still pretty vague.'

'I tried to get you out, but the doors were locked, and because of how the car had crashed, the metal had deformed, so I couldn't get you out anyway. The fire brigade had to cut you free eventually.'

Lola smiled in acknowledgement of the shared memory. 'I do remember the sound of the machine they used to get me out. I was terrified because I thought they were going to take my legs off or something.'

'I was scared too and the sound was pretty horrific, but it didn't take them long to pull you free.'

'What happened in the hour that we were waiting?'

Aidan needed to sit back so that the bench supported his frame. 'I kept talking to you because I could see that you were bleeding from your skull, and that you were getting cold the longer we waited, and your eyes were closing, which terrified me,' he replied with a sense of acceptance, his expression pained, his eyes glossy. 'I was so scared that if you closed your eyes, you might never open them again,' he revealed, turning to face Lola, who had been looking at him the whole time. 'And every time that your eyes began to close, I'd tell you that I could hear the ambulance coming in the distance, even though I couldn't, just to try and give you hope, and to keep you awake.'

'Was there nobody else around? Did nobody else see us?'

'No, and I wanted to run and find some help, but you wouldn't let me leave.'

Lola turned her body so that she was now more facing Aidan than the road.

'You sang bits of an Oasis song, didn't you? It was the one that came on the radio when I was at your shop that Saturday.'

Aidan smiled. 'I was getting cold myself and losing my mind, and I couldn't think what else to try to keep you awake, and then those lyrics came to mind. I think I must have heard that song on the radio that morning.'

'Thank you, for everything,' Lola said. 'You saved my life, and I'll never be able to thank you enough.'

'All I did was call an ambulance and bore you with the sound of my own voice,' Aidan replied, brushing off the magnitude of what he'd done.

The pair sat back on the bench and fell silent for a few moments. The sound of the river in the background swelled, the wind sweeping the water downstream with gusto. The clouds parted and the sun shone through, warming their faces, which had caught a chill.

'Are you okay?' he asked when she remained silent.

Lola puffed her chest out and spoke in a steady, confident voice.

'Despite everything, I really am okay,' she confirmed. 'I mean, it's not great, I didn't really want to start the year recovering from concussion, getting divorced, and being homeless, but worse things happen,' she laughed.

'Homeless?'

'I'm being a bit dramatic. I could have stayed at the house and asked Parker to leave, which I'm sure he would have done, but I wanted to get out of there, and anyway, I have the van in my life now,' she grinned.

'The van?'

'My campervan, which is currently parked on Carrie's driveway.'

'That's the van you bought for Parker so that you could both go travelling?'

'The very same one,' Lola confirmed. 'Only now it's my van,

and I'll be travelling alone.'

'Really?' he questioned, the thought of her leaving York secretly shattering his heart.

'Yep. Carrie is going to take on an assistant, and then I'll be leaving,' she stated.

Remaining hidden in a secluded nook of her heart, there was a hope that Aidan would persuade her to stay in York, or at least show signs that he'd miss her if she were to leave.

'Wow, that's brilliant. Good for you,' he said in the chippiest voice that he could muster, concealing his true feelings.

'What does life hold in store for you?' she asked, masking her disappointment.

'Well, I really need to go to France and sort the business with the will, but beyond that, I really don't know. I thought I was getting married and about to start a family, so I think I need to reconsider, go back to the drawing board, as they say,' he joked, though Lola could hear the hurt hiding behind his words. 'But I am going to start the search for my dad, and see where that leads me.'

'Exciting times, in a way, then,' Lola smiled. 'Hopefully this could be the start of a new relationship between you and your dad, if you manage to find him. I don't know how easy the process is.'

'I don't either, but I guess I'm about to find out.'

'Maybe once you get to France, you'll never want to leave, and that will be your new path in life, and you'll fall in love with a French mademoiselle and live happily ever after. Isn't that how the story goes?'

Aidan's shoulders fell and his body relaxed. 'I think this fresh air has got to your head, or maybe you've still got a concussion. I don't know you well enough to gauge which it is,' he laughed.

'After all I've been through, I've come to learn that anything can happen in life, especially when you're least expecting it.' Lola stood and shook her body, trying to warm up her freezing limbs. 'Well, thanks for taking the time to come and meet me. I hope we'll be able to meet up again before I leave for wherever it is I'm going.'

Aidan stood up too. 'That sounds good,' he began. In his heart, he wanted to tell her how he was really feeling, but he couldn't conjure up the courage. 'Take care, Lola,' he concluded, before turning to walk away.

Lola watched as Aidan disappeared down the road, a heaviness settling in her chest, along with a lump in her throat. Just when she felt like the pieces of her life were finally coming together, she felt one piece slipping away. Her heart ached at the prospect that she would now be leaving York, alone.

38

*L*OLA STOOD NEXT TO THE KETTLE AND WAITED FOR IT TO BOIL, rolling her eyes at the stream of romantic gestures that kept appearing on her social media feeds.

'Valentine's Day is awful when you're single,' she sighed when Carrie appeared in the kitchen. 'It's more like Alone-and-Miserable Day for me. I might just hide myself away from the world and pretend that today never even happened.'

'I wish I could do the same, but I've agreed to go on that bloody blind date.'

'Are you still going through with it? That's brave of you. I thought you'd have come up with an excuse by now.'

'I can't stand someone up on the most romantic day of the year. Even I'm not that thoughtless.'

Lola took a seat and rested her head on the table. 'You're always thinking of others.'

Carrie went and sat with her. 'Listen, I know these past few weeks have been hard for you, so why don't you put it all behind you and just set off into the sunset? Go and explore the world,' she said, placing her hand on Lola's arm. 'I've found someone to help me at work, so there's really nothing holding you back now.'

'I don't know if I can do it on my own, and I hate admitting that.'

'I get it, I wouldn't have the nerve to do it on my own either. So, why don't you just take a trip somewhere in this country?

Drive to the Lake District or head up to Scotland, just to test the water. Then you'll know if it's something you really want to do, or you can have a rethink without being a thousand miles away from home.'

'I don't have a home,' Lola cried, allowing her hands to catch her face when she raised her head. 'I know I said I wouldn't do any more crying, it's just hard.'

Carrie moved her chair so that she was next to Lola. 'Cry all you need to. Why don't you message Aidan? He's probably feeling just as low as you are right now, and I know you've been thinking about him, I can tell by the way you check your phone all the time. Unless you're hoping to hear from Parker?'

'Definitely not. I couldn't think of anything worse than getting any more messages off that bastard.'

'Well, that's a relief to hear,' Carrie declared. 'So, who *are* you waiting to hear from?'

Lola brushed her hair back with her hands and wiped her face. 'I thought Aidan might have messaged me, you know, just to meet up to say a proper goodbye if nothing else, because he knows I'll be leaving soon. We were friends, or at least I thought we were.'

'Then message him.'

'If he'd wanted to keep in touch with me, he would have done it by now. It's been a few weeks since we met up for that chat down by the river.'

Carrie pointed her finger in a playful way. 'He could be sat waiting for you to reach out to him. Why does the man always have to make the first move?'

'Even if I wanted to, I'm definitely not going to message him on Valentine's Day, that sends completely the wrong message.'

'Agreed. But you could always call into the shop, buy yourself some fudge, and that way keep the meeting casual.'

Lola got up and peered out the window, mixed feelings brewing in her stomach when she caught sight of the campervan. 'I'm about to go travelling, the last thing I should be doing is making new–'

'Making new what?' Carrie interrupted, intrigued.

'Oh, I don't know, I'm just confused. I'm going to have a drive somewhere. I don't want to stay in, alone, otherwise I'll drive myself mad and end up drowning myself in a bucket of self-pity.'

'Let me cancel this stupid blind date and we can stay in and binge watch something together,' Carrie suggested.

Lola shook her head. 'No, this mystery man could turn out to be the love of your life. I'm absolutely fine, honestly. I'm going to get my coat on and go for a drive, clear my head. I'll see you later.'

When Lola stepped outside, the air felt a little warmer against her skin than the few harsh, bitter days that had just passed. She plunged herself into the driver's seat of the van and buckled herself in, turning the key and waiting for the engine to roar. Without any idea of where to go, she set off, following the road that led her to the outskirts of York. With nothing but love songs playing on the radio, she spent the entire journey crying, one song after another acting as a reminder of what her and Parker had once shared. The thin, white line on her wedding finger served as a constant reminder of what she no longer had, her hand looking bare without the rings she once cherished. She pulled up at a local beauty spot about half an hour into her drive, ready to give her watery eyes a rest. She exhaled and felt a sense of comfort, knowing that there was now some distance between her and the romantic ghosts of her past.

'So, I just wanted to wish you luck before your big date,' she said when Carrie answered the phone. 'Did you go for the blue dress?'

'No way,' Carrie laughed. 'I'd hate to give off the impression that I'm eager. So, where are you?'

'Well, I thought it was a good idea to get out of York because I didn't want to run the risk of seeing Parker on Valentine's, especially if he's out with another woman, which he probably is, so—'

'So, where are you?' Carrie encouraged.

'I'm sat at the top of Franklin Hill.'

'Well, I guess that's a nice place to spend the evening.'

'I have a great view and I'm going to nip across the road and buy a bag of chips,' she began to explain just as someone knocked on the driver's window, making her jump. Lola turned to see who it was and saw Aidan standing outside, smiling and holding his hand up. 'I have to go,' she said, the disbelief showing in her voice.

'Are you okay?' asked Carrie.

'Absolutely fine,' she reassured. 'Have a fab night and I'll text you later.' Lola put her phone away and wound the window down.

'Hi,' said Aidan through a beaming grin.

Looking into his sparkling eyes, Lola's insides lit up.

'Hi. Have you come here to escape the ghosts of York too on this ghastly of all nights?' she joked. 'Or are you actually here with Holly?' she quickly added just in case she'd put her foot in it, looking round to see if he had a plus-one.

'I haven't seen or spoken to Holly in weeks.'

'Oh, I'm sorry.'

'I'm not,' Aidan was quick to add. 'So, this is the van,' he commented, swiftly changing the subject.

Lola beamed with pride. 'Indeed. Would you like to come and have a look?'

'Sure.'

Lola stepped out and walked to the side, pulling back the door to expose all that the camper had to offer. 'What do you think?'

Aidan poked his head in and admired the heart of the van, the warmth from inside brushing over his face. 'It's amazing. From the outside you'd never really expect all this,' he said looking back at Lola. 'You've had it done up really nice.'

'Come and take a seat if you want,' she offered, signalling with her hand. 'That's if you're not rushing to get somewhere?'

Aidan tried to reign in the beaming smile that was threatening to break through, the invitation to join Lola the best possible outcome of his night. 'I'd love to, thanks.'

He stepped inside and took a seat, followed by Lola, who turned her attention to the wood burner and switched the kettle on.

'Can I offer you tea or coffee?' she asked, pointing to the canisters strapped to the wall.

'Tea would be great, thanks.'

'Apart from Carrie, you're my first van visitor,' smiled Lola.

'I'm honoured,' he said, trying not to stare, her smile making him feel giddy inside. 'So, have you been anywhere on your travels yet, or are you still stuck in the planning stages?'

Lola met his gaze and a look of embarrassment shone from her face. 'I haven't really left Carrie's driveway, to be honest,' she began, releasing an uncontrolled moan. 'I was full of enthusiasm and then we had that avalanche of snow, and then the snow turned to ice, and we all know that I'm not a great driver on ice,' she joked. 'And then once the weather did buck up a bit, after all my research, I wasn't really sure where I wanted to go,' she confessed, allowing her chin to drop to her chest. 'So, I guess it's accurate to say that Franklin Hill is the first place I've visited on my great travels of Europe.'

Picking up on her vulnerability, Aidan attempted to raise her spirits. 'You've been through so much, it's understandable if you feel a little lost, if that's the right terminology to use.'

Lola smiled and raised her head. 'I woke up one morning and realised that my whole life had been turned upside down, and I didn't know where I belonged anymore, and I still don't, I guess, which is why I'm sat alone at the top of Franklin Hill on Valentine's evening.'

Aidan purposefully coughed and raised his eyebrows.

'Well, I know I'm not alone now,' she corrected, acknowledging the butterflies that had now made their way to all extremities of her body. 'I've missed you these past few weeks,' she blurted, immediately regretting it. 'Did you sort that stuff out with your auntie's will?' she asked, trying to divert attention away from her moment of honesty.

Aidan shook his head. 'I've been putting it off,' he began, his tone flat and emotionless. 'I've been spending all of my free time decorating my new flat to try and make it feel like home.' Aidan forced a smile onto his face. 'I've had to try and sort financial stuff out with Holly, which has been like pulling teeth, and on top of all that, I've been keeping the business on track. People in York like to eat fudge on Valentine's Day so it's been pretty busy all round.'

Lola watched how Aidan fidgeted with his fingers when he felt nervous, an endearing trait that she admired. 'And the stuff to do with your Auntie Alice's will can wait?' she asked, trying not to make it obvious how she was feeling.

'Not really. The solicitors in France have been really shortcoming with information apart from informing me that it is a property, so it's a bit of a liability at the moment.' Aidan paused when he felt his phone vibrate in his pocket. 'Sorry, I best just check to make sure this isn't anything to do with work,' he said, taking his phone out of his pocket. 'We've had a special event running tonight and I told the guys to contact me if they were struggling.'

While Aidan looked at his phone, Lola tried to check herself in the reflection of the window, running her fingers through her unbrushed hair, now wishing that she'd left the house wearing something other than just an old pair of jeans and an unflattering jumper.

'Everything okay?' she asked, spotting Aidan's frown.

'It's Holly,' he announced.

Lola felt her heart fall through her body at the mere sound of Holly's name, and she spotted Aidan biting the inside of his cheek, which put her on edge.

'How is she?' she asked out of politeness.

Aidan held his phone in his hands and looked up, unable to hide his feelings. 'She's just told me that she's eight weeks pregnant.'

Lola felt her heart stop and her emotions tumbled, confirming what she'd known for a while, even if she hadn't admitted it to herself or anyone else – she really did like Aidan.

'Oh, right.'

An air of awkwardness lingered between the two, and Lola could see the look of sadness in his eyes. The cosy ambience that the pair had created inside the shelter of the van dissolved and Aidan stood up.

'Anyway, I best get going,' he announced, finishing his tea and placing his cup down. 'Thanks for the drink.'

'You're welcome, anytime,' she said, swinging open the door for Aidan to leave.

'See you soon,' he said, before running across the road and disappearing into the night.

Lola grabbed her phone and, with shaky hands, rang Carrie.

'I think I'm in love,' she blurted the moment her friend picked up the phone. 'But you already know that, don't you?'

'I wish I was in love,' Carrie whispered, 'But instead I'm currently hiding in the ladies' room trying to think of any excuse to leave this bloody awful date that I'm on.'

'Oh, I'm so sorry, I thought you'd be done by now,' Lola apologised, taking a glance at her watch.

'Me too, but he just doesn't stop for a breath. I swear to God, I know this man's life story,' Carrie mocked. 'Anyway, this sounds like an emergency situation, so he'll just have to wait if he's really interested in me,' Carrie said with a laugh. She manoeuvred herself over to the window to get a better signal. 'So, have you realised that you're still in love with Parker, and you're willing to give him another chance?'

Lola lay her hand over her breastbone with a sense of drama.

'Tonight has made me realise that I have a bundle of feelings swirling around in my body like I'm living my teenage years all over again,' she declared with a broad smile, a genuine look of excitement that couldn't be faked, or forged. 'And when I think of him, I get a flurry of butterflies in my heart and I can't stop myself from smiling,' she continued, a lightness in her voice conveying her sense of happiness. 'And when I'm not with him, I miss him, I crave his company and I wonder where he is, and what he's doing.' She paused for breath and inhaled with purpose. 'And that's how I know I'm in love,' she concluded, resting her back against the chair and grinning at her emotional breakthrough.

'But who are you in love with?'

'Aidan Fogg. I'm so in love with Aidan Fogg that I can't believe it's taken this long for me to figure it out, and actually say the words aloud.'

Like the inside of York cathedral during a National Day of Remembrance, the once dusky horizon sparkled with speckles of light in Lola's eyes, the brightness working to erase the ghosts of her past while carving the way for new love to follow.

39

MARIE ONCE AGAIN ARRIVED AT MATTY'S FRONT DOOR AND rattled her knuckles against the wood.

'Matty,' she called through the letter box in the same manner that she had done a few days earlier. 'I swear, I'm not leaving this time until I've at least seen you. So, you either let me in, or I'll stand out here shouting all day.'

Upon releasing the letter box, she knocked again, the noise bouncing its way down the cobbled street. She stepped back and saw that the curtains were still drawn, like nothing had changed since her previous visit. After a few minutes of incessant banging, the door creaked open.

'Hi,' he said, peering around the narrow gap in the door that he had permitted to be open.

At the first opportunity, Marie pushed her way in and made her way straight up the stairs without an invitation.

'Oh, so you are in then,' she said, struggling to mask the frustration in her voice.

Matty's voice cracked with emotion. 'How do you know where I live?' he asked, following her up the stairs, a disgruntled look lodged on his face at the obtuse means of entry.

'Never mind about that. I need to know that you're okay,' Marie replied upon reaching the top of the stairs.

'You looked in my file at work, didn't you? How else could you possibly know?'

Marie took a long, slow look around the dreary interior, darkness eating up most of the snippets of natural light that were trying to seep in through the cracks in the curtains.

'Maybe,' she confirmed. 'And as your nominated next of kin and emergency contact, I feel that I have a responsibility and duty of care to know that you're okay,' she said in a firm, unapologetic voice.

Matty took a seat, resting in his usual spot on the sofa. 'I had nobody else to put on the stupid form, sorry for not asking first.'

She went and took a seat by his side, resting her hand on his lap. 'I'm not angry that you put my name. I'm just angry that you didn't tell me,' she began. 'Look at yourself, Matty, hiding yourself away like this. It's just not healthy,' she said, peering around at the lacklustre flat. 'You're obviously struggling and I'm here to help you, and this time, I won't be taking no for an answer.'

Matty allowed a small smile to slowly make its way across his lips.

'I'm just trying to sort myself out, which is harder than you'd expect once you retire,' he confessed. 'It's not all it's cracked up to be, at least it hasn't been for me.'

'So, tell me, how can I help you?' she asked, standing up and walking over to the window, peering through the gap in the curtains before opening them wide, a large splash of natural light taking the opportunity to flood the room and eradicate some of the ingrained darkness. 'You name it and I'll do it. Anything.'

He squinted at the brightness having habituated to the dimly-lit conditions. 'You could sit and talk to me, I guess,' he said. 'I can't remember the last time that I actually spoke to someone.'

'Of course, I'll sit and talk to you. You're my friend and I'd do that without you having to ask. But you need to be more willing to open the door to me. I can't have a conversation with you if I'm down on the street, can I?' Before she sat down, she flicked the kettle on and checked the fridge for milk.

Matty scratched his forehead, trying to soothe the dull ache that was gnawing its way deeper inside his brain. 'I know, it's just difficult.'

'Then talk to me about what's going on, talk to me about what feels difficult.' Marie spotted the brown gift bag that was sitting on the table, the only item in the entire space that looked out of place. 'Are you in trouble financially?' she asked, unable to ignore the sparseness of the room. Matty shook his head.

'Are you in trouble with the police?' she asked tentatively, scared, partly, of what his answer might be.

'No, nothing like that,' he replied, avoiding eye contact.

'Then what?' she asked, taking another look around the room, searching for clues. 'Is it to do with the photo that you carried around in your ID badge at work?' she asked, her eyes spotting the same photo that was on display in a small frame. 'Who are the people in the photo, Matty?' she probed, spotting that his head had dropped, his body language defeated.

Matty raised his head and looked her in the eyes, and for the first time in his life, spoke the truth aloud. 'They're my children.'

Marie's face lit up. 'You have children? I never realised,' she beamed. 'What are their names?'

Matty took an intake of breath. 'Aidan and Faye,' he began. 'You've actually met Aidan before,' he revealed, turning to look at her.

'Really? When?'

'Remember Lola, our Christmas Eve patient in bed number two?'

Marie nodded in recollection. 'Yeah, the car accident lady with concussion, and the stranger who saved her life.'

Matty smiled. 'That stranger was Aidan, my son,' he revealed.

Like a light had switched on, Marie fitted the pieces of the puzzle together. 'That would make sense then, because you were acting so strange that day, and I was worried that something was wrong. Why didn't you introduce me?'

'Aidan doesn't know that I'm his father.'

'Really? Why?'

Matty took a moment to compile his response. 'I've never been a part of his life,' he began, his expression pained.

'Oh, Matty. I'm so sorry,' Marie consoled, witnessing the hurt in her friend's eyes. 'What happened?'

Recalling the events like it only happened yesterday, Matty explained. 'It was a tough situation right from the start, for many reasons,' he conveyed, his eyes portraying the situation better than any words could have conveyed. 'His mum and I were no longer together, and not that long after he was born, things became too difficult and I was asked not to go over anymore.'

'And you've never had any contact since?'

Matty produced a slow shake of the head. 'Not as father and son.'

'And now you feel that the time is right to make amends?'

'If I don't do it now, I'll have lost him forever,' he replied, the heaviness in his words enough to create a glossiness in Marie's eyes.

'And what about your daughter?'

'I lost touch with her a long time ago, I think she lives abroad now,' he admitted in shame.

Marie placed her hand on his thigh in an attempt to settle his nervousness. 'Well, Aidan is here and I understand that the thought of telling him must be terrifying, but like you said, do you really want to lose him forever?'

The room fell momentarily quiet, only the faint sound of people passing The Shambles echoed in through the window.

Matty turned to look at Marie. 'Would you mind staying with me for a little while?' he asked. 'I'm not sure what I want to do, but I know that I don't want to be alone right now.'

She kicked off her shoes and eased her body onto the sofa so that she could put her feet up and get comfy. 'I thought you'd never ask,' she replied, offering him a reassuring smile.

40

$\mathcal{L}$OLA CARRIED THE REMAINDER OF HER BELONGINGS FROM Carrie's spare room and took them out to the camper. Inside the van, she arranged her belongings with care, like she was moving into a brand-new house. With the addition of a few photos and some vintage bunting hung around the interior, the van felt more like home than ever before.

'Hi,' announced Parker as he lingered on the edge of Carrie's driveway. His stomach churned the moment he saw Lola loading the van, the meek smile he was trying to hold onto dropping from his face.

Lola turned when she heard the sound of someone's voice.

'What are you doing here?' she questioned upon seeing Parker, a large brown envelope clutched in his hand. She loathed the way her heart still skipped a beat whenever her eyes landed on his familiar features, the dimples in his cheeks the first thing she'd noticed about him when they first met.

'I needed to see you before I sign these,' he replied, holding up the envelope. 'The divorce papers came through this morning.'

Lola stepped out of the van and slouched her body on the garden wall. Parker followed and took a seat beside her. Lola shuffled her feet in the stones and took a deep, weighted sigh.

'There's nothing to talk about, we've been through it all before.'

'If I didn't try one last time to save our marriage, I'd never forgive myself,' he declared. 'I made a mistake, Lola,' he began, turning to look at her, trying to encourage her to return his gaze. 'But that doesn't change the fact that I still love you. I have always loved you, and I will always love you.'

When Lola spotted Parker reaching out his hand, she placed her hands in her pockets, urging herself not to touch him, knowing that even the briefest act of intimacy could weaken her resolve.

'All I see when I look at you is you and her naked together,' she cried, the image in her mind still raw, and so hurtful. 'Do you know how that feels? You've destroyed all the amazing memories that we created together, and I hate you for that because it's like the past ten years didn't happen,' she sobbed, turning her face away from him, rubbing her cheek on her shoulder. In a moment lost within her loneliness, Lola craved the comfort that Parker had once offered.

He looked down at the envelope in his hands, the hurt he was feeling in his heart intensifying at the sight of Lola crying. 'If you want me to sign these, then I will. I just want you to be happy,' he said, taking out the forms and scribbling his name on each page where indicated to do so.

Out of the corner of her eye, the sight of Parker signing the papers made Lola feel sick, the finality of her marriage coming right before her eyes. She watched how his hand moved across the papers, his wedding band still placed on his finger. The smell of his aftershave drifted through the air, the scent she had once loved now making her feel sick with conflicting emotions. When she turned her head, she noticed that Parker had worn her favourite jumper, a gift she had bought him for his last birthday.

Parker stood up and handed her the envelope.

'Just so you know, I officially put in my request and my career break application has been confirmed,' he announced. 'I'm ready to leave everything behind and go travelling with you, make a fresh start and live the rest of our lives together, just like we vowed to do.'

With that, Parker turned and began to walk away, the stones crunching beneath his feet as he navigated the driveway.

In a moment of weakness, Lola felt her heart crave for everything that Parker was promising, and felt a deep-rooted desire to chase after him, but just as she did, her phone rang. By the time she'd checked to see who it was and looked back up, Parker had gone.

'Hi.'

'You're crying, aren't you?' asked Carrie the moment she heard Lola's cracked voice. 'I was just calling to see how the packing is going, and by the sounds of it, not very well.'

Lola walked towards the road, peering up and down. 'Parker has just been over,' she announced, crying when she saw that he'd gone, the lane deserted.

The anger in Carrie's words travelled down the line. 'Why won't he just leave you alone? Should I speak with him?'

Lola cleared her throat while trying to curtail her overflowing emotions. 'He's signed the divorce papers.' Lola held the envelope in her hand and peered inside, checking to see if he had really signed them all, crying harder once again when she spotted his trail of signatures.

'Brilliant, now you can finally move on, and you still don't have to go exploring the world. You can unpack the van and stay here, give yourself some time for life to sort itself out.'

'His career break is all sorted and he's ready to leave, Carrie,' Lola sobbed. 'He said that he still loves me and that he's ready to give everything up, for me, and to go travelling together.'

Carrie stared through the hatch of The Brownie Box where she was standing, shaking her head as she slumped herself on a stool.

'Oh, Lola, it might be what you want to hear right now, when you're feeling lonely, but he's not the man you deserve. He's a liar and a cheat.'

'I know but–'

'There are no buts,' she interrupted. 'As your friend, I'm telling you that you deserve better, and we both know deep down how you really feel about Aidan.'

'It doesn't matter how I feel about Aidan because he doesn't feel the same way about me. I told him that I'd missed him, and he didn't say it back, and on top of that, his ex-fiancée is now expecting his baby. I'd say that's all the news I need to step away from the whole situation.' Lola walked inside the van and slumped her body down, allowing her aching limbs to rest. 'Oh, Carrie, what should I do?' she exhaled.

'Sign the papers and move on, and I'll be right here by your side,' she reassured. 'It's better to be alone than to give your heart to someone who really doesn't deserve it.'

'You're right, you're always right,' she laughed, wiping her face with the back of her hand. 'I'm so done with all this crying. Have I said that before?'

Carrie smiled and looked at an old photo of her and Lola that was pinned to the wall of The Brownie Box. 'You might have said that a few times over the years.'

'Well, I mean it this time. I'm never going to cry over a man again, they're just not bloody worth it,' she laughed.

'So, what's the new plan?'

Lola took a moment to compose herself before replying. 'Well, I'm going to finish packing, and then tomorrow I'll be leaving York.'

'And what about Aidan. Don't you want to see him before you go?'

'What's the point? They're expecting a baby together and he's told me before that, more than anything, he wants a family of his own, and now he has it.'

'And you're okay with that?'

'I can't be upset about something that never actually happened, can I? I don't even know if he had feelings for me anyway,' Lola sighed. 'He could look at all women in the same way that I thought he just looked at me, or maybe I was just desperate and seeing something that was never really there in the first place. Either way, I don't think he's over Holly and now they're expecting a baby. End of story.'

'How about this - I'll make us some tea tonight and we can drown our sorrows over a few bottles of wine. How does that sound?'

Her posture transformed and became relaxed. 'What would I do without you?' she said. 'That sounds fab, thanks.'

'It's a date then, see you later.'

The moment Lola hung up the phone, she grabbed a pen and scribbled her name on the divorce papers, sealed the pre-paid envelope, and made her way to the nearest postbox, before pushing the documents through and walking away.

41

With a mixture of emotions swirling through her mind, Lola watched Holly's front door from afar. From her vantage point across the road, hidden from view by a cluster of trees, she hoped that her instincts were wrong, and that she wouldn't see Aidan.

'What on earth am I doing?' she whispered when Carrie answered her phone.

'I don't know, what are you doing?'

Ashamed, Lola pressed her free hand against her forehead. 'I'm sat on a bench, hiding, at the top end of Poets Nook, again.' The moment she said the words aloud, she realised how insane her behaviour was. 'I've turned into some kind of mad stalker, haven't I?'

'It all depends on who lives on Poets Nook,' Carrie questioned.

'Holly,' she replied, the word so quiet that Carrie was only just able to hear her.

'Why are you stalking Holly?'

'Well, after what you said yesterday about seeing Aidan before I leave, and after our chat last night, I came to the conclusion that I do want to see him,' Lola explained. 'I know I have these feelings for him and if I left without telling him, then I'd always wonder what could have happened. And after the amount of wine I drank last night, I thought it best not to set off until late afternoon, so here I am.'

'So how does any of that result in you being at Holly's house instead of over at Aidan's flat?' asked Carrie, confused.

'Well, I knew he'd be at work, so I decided to pop over to the shop first thing.'

'And?' Carrie questioned when Lola didn't elaborate.

'And he wasn't there, and while I was lingering in the shop pretending to be a customer, waiting to see if he'd appear from the back workshop, I overheard his colleagues say that he'd gone to the bank, and then he was going to Holly's... and now here I am like some kind of mad woman stalking him from afar.'

'You're not mad, a little erratic maybe, but that's just you,' Carrie joked. 'And what are you planning on doing now you're there?'

'Well, if I see him coming out smiling, or going in looking all loved up, I'll know the answer to my question, won't I? I'll know how he feels without even having to ask him.'

'It's not the best plan I've ever heard of,' Carrie grimaced.

Every time a car travelled down the road, Lola slouched on the bench or pretended to pick something up off the floor in an attempt to shield her face.

'Agreed, but I need to know, Carrie. I need to know if he still has feelings for her and if he's going to give her another chance.'

'How long are you going to wait?'

'Oh God, he's here,' Lola announced, her voice muffled as she tried to hide her face with her scarf. 'He's walking up the road.'

'Lola, just breathe. It sounds like you're about to pass out.'

Lola took a breath, trying to steady her nerves, her eyes going glossy.

'I really like him, Carrie. I've fallen in love with him, which is so crazy after such a short space of time, so utterly ridiculous, and the thought of getting my heart broken for the second time in nearly as many months is just too much to bear. But I can't help the way that I feel.'

'You're right, you can't blame yourself for falling in love, even if the timing could have been better.'

'He's walking up to the house, and now he's tapping on the

door,' she said, providing a running commentary on the unfolding scene. 'Is it a good sign that he's not using his key?' she asked before continuing to speak. 'I can tell he's nervous because he's fidgeting.'

'Are you sure you really want to see this?' Carrie asked.

'She's opening the door,' Lola blurted. 'Now they're hugging,' she cried in the same breath, her tears falling the moment that she watched the tender embrace. 'They're still hugging.'

'Lola, walk away, please, don't do this to yourself,' Carrie begged.

'They're going to get back together, aren't they?' she said, crying. 'I'm leaving. I can't watch this anymore.' Lola got up and turned her back, heading in the opposite direction. 'I'm on my way to yours to pick up the van,' she added. 'And then I'm leaving York, I'll be gone by the time you get home from work so I'll call you tonight,' she concluded, hanging up the phone.

Back down at the far end of Poets Nook, Aidan's body seized the moment Holly greeted him with an unexpected embrace, her arms gripping his body with such a sense of purpose that all he could do was stand still until she released him, refusing to reciprocate the affection.

'Why didn't you just use your key?' Holly whispered into Aidan's ear. 'This is still your home, *our* home,' she added, pulling herself away and indicating for him to follow her inside.

'Shall we sit in the lounge?' he asked upon entering, the house feeling strange as he peered around the space that had once felt like home. He noticed that Holly had hung some new pictures on the wall, photos that he had always loved.

'Yeah, perfect. Can I make you a coffee?' she replied.

'No, I'm alright, thanks.' Aidan strolled through to the lounge.

'So, how are you?' Holly asked, taking a seat on the sofa at the opposite end to Aidan, her foot outstretched. 'I've missed you,' she added with a cheeky smile.

Aidan's lips remained pressed tightly together, his eyes downcast. Just being back in the house stirred up his buried emotions, the room serving as a reminder of what he and Holly had once shared. His skin crawled as he wondered if Holly and Parker had been in the lounge that night, right where he was now sitting on the sofa.

'I was shocked when you sent me the message about the baby,' he announced.

'Shocked but happy, I hope?' she questioned, allowing her foot to drift further over to his side. 'Isn't this what you've always wanted?'

He released an uncontrollable moan. 'You're kidding me?' he muttered, shaking his head. 'This isn't at all what I wanted.'

The crease in the centre of his eyebrows became more prevalent and he found that he couldn't even look at her.

'I know I made a mistake, Aidan, but I still love you, and we can still make this relationship work. We can still be a family if you want.' Holly nudged herself further towards the centre of the sofa and took hold of his hand. 'I still love you and I know you love me, and our baby.'

For the first time, Aidan angled his head to meet her gaze, releasing his hand from her grip.

'Did you meet up with him again after that initial night?' he asked in a direct manner, momentarily deflecting all affection.

Shocked, Holly manoeuvred her body back to where she had been sitting at the other end of the sofa. 'I thought we'd moved on from all that. What does it matter?'

'It matters to me.'

Holly's hands slid loosely until they rested in her lap. 'It was just that one night,' she replied, looking down at her intertwined fingers.

'Really?' he quizzed, refusing to divert his gaze.

'Really.'

Aidan stood up and walked towards the window, his arms folded across his body.

'You're such a liar, it's like you can't stop.'

Holly sat up straight. 'What are you talking about?'

'I know he was here again the other week,' he laughed, rubbing his forehead.

'How do you know? Have you been spying on me?'

Aidan's voice adopted a tart tone. 'Don't flatter yourself, Holly,' he said, shaking his head. 'I've got better things to do with my life than follow you.'

'Nothing happened, we just talked.'

Aidan thrashed out his arms. 'That's not the point. Don't you get it? You're always lying, so how could you ever expect me to trust a single word that you say?'

'It's over. I promise you, it's over.'

'It's over because he ended it and chose to try and make it work with his wife. Isn't that what you mean? Isn't that the truth?'

'How do you know he was married?' she asked, the shock evident in her voice.

'It doesn't matter.'

'Have you met someone else?' she asked out of the blue, pangs of jealousy surging through her body. 'Someone I know saw you on Valentine's Day at the top of Franklin Hill.'

Aidan looked over at Holly. 'It's really no business of yours, or anyone else, for that matter, who I spend my time with,' he replied, turning back to face the window.

Through glossy eyes she looked up at Aidan and asked another question.

'What about the baby?'

Aidan took a prolonged breath in an attempt to steady his nerves.

'I've always wanted to be a dad, you know that more than anyone,' he began, trying to hold back his tears. Deep down, all he wanted to do was crouch on his knees and press his hands against Holly's stomach, savouring the feeling that he was finally, after so many years of longing, going to be a father.

Holly stood up and walked over to where he was standing in the window, placing her arms on his. 'We can make this work,' she said.

Aidan moved away and shunned the offer of affection.

'Is it mine?' the question landed like a bomb in the room. Holly's silence instantly shattered his heart. 'You're not even sure, are you?' he added, his face snarled. 'You're unbelievable, Holly.'

She turned and walked away, resting her body on the sofa.

'What were you going to do? Just pretend like it's mine and hope for the best, hope that I wouldn't put two and two together when the child is born and looks nothing like me?'

Holly's chin dropped to her chest. 'Because of what happened, I can't be sure, not 100% anyway, so I've done a test and now I'm waiting for the results.'

'And you didn't think to wait before you told me?'

'I want so badly for it to be yours, Aidan. I feel in my heart that it's yours,' she sobbed.

Aidan's eyes reddened and the pain that he was hiding inside broke through to the surface, a harsh grimace appearing on his face.

'I can't believe that I actually thought about giving this another go, because of the baby and how much I want to be a dad. What was I thinking?'

'I know you love me.'

Aidan turned to face the room. 'I did love you, Holly, so much that it hurt. But not anymore. I don't even like who you are anymore, I almost don't recognise you.'

Holly hid her face in a tissue, her tears uncontrollable. 'I can't do this without you, Aidan.'

'And I can't do this with you,' he was quick to add. 'I won't be second best for anyone, and I know deep down that's what I am to you, just the best of a bad situation.'

He walked towards the door, avoiding eye contact.

'Where are you going?' she asked, her voice raised and shaky.

He paused in the doorway, allowing his head to rest on the wood. 'I'm leaving, Holly,' he sighed. 'This was over the night you slept with someone else, it's as simple as that. There's no going back, not for me. I don't love you anymore,' he concluded, shrugging his shoulders.

Holly jumped out of her seat and scurried after him.

'What about the baby?' she shouted the moment she heard Aidan press the front door handle ready to leave. 'You can't walk out on me, on our baby.'

'If the baby does turn out to be mine, I'll fight for equal custody and I'll be the best father that I can be,' Aidan admitted. 'But until you know for certain, I can't even be in the same room as you.'

He pulled the door open and stepped outside, walking down Poets Nook without even a single glance back.

The sun shone brightly, the warmth comforting on Aidan's face and serving to dry out his skin where he had allowed his tears to fall. After days of grey, bleak skies, in Aidan's eyes, the sun finally shining through the mass of clouds felt symbolic. Without thought, he strode with purpose in the direction of Carrie's house. He'd walked past her driveway at least a handful of times over the previous few weeks, and had seen Lola's van parked up. But each time his nerves had gotten the better of him, and he'd walked away without knocking, not really knowing where to start, or what to say.

The moment he turned the corner and saw Carrie's driveway empty, his hopes scattered at the thought that he was too late. This time, he walked up to the house and rang the bell, stepping back and taking a breath.

'Hi,' said Carrie, opening the door.

'Hi, erm, is Lola here?' he asked.

She shook her head. 'No, she isn't,' replied Carrie, her bag over her shoulder having just walked through the door.

Aidan couldn't hide his disappointment, a sense of sadness evident in his eyes.

'Do you know when she'll be back?'

'She's left, Aidan. She's already left York.'

Unable to hide his feelings, Aidan lowered his head, unable to speak.

Carrie leaned against the doorframe. 'After what you told

her on Valentine's night, about Holly and the baby, she decided it was time to leave, go travelling like she'd been planning, and escape from York.'

A lump appeared in Aidan's throat as he listened, his limbs weak.

'She did want to see you before she left because there was something she wanted to tell you, so she went over to the shop, but someone told her that you'd gone to see Holly.'

Aidan looked up, defiant. 'I have been to see her, but to finish things, to let her know how I felt.'

Carrie shook her head. 'Lola was watching from afar. She saw the way that you and Holly were hugging, and made her own assumptions.'

'Holly did hug me, but I swear there was nothing more to it. She opened the door and flung her arms around me. Is that what she saw? Is that why she's left? Because she thought I was getting back together with Holly?'

Carrie nodded. 'Was she wrong to assume that you and Holly are back together?'

Aidan offered a slight nod while his head spun, his breath wheezing. Panic set in and he felt a tingling in his chest.

'I think I'm in love with Lola, Carrie,' he declared, allowing himself to voice his feelings aloud for the first time. 'I didn't think it was possible to love again so soon after everything that's happened, and I told myself not to rush in because I didn't want to risk her being hurt again. But I do love her, and I think I have since the day of the accident.' Aidan caught the look that appeared on Carrie's face. 'Why are you smiling?' he asked.

'Because she's in love with you, too.'

With a slow-burning smile, Aidan stood up straight and looked at Carrie.

'Then I need your help.'

42

'SHE STILL ISN'T HERE,' AIDAN SAID AS HE HEARD CARRIE ANSWER his call. 'I'm getting worried.'

Carrie checked her Find My Friends app to identify Lola's whereabouts. 'She's definitely still on her way, so unless she diverts or stops for a break, she should arrive there in about ten minutes.'

'And you definitely spoke to her last night, and she confirmed that she was still planning on staying here tonight?'

'Yes, and yes,' agreed Carrie, trying to recall the exact conversation from the previous evening. 'Have faith. She's been wanting to visit that place for so long now, so I very much doubt that she'll have a change of heart.'

'Okay, I'll keep you posted,' he concluded before hanging up. Aidan continued to linger at the main entrance to the campsite that Lola had frequented during her childhood summer holidays before her parents divorced, the rustic barn that had captured her heart now acting as Aidan's backdrop.

'Any sign of her yet?' asked Annie when she appeared.

'Nope, but Carrie thinks she'll be here within the next ten minutes. Is everything ready in there?' he asked, peering back into the barn.

'Yep, I think we're all set. You stay here and keep watch, and I'll go and double-check inside,' she suggested before heading into the building.

Aidan paced the veranda in front of the barn, nerves causing his limbs to bounce.

'Great, then all we can do is wait,' he mumbled to himself, trying to calm his nerves.

He ran through what he wanted to say to Lola, urging himself not to stumble over his words when the big moment finally arrived. White mist dissipated through the air the moment his warm breath collided with the cool, outdoor conditions, the rest of his body oblivious to the chilly temperature, adrenaline taking control of his senses. Over in the distance towards the main road, he saw the flicker of headlights as a vehicle approached. His heart raced and he found himself dancing on the spot, stretching up on his tiptoes to try and set eyes on the distinctive colours of Lola's van.

'I think she might be here!' he shouted, hoping that Annie would hear, himself reluctant to leave the spot. As the vehicle approached with care over the set of four speed bumps, Aidan squinted, his focus glued to the lights as the vehicle neared. After a couple of seconds, the approaching vehicle passed under a streetlamp and the distinctive colours of Lola's vintage van shone in Aidan's eyes.

'She's here!' he called out when the van came into view.

Annie appeared on the veranda.

'Right, you go inside and prepare yourself, and I'll take over out here,' she confirmed, smiling at Aidan as he disappeared inside.

Pulling her jacket up to her chin, Annie took hold of her cardboard signs and walked down the steps of the barn, waiting by the side of the road next to an old-fashioned lamp post. When Lola's van was nearly upon her, she held up the first sign that read: *Hi Lola…*

Once she had navigated the winding road leading up to the campsite, Lola spotted Annie standing in the distance, a sign held in her hands. She eased her foot off the accelerator and drew to a complete stop in front of where Annie was standing on the veranda. With a slight tremble to her hand, she wound the window down and read the words, *Hi Lola…* She immediately recognised Annie from Fudgy Nook, and a look of confusion soon appeared on Lola's face.

'Hi,' she said through the open window. 'What's going on?' she questioned, a moment of panic causing her composure to waver.

Without speaking, Annie held up another sign.

Aidan asked me for a bit of help...

'Okay,' Lola replied slowly, peering around to see if anybody else was about, the grounds deserted.

Annie held a third sign up for Lola to read. *Would you come and follow me?*

'What? Now?' Lola asked, unsure what was going on, her heart pounding from within her chest, and her mouth dry. Turning off the engine and unbuckling her seatbelt, Lola grabbed her coat and opened the door, closing it behind her. She took a moment to straighten out her hair, feeling a little dishevelled after the journey. 'I'm ready.'

Annie guided Lola towards the barn, stopping when they reached the front of the double doors. Annie took out another sign, allowing Lola to stop, and read.

Do you remember what you loved about this place when you were growing up?

Lola immediately nodded and smiled with a warming sense of sincerity. 'The bunting and the hay bales in the barn?' Annie put down the signs and turned to open the doors, allowing Lola to step inside.

'Oh, my goodness!' she gasped, looking around, her feet planted to the spot. Shock brought her hand to her mouth and she felt her muscles weakening as her legs began to wobble. Inside the dilapidated barn, Lola first saw rows and rows of bunting hanging from one side of the building to another, and strips of festoon lighting lining the perimeter, the twinkling lights shining in her retinas and causing her pupils to dilate.

'Go inside,' Annie whispered into Lola's ear, gently nudging her to take another step forwards.

Once she had entered the barn, she spotted Aidan at the far end, a backdrop of hay bales framing the quaint table he was standing beside. Her heart skipped and for a moment, life once again felt perfect, and safe.

'Hi,' she cried, producing a slight wave. Unable to control her outpour of emotions, Lola turned back around in disbelief, Annie's smile and hand gestures indicating for her to carry on walking.

Lola's tears fell as she made her way across the room in slow motion, her gaze focused on nothing but Aidan's broad, beaming smile. She wiped her face with the back of her hand, her lips moist with tears.

'This is what I'd have planned had I known that we were going to be spending Valentine's night together,' he began, wrapping his arms around her and kissing her on the cheek. 'Will you be my date tonight?' he asked, pulling out a chair so that she could take a seat at the candlelit table.

Still revelling from their embrace and feeling lightheaded from the comforting aroma of his familiar aftershave, Lola smiled and took a seat.

'I'd love to be your date.'

Taking in her surroundings, she peered around the barn, a smile beaming from her face.

'I'm in shock,' she confessed, still trying to fathom how such a big surprise had been planned without her knowing. With a sense of déjà vu, Lola peered around the barn and it was like she had momentarily stepped back in time, witnessing the architectural features through her childhood eyes.

'You remembered our very first conversation?'

Aidan nodded. 'We spoke about travelling because I saw you looking at a map on your phone, and you told me about this place and how you'd loved it as a child, and if you could go anywhere in the world, this place would be top of the list.'

Lola looked puzzled. 'But how did you know where I was? How did you know that I would even turn up?'

'I had a little help from Carrie.'

Lola shook her head and grinned. 'I spoke to her last night and she was asking about what I was going to do tonight. She knew about this all along?'

'Yep.'

'Are we the only ones here?' she asked, peering around.

'There are other people on the site, as far as I know, but I've hired out this whole place just for the two of us tonight,' he said, looking around and admiring his work.

Lola turned back and, with a coy expression, looked Aidan in the eye. 'I'm a little confused,' she revealed. 'I mean this is all very lovely, and I'm thrilled to see you, but I saw you with–'

Aidan lowered his head and finished her sentence. 'You saw me at Holly's.'

Lola nodded, her restless legs tapping beneath the table. 'You were hugging her, and you both looked really happy, so I assumed–'

Aidan shook his head and interrupted. 'It wasn't like that, not at all,' he began. 'I just went there to talk to her about the baby, and when she opened the door, she hugged me like nothing had happened, like we were still a couple, and it took me by surprise,' he explained. 'But we're not together, and we never will be,' he added. 'I don't love her anymore. If the baby does turn out to be mine, then I'll be the best parent that I can be, but that's it.'

Lola processed what he'd just said, shaking her head from side to side.

'What, so the baby might not even be yours?'

Aidan looked down in an attempt to hide his tumbling emotions. 'She's taken a paternity test and is just waiting on the results,' he said, looking back up when he'd finished his sentence.

'So, the father of Holly's baby could be Parker, is that what she's implying?'

Aidan nodded, hoping that by confirming the answer to her question with an action rather than a word, it would somehow make his answer less hurtful.

Lola sat up in her seat and took a sharp intake of breath. 'Well, it looks like the accident really did happen for a reason. It made me miscarry. Otherwise Parker could have had two women pregnant at the same time. Imagine that.'

'I didn't know you were pregnant?'

'Only the early stages, but it wasn't meant to be, and now I know why.'

'Can we promise something to each other?' Aidan began to ask. 'Can we promise that we won't speak about Holly or Parker for the rest of the night?'

He unscrewed the cap on the chilled bottle of wine and poured them both a glass before raising his to make a toast.

'Cheers.'

'Sounds good to me – cheers,' Lola replied. 'Have you done all this for me?' she asked, blushing to a level that she couldn't control.

Aidan nodded, taking a sip of his drink to try and conceal his own speckles of shyness.

'Why?' she questioned, her heart needing to hear the words from his mouth.

Aidan put his drink down and took a breath.

'From the day of the accident, I knew that I had feelings for you, and I haven't been able to stop thinking about you ever since,' he began, maintaining eye contact and reaching over to take hold of her hand. 'And I know that both of our lives are a bit messy right now, and that all this has happened in a bit of an odd way, but I like you, Lola, and I love spending time with you.' He kept his hand outstretched, hoping that she would take hold of his.

'I don't regret anything that happened that morning, or any of the crazy stuff that happened in the lead-up to the accident, because it all meant that I met you,' she said, her voice cracking with emotion. 'And I really like you too,' she concluded, leaning forwards, taking hold of his hand and maintaining eye contact, her lips parting to reveal a broad smile.

Aidan relished the moment of physical contact. 'So, what happens now?'

'What do you mean?'

'Well,' he began, 'the big question is, where's your life going to be? You've got all your belongings packed into the back of the van and you've left York to go and travel the world.'

She smiled. 'I was running away from York because of everything that had happened,' she explained with a shrug. 'But, if you'd like me to stick around so that we can get to know one another, then that sounds more tempting than sleeping in a cold van by myself.'

Aidan smiled like he hadn't done in a long time, his cheeks aching with happiness. 'I was hoping that you'd say that.'

At that moment, Annie walked into the barn carrying two pizza boxes like she was a waitress about to serve a fancy restaurant meal.

'I have two pizzas for you,' she announced, placing them on the table. 'I'll leave you two to eat and I'll get going now, if there's nothing else you need help with?' she asked, looking at Aidan.

'You get going, and thanks again for all your help, Annie. I couldn't have done any of this without you.'

'I'm starving, are you?' Lola asked when Annie walked away, taking a slice and savouring the warm pizza.

'Once we've had this, I have one other surprise for you,' Aidan responded.

'More surprises? I don't know how you're going to top this,' she said, admiring the barn. 'This place has so many special memories. There used to be a stage over there,' she explained, pointing to the far end. 'And on Friday and Saturday nights, there would be a band playing and my parents would let me have a late night so that I could watch it.'

'Whereabouts did you stay?'

'It was over on the far side of the lake. There used to be a little play area and our caravan was parked right next to the swings.'

'No wonder you have so many great memories,' Aidan remarked. 'But why haven't you ever come back here? It's not like it's a million miles away.'

Lola rolled her eyes. 'Because Parker was never keen on spending our summer holidays here in the UK. He preferred the all-inclusive beach type of holiday, my nostalgic memories of this little lake didn't compare.'

'I haven't really had time to look at the lake – should we go and check it out?' he asked once they'd had enough to eat. 'I'm not sure how much we'll see with it being dark though.'

Lola finished her drink and pushed her chair back. 'The lake was always the best part for me because it provided endless hours of fun, everything a child could need,' she explained, getting to her feet. 'I just hope that you can see it in the dark, I don't know if they light it up during the winter months.'

Aidan and Lola walked the length of the barn, their shoulders touching. Lola allowed her hand to dangle, a smile appearing on her face when Aidan took hold of it, wrapping his fingers around hers.

'After you,' he said once they reached the door, holding it ajar for her.

'Shall I just leave the van here?'

'Yeah, we won't be long,' he said, leading Lola down towards the lake.

The pebble path that stretched from the barn to the lake was only lit by the flickering light emanating from the barn, the walk getting darker as they navigated their way down.

'It seems pretty quiet,' she commented, spotting only a few tents pitched up alongside a handful of vans. She then looked out towards the lake. 'Okay, so I admit it, it doesn't look much now,' she explained when they reached the end of the path, the lake before them appearing dismal beneath the cloudy, sombre sky. Despite the stark contrast to how she had remembered the lake from her childhood, in her mind, Lola could still picture herself swimming in the lake as a child, recalling how cold the water had felt against her skin, and how cut blades of grass had stuck to her feet each time she had made a dash back to her family caravan.

Aidan took out his phone and unlocked the screen. 'Are you ready?' he asked, turning to face Lola.

'Ready for what?' she asked.

'Watch this,' he said, indicating towards the distance. After a few seconds, the entire circumference of the lake became illuminated with festoon lighting, the bulbs hanging from tree to tree, acting as a crown.

Aidan turned to look at Lola, the brightness of the lights reflecting in her eyes, a slow look of amazement spreading across her face.

Lola couldn't draw her attention away from the lake, another feeling of déjà vu overwhelming her mind, more images of her childhood flashing like bolts.

'Did you do all this too?' she asked without turning her head.

'I wanted it to be special for you, and for it to live up to all your memories,' he explained. 'This was the beginning of your adventures in the van, and I wanted it to be amazing so that you'd want to continue travelling, hopefully with me.'

It took a few minutes for the words to register in Lola's mind and when they finally did, she turned her head. 'Did you say travelling, with you?'

Aidan's face seemed to shine, and he maintained strong eye contact, holding his breath.

'I was hoping that maybe you'd come to France with me,' he began, a sense of cautious hope audible in his voice. 'I have to go and sort out the inheritance stuff from my auntie's will, and I thought that maybe you'd want to come with me.' His feet wriggled on the spot and he held his body still in expectation while he waited for her reply.

Lola let go of Aidan's hand and looked out towards the lake. 'France?' she questioned.

Aidan nodded and held his breath, preparing himself for a rejection that would hurt more than he was willing to admit. He watched Lola's face, the smile that had been evident all evening slowly falling from her lips.

'I understand if you're not too sure about the idea,' he replied when Lola remained silent.

She turned to look at Aidan, her smile soon returning. 'I think I'd follow you just about anywhere,' she beamed.

Aidan exhaled, taking a brief glance towards the stars. 'I thought for a moment you were going to say no,' he confessed, before turning back to look in her eyes. 'Really? You'll come with me?' he asked again.

Her radiant smile confirmed her answer. 'But I won't drive us there, not in the van, or any other type of road vehicle. Maybe we'll fly instead,' she laughed. 'I know I've only done one night so far, but this life on the road isn't all it's made up to be.'

Aidan stepped closer and pressed his hands to either side of Lola's face, delivering a gentle, first kiss to her lips. 'I love you, Lola,' he declared in the moment. 'I know it's soon, and I know we've only known each other for a few months, and I know that I'm recently separated, and yet despite all of that, I know that I love you, and I have done ever since we met on Christmas Eve.'

Without pausing for a breath, she replied. 'I love you, too,' she whispered, allowing her head to rest on his chest, their warm breath escaping into the cool air. 'And I'm not just saying it because you have. I'm just telling you the truth about how I feel, something I've wanted to do for so long.'

Looking out across the lake, Aidan and Lola remained in their embrace, neither one wanting to be the first to let go.

'Where are you staying tonight?' she asked, looking out over the water, the glow from the moon reflecting on the surface.

'Annie booked me one of the caravans for a night. I'm not sure which one it is though,' he replied, trying to recall which pitch number she had confirmed earlier on in the day.

Lola remained still, her voice almost a whisper. 'Will you come and stay in the van with me tonight?' she asked, her gaze still cast out across the lake.

'I'll stay with you forever, if you'll let me.'

43

THE TRAY OF BROWNIES THAT CARRIE WAS HOLDING SLIPPED OUT of her hands, The Brownie Box floor becoming covered in fragments of chocolate.

'What do you mean you're in France?'

Lola stood back and watched Aidan at the luggage conveyor belt, his body language indicating that maybe their bags hadn't made the trip.

'I'm here with Aidan,' she replied.

'What? When? I only spoke to you yesterday and you didn't mention anything about going to France.'

'It was a last-minute thing. We found some cheap cancellation flights, so decided to just do it.' Lola's smile hadn't faded for over two days while she and Aidan had remained tucked away at the campsite.

Carrie sat herself down and looked out across The Shambles before peering over to the corner of the van, smiling to herself at the sight of Lola's empty stool.

'I can almost see your smile from here in York,' she said. 'You sound so happy.'

'I really am, Carrie,' she began to gush. 'But it's like he's almost too perfect and I feel like I'm waiting for the punchline to hit me, you know, the part where I find out he's been married ten times or has a string of children somewhere.'

The sound of Carrie's sigh travelled down the phone.

'Your husband cheated on you, twice. You were in a serious car accident and you could have died, and now you've fallen in love with the man that helped to save your life. I think you've had all the punchlines possible,' she laughed. 'You just need to allow yourself to be happy. Be in love and see what life has to offer outside of this van, outside of York. Aidan is different to Parker, I just know he is.'

'I miss you,' Lola whispered.

Carrie turned to look at the photo of them both that was pinned to the back of the van, taken the very first day that they had opened up The Brownie Box.

'I miss you too but it's not like we're never going to see each other again. You're just on holiday, that's what I'm telling myself at the moment. Anyway, forget about me, what on earth are you doing in France?'

Lola continued to watch Aidan as he attempted to communicate with the French airport staff, gesticulating with his hands as the conversation unfolded.

'It's to do with Aidan's auntie who I told you about, the one whose ashes we scattered the other week. Anyway, this auntie has left something to him in her will. So, we're here so that Aidan can meet with the solicitor and sort out all the paperwork and legal stuff.'

'Sounds exciting. There could be a lovely little French gite waiting for him,' Carrie romanticised.

Lola made a noise to indicate the contrary. 'Unlikely, from what he's told me,' she explained. 'Aidan has said that his Auntie Alice hated him, literally resented the fact that he'd been born, and when his mum passed away, she refused to look after him – his only family – I mean, what kind of human being does that?'

'Yeah, maybe not so exciting then. So, what's the plan?' Carrie asked.

'We'll stay here for a few days so that he can sort this stuff out, and then we'll be coming home.'

'What? Really? Coming home to York?'

'Yep, I was only going travelling because, well, I wanted to get away from Parker, away from all the reminders, but now—'

'Now?' Carrie added when Lola didn't finish her sentence.

Lola gazed at Aidan, who was now walking towards her with a cross expression wedged on his face. 'Now I can see a future with Aidan, so why would I run away from that? He needs to be in York because of the business, so therefore I want to be in York, too.'

'And what about our business?'

'We pick up where we left off, if you're still happy with that? Maybe we could develop our product range, like you've been suggesting for ages.'

'Of course, I'm happy with that, and I'd love for us to try something new,' Carrie jumped in with excitement, her face lighting up at the prospect.

Lola spotted Aidan approaching. 'Great. Anyway, I best get going. I think we're about to leave so I'll speak to you soon.'

'Okay, keep in touch, and stay safe,' replied Carrie before hanging up.

'I'm guessing that we have no luggage?' Lola laughed, trying to make light of the situation. She took hold of his hand and smiled, her reassuring act of affection immediately suppressing Aidan's frustration.

'They're clueless,' he began, shaking his head with annoyance. 'All they know is that our luggage isn't here, it's not even in France. At their best guess, our case is on its way to Rhodes.'

'So, let's get going and we'll just buy a change of clothes to last us a couple of days, and if we do end up being a little stinky, nobody knows us here anyway,' she laughed, taking hold of his other hand. 'I'll put up with your smelliness if you'll put up with mine.'

She stood on tiptoes and kissed him on the lips, christening their first public display of affection.

Aidan released an appreciative sigh. 'You're amazing,' he beamed. 'Let's get going,' he added, leading her towards the exit.

'The sooner I get this stuff sorted, the sooner we can go home and–'

'And?' Lola asked.

'The sooner I can introduce you to everyone at home as my girlfriend, if that's okay with you?' he smiled.

Lola walked closer to Aidan so that their arms were pressed against each other, and she squeezed his hand, her free arm stretching out across his body.

'I'd love to be introduced as your girlfriend.'

The automatic doors to the airport swung open, permitting them to step outside.

'Blimey,' Aidan choked as the heat from the early March sun beamed onto his face. 'I'm not sure we'll need our coats,' he said, opening the taxi door to allow Lola to climb in first.

She unzipped her jacket. 'Well, this is nice,' she relished, tilting her head towards the sky before getting into the car. 'I think this is called sunshine,' she added, savouring the comforting feeling on her skin. 'Should your business take a little longer than a couple of days to sort, then that's absolutely fine with me,' she concluded, buckling in her seatbelt.

'Collonges-la-Rouge, s'il vous plait,' Aidan attempted his best French.

Lola raised her eyebrows at his impressive attempt at the accent. 'Nice! Do you actually speak French?'

'Nope, but I can do a good fake accent.'

'How are you going to get on with the solicitor?'

'I'm told I'll be meeting with someone who is fluent in English, thankfully.'

The journey to Collonges-la-Rouge was about a half-hour drive from Brive-Souillac airport, and Lola spent it trying her best to take in the French countryside as it whizzed past her window. As she peered out in a daze, her eyes drank in the sight of all the fields that were growing an abundance of sunflowers, the vibrancy encouraging her to smile in a way that reflected her inner state of happiness.

'Are you nervous?' she asked, turning to look at Aidan and

noticing that his hands were fidgeting in his lap.

'I just want it sorted now, and to deal with whatever it is that Alice has left me.'

Lola adored the way that Aidan fiddled with his hair when he was nervous, something she'd noticed during their first night together at the campsite.

'I'm here, so we can face it together,' she reassured him, pressing her hand against his leg. The further away from the airport they travelled, the more remote the landscape became, with uninterrupted views of lush green fields and vineries in every direction.

'It's amazing, isn't it?' she commented, her eyes still drawn to the views, secluded villages sunken into the mountainous backdrop. 'I haven't even got out of the car yet, and already I don't want to leave.'

'Should we run away and never go home?' he asked in a manner that didn't reflect he was joking.

'Don't tempt me,' she replied. 'So, where are you meeting the solicitor?'

Aidan opened up his emails. 'Apparently he'll be at a café called La Bonte at 1 o'clock today.'

Lola gazed out of her window again, her eyes drinking in the scenic view that felt typically French, boulangeries brimming with baskets of freshly baked baguettes in every village they passed.

'Well, at least it's not in some stuffy office.'

In the distance, a muddle of red rooftops poked out from the green foliage. The winding road down enabled Lola to admire the quaint, French villages, looking exactly how she'd pictured them in her mind.

'Collonges-la-Rouge?' she said to the taxi driver, pointing to the village.

'Oui, madame.'

Lola rested her head on the glass, relishing the feeling of being hundreds of miles away from home, and finding herself in what looked like a little patch of paradise.

Aidan squeezed her hand. 'Are you okay?'

'I was just thinking how grateful I am to be here, with you. And I know the circumstances aren't the best, but it beats travelling alone up the A1 on a dark, wet, miserable British day.'

The taxi driver slowed down before pulling up beside a sign that welcomed them to Collonges-la-Rouge.

'Merci,' he replied when Aidan paid the fee.

Lola swung her hand luggage over her shoulder and took a moment to take in her surroundings when she got out of the car.

'Are you sure we're in the right place?' she asked, watching the taxi drive away, the battered car soon disappearing into the fields. 'It doesn't look like there's anybody here.'

Aidan took a glance at his watch. 'It's only just coming up to one o'clock, so maybe people are still on lunch. Isn't that a thing here, where nothing happens during lunchtimes?'

'Have you got any directions for the cafe?' she asked, looking around to see if she could spot any signs.

'No, which means this place can't be very big. Let's head this way,' suggested Aidan, taking hold of Lola's hand and guiding her into what looked like the centre of the village.

'Do you think we stand out as tourists?' she laughed. 'It feels like the kind of place where everybody will know everybody else's business.'

Down a winding cobbled path, in the distance, Aidan spotted a sign for the café.

'There it is,' he announced. 'Let's hope everything pans out just as easily.'

As they strolled into the heart of the village, Lola could sense Aidan's nerves, his palm sweaty. The pair stopped outside the café and peered inside, spotting only two people seated.

'I'll go and have a mooch if you like, while you have the meeting,' she suggested, 'and I'll try and get us something to eat, though I'm not promising anything because apart from hello and goodbye, my French is pretty much non-existent.'

'Okay. Hopefully I won't be long, but I'll text you once it's done.' Aidan kissed Lola on the lips, reluctant to let her hand go.

'I'm here for you, remember,' she reassured him, before Aidan turned and walked into the café. Within a few seconds, a smart-looking man carrying bundles of paperwork appeared from out of a side street and entered the café, walking straight past Lola. She turned and peered back through the window, giving Aidan the thumbs up before setting off down the street.

Within only a few minutes of meandering the cobbled streets of Collonges-la-Rouge, the burdens that had been weighing down on her shoulders floated away like the scattered parts of a dandelion clock, and she lost herself in the beauty of the village.

'Guess what?' she began when Carrie picked up her phone.

'Aidan's asked you to marry him,' she replied without thought.

Lola laughed and shook her head. 'Er, no,' she was quick to correct. 'Given that I'm technically still married, and I've only known Aidan for three months or so, I think we're a little way off marriage proposals, at least I hope so anyway.'

'So, what's going on then? Where are you now?'

'We've just arrived in this village called Collonges-la-Rouge and I kid you not, it's the French equivalent of The Shambles, only prettier, warmer, and without all the noise pollution,' Lola said excitedly, the enthusiasm in her voice spilling through her words. She arched her head as she strolled through the narrow, winding streets, each as picturesque as the previous. 'All the buildings are even more higgledy-piggledy than they are back home, and they're made from red sandstone. It's just so pretty, unlike anything I've ever seen before.'

Lola admired the way that all the houses boasted charming balconies and stretching, vibrant vines that snaked the length of the brickwork, creating a type of jewellery from the foliage.

'There are hidden courtyards with little eateries everywhere,' she boasted.

'I bet our coffee is better though,' Carrie interrupted.

'The smell of baking pastries and bread just lingers down each street, and there's not a Costa or Tesco Extra in sight,' she explained, her head turning from side to side as she walked, trying to take in everything as she passed. 'All the shops are selling local handmade crafts, and they put the artwork and textiles in the street. You just couldn't do that in York because someone would be off with it,' she laughed. 'There's such an artisan vibe and The Brownie Box would fit in perfectly,' she added.

Carrie peered out from The Brownie Box hatch, the sky heavy with clouds making it appear that the day was losing light before the sun had even made an appearance.

'Well, you've sold it to me already. I'll get on a plane and come and join you, I'm sure Aidan wouldn't mind. I could do with a holiday right now.'

'He's just in with the solicitor, and I'm a bit nervous, to be honest. He's no idea what's going to happen, but dare I say it, if she's left him anything here, I can't imagine it being a ruin. The properties and scenery are lovely — postcard-worthy, in my opinion.'

'At least you're there with him. I take it things are going well between the two of you?'

Lola couldn't hide her warm smile. 'It's amazing, Carrie. He's amazing. I thought I was happy with Parker, but compared to this, I've realised that I was never *really* happy with Parker, I was just settling, thinking that it was as good as it was going to get, as good as I deserved.'

Lola admired the collection of terracotta pots decorating the streets, each one brimming with scents of summer. In the distance, a low-lying archway framed a cluster of slated turrets, the peaks stretching above the rest of the village rooftops.

'It sounds like a dream, and I'm very jealous. Anyway, I best get going, I've got customers. Take care of yourself.'

'Speak to you soon,' Lola concluded before hanging up.

Beneath the warmth of the sun, she ventured into one of the bakeries, her nerves following her in.

'Bonjour,' she said in a quiet voice. The lady behind the counter smiled and began speaking, the only word Lola could pick out was *hello*. With flushed cheeks, Lola pointed to one of the trays of pastries.

'How many?' the lady asked with a smile.

Relief flooded over Lola's face when she realised the lady spoke English.

'Oh, two please. Thank you so much.'

Just as she was paying, her phone buzzed.

'Au revoir,' she said, before walking outside and heading back in the direction she'd left Aidan. His message indicated that the meeting was already over. Having not been paying attention, all the streets looked the same, and she couldn't recall the direction she'd come from. Panicked, she recalled the prettiness of the slated turrets and so arched her head, hoping to use them as a point of reference, and upon spotting the peaked buildings, turned and began heading in the right direction, her feet soon blistering beneath the soaring temperatures.

'Hi, how did it go?' she asked when she spotted Aidan sitting on the bench opposite the café. 'Are you okay? I thought it'd take much longer?' she added, witnessing the expression on his face and the ghostly appearance of his complexion. Taking a seat next to him, she rested her hand on his leg. 'What is it?'

Aidan looked up, a glossiness clouding his vision. 'I've got the keys,' he began, opening his palm to reveal two brass keys.

Lola placed her bags down and rubbed her forehead, the heat of the midday sun catching her off guard.

'Right, and what else did he say about it all? Do you know where it is, or even what it is?'

Nodding his head, Aidan looked to his right at the little corner shop only a handful of metres away.

'Alice has left me that.'

Lola looked in the same direction, following Aidan's gaze until her eyes rested on a quaint sweet shop, packets of fudge and other sugary treats on display in the window.

The pair kept looking at the entrance to the shop, people bobbing in and out all the while.

'What? She's left you that shop in her will?' Lola questioned, her face reflecting her state of confusion.

Aidan nodded slowly. 'But there's more,' he revealed, peering a little further down the street to the house that was attached to the shop. Two turret towers sat either side of a central, circular slated roof, and a handful of steps led up to the front door.

Lola followed Aidan's gaze again and then looked back at him in disbelief.

'What, she's left you the house too?'

All Aidan could do was nod his head, the enormity of the situation stealing his words.

Lola dragged her attention away from the house and looked back at Aidan.

'I don't understand. All you've ever told me about Alice is that she hated you, and your mum, and that she refused to have anything to do with you.'

Lowering his head, Aidan took a few shallow breaths, his voice quiet.

'She never had anything to do with me, or my mum.'

'Then why would she leave you all this?' she asked, admiring the turrets that she'd described down the phone to Carrie. 'It doesn't make any sense.'

'That's not all,' he added. 'My Auntie Alice had a daughter, which means that I have a cousin,' he declared in one quick breath, his mind still trying to process the information. Aidan wiped his arm across his face, taking with it his sadness and tears of disbelief. He turned to look at Lola, a smile of sincerity shining through his upset.

'I have family that, all this time, I didn't even know about.'

44

'Y OU CAN DO THIS,' ENCOURAGED MARIE, STANDING BY MATTY'S side and giving him a gentle nudge as she stepped out onto The Shambles. Matty retreated back to the safety of his door, stepping back inside the flat and lowering his head.

'I just don't know what I'll say,' he replied, his hands shaking.

'We've talked about this, and the good thing is that you don't really have to say anything, do you?' Marie encouraged, indicating for Matty to follow her outside. 'You just walk in and say that you've bought a gift, and if that's all you can muster, the present will tell him the rest,' Marie smiled. 'So, come on, let's go. I'll be by your side to fill any awkward gaps in conversation.'

Matty looked across the street and took in a deep breath.

'But what if–' he stalled, not really knowing how to finish his sentence.

'If it all goes wrong,' she began, knowing what Matty was alluding to, 'then at least you'll know where you stand, and then you can move on with your life knowing that you tried your best to make things right.'

Matty stepped out onto the cobbles, The Shambles bustling with activity, the Yorkshire fair weather enticing people out of their homes to shop and mingle.

'And you'll come with me?' he asked.

'I'm right here,' Marie reassured him.

Weaving their way across the street, Matty stepped through

the door to Fudgy Nook.

'Hi, Matty,' Annie greeted. 'It's been a while since we've seen you in here,' she said, a broad smile beaming from her face. 'How are you?'

Marie nudged Matty in the back when he hesitated. 'I'm good, thanks. I've just been a bit busy lately.'

'Well, that's good to hear. Aidan and I were actually getting worried about you.'

'Really?' he questioned.

'Yeah. It was actually Aidan who mentioned that he hadn't seen you in a while, and he was getting a bit concerned. He even went over to your flat to make sure that you were okay, but you must have been out. I told him not to worry, but that's just Aidan,' she smiled. 'Some of our regulars are much more than just customers, and you're one of them.'

Marie looked up at Matty, knowing what Annie's words would have meant to him. She placed her arm around his back, sensing that his composure had been rattled.

'Anyway, what can I get for you today?' asked Annie. 'We have some new flavours to try, if you're interested?'

Matty took a moment before replying, his gaze darting to see if he could spot Aidan in the back workshop.

'Erm, I was actually just hoping to see Aidan. Is he here?'

Annie shook her head. 'No, he's not. I'm sorry.'

Marie spotted the disappointment in Matty's eyes, so she gave his hand a gentle squeeze of reassurance.

'Do you know when he'll be back?' Matty asked.

'He's in France, a last-minute trip, so I'm not really sure when he's planning on returning. I don't think he mentioned that on the phone when I last spoke to him. Hopefully he'll be back before we run out of stock!' she joked. 'Is there something that I can help you with?'

Matty looked at Marie for support and guidance.

'Could you just pass him this when he returns? I've been

meaning to give it to him for some time, but with one thing or another, it just slipped my mind,' he explained, reaching out and placing the brown gift bag on the counter.

'Sure, no problem at all. When he gets back, he'll come here first, I suspect, just to check everything is okay. So, I'll leave it behind the counter and then he'll be sure to see it,' she explained, taking hold of the bag and placing it on the desk behind the counter.

'Thanks, see you soon,' he said, before turning to walk away.

Outside on the cobbles, Marie turned to Matty and congratulated him.

'See, I told you you could do it!' she said with a reassuring smile. 'You've placed the ball in his court so there's nothing more you can do, at least not until he returns.' Marie took a look at her watch. 'Is it too early for a drink?' she asked, her eyebrows raised. 'I think we deserve one, don't you?'

Matty arched out his arm so that she could form a link. 'No, I think we deserve a couple,' he proclaimed, leading her down The Shambles. 'And I know the perfect pub,' he concluded, a lightness evident in his stride for the first time in years.

45

STRIPPING DOWN TO NOTHING BUT HER UNDERWEAR, LOLA LEFT her clothes scattered across the floor and grabbed her bath towel before walking into the living room of the holiday home where she and Aidan were staying.

'Once you leave, I'm going to have a shower and try to cool down, my feet are crippled after so much walking,' she moaned, inspecting the blisters on her ankles. 'But the pain has been worth it. Spending all day wandering around this incredible village with you has been amazing, today has been amazing full-stop,' she boasted, wrapping her arms around Aidan's torso. 'Waking up next to you this morning and then looking out to this view,' she explained, indicating towards the vibrant landscape that stretched beyond the window. 'I mean, how perfect is life right now?' she gushed, feeling the warmth of the afternoon sun as it rested on her face, the French air rejuvenating the zest for life that in recent months, Lola felt she had been missing. 'I haven't felt this much at peace in such a long time,' she added, staring deep into Aidan's eyes like she was looking at him for the very first time. 'York, the accident, St Jude's, it all feels like a lifetime ago now that we're here.' She gazed out the window again and rested her hand on the ledge, peering down at the locals who were meandering the winding streets, carrying baskets of fresh produce purchased from the outdoor market.

He pulled her back and placed his hands at either side of her face, delivering her a tender kiss to her lips. 'Let's pretend that nobody else exists and then I can stay here with you all night,' Aidan mused.

Sensing his nerves, she sat him down on the sofa, her smile broadening.

'It'll be fine, she'll be fine,' she encouraged. 'All you need to do is go and meet with this cousin of yours, introduce yourself, and then the rest will all fall into place,' she said, placing a kiss on his soft lips. 'And I'll be here waiting for you when you get back.'

Aidan peered across the room at the clock, noticing that it was time he should be leaving. 'I know, it's just a lot to take in. I mean, what if she hates me?' he asked, standing up and walking towards the window, opening it wide in the hope that the cool, late afternoon breeze would lower his rising temperature. 'What if she hates me because, for reasons that I don't understand, her own mum has left everything to me? I mean, it's not great news for her, is it? I think I'd have a bit of resentment if the roles were reversed.'

He stuck his head out of the window, trying to capture any snippets of freshness making their way through the humidity.

Lola went and grabbed a chilled bottle of water out of the fridge, handing it to Aidan.

'I need you to be strong,' she began. 'Isn't that what your mum told you? Isn't that what you told me?' Dipping her head, she encouraged him to look her in the eye. 'So, I need you to take a breath, be strong, and go and meet with this woman. Otherwise, you'll always regret it. If you hide behind lawyers and solicitors to work all of this out, you'll never forgive yourself. She'll have a story to tell you, Aidan, her story, and you need to hear it, no matter what it is.'

She went and sat back down, putting her feet up to ease the throbbing.

'You've always wanted a family, haven't you? Well, now you have it. And you know what they say – you can't pick and choose.'

Aidan maintained eye contact, his expression softening as he gazed. He crouched down by her side, laughing internally at her mismatched selection of underwear.

'Why are you so amazing?' he replied. 'You're caring, you're funny and you're gorgeous, even in your faded blue knickers and grey bra,' he added, kissing her slowly. 'I've loved exploring with you today,' he explained. 'It's just been the two of us, no ghosts from home following us around, and it's been the perfect way to take my mind off tonight.'

'This is just the start of our adventures,' she began. 'The accident and all the stuff that happened in York was just a warm-up, we were just trying each other on for size, and guess what?' she smiled. 'We're a perfect fit.'

He kissed her like he meant it, like it was their first time, and last time.

'Thank you for being everything I expected, and more.'

He stood up and walked towards the door.

'Right, I'm going to go. I'll be back as soon as I can.'

Outside on the street, Aidan noted that the cafés and shops were showing signs of closing. He paced towards the heart of the village, his feet feeling heavy, his legs sluggish. In the pit of his stomach, a churning sensation served to rattle his composure and the thought crossed his mind to turn back and give himself more time to think of what to say, but in the distance, he saw the shop come into view, the sign above swaying in the breeze.

The street was pretty quiet, the hustle from the day showing signs of subsiding as the sun began to set. His mouth felt dry, and he couldn't recall ever feeling quite so nervous. With Lola's words of encouragement still fresh in his mind, he took a few more paces and then stepped through the shop door.

'Hello?' he announced, a bell above the door jingling when he entered.

Inside the snug interior, all the walls were clad with rustic, wooden shelving units that displayed rows of Victorian-style glass sweet jars, each brimming with various flavours of fudge. The floor was finished with traditional tiles, and there were wicker baskets dotted around, all boasting bags of beautifully wrapped fudge. In the air, the smell of sugar drifted in invisible trails, and on the countertop, a large stash of brown paper bags sat next to an old-fashioned pair of weighing scales that looked well worn.

'Bonjour,' a female voice called, a lady appearing from out of a back room.

The moment the woman appeared, Aidan recognised her and froze, all his thoughts blowing away with the warm, incoming breeze.

'Hi, Aidan,' she added with an English accent, resting her back against the wall.

'It's you,' he replied, recognising her from the bridge in York, the day that he had scattered Alice's ashes.

'It's me,' she repeated with a smile. 'My name is Faye, I'm Alice's daughter.'

Overcome with emotion, Aidan wanted to give Faye a hug, and yet all he could do was stand still and stare.

'I'm not sure what to say,' he announced after a few seconds of silence.

'Let me close up and we can go and have a chat, if that's alright with you?'

Aidan nodded. 'Sure, I'll go and wait outside for you.'

Faye took off her apron before turning off the lights and locking the door. 'Shall we go and sit on a bench?' she suggested, pointing towards the far end of the street where there was a vacant seat under a tree.

'This is all a bit of a shock to me, so I apologise if I seem a bit dazed.'

'Don't worry, I understand. I've had a bit of time to digest all of this, it hasn't just been thrown on me like it has with you.'

The pair sat beneath one of the many trees dotting a secluded courtyard, the bench wrapping around the tree, offering maximum shade from the sun that was still shining.

'So, you've known about me for some time?' Aidan asked.

'Well, no, not really,' Faye replied. 'About six months ago, when my mum became really ill, she told me everything at that point.' Faye took a deep breath and looked up towards the azure sky, her heart still learning how to deal with the loss of her mum. 'For most of my life it's just been me and my mum, and now I have you,' she added, turning to Aidan and smiling.

'And I have you,' he smiled in reciprocation. When he looked at Faye, he saw similarities between her and his own mum; the shape of their face, the fullness of their lips, and the dark, bouncy nature of their hair. 'You remind me of my mum so much, the way you smile, it's just like her,' he added. 'I guess with our mothers being twins you were bound to remind me of Mum in some way, I just never even thought about that.'

'I've seen photos of them both, of my mum and your mum, and even though they weren't identical, they looked so similar. I guess I inherited their features, too.'

Aidan lowered his head. 'None of this makes any sense,' he added, his brain starting to function with clarity, all his questions and concerns coming to the forefront of his mind. 'I feel so terrible for what I'm about to say, but I feel like I need to tell you the truth before we start to chat and get to know one another, just so that I'm not hiding anything from you.'

Faye took in a deep breath and braced herself, anticipating his next words. 'Go ahead.'

'All I know is that your mum, my Auntie Alice, never wanted anything to do with me or my mum,' he began. 'Alice refused to look after me when my mum passed away, did you know that? I had just turned seventeen and had nobody else in my life, except for Alice,' Aidan added, all the hurt from his childhood flooding back, his eyes filling with forgotten emotions that, despite over a decade having passed by, would never fully fade. 'And now I learn that she's left me a house plus a business in her will,' he explained. 'It just makes no sense.'

Faye looked up, and with a soothing voice, began to explain her side of the story. 'She wanted so much to be there for you, but she just didn't know how to go about it,' she explained. 'So much had happened in the past that she was embarrassed of, and right up until the very end, she thought that you wouldn't have wanted anything to do with her, knowing how badly she'd treated you and your mum.'

Aidan listened with intent, taking in the side of the story that he'd always wanted to hear for himself.

'Even though it wouldn't have been easy, for anyone, she could have tried to make things better.'

Faye nodded her head in agreement. 'She just didn't know how to say sorry. The feud had gone on for so long, and I don't think words could have healed it at that point.'

'Is it true that Alice didn't approve of my mum being a single parent? Is that why she didn't want to have anything to do with us?'

An uneasy look appeared on Faye's face. 'I think the reasons behind it all were complicated, and my mum found it hard to talk about, especially when she became really ill.'

Aidan spotted the sadness welling in her eyes, a sadness that conveyed her loss was still raw, and recent. 'And you only found all this out in September?'

Faye nodded her head again.

'And you know about the will?' he asked.

A beaming expression developed on her face. 'I do. Mum worked so hard and was really successful at what she did, and it was all for me, and for you,' she explained, turning to Aidan. 'It was her way of making it up to you, her way of proving that she really did love you, and your mum, all along.'

A look of sombreness appeared on Aidan's face and all traces of a smile fell from his expression. 'It's all just so sad,' he explained. 'It sounds like my mum and your mum went through such similar, tough times, when all along they could have turned to each other for support, and we wouldn't have been left feeling so alone.'

A flicker of happiness could be seen on Faye's face. 'Our mums used to bake together as children, did you know that?' she asked.

Aidan shook his head.

'That's where their love of fudge came from. Then your mum opened the shop in York, and my mum opened up shops over here.'

'How long did Alice live here for?'

'As far back as I can remember, probably when she found out that she was pregnant with me, because I've lived here all my life. I think she just ran away from all the memories that York held for her, and she wanted to make a fresh start for herself, and for me.'

Aidan's expression became pulled. 'Why did you come to York? Why didn't you introduce yourself when you saw me on the bridge that day?'

Faye took in a deep sigh. 'I wanted to know for myself if you'd ever be able to forgive her, forgive my mum for everything that she did, and the moment that I saw you on the bridge, saying those few words before you released her ashes, I just knew that you were the kind of person that I wanted in my life, the kind of person that Mum knew you were all along.'

'And you had a funeral for her over here?'

'Of course, and I've scattered some of her ashes here, like she wanted, and in a place that meant a lot to her.' Faye gazed out into the distance, her nerves being replaced by a sense of peace. 'Have you been to the house yet?' she asked, standing.

'No, I wanted to see you first.'

'Would you mind if I show you around? Have you got time? There is something I really think you need to see for yourself.'

'Sure,' he replied.

Faye walked the few paces down the street and climbed the handful of steps to the front door of the house, and Aidan followed.

'This was the home that I shared with my mum for so many years,' she said, pausing at the top of the steps and looking back at Aidan. 'Are you okay with me still using my key? I know that this is legally your house now,' she asked, revealing the keyring in her hands. 'Mum wanted me to keep an eye on things until all the legal stuff was sorted out, knowing it could take some time with you being back in England. She didn't want any harm coming to the place. All these arrangements are in the paperwork from the solicitor.'

Aidan indicated with his hand for her to carry on.

'Of course.'

Faye unlocked the door and walked inside, Aidan following behind.

'You might think that it was easier for my mum to forget about things by moving over here, but nothing could have been further from the truth.' Faye walked down a narrow hallway and into the lounge, one wall covered in photo frames of various sizes. 'They're all of you,' she said, admiring the photo gallery. 'When Mum told me about you, she showed me all these that she'd taken of you over the years and had then hidden away, and so I put them up on the wall for her.'

Aidan gazed at the wall, the sea of personal photos so overwhelming that he couldn't find a single word to say.

'My mum actually made so many visits back to York over the years to see you, to check that you were doing okay, to make sure that you looked well, and happy. You just didn't know that she was there, keeping an eye on you all along, in the background.'

'There are so many,' he finally said after taking the time to digest each photo, recalling the specific memories that each of the pictures portrayed. 'I remember this day so well,' he added, looking closely at a specific photo. 'She must have been standing right behind me, making sure that I went into college okay.' Aidan's chin dropped to his chest and his posture weakened, a visible grimace appearing on his face. 'I feel so bad,' he muttered. 'For all these years I have hated her, and thought so badly of her, and yet she cared all along, I just didn't know it,' he concluded, looking up to meet Faye's glance.

'Don't feel bad. As far as you knew, she wasn't there for you, so it's understandable that you felt hurt and let down, and she understood that,' she explained. 'I can assure you that it was never Mum's intention to make you feel guilty, and it definitely wouldn't have been what she wanted,' she added. 'All Mum wanted to do was show you that she really did care about you, and to make sure you'd always be okay, financially.'

'I don't want her money, really I don't, and I don't want to come across as ungrateful or disrespectful,' he was quick to reply. 'My mum worked hard to make sure that I would be okay, and I'm doing fine,' he reassured her. 'I don't know how much you know about me, about my life back in York, but I inherited my mum's shop, Fudgy Nook, and it's doing great. I'm doing great.' Aidan looked at one of the photos on the wall, recalling the day that he had graduated without any family by his side. 'All I ever wanted from Alice was to know that she cared about me, and now I have that,' he smiled, 'so I don't need anything else.'

'The problem is, you can't really argue with my mum now, and I'm guessing she probably knew that all along,' Faye smiled.

'Are you not upset by any of this? I mean, isn't this your home? And I assume the shop is your business.'

Faye shook her head and offered a smile of sincerity. 'Not at all. My mum spoke to me about all this before she passed away, making sure that I was okay with the arrangements, which I was, I am,' she reassured. 'I haven't lived here for some time, and I don't class this as home anymore,' she said, looking around. 'We have a place over in Nantes, that's where Mum and I spent a lot of our time, and that's where I have my own shop, a business that me and Mum set up together,' she added. 'Everything that she worked hard to achieve here in Collonges-la-Rouge was all for you, right from the very start.'

Aidan took in a deep breath. 'It's all just so hard to take in,' he replied, peering around the house that he now owned, a warming smile spreading across his face when he spotted an old picture of Alice and Faye baking together. 'It looks like our mums wanted to keep fudge-making in the family all along,' he commented.

Faye could feel her emotions welling in the back of her eyes. 'I'm just so glad that you're here,' she added.

Aidan stepped closer and tentatively wrapped his arm around her, the embrace feeling safe, and strangely familiar. 'I'm so sorry that I never got to meet your mum,' he whispered. 'She sounded like an incredible person, and I'm just sorry that I never had the opportunity to get to know her for myself.'

Faye closed her eyes and relished the special feeling that fluttered through her body when she was able to be comforted by family.

'And I'm so sorry that I never got to meet Heidi,' she replied. 'I would have loved to have had an auntie in my life, it would have made my family tree feel more complete.'

Aidan pulled away when he sensed she was upset and reached for a tissue, placing it in her hand.

'My mum would have loved you,' he smiled, admiring Faye's mannerisms. 'And she was always doing exactly what you're doing now,' he commented, noticing the way that Faye pulled at the tissue, breaking bits off in her hand. 'I would always know where my mum had been sitting because there would be bits of tissue scattered everywhere, especially in her bedroom window. That was her favourite place to sit because she loved the views it offered of York,' he recalled with fondness.

Faye dabbed away her tears. 'Let me show you the views from over here,' she suggested, walking over towards the balcony and pushing the doors wide open. 'My mum was also a big fan of views, and she hoped that they would win you over, too.'

Aidan followed Faye and stepped outside onto the terrace, the warm evening breeze caressing his skin. He looked out and admired the picturesque view, nothing but blankets of green in all directions, a wave of unfamiliar scents rolling in off the fields and awakening his senses. He closed his eyes and relished the tranquillity, a welcome feeling of familiarity brushing away any lingering nerves that were bouncing around in his body. He and Faye rested their arms on the balcony railings and stood side by side in silence for a few minutes, relishing how special it felt to once again be in the company of family.

Without trying to understand or overthink how he was feeling, he turned to Faye and offered a reassuring smile.

'I'm so glad I'm here.'

46

'So, how did it go last night?' Lola asked when she stirred, spotting that Aidan was already up and sitting on the balcony, the doors wide open to allow the warm, morning breeze to seep in. 'You must have got home late, because I didn't hear you get back.'

Aidan swung round in his seat so that he could face Lola.

'It was amazing,' his beam of happiness was unmistakable. 'After I went to the shop and met with Faye, we went to the house and sat talking for hours, just sharing stories about our mums,' he began to explain, getting up and walking through to the bedroom.

'That's her name? Faye? She's your cousin?'

Aidan smiled and nodded, grabbing a brown paper bag before draping himself across the bed. 'Yep, she's so nice and I can't wait for you to meet her,' he added. 'Here, try one of these. I bought us some pastries for breakfast,' he said, opening the bag and offering one to Lola.

'Thanks,' she said, sitting up and straightening out her hair. 'Wow, this is amazing,' she added, taking a bite out of the buttery, flaky pastry, her free hand catching the crumbs.

Aidan leaned his back against the foot of the bed and rested his legs alongside Lola's, taking out his phone when it buzzed.

'Everything okay?' Lola asked when the sparkle in Aidan's eye vanished.

'Holly has just sent me a message to let me know that the

baby isn't mine,' he confirmed, a moment of heaviness apparent in his demeanour.

Lola raised her eyebrows at the news, an internal feeling of relief sweeping through her body. 'How do you feel about it?'

'It's good news,' he confirmed. 'Even though, for a moment, I had allowed myself to imagine what it would be like to be a dad,' he added, shrugging his shoulders at acknowledging his true feelings.

'And when the time is right, you'll experience all of those feelings,' Lola reassured. 'And hopefully, so will I,' she smiled. 'Does this mean that Parker is the father?' the realisation stealing her smile.

'She hasn't said,' Aidan replied, re-reading the message.

'Anyway, let's not talk about Holly, let's talk about much nicer things. How was last night?'

Aidan overhauled his expression with ease. 'Last night was just so amazing because I got to hear about Faye's experience of living here, with Alice, and she got to find out about my childhood back home with Mum, the auntie she never knew.'

A warmth spread through Lola's chest and her eyes softened, her inner glow appearing across her external features. 'You seem so happy.'

'It's just such a nice feeling to know that I have family, albeit just one cousin that lives in another country, but it's more than I thought I had two days ago,' he grinned. 'Ever since mum passed away, I've longed to feel part of a family, and even though I'm going to try and find out who my dad is, I now already have a cousin, and Faye is amazing.'

'That's great.'

Aidan sat up a little. 'Faye told me that my Auntie Alice made quite a few trips to York over the years, just to make sure I was doing okay after Mum passed away,' he began to explain, a sparkle appearing in his eyes that Lola hadn't seen before. 'There's this wall of photos at the house, and they're all photos that Alice took of me, you know, like the day I left high school, my first day at college, the day I took my driving test. She was there all along in the background, watching to make sure that I was okay.'

Lola looked puzzled. 'How did she know what you were up to? How did she know what days to be there?' she asked.

A puzzled expression also appeared on Aidan's face. 'I'm not too sure, you know. I never thought to ask. But isn't it amazing that she did care about me after all?'

'It's brilliant, and I'm so happy for you,' she expressed, placing a hand on his leg.

A sudden feeling of apprehension tumbled through Lola's mind at the realisation that, given all he had discovered, Aidan might not be so willing to just leave France and return to York. The time away from her home city had allowed Lola to realise that, deep down, Yorkshire was where her heart, and her future, lay. All the romantic scenarios that she had been imagining about her future now appeared less certain. She also sat up in bed, trying to cast away her doubts.

'So, what's our plan?' she asked, trying to hide her sense of apprehension.

Aidan looked at his watch. 'The plan for today?'

'Today. Tomorrow. Life, in general,' she replied, ruffling her hair.

'Well, I think I know a rough plan for today,' he began. 'I said I'd meet up with Faye at the shop in about half an hour because we didn't really talk about the business and how it's all going to work. And then I'm meeting up with the solicitor at 11:30, because I have a few more things to iron out.'

'How are you feeling about everything?' she began, turning her body so that she could gauge Aidan's reaction. 'You came out here with limited expectations, and now you have all this, and Faye,' she added, pointing out of the window.

Aidan rubbed his forehead in an attempt to straighten out the frown lines that had appeared. 'I'm just not sure,' he admitted in one quick breath. 'It's a confusing and unexpected situation to find myself in,' he began, his expression blank. 'I spent so long hating her, and now I find out that Alice worked so hard to leave this legacy for me, to make up for the past, which was so thoughtful of her, but it's here, in France, which makes it even more complicated.'

He draped his arm over his face, hoping that it would alleviate his pounding headache.

Witnessing his turmoil, Lola tried to unpick his thought process further, seeking reassurance that their fledgling relationship was still flourishing on stable ground.

'Are you thinking you'll want to keep the business open, and maybe rent the house, or even move in yourself?' she asked, her hesitation audible in her words. Once she'd asked the question, the butterflies tumbling through her stomach made Lola realise how strongly she felt about the answer, how intense her feelings already were for Aidan, and just the thought of him wanting to stay in France threatened to rock the composure that she had slowly re-established.

Aidan removed his arm, his own emotions visible in his eyes. 'I already know that it would feel so wrong to just sell everything and return to York with the money,' he began, looking at Lola. 'And on top of that, I'd be leaving Faye here after we've only just found each other.'

Upon having her fears confirmed, Lola turned away and gazed outside, taking a moment to admire the uninterrupted blue sky, a sinking feeling in her stomach telling her that life was pulling Aidan away from her embrace.

'Well, while you meet up with Faye, I might wander out and have another mooch in the village, then I can prepare some dinner for us tonight back here. Maybe I'll do something romantic out on the balcony, how does that sound?' she asked, doing her best to hide her true feelings, and offer the support and encouragement that she knew he needed.

Aidan leaned over and kissed her on the lips.

'Are you sure you don't want to come with me this morning? Faye wants to meet you, and I shouldn't be that long with the solicitor.'

Lola kissed him back, her insides still fluttering. 'You and Faye must have loads of business things to discuss, so how about I tag along next time when the conversation will be less intense?' she replied. 'And anyway, I need to call Carrie and let her know I'm still alive. We never go so long without speaking to each other.'

Aidan slid his arms around Lola's waist and kissed her, squeezing her tightly and lifting her feet off the ground. 'I'll be back as soon as I can,' he reassured her. 'But have another fab day as a tourist. This is why we did that practice in York, you'll be an expert at it now,' he added, before lowering her down and walking towards the door. 'I'll see you a bit later.'

'Bye,' she replied.

Still without her suitcase, Lola changed into her clothes from the previous day and headed outside. The village was beginning to come to life, shutters on windows opening and people emerging on the streets, queues forming outside each boulangerie she passed. Following her instincts, she had second thoughts about her morning plans, and instead chose to head in the direction of Faye's shop. Despite carrying around a bundle of nerves, she knew deep down that, no matter how insecure she felt, introducing herself to someone that meant so much to Aidan was the right thing to do.

As she approached the door, she could hear laughing coming from inside the shop. Standing a little way back, just out of sight, Lola peered through a side window, spotting Aidan standing behind the counter wearing an apron, alongside a woman she assumed was Faye. Lola watched for a moment, seeing how happy he looked, and how he was trying to serve a customer, more rumbles of laughter echoing out of the door when Aidan attempted to speak French.

She walked a little closer towards the shop window whilst remaining out of sight. She watched the customer leave, and just as she was about to push aside her nerves and enter, she overheard a conversation through the open window.

'This place is amazing,' she heard Aidan comment. Lola pressed her back against the wall and continued to listen to the unfolding conversation. 'People here just seem happy, so carefree and I can see myself fitting in nicely. Back home there is always something to complain about, the awful Yorkshire weather doesn't help I guess.'

Hearing Aidan's comments about home made her heart sink, her tears welling behind her eyes.

'So, what are your thoughts about the shop, the house?' she heard Faye ask him. 'Have you thought about what you are going to do?'

Lola held her breath, waiting to hear what his honest answer would be. She looked down at her feet and fidgeted with her hair, trying to prepare herself for what was to come, neither her nor her fragile heart ready for the truth.

'Well, I'd love to stay here in France, it would just feel like the right thing to do. After all, this is a family business that started with my mum and Alice around the kitchen table with a bowl and wooden spoon,' she heard Aidan begin. Lola's heart broke and she felt her body weaken. Pulling herself away from the wall, she began to walk away, her tears falling onto the cobbles and drying immediately beneath the early morning warmth from the sun. With her head lowered from sight, she walked away, her heart lying broken on the floor. Keeping herself out of sight, she perched herself on a bench across the street, the shop still just in her line of view. She tried to shake away her sadness, punishing herself for having fallen for someone so soon. For once in her life, she wanted to feel like her feelings were being put first, knowing that this time, she wouldn't settle for anything less.

Across the street, the conversation continued. Inside the shop, Aidan took off the apron and walked around to the other side of the counter.

'But I know that I can't stay here, because I love Lola, and I can see a future with her,' he continued. 'And even though I haven't talked to her about it yet, I can't imagine that she'd want to settle here in France, not permanently anyway, and to be honest, neither would I. My life is back in York. I have my business there, and keeping my attention on that is important to me. It's my mum's legacy.'

Aidan took a moment to compose his feelings, a forlorn look appearing on his face.

'And I don't want to seem ungrateful, that's the last thing I want. I appreciate so much what your mum has done for me, I really do. But for this business to continue to be a success, it needs stability and focus, and I'm just not sure that I'll ever be able to offer those things.'

A look of disappointment haunted Faye's face. 'I understand that York is your home, I would probably feel the same if I were in your shoes.'

Aidan offered Faye a hug, witnessing the disappointment in her eyes.

'Please don't think that my decision means that you're not important to me,' he explained. 'You're my family now, so we'll always be a part of each other's lives, even if we're not always in the same country. I guess we just need to figure out some logistics to ensure that we'll never lose touch once my time here comes to an end.'

'Sounds good,' she smiled, releasing herself from the embrace and trying her best to reign in her emotions.

'Anyway, I best get going to meet up with the solicitor. There are a few things I need to discuss with him,' he said, walking towards the door. 'Shall we all meet up for tea tonight? Lola was going to cook, but I'm sure she'd love to go out instead. She's been looking forward to meeting you.'

'Sure, that'll be great.'

'Perfect, I'll message you later on,' he said, before disappearing down the street.

Remaining seated on the bench, Lola caught sight of Aidan leaving the shop, a smile on his face and a visible spring in his stride. Once he was out of sight, she stood up and walked across the street, pushing open the shop door and walking inside.

47

'Bonjour,' announced Faye when Lola entered, although she didn't really look up but instead carried on with what she was doing behind the display cabinet.

Lola perused the shelves, and with her back to the counter, tried to summon up the courage to introduce herself, but before she could speak, Faye said something else in French.

Lola looked across the shop before turning to face Faye.

'Hi, I'm so sorry but I don't understand French, so I'm not sure what you just said, or if you were even talking to me. Do you speak English?'

Faye immediately looked up. 'Yes, sorry. I just assume that at this time of year all of my customers will be locals, or at least French. It's only in the summer months that we tend to get a lot of tourists here. I was just saying that I'm closing for lunch.'

Upon first sight of Faye and listening to her talk, Lola immediately liked her, finding her demeanour and charm endearing.

'I'm Lola,' she revealed in one quick breath, not really knowing what else to say. 'I wanted to just say hi and introduce myself. I'm Aidan's, erm…'

'You're his girlfriend, I recognise you from the bridge in York,' she smiled. 'Aidan has talked about you a lot,' she added, before walking to the other side of the counter and holding out her hand. 'It's so nice to meet you in person, Lola. I'm Faye.'

The pair shook hands.

'I love your shop, and if your fudge is as delicious as Aidan's, then I'd like to taste all of your flavours,' she said, looking around. Although she was unable to read the fancy French labels, her mouth began to water at the sight of all the treats.

Faye's cheekbones became more prominent as her smile developed. 'And I'm excited to try his,' she replied, grabbing her handbag. 'I'm just about to go on my lunch break. Would you like to join me? It'd be nice to have a chat.'

Lola felt a little unsure. 'Well, I'm meant to be out buying some ingredients so that I can cook tea tonight,' she explained.

'Oh, I might be about to spoil a surprise then, but Aidan asked me if I'd like to go out for tea with you both tonight.'

Lola checked her phone, spotting the message from Aidan.

'You're right, he's suggested that we all go to a restaurant. That saves me the ordeal of trying to shop for ingredients,' she laughed, wiping her brow with relief. 'My French doesn't stretch much further than *hello*.'

'Perfect, I usually just sit outside underneath one of the trees. All this lovely weather and I spend most of my time indoors unable to enjoy it.'

Faye locked the shop door and the pair meandered down the street.

'There's usually a bench free over there that's in the shade,' she suggested, pointing to her left.

Lola arched her neck and allowed the sun to rest on her face.

'This sunshine makes me feel so jealous. The UK isn't known for its great weather, and we certainly do get more grey days than sunny days in York,' she replied, the women taking a seat beneath a cluster of trees.

'So, I hear that you and Aidan had quite the interesting start to your relationship,' Faye said in a playful way, her eyebrows raised.

Lola nodded. 'Definitely interesting,' she replied. 'But I bet that he didn't go as far as telling you that he actually saved my life.'

Faye turned to look at Lola. 'He saved your life? No, he didn't tell me that bit.'

'I thought not. He's so modest about it all, but he really did save my life.'

'Wow, that's amazing.'

Lola turned to look at Faye. 'So, how are you feeling about everything? All this must be a lot for you to take in, too,' asked Lola, taking the opportunity to gauge Faye's true emotions.

Faye took a salad box out of her bag and unwrapped her disposable cutlery. 'It's been a lot to wrap my head around,' she began. 'I've had a little more time than Aidan to digest everything, but not that long, not really.'

'I'm sorry to hear about your mum,' Lola offered, sensing that there was a raft of emotions bubbling beneath Faye's calm exterior.

'My mum was my best friend and I thought I knew everything about her, but when she became poorly and told me about what had happened in the past, I just felt so bad that she'd been carrying around all these secrets for so long, and with nobody that she felt she could talk to.'

'I know that Aidan is thrilled to have you in his life. I know that he's suffered from feelings of loneliness in the past.'

'It's just a shame that we're so far away from each other now.'

Lola's chest expanded as she drank in the warm air.

Lola cast aside her own feelings and insecurities. 'Well, maybe Aidan will consider moving over here, or at least spend some quality time here in France with you, and who can blame him?' she replied, looking out across the cobbles. The sun was dripping from the sky, its rays shining down over the buildings, making it appear as though the red stones were sparkling.

'I don't think his heart is here,' she replied, looking Lola in the eyes and smiling. 'His heart is with you.'

A downturned expression appeared on Lola's face. 'I overheard Aidan talking to you just as I arrived at the shop, and I heard him say that he'd love to move here.'

Faye thought back. 'Are you sure that you heard everything that he said?' she questioned.

'I walked away after a few minutes,' she stated, trying to conceal her upset.

Faye smiled. 'That makes sense then, because you missed the end part of the conversation where he told me how much he loves you, and that his future will be wherever you are. He knows York is your home, and that's home for him, too.'

'I just want him to be happy, and if that means spending more time here, then I'd never try to stop him.'

An odd look appeared on Faye's face that she couldn't disguise. 'Are you okay?' Lola asked.

'There's something I want to tell Aidan, but I made a promise to my mum, and now I really don't know what to do.' Faye gave a slow shake of her head in an attempt to dispel her quandary.

Without realising it herself, Lola's posture stiffened, and she wasn't really sure what to say. She could feel her heart rate increasing, her mind conjuring up all sorts of possible scenarios.

Faye lowered her stare until it fell into her lap.

'I made a promise to my mum, and it's so hard to think about breaking it, breaking her trust, and yet I think Aidan deserves to know the truth. If it was me, I'd want to know the truth.'

Lola witnessed Faye's turmoil and sympathised.

'It's hard trying to please everyone, especially when they're not here to talk to.'

Faye remained silent, her expression perplexed. 'Had I had just a few more days with Mum, I would have spoken to her about it, but there just wasn't time. It was one of the last things that she told me, and then just like that, she was gone.'

'I'm so sorry,' Lola replied, reaching out her hand and holding Faye's when she could see her tears. 'Please don't get upset,' she added, passing Faye a tissue. 'Your mum wouldn't have wanted you to be upset.'

'I don't want to hurt anybody. I just think he deserves to know the truth,' she sobbed, her emotions pouring into her tissue.

'Then talk to him. Your mum would understand, I'm sure she would.'

Faye took out a crumpled photo and handed it to Lola.

'What's this?' she asked, looking down at the picture. 'I've seen this before,' she added, studying the people in the photo.

'You have?' questioned Faye.

'Yeah. Aidan has a copy. I think it was his mum's, and after she passed away, he found it in her purse.' Lola pointed to the pregnant lady in the photo. 'That's Aidan's mum, Heidi, when she was pregnant with him. And that's your mum, isn't it? It's crazy that even in their twenties, they looked so similar, apart from the baby bump.'

Faye began to cry.

Lola put her arm around her shoulder. 'What's wrong? I don't understand,' she said in an attempt to offer comfort. 'Aidan isn't upset about what happened in the past anymore. He's made his peace with your mum, and he's just so happy that he's found you.'

Faye took a deep breath and turned the photo over, revealing the handwritten words scribbled onto the back.

Me, pregnant with Aidan, front garden. York.

'I'm confused,' said Lola, her eyes squinting to read the faded words.

'That's my mum,' she said, pointing to the pregnant lady. 'She was the one who was pregnant with Aidan, not Heidi.'

Lola looked at Faye, and then looked back at the photo, studying it again. 'So, you're saying that Alice is Aidan's biological mum?'

Faye nodded, her tears still streaming. 'Mum told me all this just a few days before she passed away.'

'I don't understand. Aidan has told me that Alice didn't want anything to do with Heidi or him. He believes that she disagreed with Heidi's decision to keep the baby, like she was ashamed.'

'My mum was ashamed, but of herself,' she replied. 'When

my mum fell pregnant with Aidan, her relationship with my father broke down,' she continued. 'As a result, my grandparents encouraged her to have an abortion, making her believe that being unmarried and pregnant was something to be embarrassed about.'

'So, where did Heidi come into it?' Lola questioned when Faye stopped talking.

Faye looked up, her eyes red and her skin blotchy.

'Heidi was financially independent having already set up her business, and even though it was only just starting to turn a profit, by that time she had bought her own place. So, she begged my mum not to get the abortion and offered to help with the baby, saying they could both move in with her,' she began. 'And even though my mum was still scared about how she would cope, she turned her back on my grandparents and accepted Heidi's offer,' she continued. 'But my mum suffered with postnatal depression, and even with Heidi's help, she couldn't cope, especially without the additional support of my grandparents. So, she left. One day she just packed up all of her things without saying anything or leaving any explanation, and left Aidan behind for Heidi to take care of him.'

Lola's thoughts turned to Aidan.

'You're Aidan's sister,' she suddenly announced when the pieces of the puzzle dropped into place.

Faye couldn't help but beam with happiness.

'I am,' she cried.

Lola held Faye's hand, herself welling up at the magnitude of the revelation. She admired Faye's soft features and saw snippets of familiarity. 'You both have the same shape of eyes, it's one of the first things I noticed about you when we met.'

'I can see similarities, too,' she nodded, a genuine smile of happiness shining from her face.

Lola dabbed her eyes, allowing the news to digest. 'But I don't understand why Alice hated Heidi so much, and why she didn't want anything to do with Aidan. Heidi had looked after Aidan and offered Alice so much support, so it doesn't make any sense that she would have any resentment.'

'Once she had gotten her depression under control, my mum wanted Aidan back, but it was too late by then. So much time had passed by, and Aidan was settled and didn't want to leave. In his eyes, Heidi was his mum, he knew no different, and he wouldn't leave her,' she said, her shoulders falling.

'How old was Aidan at that time?'

'Well, my mum got back together with my dad for a short while, and that's when I came along. I think Aidan would have been about three.'

'So, that's the reason that they were never a part of each other's lives?'

Faye nodded. 'My mum admitted that she was jealous of the relationship that Heidi had formed with Aidan, and that it was just too hard for her to watch.'

'And after Heidi passed away?'

'By that time, there'd been too much damage done and my mum didn't know how to make things better with Aidan, she didn't know where to start to explain. And so, she did what she thought was best at the time, and that was to watch over him from afar, make sure that he was okay and that he had everything he needed, and all the while, she was working so hard to create all this for him.'

'So, everything that Aidan knows is a lie?'

Faye's shoulders loosened and her gaze became focused.

'Yes, which is why I feel like I should tell him the truth.'

'Do you know who his father is?'

'I do but I've never had a relationship with our dad because once I was born, we moved here. I think he still lives in York.'

'Really?' she replied, her shock evident in her voice. 'Aidan has already mentioned trying to find out information about who his dad is, so that he can maybe have some kind of relationship with him. I can't imagine how he'll react when he knows that his dad is actually in York.'

'When I was much younger, we would speak occasionally, but we don't have a relationship. The distance just made it too hard, I guess. My mum broke up with him just after I was born, and they never rekindled.'

Lola shook her head, anticipating how Aidan would react upon hearing the news.

'Mum visited the UK to check on Aidan over the years, but it was his dad who was the one keeping a close eye on him and making sure that he was doing alright.'

Lola sat back on the bench. 'You're right about one thing. You have to tell Aidan the truth,' she began. 'Everyone deserves to know where they come from. Everyone deserves to know who their family really are.'

48

A HEAVY, THUNDEROUS CLOUD HUNG ABOVE THE MINSTER; York city below drenched in an early spring storm. Sneezing and sniffling, Lola got out of the taxi and wrapped her coat tight, her body shivering beneath it. In comparison to Collonges-la-Rouge, the air in Yorkshire felt thick with smog, the dense clouds oppressive, and she immediately felt like she'd been too hasty, regretting her rash decision to leave France, alone. Without any prior warning, she tapped on the side door to The Brownie Box.

'Thanks, just leave it there,' Carrie shouted, expecting the person knocking on the door to be a delivery person.

Lola tapped again.

'Bloody hell,' muttered Carrie, drying her hands and walking to the door, pulling it open.

'I said–'

'Hi,' interrupted Lola.

Carrie jumped out and wrapped her arms around her best friend.

'Oh, my goodness, you're home!' she shouted. 'I've just sent you a message asking how you are,' she said, pulling her body away from Lola's so she could look at her face. 'I'm assuming not great, as you're here, alone,' she added, peering outside to see if Aidan was there too.

'I'm alone,' cried Lola, leaning her head forwards and sobbing into Carrie's shoulder.

Carrie wrapped her arms around her friend again.

'Oh, Lola, I'm so sorry,' she whispered into her ear. 'Come on, let's go inside.'

Carrie led Lola into the van and pulled out her stool.

'Here, sit down.'

Lola sat and dried her eyes while Carrie served the trickle of customers.

'It feels so strange to be sitting back here,' Lola began when Carrie joined her on a stool.

Carrie handed Lola a box of tissues. 'Why are you here, and where's Aidan?'

'He's still in France,' Lola began to explain. 'I didn't even tell him that I was leaving.'

Carrie's facial expression conveyed her sense of shock. 'Why? What happened?'

Lola dabbed her face, her skin blotchy and chapped from her tears. 'Without Aidan knowing, I went and met with Faye by myself.'

'And what's she like?'

'She's so lovely, everything that I didn't really want her to be,' Lola cried. 'I wanted her to be horrible so that it would be easy not to like her.'

'Why don't you want to like her?'

'She's the reason that Aidan is probably going to choose to spend more time in France than York, maybe even move there. Who knows?'

'How do you know that? Did you ask him?'

Lola looked up, ready to deliver the news.

'Faye is Aidan's sister.'

Carrie's mouth dropped and she accidentally spilled her tea. 'What?' she spluttered.

'Alice is Aidan's biological mum, and Faye is his sister.'

'Oh, my goodness, you're joking?'

'Nope, and there's more. Aidan's dad lives here, in York,' she

300

added. 'All these years his dad has been watching him from afar, sending updates to Alice in France about how he's getting on.'

'And what has Aidan said about all this?'

Lola shrugged. 'I don't know.'

'What do you mean?'

'When Faye told me everything, I just felt like I should leave. I didn't want to confuse the situation for him anymore than it already was. If Aidan wants to be in France with his sister, then that's what I want him to do if it'll make him happy. Had I stayed there any longer, it would have only made his decision that much harder to make.'

'So you left, without even talking to him, or saying goodbye?'

'I know it sounds awful, but I was only thinking of him. I want him to do what's best for *him*, and not be influenced by me, or come to resent me. I know for a fact that I don't want to put roots down in France, not long-term anyway, so it's as simple as that.'

'But you still love him?'

Lola couldn't bring herself to say it out loud for fear of bursting into tears, so she nodded in agreement.

'Have you heard from him at all since you left?'

Lola shook her head. 'I left him a note saying I think it was best that I return to York alone, so who can blame him for not messaging?'

'Blimey, I wonder how he's feeling.'

'I wanted to message him, but what's the point? That would just make the situation worse. He hasn't been in touch with me, he hasn't rung to say that he'll be coming back too, so I think his silence speaks volumes about his decision, wouldn't you agree?'

'Well, maybe it's for the best. Like you said, you didn't want things to get too serious with him and then end up heartbroken, again.'

'But I'm heartbroken now,' Lola cried, shaking her head, releasing her bottled up sadness. 'I really do love him, Carrie, and I know we'd only known each other since Christmas, but we'd formed such a close relationship in those three months, especially because of the accident and what happened between Holly and Parker, and I really wanted him to choose me. I wanted him to want to be with me more than he wants to be in France.'

Carrie stood up to serve a customer.

'Hi, what can I get you?' she asked.

As she listened to the lady's order, in the distance, she saw Parker and Holly walking up The Shambles, holding hands. Unsure what to do, she fumbled to prepare the order while keeping her eye on them, hoping that they weren't heading in her direction. Out of the corner of her eye, she then looked down at Lola, hoping that her attention was distracted.

'Here you go, see you again,' she said to the customer, placing the cup on the countertop and processing payment.

'Lola, duck down,' Carrie insisted when she saw Parker and Holly heading straight towards them.

'What?' she replied, looking up in confusion. When she saw Carrie gesticulating to hide, she jumped off the stool and squatted down beneath the counter, hidden from view.

'Hi, Carrie, how are you?' asked Parker when he approached the hatch.

'I'm good, thanks for asking.'

'This is Holly,' he introduced, turning to Holly and smiling.

'Hi, Carrie.'

Carrie smiled meekly at Holly and turned back to address Parker. 'So, what can I get for you?'

Beneath the counter, Lola pressed her hands to her face. She held her breath, scared that Parker might hear. The sound of his voice made her sadness fall in torrents, a voice that once made her tingle inside. The smell of his familiar deodorant wafted through the air and into her nostrils, her senses rebelling to a scent that once felt so provocative. Her body shook with nerves, and she wrapped her arm around Carrie's leg, so thankful that her friend had saved her from a moment of potential humiliation.

'I actually wanted to speak with Lola. There's something I need to tell her, and I think she's blocked my number so there's no way of me getting in touch with her. I thought she might be here.'

'Well, you can't really blame her for blocking your number, can you?' smiled Carrie in her most polite manner, turning to check that what she was seeing was correct; Holly had a blossoming baby bump. 'So, I'm guessing the news you want to tell her is that the two of you are expecting, is that right?' she added, unable to hold her tongue any longer. Through a fake, forced smile, Carrie continued before Parker had time to reply. 'I don't think Lola will really be interested in your news, if I'm being honest, she's far too busy having an amazing time on her travels. She'll be somewhere in the middle of France by now, and I can assure you, she won't be thinking about you, or you,' she said, turning to look at Holly.

'We never meant to hurt her, Carrie,' Holly muttered.

'Oh, please don't flatter yourself,' she replied, looking Holly in the eye. 'Lola won't be hurt by this at all. She's actually celebrating her divorce right now, and thanking her lucky stars that she's no longer married to someone as pathetic as you,' she concluded, directing her final comment at Parker.

'I'm just trying to do the right thing, Carrie,' Parker explained. 'I didn't want to run the risk of us bumping into her with her not knowing that we're having a baby. We're giving it a go between the two of us,' he said, smiling and turning to look at Holly.

Carrie released a laugh and shook her head.

'Do the right thing? It's a little late for that, isn't it? You slept together when you were married – how on earth is that doing the right thing?'

'Just let her know that I've tried to reach out to her, that's all I'm asking for.'

Carrie diverted her attention and began making a coffee.

'Please don't come back here again, there are plenty of other places to get coffee from in York,' she said, refusing to give the pair another glance.

Until Parker and Holly had walked away, Lola remained hidden, crouched on the floor.

'They've gone,' Carrie announced, lowering herself down to sit alongside her friend on the floor.

Lola kept her eyes covered with her hands, trapping her tears. 'I'm not upset that the baby is his, we found that out whilst Aidan and I were still in France,' Lola sobbed. 'Because I don't care, honestly I don't,' she explained, slowly removing her hands, uncovering her red, bloodshot eyes. 'I'm upset about the fact that I did have a husband, and now I don't, and I did have a baby, and now I don't, and then I did have a boyfriend, and now I don't. And now I'm sat on the floor, hiding from the world like a pathetic mess.'

'Things will get better, I promise. I think you just need to take a break from men,' joked Carrie, trying to make her smile. 'You go home, and when I've finished here, we can chat properly tonight over a few glasses of wine.'

Lola turned to Carrie and asked, 'Where is my home?'

'Your home is with me, for as long as you need. And I don't mean outside on the driveway, staying in the van. I mean in your bedroom, in your home.'

Lola leaned across and rested her head on Carrie's shoulder.

'Thank goodness I have you in my life,' she began. 'It's crazy, you know, but I've missed being in here so much.'

Carrie leaned her head so that it rested on Lola, her demeanour relaxed. 'We're living the dream, you and I. We have our own business with nobody telling us what to do,' she said. 'Who needs a man anyway?' she laughed as their conversation was interrupted by a knock on the door.

'Leave it outside, thanks,' shouted Lola like she'd never been away, knowing it would be a delivery driver dropping off supplies. In her pocket, she heard her phone ringing. 'It's Faye,' she said to Carrie, pulling out her phone and looking at the screen.

'I wonder what she wants.'

'I have no idea.'

49

*L*OLA OPENED HER EYES TO FIND THAT, NOT ONLY COULD SHE not recall what day of the week it was, but she also wasn't entirely sure where she was. Allowing her eyes to close, she reopened them a few seconds later when her brain caught up, realising it was Sunday, and that she was in Carrie's spare bedroom. Before she had time to stretch and think about the day ahead, she heard a knock at the front door. Remembering that Carrie was going out for an early-morning Yoga session, Lola opened the curtains and peered down, spotting Aidan standing at the front door.

'Hi,' he beamed at the sight of her through the window, a bunch of pale pink roses, speckled with white buds of gypsophila, gripped in his hand. Lola brought her hand to her mouth, tears immediately tumbling down her cheeks. She opened the window and leaned out.

'You're back!' she cried. 'Don't move, I'm coming down.'

Grabbing her sweater and a pair of shorts, Lola scrambled to get dressed and ran her fingers through her hair on the way downstairs. She unlocked the door and stepped out, immediately wrapping her arms around him.

'I love you, Lola,' he whispered in her ear, his embrace keeping her secure within the comfort of his arms.

'I love you, too. I'm sorry that I left without seeing you, I just thought–'

'You don't need to explain,' he interrupted. 'It was actually the best thing that you could have done,' he added. 'It gave me some time and space to figure out what I really want in life.'

'When did you get back?' she asked, still in shock, unwilling to release her grip of him.

'I've come straight from the airport now,' he explained, trying to indicate to the bag flung over his shoulder. 'I haven't been to the flat or the shop. I just needed to see you,' he whispered into her ear.

Lola could feel his heart beating beneath his chest, and she savoured the closeness, and the feeling of love and safety once again swirling through her own heart.

'There's somewhere I want to take you, if you'll come with me,' he asked, before releasing his grip and taking her hand.

'Right now?' she replied, looking down at her scruffy appearance.

A silly smile appeared on his face. 'Well, it's probably best to get dressed first, but if you want to come out with me in your pyjamas, then that's fine with me, too.'

'Just give me five minutes. Carrie is out, so just make yourself at home while I change,' she said, disappearing upstairs.

Like a hurricane, Lola whizzed herself in and out of the shower before throwing on a dusting of makeup and checking herself in the mirror, wanting to look and feel her best.

'I bet you've never seen someone get ready so quickly,' she announced when appearing in the lounge doorway, spotting Aidan peering out of the window. 'I'm ready.'

'Wow, you look amazing,' he complimented. 'Then let's go,' he said, holding out his hand for her to take.

Still beaming with happiness, Lola relished the feel of Aidan's hand as they strolled towards the town centre. 'I can't believe you're actually here,' she said, interlocking her fingers with his. 'I'm sorry again for leaving the way that I did, it's just I knew that you had some hard decisions to make, and I didn't want to make it even tougher for you.'

'You don't need to explain, honestly, it's fine,' he replied, navigating them through the bustle of the city centre, weaving their way down The Shambles and towards York Minster.

Lola looked down, a wave of guilt washing over her.

'I could see in your eyes how much the French shop meant to you, how much Faye meant to you, and I just wanted you to make the right decision, the best decision for you.' Lola then recalled the surprise telephone call that she had received from Faye, and the somewhat cryptic conversation that at the time hadn't made much sense, now all started to become clear.

Aidan looked Lola in the eyes. 'And I love the fact that you always put others before yourself,' he replied, kissing her hand. 'But the best decision for me is to be with you.'

Just outside York Minster, Aidan paused and turned to look Lola in the eye again.

'When I met up with the solicitor for the second time, it was to sign everything over to Faye. My decision had already been made and I knew deep down that I didn't want to stay in France, or even split my time. I knew that I wanted to come back to York with you, this is my home. I just wanted to get it all in writing before I told you about my decision.'

'Really? So, you don't own the shop or the house anymore?' she asked, taking hold of his hands.

'No. It would never have sat right with me to take any of it, especially given that I couldn't check how my mum would have felt about it all,' he began, looking over to the entrance of the cathedral. 'I got what I needed,' he added, looking back at Lola with a beaming smile. 'I got closure to the whole situation, closure to all the childhood bitterness that I've been holding on to for too long,' he explained. 'And better still, I learnt that Alice had been in my life all along.'

Lola picked up on who he referred to as his mum. 'Did Faye talk to you?'

He looked up at the Cathedral with a sense of peace shining from his face. 'You mean about Alice being my real mum?'

Lola nodded. 'How do you feel about it?' she asked.

'I don't know if this sounds awful, but I'm going to say it anyway because it's how I feel, but it doesn't change anything, not for me,' he began. 'I never knew Alice, so although she's my biological mother, Heidi was my mum, and she'll always be my mum in my mind.'

'And you're okay with what happened?'

'It's not a great feeling knowing that Alice abandoned me, but I understand why she did it, and what happened is in the past. Alice isn't here for me to talk to, but if she was, I would make amends with her. So, that's it. I don't hold a grudge for the decisions that were made, I think it was just a tough time for everyone involved. I had an amazing childhood and an amazing mum. What's there to be bitter about?'

'And how do you feel about your dad being here, in York?' she asked, taking a glance at the cathedral, relishing the feeling of being back home.

Aidan couldn't help but smile. 'I mean, it's a weird thought that after all these years he's been so close by, but Faye and I didn't really get time to talk about him that much. I didn't even ask for his name because I managed to book a flight that was leaving within a matter of hours, and I only thought about it afterwards. Not that it makes any difference, it's not like I was going to try and call him straight away.'

'But you are still thinking about reaching out to him?' she asked, sensing his underlying reservations.

He shrugged his shoulders. 'I think so. But then again, if he's known about me all along, but has never made any attempt to contact me, then maybe he doesn't want to be a part of my life, and maybe I should respect that.'

A playful look appeared on Lola's face and she peered around at those people who were also lingering near the cathedral. 'But you must be curious? I know I would be. He could be someone here, standing right next to us and you'd never know.'

'Every time I walk past a guy in his late fifties, early sixties, I'm going to be second-guessing if we're related,' he joked, finding the lighter side of the quandary.

'And what about Faye?' she asked. 'How did you leave things with her?'

Aidan's smile developed into a more forlorn expression.

'After I had explained everything to do with the solicitors, it was time to leave for the airport,' he sighed. 'To be honest, I think I'm still in shock. I mean, it's amazing that I now have a sister, it's definitely an upgrade from finding out that I have a cousin,' he beamed. 'And she's so kind, and so thoughtful. It's just a lot to digest.'

'Did she seem okay about your decision to hand back the business?'

'I think she'd have liked for me to be involved, but she understood my reasons. She's going to run the shop in Collonges-la-Rouge and will probably move back to the village temporarily because she already has a good manager running her other shop in Nantes. And we'll just keep in touch whenever we can via video calls, messaging, and maybe some summer holiday trips in the future.'

'And you're okay with that?'

'I'm okay with it,' he smiled. 'She's hopefully going to be an important part of my life, but not as important as you.' He looked at Lola and then gazed up towards the cathedral, a warming smile appearing on his face.

'So, why have you brought me here?' she asked, perplexed at his expression.

'One of the last things that I did with my mum before she passed away was to go to the top of the tower,' he explained, peering up at the pinnacle of the cathedral. 'And she said that whenever I met *the one,* as she liked to call it, I should bring her up here, and if the bells are ringing, it'd be a sign that she approves.'

Lola looked a little sheepish. 'Right?' she questioned, unsure what to make of Aidan's comment.

'And she was only joking, she was just being silly and trying to make light of what was happening, I knew that, but I've never forgotten what she said to me that day.'

'It's a nice thought,' Lola replied, sensing Aidan's breaking emotions.

'And although I really don't believe in anything like that, I did take Holly to the top of the tower before I proposed to her, and that day couldn't have been quieter,' he laughed. 'There wasn't a breeze, there wasn't the sound of a bird chirping, there wasn't anything. It was the most bizarre experience, because I've been up there quite a few times in the past, and there's always some kind of noise or commotion,' he explained. 'Holly was actually more bothered about getting the perfect Instagram shot, which says it all, really.' Aidan looked up towards the top. 'So, I just want to see what happens when I take you up there, see how I feel, see how you feel.'

Lola peered up in dismay, a sudden and overwhelming sickness rumbling her composure. 'I'm actually not great with heights, I think you saw that during the flight to France,' she said. 'And somehow, I've always managed to get out of climbing those stairs up to the top,' she explained, peering up at the Minster tower. A whiteness stole Lola's usual peachy complexion, and her grip on Aidan's hand tensed.

'Do you trust me?' he asked, moving his head so that he was blocking her view. 'Do you trust me?' he asked again.

Lola nodded, but unconvincingly so.

'Did I or did I not save your life?' he asked, smiling.

'You did save my life, but I'd like not to put myself in the situation where my life might need saving for a second time.'

'Just trust me. You'll be fine, and once we're at the top, you'll never want to come down.'

Aidan guided Lola through the cathedral until they reached the passageway which would lead them up to the top of the tower, a uniformed man standing at the entrance. Lola spotted the sign, notifying the public that, due to unforeseen circumstances, trips up to the tower were cancelled for the afternoon.

'That's a shame, maybe we can do it another day,' she said to Aidan, reading the notice.

'Thanks, Seb,' said Aidan when the man smiled and opened the door for them.

'How are we being allowed through?' she asked, looking back and seeing that the door had been closed behind them.

'I know a few people and they've pulled some strings for us,' he replied. 'I want this to be special, just you and me,' he added. Aidan paused at the foot of the first step. 'Are you ready? All you have to do is put one foot in front of the other, and follow me.'

Lola did as Aidan instructed and began the climb. 'How many steps are there, do you know?' she asked when she was only ten steps in.

'Erm, 275,' he confirmed in one quick breath, hoping that Lola wouldn't hear. 'But let's not focus on how many there are, let's just keep going, you're doing brilliantly,' he encouraged, looking back to make sure that Lola was still following.

'It's so narrow,' she said, her voice a little panicked when she felt the narrow, spiral staircase tightening around her body, her breathing laboured. Lola ran one hand along the metal stair rail, the contour guiding her upwards, and her other hand pressed against the cool stone walls, the solidity of the structure offering her some kind of reassurance.

'We're almost there,' Aidan encouraged. 'Another few minutes and we'll be at the top.'

Battling with panting breaths and dizziness, Lola broke free and emerged out into open air at the top of the tower. Aidan looked back and took her hand, leading her outside. The cool, fresh air swept Lola's hair, the breeze refreshing against her clammy skin.

'I knew you could do it,' he smiled, stopping and hugging her. 'Are you okay?' he asked, waiting for Lola to catch her breath.

'I'm fine,' she huffed, leaning down and concentrating on her breathing. 'Just give me a second.'

'Before you look out, I want to take you to where me and Mum used to stand. We had our own special spot,' he explained when Lola stood up straight. He took hold of her hand and guided her around the top of the platform, hugging the inside curvature of the building. 'You sure that you're okay?' he asked again.

'I'm better now that I can breathe,' Lola smiled, her eyes still focusing on her feet rather than the horizon. 'Let me know when I can look.'

'We're nearly there,' he said before stopping. 'Right, close your eyes,' he instructed.

Nervous, Lola pressed her eyelids shut. 'Do you know how scary this is?' she said when Aidan encouraged her to take a few steps forward, away from the safety of the inner wall.

Aidan positioned her in the exact spot that he and his mum had stood so many times before. He stood behind Lola with his arms outstretched, enclosing her body, his chin poised on her shoulder. 'Right, open your eyes.'

Lola's eyes opened wide, the view of York opening up before her like a magical pop-up book.

'Oh my goodness,' she gasped, her jaw agape when she felt like she could reach up with her hand and touch the sky with her fingertips. The collection of ominous clouds that had gathered overhead tumbled away over the cathedral, allowing the sun to beam with righteousness over her face. Instinctively, she closed her eyes and took a moment to relish the feeling of warmth on her face.

'This is amazing,' she said, turning to Aidan and witnessing the expression on his face. 'And we have this all to ourselves,' she added. With the platform deserted, Lola felt like only she and Aidan existed, just like she had done on the day of the accident. 'Thank you for arranging this for me,' she beamed, before kissing him and turning back around.

Through a purposefully crafted gap in the safety railings, Lola peered out between the North and South transept, the horizon stretching for as far as she could see.

Aidan bowed so that their heads were level, their cheeks touching. 'So, this is where my mum would bring me, and she would make me look through this gap before telling me that I could go anywhere and do anything that I wanted in life,' he explained.

Lola looked down and admired the ribs of the cathedral, the stone arches protruding, acting to cement the building to the ground like anchors.

'I can see why she brought you up here, it's so inspiring,' she said.

With their thoughts lost in the view, both Aidan and Lola relished the moment, the silence and tranquillity offering a sense of peace. And then, in their next breath, both of their bodies physically jumped when the cathedral bells began ringing, the sound deafening and causing a series of vibrations to rumble right through the core of their chests.

'Blimey, that made me jump!' Lola shouted, turning to Aidan with her hand over her heart, trying to calm her scattered nerves. She noticed the glossiness in Aidan's eyes, his arms remaining around her body, drawing her closer.

'I didn't pull any favours for this, I promise,' he beamed, looking over towards the tower, witnessing the men pulling on the ropes in order to ring the mighty bells. 'This is all my mum's doing. I knew that she would approve of you,' he smiled, relishing the moment and taking a minute to remember Heidi, his love for her even stronger now that he understood everything that she had sacrificed for him. 'Can we stay here for a while?' he whispered, wanting to relish the feeling of gratitude, the feeling of contentment, the feeling of optimism and the feeling of love that were all swirling around his body in a manner that he'd never before experienced.

'This is our home, we can stay here forever,' she replied, delivering a kiss to his lips before looking back out across York, admiring the place that she now loved to call home.

50

THROUGH HIS LOUNGE WINDOW, MATTY PEERED DOWN OVER The Shambles, the street deserted apart from a lone, late-night dog walker. Over the years - and past few days, in particular - Matty had spent so much time observing the view beyond his window that he could recite the architectural details of the buildings opposite, like where all the original butcher's meat-hooks were positioned on the listed buildings. But even when his eyes became distracted and wandered, his attention soon turned back to Fudgy Nook, and to the gift bag that he could see was still sitting on the desk behind the shop counter.

With his hand gripped on the curtain, Matty was just about to close it when a figure appeared at the top end of the street; a single male walking with purpose. After only a few seconds of watching the person approach, Matty's pulse began to race and a surge of adrenaline caused his mind to feel energised. Without thought, he grabbed his phone and sent a message to Marie that simply stated, *Aidan is back.*

With a flick of the switch, Matty turned off the lamp and stood to the side of the window, concealing his frame from sight. He watched with bated breath the moment that Aidan arrived outside the shop, and within seconds, he saw the lights inside illuminate, and he could see everything that was unfolding.

'What's happening?' asked Marie when Matty answered his phone.

With his eyes glued to the shop, he replied. 'Aidan has just arrived and now he's gone through to the workshop, I think,' he explained when Aidan disappeared out of sight.

'Has he seen the bag?' she asked, her voice full of apprehension.

'No, I don't think so. He hasn't been to that side of the counter yet.' Matty could feel his heart pounding, a tingling sensation raging through his chest. 'I've waited so long for this, for him to find out who I am, and now, I can barely bring myself to watch,' he explained, pulling himself away from the window and pressing his head against the wall. 'What if he's not interested, Marie? What if he hates me? What if he doesn't want anything to do with me? What then?' he continued, the sound of his voice shaky and unsettled.

'Then you'll know, Matty. You'll know that you tried your best to make amends. You can't do any more than that,' she sympathised, her voice sounding soft and caring.

'I just don't know how I'd cope,' he confessed, turning around and pressing his back against the wall. 'And this is the reason that I've never reached out before, because at least now I still have hope of a relationship. Without hope, I have nothing.'

Marie wanted to be able to wave a magic wand and transport herself to Matty's side, enabling her to put her arms around his body and offer him the physical support that she knew he needed.

'It would be disappointing to learn that he wasn't interested. But there'd still be a wonderful life for you to lead, with or without your family. And you'll always have me.'

Matty's brain and heart were engaged in an internal battle, his heart winning the war.

'There's something I need to tell you, Marie, and I didn't want to at the time because I knew it'd make you upset. But I know I need to talk to someone, and you're the only person I have,' he continued.

'What is it?' she asked. When no reply came, she asked again. 'Matty, what is it?' she asked in a more encouraging tone.

'The other day, I went to the main bridge on the outskirts of town, and I thought about ending it all,' he began, the words hurting as he spoke. He could hear Marie weep down the line.

'Oh, Matty.'

'I only thought about it, and I don't think that I was actually going to do anything, I probably wouldn't have had the guts. But I did consider it, and as my friend, I wanted you to know.'

Silence fell between them.

'Matty,' Marie began. 'I need you to promise me something,' she requested, her voice breaking the more she spoke. 'I need you to promise me that, before you ever get to that stage again, you'll call me, you'll come over to my house, or you'll come and find me at work, whatever it takes. Just talk to me, okay? Will you promise me?'

The line went silent again.

'I promise,' he finally replied. Beneath the darkness of the room, a weight lifted off his shoulders at sharing one of his darkest secrets, and for a moment, life didn't feel quite so lonely.

'Are you okay? Shall I come round?'

'No, I'm fine, honestly. I know that I've reached the bottom now and the only way must be up,' he explained, his voice still shaky.

'Maybe this is the start of a new chapter in your life.'

'I hope so,' he mumbled.

'What's Aidan doing now?' she asked in a brighter tone, trying to lift his spirits.

'I don't know, I walked away from the window.'

Marie's tone went up an octave. 'Well get back over there and look!' she laughed. 'We need to know what's going on.'

Matty crept back towards the window, the lights in the shop still illuminated. 'He's just walked back into the shop,' he narrated.

'And what's he doing?' Marie asked with an abundance of enthusiasm in her voice.

'He's walking behind the counter now,' he said in a lively

tone. 'He hasn't spotted the bag yet,' he added, watching how Aidan methodically checked the shop. 'Oh, my goodness,' Matty whispered.

'What?' she asked, jumping on his words, her nerves equally rattled.

'He's just seen the bag and he's picked up a piece of paper that was next to it. I'm guessing that a note has been left saying who it's for,' he explained. 'Now he's looking inside it.' Matty could barely breathe, anticipation constricting his windpipe. He wanted to run across the street and explain everything in person, look Aidan in the eye and say what had been on his mind for so many years, and yet all he could do was stand still, watch, and wait.

'What's happening now? You need to tell me everything,' Marie demanded, feeling like she was experiencing the ordeal blindfolded.

'He's opening the wrapping paper,' Matty replied in a calming tone, his eyes rarely blinking.

'And?' she probed.

'The paper is off and he's holding the frame in his hand, he's holding it close to his face and having a good look at the picture.' Matty squinted, trying to see Aidan's reaction. 'He's looking at the tag on the bag now, he'll know it's from me, and that I'm his dad,' Matty explained, a lump wedged in his throat, his heart feeling like it was pumping to an irregular beat.

'Is he smiling? Is he crying? What's his reaction?'

Matty lowered his head, he couldn't look anymore.

'Matty, what's he doing?' Marie asked again.

'He's turned off the lights and now he's leaving,' he commented, his voice broken and flat.

'Going where? Has he taken the frame with him? Maybe he's on his way over to you.'

'I was wrong,' he commented in a flat, lifeless tone.

'Wrong about what?' she quizzed.

'Now I've reached rock bottom.'

With a sense of helplessness, Marie pressed her free hand over her face.

'What's happening?'

Inconsolable, Matty's posture began to collapse, like the life was draining from his limbs.

'He left the frame in the shop and now he's leaving.'

Having interpreted Aidan's reaction to the picture as a brutal, personal rejection, Matty ended the call and dropped his phone onto the floor, before closing the curtains and walking away from the window, retreating into the darkness and safety of his flat.

51

'WHERE ARE WE GOING?' ASKED AIDAN WHEN HE AND LOLA got out of the campervan, a blindfold pressed against his eyes. 'There really is something that I want to talk to you about, I'm not just making it up because I don't like surprises,' he explained, Lola having ushered him into the van the moment he had returned from checking up on the shop.

Lola ensured that his eyes were completely covered. 'Step up,' she instructed, helping him onto the pavement. 'Whatever it is you want to talk to me about can wait.' She linked his arm to serve as a guide, and the pair set off on foot, walking towards the city centre.

'Why are we coming out so late?' he asked. 'Don't normal people go out at like six or seven o'clock? Eleven-thirty is more like bedtime. Or am I just getting old?'

Illuminated by the glow offered from the streetlights, Lola and Aidan walked towards the cobbled maze of side streets that encompassed The Shambles, the town centre deserted while the restaurants and bars on the periphery prepared to wind down after a busy night of service.

'Well, what I have planned just wouldn't have worked had we come earlier,' she explained. 'You'll soon understand.'

'I understand that, no matter what time of the day or night, if I'm with you, life is perfect,' Aidan replied.

Lola checked that the road was clear before crossing. 'You can't be saying lovely things like that during my surprise. I'm meant to be the one trying to be romantic,' she joked.

'Oh, so, you're wooing me, are you?' he laughed. 'I'm not sure that's what this feels like.'

'I actually want to take you back in time to Christmas Eve,' she began to explain. 'Apart from the accident, something else happened during that morning, and until only a few days ago, I couldn't remember what it was, and it's been annoying me ever since,' she continued to explain, spotting The Brownie Box coming into sight in the distance.

'Can I look now?' he asked, sensing Lola's nerves.

'Yep, you can look,' she confirmed. The Shambles had been put to bed in complete darkness, the main streetlights turned off, and there wasn't a soul to be seen.

'I'm confused,' he announced, realising his location. 'I was here only an hour ago, checking up on the shop.'

'I remembered a promise that I made to you on the morning of the accident,' she said, at which point she waved her hand. In the next blink of an eye, the entire street became illuminated by rows of festoon lighting, The Brownie Box the focal point, the only business which was open, with its hatch draped in plumes of lights. 'I said that I would make you some of my brownies, didn't I? You gave me your wristband, and that's what I offered you in return.'

The lights shone in Aidan's eyes and his pupils dilated. 'You did,' he grinned, recalling their pact. 'So, does this mean that your memories have now fully returned?' he asked, a sense of relief in his words. 'You're back to how you were before the accident?'

She nodded, tears welling in her eyes. 'And I'm now ready to leave the accident in the past, and concentrate on the future,' she said with a great sense of satisfaction, her beaming expression conveying her sense of relief.

'That's great news,' he replied, kissing her on the lips, relishing the moment. 'How did you do all this?' he asked, amazed that the entire street had been transformed. Lola looked over to Carrie and gave her a thumbs up before her friend disappeared from sight. 'I had a few little helpers,' she explained. 'And having always lived and worked in York, I know a few people in high places myself,' she laughed. 'It might not be top-of-the-tower views, but it's the best that I could do.'

'It's amazing,' he gushed, leaning in and kissing Lola on the lips.

'So, would you like to join me for a little midnight treat? I know it's a bit out-there, but Carrie and I have done extensive research, and this is *the* best time to savour our brownies.'

'I'd love to,' Aidan replied, taking hold of Lola's hand and walking towards The Brownie Box.

She unlocked the door and stepped inside the van first, indicating for Aidan to join her.

'Take a seat on my stool and I'll get to work,' she said, donning her apron and reaching down to the fridge. 'Luckily, here's a batch my little helper prepared earlier for us,' she laughed, taking hold of the tray and placing it in the pre-heated oven. 'These are best served with a cup of tea or milky coffee, which would you prefer?'

'Well, considering I was in France this morning, I'll have a coffee to keep me awake, thanks,' he replied, getting cosy on the stool, wrapping his coat snug around his body. 'So, this is how it feels to be on this side of the counter,' he commented, looking out through the hatch. 'It's much bigger in here than I thought.'

'After a few years, I can assure you that the space doesn't feel so big,' she laughed. 'But Carrie thinks she's found us a unit to rent, so maybe a coffee shop won't be just a dream anymore, and we can upgrade ourselves from the van.' Lola sat on the other stool next to Aidan, pressing her hand against his thigh. 'Who would have thought we'd be sitting here now?' she commented. 'The accident, Parker and Holly's affair, my pregnancy, Holly's pregnancy, my divorce, your inheritance, Faye. I feel like we've had our fair share of obstacles to overcome since meeting, and yet here we are, still together and smiling despite everything that has been thrown our way.'

'I just can't picture my life without you in it now,' he continued. 'And I wanted to talk to you about the future, about how you see it looking.'

Lola raised her eyebrows. 'This sounds serious. We haven't really had any deep and meaningful conversations about the future.'

Aidan took hold of Lola's hand. 'I know, but because of everything that's happened recently, I've been forced to think about the future, and how I want it to look.'

Lola looked out across The Shambles. 'Well, after everything that happened with Parker, I was pretty sure that I wanted something more out of life, I thought there was more to life than this,' she said, looking around the van. 'But what the whole situation has taught me is that I actually do really love this life. I love the daily norm, I love coming to work with my best friend and going home to someone at night,' she explained. 'All I want is to be happy. I'm not asking for the world and I'm not asking to be swept off my feet. I just want to be loved by someone who loves me for who I am, and who isn't always waiting for the next best thing to come along. I want to grow old with someone.'

Aidan produced a silly little grin, a yearning look appearing in his eyes. 'And do you see that person being me?' He looked away, his nerves stealing his confidence to maintain eye contact.

'I do see that person being you,' Lola replied, her pulse racing, a fluttering sensation warmed her stomach. 'But I do want you to know that, despite everything that's happened, I'm still ready to settle down. I'm ready to dedicate my life to someone and raise a family of my own. Those are things that are important to me, and I'm looking for someone to be on the same page, in the same country. I'm tired of being the person who has to convince someone to want the same things as me, it's exhausting.'

Aidan budged his stool a little closer so that their knees touched.

'From the moment I saw you trapped inside your mangled car, I knew you were special, I could see it in your eyes,' he began. 'There's nothing more I want in life than to be with you.'

Lola had never felt so content, so loved as she listened to his words. 'So, your heart is here, in York? You don't see yourself moving to France, or making extended, frequent visits back there?'

'I mean, I'm going to miss Faye. I wish we weren't so far apart, but my home is here and that's one of the main reasons why I've handed the business and house back to her. My home is here with you, and always will be, and she understands that,' he reassured, kissing her and stroking her face.

'Well, with all that being said, I do have one last little surprise for you,' she said, taking hold of a hand-held bell that was on the countertop and jingling it while standing, the sound of the bell echoing down the street.

'What are you doing?' Aidan asked, a puzzled expression on his face.

'I might not be able to make the cathedral bells ring on demand, but I do have other skills,' she revealed, a genuine beam radiating from her face. 'Look who I found roaming the streets of York,' she said as Faye appeared from around the corner.

'Oh my God!' he announced the moment he set eyes on his sister. With tears welling, he stood up and took hold of Lola, whispering in her ear, 'Thank you so much.'

After kissing Aidan, Lola walked out of The Brownie Box and round to the front near the hatch, her and Faye hugging like they were best friends.

'Thanks for helping to make this happen,' Faye said during the embrace, tears welling in her eyes too. 'I've never felt so lonely in my whole life since losing my mum,' she cried. 'And you have just made life a little easier for me.'

'Well, now you have a brother and a new friend,' Lola replied, wiping away Faye's tears.

Aidan followed Lola, still unable to comprehend the situation. 'I can't believe you're actually here. I thought it was going to be ages before we could see one another again,' he said, pulling his sister into an embrace of his own. 'You said that you were going back to Nantes,' Aidan questioned.

'I was lying so that we could keep all of this a surprise. I had actually already packed my bags in the hope that I could come here instead,' Faye smiled. 'I rang Lola and she helped to set it all up.'

'How long are you staying for?' he asked with excitement.

'For a while, if that's okay?' she replied. 'My mum had so many regrets and I don't want us to make the same mistakes,' she began. 'And at least for a while, I'd like us to be on the same side of the English Channel, that's if you'll have me.'

Aidan glanced over at Lola, who was smiling and nodding her head.

'Absolutely,' Aidan agreed, turning back to Faye. 'I'd love for you to spend some time with us here in York, and it'd be great to have you over at the shop.'

Lola stepped back into the van, admiring the way that Aidan and Faye were grinning at each other, thankful that the reunion had unfolded as she hoped. She looked at her watch, counting down the seconds until midnight, knowing that the cathedral bells were going to be ringing during a special service.

Just as Aidan and Faye stepped closer to the van's hatch, the sound of the cathedral's heartbeat caused Aidan to pause. He looked over towards York Minster as it rose from the city grounds in the distance, thoughts and warm memories of his mum rushing to be by his side. He smiled in appreciation and gazed towards Lola, his heart melting.

Lola raised her cup through the hatch. 'Here's to making new memories, memories that I know the three of us will never forget,' she toasted. 'You two move back just a little bit so that I can take a photo of you both with the cathedral in the background,' she requested, rooting for her phone. 'This is one of those moments that we need to capture, a moment in your family's history.'

Aidan and Faye took to their positions and waited for Lola, the pair continuing to smile at each other in disbelief.

'Now we just need to find Dad,' Faye commented. 'I haven't

spoken to him in so long, but I'm hopeful that he's still here, in York,' she added.

'Smile,' Lola said, the flash from her phone dazzling.

Aidan turned to Fay before speaking. 'I know that our dad is here, in York,' he announced, his eyes wide and alluring.

'Really? How?' Lola questioned upon hearing his revelation.

The three of them gravitated back towards the hatch once the photo had been taken. 'That's what I wanted to talk to you about,' he continued, looking up at Lola. 'But we headed straight here once I'd got back from the shop, so I didn't get chance to explain.' A ruddy complexion could be witnessed on Aidan's face, an innate happiness shining through his expression.

'So, what happened while you were at the shop? How do you know he's here in York?' Lola continued to question.

'A gift bag had been left for me while I was away. Inside, there was a photo frame with the words *Love Dad* engraved onto the front,' he described. 'And the picture within was of a man cradling a baby in one arm, and a toddler in the other.'

Faye immediately smiled, the description familiar. 'Was it this photo?' she asked, taking hold of her purse and pulling free a little crumpled picture.

Aidan looked up. 'Yeah, that's the same one.'

'This is the only photo that I have of you, me and Dad,' she continued, her smile unrelenting. 'I was going to show it to you before you left France, but we just ran out of time, and we were rushing to get you to the airport.'

'Why are you smiling?' Lola asked, catching the grin that had appeared on Aidan's face.

'Because I know who our dad is,' he beamed.

'Really? Who?' Lola questioned, taking a closer look at the picture.

'It's Matty Smith.'

'Matty? The nurse from St Jude's? The one who looked after me while I was in ICU?' Lola questioned.

Aidan offered a warming grin of confirmation.

'Yeah, Matty Smith. That's our dad's name. Do you already know him?' Faye asked, puzzled.

Aidan was quick to reply, an innate look of happiness shining from his face. 'I do, I've actually known him for a long time,' he explained, his eyes welling with emotion. 'I just can't believe that he's our dad,' he cried, so many feelings of love rushing through his heart. 'And he's been here, in York, living across the road from the shop for as long as I can remember.' Aidan gazed down The Shambles, peering up at the flat that he now knew belonged to his dad.

52

WITH HIS HANDS STUFFED INTO HIS POCKETS, TO AIDAN, THE Shambles had never felt quite so eerie as he meandered his way down the winding, cobbled street. He noticed that the lights had already been turned off in most of the flats, the closed curtains shielding those residents who were sleeping. During the nighttime hours, Aidan felt like the street he knew so well seemed to take on a different personality, unfamiliar noises and shadows tracing his steps, causing him to turn and check his surroundings with caution. Reassured that he was alone, he paced onwards, his feet navigating the uneven cobbles, each stride taking him one step closer to his destination. His mind raced with a million and one thoughts and his emotions tumbled; one minute he felt overwhelmed with excitement, the next he was fighting back tears and battling feelings of judgement. With Lola and Faye's words of encouragement playing through his mind on a non-stop reel, he soon arrived at Matty Smith's front door.

His hands jiggled in his pockets and his feet fidgeted. After taking in a deep breath, Aidan pulled his hand out of his pocket and tapped his knuckles against the wood before taking a pronounced step backwards. Conscious of the time, he glanced upwards and saw that a light was on in the flat above, providing him with hope that Matty might still be awake. After a minute had passed without any answer, he knocked again, only this time, a little louder. Beneath his chest, his heart pounded, his nerves causing him to feel breathless, and for a brief moment, he felt like changing his mind and taking the easier option; turning and walking away.

Tucked away inside his flat, Matty jumped upon hearing the knock at the front door. He checked the time, noting the late hour, and put down the book that he was reading. Remembering that Marie was away on holiday, his heart raced at the thought that it could be Aidan standing outside his front door. He couldn't think who else it could possibly be. After a lifetime of praying, a lifetime of hoping and wishing for this exact moment to happen, Matty found himself unable to move, momentarily paralysed on the sofa. Fear nailed him to the spot and prevented him from running to open the door, and wrapping his arms around his son.

When the person knocked again, Matty finally summoned the courage to walk towards the window, move the curtain aside and peer down. The moment he did, he spotted Aidan turning and walking away.

'Hi,' shouted Matty when he rushed down the stairs and opened the door, his word bellowing down The Shambles and preventing Aidan from walking a step further. 'Would you like to come in?'

The pair stood in silence for a moment and looked at each other in a way that they'd never done before; through fresh eyes and with new perspectives. After a few seconds, Matty opened the door a little wider and stepped further inside, his action working like a magnet to draw Aidan back.

'Please, come in.'

Aidan gazed up and down the street in a moment of uncertainty, hoping to find encouragement and strength in one form or another.

'Okay,' he replied, before turning and walking towards the door, doing his best to push away his feelings of doubt and apprehension. He stepped foot inside the flat and waited for Matty to close the door before following him up the steep, narrow staircase.

Once at the top, Aidan peered around Matty's home and digested his first impressions of the flat. In his opinion, the snug apartment had a very minimalistic feel, the living space free from all clutter, free from any personal possessions, and in Aidan's eyes, free from any signs of love, or happiness.

'I'm not even sure what to say,' he began, all his pre-prepared words now evading his memory. 'I'm sorry it's so late, but I saw that your light was on, so assumed you were still awake.'

'It's okay. I tend to stay up late reading. Please, sit down,' Matty offered, indicating towards a seat. 'Can I get you a drink?'

'No, I'm fine, thanks,' Aidan replied, taking a seat near the window, catching sight of his shop across the road.

Matty also took a tentative seat, his words and composure all becoming scrambled in a moment of shock that was taking time to subside.

After an awkward silence, Aidan spoke.

'So, is it true?' he asked, his gaze remaining on the floor, his thoughts also scrambled and his heart aching like it had never pained before. 'Is it really true that you're my dad?'

Matty couldn't look up either, he didn't know how to, and his heart wasn't strong enough to sustain any form of rejection towards the truth that he was about to declare.

'I am,' he confirmed.

For a few more seconds, both men remained silent, each one digesting the information, seeing how their hearts responded, and waiting for the other person to show their emotions first.

'Please, don't hate me,' Matty added, the silence feeling worse than the anticipation of rejection.

'I don't hate you,' Aidan was quick to reply, building the courage to look up, and for the first time in his life, he gazed at Matty and saw him as the person he really was; his dad. 'I'm curious, more than anything, and I'd like to hear your side of the story.'

Matty's voice cracked with emotion. 'And that's all I've ever really wanted.'

He experienced a surge of paternal love flow through his heart, his emotions brewing beneath the surface.

'There hasn't been a day gone by when I haven't thought about you, and every night I have prayed for this very moment to come,' he continued. No longer able to conceal his regret, a wave of emotion broke free and Matty lowered his head, tears falling from his eyes when he blinked. Embarrassed, he quickly excused himself from the room. 'I'll just go and put the kettle on, in case you change your mind about that drink. Give me a minute,' he explained.

Aidan took the opportunity to look around again, taking in the simplicity of the room. Through his eyes, he was still unable to find any traces of a family, any signs of love, or any evidence to suggest that the person living here had led a meaningful life. From Aidan's perspective, there was nothing to be found except a sense of loneliness. He spotted indentations on the sofa where a single person must have spent a long time sitting, a lone pair of slippers abandoned beneath a side table, and a single coat hook near the stairs. The room felt dark, no additional home furnishings to offer softness, light or a sense of personality. Then he got up out of his chair after spotting a tiny picture on the windowsill. Upon closer inspection, he saw that it was the same photo that had been left in his shop, the same photo that Faye had produced from her purse, and an indescribable feeling warmed his heart like never before, the tiny photo suggesting that maybe it was true that he had always been an important part of Matty's life.

Matty reappeared, carrying two mugs in his hand.

'Sorry about that. Here, I made you a coffee anyway. I know that you like it with milk and two sugars, you've told me that before when I've been to the shop,' he explained, his emotions pushed away so that, for now at least, they remained out of sight.

'Thanks,' Aidan replied, taking hold of the drink and sitting back down. 'This is all a bit of a shock,' he continued. 'I've only just found out the truth about who my real mum is, and about Faye, and now this.'

Matty focused his gaze and his eyes brightened. 'I know it's a lot to take in, and I'm sorry that it's taken so many years for the truth to finally surface.'

Aidan jumped on the statement. 'Why has it taken so long? Why have you never told me? You live right across the street and have done for so many years,' he began, pointing out of the window. 'You come into my shop all the time, we've spoken so much in the past, and yet all along, you've never told me the truth about who you really are. Why?'

Matty took a moment before replying, reigning in his eagerness to defend himself, to defend his behaviour. 'For so many years, I was prevented from being a part of your life, and then once you were old enough to understand, and make your own decisions, I just didn't know how to tell you. I was scared and I didn't want to hurt you anymore,' he explained, his voice strained as his gaze fell away. 'But I know now that I should have tried harder,' he confessed, his words heavy and filled with sincerity. 'I should have fought harder to be a part of your life, and the only reason that I didn't is because I thought I was doing the best thing for you.'

Aidan shook his head, Matty's explanation failing to clarify his muddled stream of thoughts. 'What do you mean, you were prevented from being a part of my life?' he asked, his mouth dry and his words cracking beneath the weight of his realisation.

Matty's chest loosened, allowing his breath to move more freely.

'When Alice left you with Heidi, it was at that time it was decided that, for everyone's sake, it was best that I didn't visit you anymore,' he said, hurt still evident in his eyes despite the passing of time. He took a sip of his tea, taking a moment to compose himself, the rawness of his emotions hard to conceal.

Witnessing the distress in Matty's eyes, the honesty in his words, Aidan tried to empathise.

'I know all this is bringing up some difficult memories for you, but could you tell me what happened, from the beginning, from when I was born?' he asked in a softer tone.

'After you were born, Alice and I went our separate ways, but she allowed me to visit you,' he beamed. 'And those days that I saw you were some of my happiest,' he added, allowing a genuine smile of nostalgia to take hold.

Aidan listened as Matty's words painted a picture in his mind.

The smile on Matty's face faded. 'But Alice wasn't coping, even with Heidi's support, and during those early days, she was really struggling with depression.' A sense of reluctance rose in his voice. 'And that's when everything changed.'

'How did it change?' Aidan was quick to question.

Matty drew in a deep breath. 'A decision was made that I had no control over, even though I was your dad.'

'What decision?' Aidan asked, encouraging Matty to continue.

'Although I desperately wanted to take care of you myself, because you were already settled in a routine at Heidi's where you were all living, it was agreed that it was in your best interest for Heidi to carry on looking after you while your mum took some time away to focus on getting better. It was only meant to be a short-term arrangement, but by the time that Alice felt well enough to take you back, you'd formed such a strong bond with Heidi that you didn't want to leave her,' he explained, pausing for a moment before looking directly at Aidan. 'In your eyes, Heidi was your mum, not Alice.'

'So, that's why I stayed with my mum?'

Matty looked up and nodded again, trying to gauge Aidan's reaction. 'Alice believed that Heidi had turned you against her, and that's when they stopped talking. I don't think they ever spoke to one another again.'

'And what about you?'

'In the beginning, I still visited you at Heidi's, but for some reason you'd get upset, you'd cry and not want to be near me,' Matty recalled, his shoulders lowering beneath the burden. 'And the last thing I wanted to do was hurt you.' He shook his head, momentarily placing his hands over his face before looking up.

'And then one day, when you were about five, Heidi asked for me not to go round anymore. She told me that you didn't want to see me, and that after everything that had happened, she needed to be able to create a safe and stable environment for you, and I couldn't argue with that.'

'Did you believe my mum? Do you think that she turned me against Alice?' Aidan asked. 'Do you think she turned me against you?'

Matty shook his head, his forehead creasing. 'No, I don't. Heidi was one of the kindest people I have ever known. She created such a wonderful home for you, and she only ever wanted the best for you. She always kept me updated with what you were doing, and we spoke most days, and she said that when you were old enough to understand, old enough to make your own decisions, or when you started to ask questions, I could try coming over again.'

'But you didn't try again?' Aidan asked in a curious tone.

'Heidi said you never spoke about me, or ever asked if you could meet me. And the more the years went by, the harder it became for me to make that first move. I was scared that if I approached you, I would make your life harder, and that's not what I wanted for you. I saw that you were happy and being taken care of, so I remained out of sight. But I was always there in the background, watching over everything that you were doing, and I was happy with that. I accepted the situation for what it was.'

Aidan took a moment to process everything. 'So, what happened between my mum and Alice?'

'As far as I know, Alice was never able to forgive Heidi. She was so jealous of the relationship that you had with your mum, a relationship that she thought should have been hers, so they never spoke again. It was such a sad ending given that they were twins, and had once shared such a close bond.' Matty saw the pained expression on Aidan's face. 'Nobody really did anything wrong, it was nobody's fault, not really. It was just such a shame that we couldn't have all made it work a bit better, for everyone, especially you.'

'What happened after Faye was born?'

'Well,' he began through a heavy sigh. 'Alice and I got back together for a time, and I still loved her, so I was willing to try and make it work, but I just served as a reminder of what she had lost, and so after a few months, that was the end. She moved to France with Faye, and I never saw either of them again,' he explained. 'Alice was the love of my life, and you and Faye have always meant everything to me, even if it doesn't appear that way,' he confessed, a great sense of relief lifting from his body at finally being able to explain his side of the story.

Aidan stood up and looked out of the window, his own emotions rising to the surface. He felt his heart aching and he wanted to believe, more than anything else, that Matty was telling the truth. 'I went through most of my childhood feeling like something was missing, like *someone* was missing, and I never told my mum because I didn't want her to feel bad, or to think that she wasn't doing a great job,' he explained, turning to face Matty, his eyes glossy. 'But maybe, had I told her how I really felt, all this could have been resolved so many years ago. Maybe we could have all been some sort of family.'

Aidan allowed his head to fall, his shoulders lowering and his hands diving into his pockets.

Upon sight of Aidan's broken demeanour, Matty's paternal instincts rose to the surface, encouraging him to stand up and walk towards the window. He stood side by side with Aidan and, in one gentle motion, raised his arm and placed it over his son's shoulder, drawing him closer.

Aidan glanced to his side and admired the way in which Matty's hand rested on his jumper. He relished the physical touch of affection, and for the first time in his life, he was able to experience the type of fatherly love that, deep down, he had always craved. He felt a bond blooming in his heart, and he couldn't help but envisage how his future may look with Matty in his life.

They both remained still, looking out over The Shambles,

Fudgy Nook coming into view across the street.

'I have thought about you every single day,' Matty commented, his arm still firmly held around Aidan's shoulders. 'And we've built a firm friendship over the years,' he explained. 'I know that you like to travel. I know that you have an interest in cycling and that, whenever you can, you like to explore the countryside,' Matty began, and out of the corner of his eye, he saw the beginnings of a smile appear on Aidan's face. 'I know that you like watching films, but not sci-fi, and I know that you have a great sense of humour, even though some of your jokes are pretty awful,' he grinned.

While still looking out across the street, Aidan began to speak, recalling all the conversations that he and Matty had had over the years in the shop. 'And I know that you worked at St Jude's, and did for many years. I know that you like watching rugby with a beer or two, and I know that you've never been keen on the winter months because of the idiot drivers,' he began, pausing a moment to think. 'I know that you like to cook, but rarely do, and you like to watch films or go for walks down by the canal, as long as you pass a pub on the way.'

Matty recalled the day that Aidan arrived in St Jude's after the accident.

'I know that you've fallen in love with Lola, and that you helped to save her life.' Aidan turned to face Matty, tears rolling down his face, and they embraced in a manner that implied they would never again become separated.

'I always want you to be a part of my life,' Aidan whispered into Matty's ear when his emotions allowed him to speak.

'I'm sorry that I haven't always been there for you, at least in the way that you needed,' Matty replied, maintaining his grip on Aidan.

Aidan felt his body relax and he savoured the special moment.

'You're here now, that's all that matters.'

After a few more seconds of embracing, they pulled away from each other. 'Do you want to sit down, and we can talk for a little while? I know it's late, but I have a few chilled beers in the fridge,'

Matty asked, eager to prevent Aidan from leaving.

'Oh, I can't. Lola arranged a surprise for me tonight and she's actually still up at The Brownie Box,' he explained. 'So, I best get going.'

Aidan saw the look of disappointment quickly spread across Matty's face.

'Would you like to join us?' he asked. 'I know it's late, but it'll be worth it.'

Matty developed a slow smile and needed no further encouragement, his tears welling behind his eyelids.

'I'd love to, if I'm not imposing,' he replied, his hands shaking, a sense of disbelief igniting his skin.

Aidan smiled. 'Great, then let's get going.'

Matty remained still, tears beginning to trickle down his face. This time, it was Aidan who offered comfort, placing a reassuring arm across his dad's back.

'It's going to be an emotional night for everyone,' Aidan commented, picturing in his mind how Matty was going to react upon seeing Faye. 'Let's go. And grab a thick coat, it's freezing outside,' Aidan said, walking towards the stairs.

Matty followed, grabbing his coat and wrapping it around his body before pulling a hat over his head. 'Blimey the temperature really has dropped,' he commented as he stepped foot on the cobbles, the freezing conditions snapping at any exposed skin.

'Luckily, we haven't got far to go,' Aidan smiled, spotting the lights in the distance.

The pair headed up towards The Brownie Box, a lightness evident in their stride, commonalities in their mannerisms already shining through.

'The surprise that Lola arranged for me is now also a surprise for you,' he explained, turning to Matty ready to gauge his reaction. 'Faye is here, and she can't wait to meet you.'

Aidan watched how Matty's eyes sparkled at the news, a flushness appearing on his dad's face.

'Really?' Matty questioned, his eyes squinting so that he could see in the distance.

'Really,' Aidan confirmed, encouraging Matty to keep walking, sensing some hesitation in his body language, his pace slowing. 'She's right there,' he concluded upon spotting Faye's smile.

'Hi,' Faye announced when they approached, her wide, beaming smile offering Matty a warm welcome.

Matty froze and after a few seconds of not knowing what to do, he opened up his arms and drew his daughter into an embrace, the pair hugging until their arms ached.

'Hi, Faye,' he replied, inhaling the scent of her hair as it brushed against his face. 'I'm so sorry for not trying harder to keep in touch with you,' he apologised, admiring her beauty for the first time in person, noticing how much she resembled Alice.

'None of that matters now. It's a fresh start for us all,' she smiled, glancing towards Lola and Aidan, who were both huddled near the van. 'I'm just happy that we're all together,' Faye added.

'You look just like your mum,' Matty beamed, admiring Faye's eyes, unable to dispel images of Alice, the woman who, despite everything that had happened, he had never once stopped loving.

Faye adored the feeling that rushed through her heart whenever anybody told her that she bore such a striking resemblance to Alice, and in her mind, it helped to keep the legacy of her mum alive. 'There were so many occasions over the years when I would catch mum looking at your photo, and I knew she longed for things to be different.'

Matty took a moment before replying. 'I knew that she loved me, I never doubted that, but I reminded her so much of Aidan, and for that reason, it just wasn't meant to be.'

Faye reached out her hand and took hold of Matty's. She relished how her dad was still able to speak so fondly of her mum, and for the first time in her life, she knew for sure that she had always had two parents who loved her.

'Let's go and stand near the van, I think it's a bit more sheltered,' she explained, feeling the cold bite of the wind that had begun to swirl up and down the street.

So engrossed in the poignant moment, they all remained unaware of the incoming weather front, a thick blanket of cloud rolling in off the Yorkshire Moors and settling over the dormant city. As though the scene was laid out inside a shaken snow globe, a dusting of snow cascaded from the sky and decorated the slanted rooftops with a flurry of glistening flakes. The unseasonal dip in temperature encouraged those residents who were still awake to once again fill their coal scuttles and stoke the fire until the flames were the deepest hue of amber. The scent of burning embers drifted out through chimney pots, before making its way through the maze of side streets.

Almost in complete unison, when the snow shower intensified, Aidan and his family arched their heads and allowed the unseasonal snow to rest on their faces.

'Does it always snow at this time of year?' Faye asked, unable to recall her last experience of such a snowy flurry.

'We have had snow in April,' Lola revealed, wrapping her coat so that it hugged her body.

'How about we all make a dash back to my place?' Matty suggested, the chill causing his warm breath to produce a pocket of white mist to scatter through the air.

'Sounds good to me,' Lola replied, reaching up to close the hatch, her fingers numb from the blustery conditions.

Once The Brownie Box was locked up, the four nestled themselves together and meandered their way down The Shambles, their shoes leaving a collective trail of footprints in the billows of undisturbed snow.

'I haven't packed for wintery weather,' commented Faye, recalling the spring wardrobe brimming in her suitcase.

'You can borrow some of my coats and jumpers,' Lola offered, linking Faye's arm when the conditions underfoot became treacherous.

'Here we are,' Matty announced, pulling his keys out of his

pocket and unlocking his front door. 'You all go up and get warm,' he added, indicating for them to head inside.

'I'll put the kettle on,' offered Aidan, leading the way up to the lounge.

Matty lingered downstairs in the doorway and gazed up at the sky, watching how the snow fell, the flakes tumbling in a haphazard fashion, succumbing to the changing wind. For the first time in years, he savoured the beauty of the wintery flurry without worrying about its dangerous consequences. He turned his head, and with glossy eyes, relished the sounds of chattering voices that were coming from upstairs. He smiled at the thought of his family finally being reunited under his snow-capped roof, in a once lifeless house that, within moments, had been transformed into a magical family home.

The End

Printed in Great Britain
by Amazon

86416321R00194